BLIND TRUST

Center Point
Large Print

Also by Natalie Walters and available from
Center Point Large Print:

Lights Out
Fatal Code

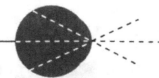

THE SNAP AGENCY
BOOK THREE

BLIND
TRUST

NATALIE WALTERS

CENTER POINT LARGE PRINT
THORNDIKE, MAINE

This Center Point Large Print edition
is published in the year 2023 by arrangement with
Revell, a division of Baker Publishing Group.

The text of this Large Print edition is unabridged.
In other aspects, this book may vary
from the original edition.
Printed in the United States of America
on permanent paper sourced using
environmentally responsible foresting methods.
Set in 16-point Times New Roman type.

ISBN: 978-1-63808-754-0

The Library of Congress has cataloged this record
under Library of Congress Control Number: 2023932174

Lyla and Garcia's story might not have happened without the joy of nope. Thank you!

1

H ow much longer?"
Lyla Fox gritted her teeth at the voice echoing through the tiny earpiece. "Working on it." She kept her voice low. "Not all of us are computer geniuses." Like Kekoa Young, SNAP Agency's cyberguru, who was now chuckling in her ear.

Casting a quick glance over her shoulder from her desk at the front of the office, Lyla checked exam room 4, where Gretchen was getting vitals on an elderly patient named Claude. The door was still closed. As was the door across from it. She exhaled. The last thing Lyla needed was for Dr. Castillo to catch her stealing files.

"I prefer hunky Hawaiian cybergod, or just hunky."

"I'll leave that nickname to Elinor." Lyla wrinkled her nose. "Girlfriend-only material."

"Oh, she calls me—"

"Can we keep the coms clear of unnecessary chatter?"

Lyla rolled her eyes at Nicolás's gruff tone. She pictured the skin between his brows pinched in agitation. It made her smile. She took far too much pleasure in getting under Nicolás Garcia's skin. He was too serious, a real— "Killjoy."

"Pardon?"

Oof, had she said that last part aloud? She *wasn't* wrong. At least not entirely. Over the last couple of years, Lyla had begun to wonder if Nicolás knew there were other emotions besides serious. She believed it had something to do with his military career, which he rarely talked about, but there were little moments when she'd seen that somber façade crack and . . .

The computer screen glitched and Lyla jerked forward, her sudden movement shifting the chair on wheels sideways so her knee hit the side of the desk. Ignoring the sharp pain, she watched the transfer stall at 47 percent.

"Something's wrong." Lyla moved the mouse, but it only caused the rotating circle of annoyance to pop up on the screen. "It's stopped. Something's not right." She tapped the Enter key a couple of times, clicked the mouse.

"Stop hitting keys," Kekoa said. "I'm going to interrupt the—"

"You'll never guess what Porridge did this time," a familiar female voice spoke up behind her.

Lyla's fingers flew over the keys, but the screen wouldn't change, so she quickly hit a button, returning it to the desktop display. She prayed Kekoa could still do whatever he was about to, and they would get the evidence they needed. Heart pounding in her ears, she spun in her chair to face Gretchen and smiled innocently. "Tell me."

Gretchen Newhouse was a nurse in her mid-fifties with two grown kids who hadn't given her any grandkids yet, so she focused all that grandmotherly love on Dr. Castillo's patients.

She dropped her clipboard on the desk and leaned against the wall. "I couldn't do it justice." Thumbing at the exam room she'd just exited, she said, "You have to hear Claude tell it."

"Don't worry, sis, file's downloading." Kekoa spoke softly in her ear. "Just need a few minutes."

"Good thing Claude likes to talk."

Gretchen gave Lyla a strange look. "He *does* . . . but it's because he's lonely, honey. You weren't here when his wife, Patty, was alive. He didn't come into the office near as much then. I think he just wants someone to talk to. Breaks my heart."

Lyla's too. Claude Miller was sweet and lonely and *loved* talking about his dachshund, Porridge. In the last month and a half since she'd been working undercover as a receptionist for Aspen Hills Medical Center, Claude came in at least once a week with a variety of issues that never really amounted to more than just a vitals check. He was a retired Army veteran unaware that the FBI suspected Dr. Castillo of fraudulently billing the VA for hundreds of thousands of dollars. And the reason Lyla was there in the first place.

"I know it causes us more work, but I'm just glad he has someplace to go."

Lyla's chest tightened at Gretchen's words. She glanced at her computer screen. Right now, Kekoa was gathering evidence that would put Gretchen out of a job and leave Claude with no place to talk about Porridge. They were collateral damage that caused Lyla's stomach to churn.

"Something isn't right."

Lyla jumped at Nicolás's voice, causing Gretchen to frown. Rubbing her arms, she forced herself to shudder again. "Sorry, I got the chills."

Gretchen looked out the window. A breeze teased the russet and gold leaves still clinging to the branches. "*Farmers' Almanac* predicts an easy winter."

"Somebody's tipped off the doc," Garcia growled. "Feds are on their way."

"We need the rest of the file." Kekoa's frustration was palpable. "If we don't—"

"I know," Lyla said and then cleared her throat when Gretchen shot her another odd look. "I'm not anxious for the snow."

"I don't know about them farmers, but my hip says otherwise." Claude ambled out of the exam room, his liver-spotted hand clutching a cane as he walked toward them. "My hip can forecast a snowstorm better than that cheeky gal on channel nine."

"Come here, Claude." Gretchen met him halfway and began fixing his misbuttoned sweater.

"I'll make you a cup of coffee while you wait for your ride."

Claude tipped his head. "I'd appreciate that, Ms. Gretchen." His cloudy gaze found Lyla. "Did I tell you about Porridge and the squirrel?"

"No, sir." She smiled, but her eyes flashed to Dr. Castillo's office. Was he in there deleting the evidence? She had to stop him. "Not yet." She picked up a stack of patient files. "But I need to get Dr. Castillo to sign some paperwork first, and then I'll be back so you can tell me all about it."

"Bridgette, honey, you're a sweet girl." Claude put a gentle hand on her arm when she passed. "Putting up with an old man's stories."

Acid slipped up Lyla's throat. Bridgette Anderson was the false identity Lyla was using. Normally she had no problem assuming an alias—she enjoyed pretending to be someone else—but she'd grown close to Gretchen, Claude, and a few of the other veterans. After today, Bridgette Anderson would disappear.

"Bridgette, you okay?" Concern laced Gretchen's eyes as she reached for Lyla's arm.

"Yes. Sorry. Tired, I guess." That wasn't a lie. Everything else was.

"Ly, you need to get into his office and stop him," Kekoa said into her ear.

"I should get the doctor to sign these so we can get home." Not waiting for a response, Lyla turned down the hall and headed for Dr. Castillo's office. Agitation gnawed at her gut. Somewhere along the way she'd allowed herself to become emotionally invested in Gretchen's and Claude's lives. The lives of all the veterans she checked in every day. Each of them had served their country and now might not get the benefits they deserve because of a greedy doctor.

That is going to stop today.

She tapped lightly on Dr. Castillo's office door and heard a grunt. Odd. She slowly turned the doorknob and entered. Restraint wasn't something Dr. Castillo favored. Photos of his extravagant travels across the globe on private planes and chartered yachts covered his walls. Pricey souvenirs worth more than most of his employees' salaries combined decorated his office.

"If you can get close enough to his computer, I can use the transmitter in your pen to trigger the spyware you downloaded to access his files." Kekoa spoke quietly as though he were afraid someone besides Lyla might hear.

Lyla felt for the pen in her pocket. "Dr. Castillo?"

Victor Castillo spun in the leather desk chair behind his mahogany desk to face her. In his late thirties, he wasn't bad looking. His dark-brown hair had a light feathering of gray near the temples, and his skin was nearly flawless thanks to Botox. The top button of his shirt was undone, his tie lopsided and loose around his neck. Lyla met his normally clear brown eyes and noticed they were glassy.

She stepped closer to the desk. "Is everything okay?"

"That's good, Lyla," Kekoa said. "Don't move."

"Okay?" A maniacal laugh slithered from the doctor's lips. "No. Everything's-s-s not okay."

His slurred speech caused her to frown. Had he been drinking? Lyla slid a quick peek to the credenza, where a crystal decanter holding aged whiskey sat empty.

"They're going to arresht me."

"*Somebody's tipped off the doc.*" Nicolás's words rang in her head. Who? Maybe others were involved in the scheme.

Three months ago, the Department of Veterans Affairs contacted SNAP to investigate the high number of insurance claims being submitted to Medicare and CHAMPVA on behalf of several veterans who complained they couldn't get appointments or they'd had their appointments canceled for no reason.

With Kekoa's help accessing the computer system, Lyla figured out in only a month that Dr. Castillo saw a light patient load but billed the government for multiple visits and made bank at the expense of the government and veterans. Since then, Lyla had been examining all the patient files to gather as much evidence as possible for the FBI to prosecute him to the fullest.

She slipped her hand into her pocket and palmed her cell phone, twisting sideways just enough so that the doctor wouldn't see her pull it out. She placed the phone on the patient files in her hand and, barely moving her fingers, opened the recording app and turned it on. If Castillo named others or was about to give a drunken confession, she wasn't going to miss it.

"I don't understand." Lyla hated playing dumb, but if there was one thing she'd learned in her job for the Strategic Neutralization and Protection Agency, it was that men, especially of the criminal sort, liked to brag about their crimes to women they believed were too dumb to do anything with the information. *Oh, I love to prove them wrong.* "Who's going to arrest you for what?" she asked.

"I almost changed my degree plan. Art." Castillo snorted. "But my parents insisted I be a doctor. They paid the bill"—he shrugged—"so I thought, *Why not?* Lots more money in medicine."

Yeah, stolen money.

"Lyla, I think you need to get out of there," Nicolás warned.

"Just a few more minutes," Kekoa said. "Lyla, can you move a bit closer? Might make it go faster."

Flipping her phone facedown, she took another step, bringing her behind his computer and

14

close enough that she could smell the alcohol.

"They don't tell you about the sacrifices. The long nights studying. The alcohol." Castillo let out a pathetic laugh. "The last girlfriend I had was my senior year of high school."

Was she supposed to feel sorry for him? Lyla's eyes slid to the pictures on the walls of the young doctor being flanked by beautiful women in scant clothing designed to emphasize their enhanced features. *Yeah, life is really hard when you're living high at the expense of those who sacrificed for their country.*

Dr. Castillo rose behind the desk. "I couldn't figure it out."

"I don't like this. You need to get to the door, Lyla."

Lyla held her ground, ignoring Nicolás. "How long?"

"Longer than it sh-should've," Dr. Castillo answered, but Lyla's question wasn't for him.

"Another minute. Two tops."

"Kekoa." Lyla flinched at Nicolás's sharp tone.

"I'm good, but I can't make it go faster, brah."

"Get out of there, Lyla. The Feds are on their way. We have enough evidence to put him away for a long time."

She could feel the agitation in Nicolás's tone, and it sparked her defiance. Once again, he didn't trust her to do her job. *Why?* They never would've gotten this close to Dr. Castillo's

15

records had *she* not been convincing enough to win his trust. *She* was the one who'd called in multiple favors from family friends—doctors—who gave her alias, Bridgette Anderson, stellar recommendations so he'd hire her. And *she'd* spent long nights comparing records until *her* eyes felt like sandpaper from the harsh glow of the computer screen. "I'm staying."

"What?" Dr. Castillo leaned his hands on his desk.

"I said I'm staying until you tell me what's going on."

Nicolás grumbled something over the coms that Lyla couldn't make out before his voice became clear. "Can she move and put the chair between her and Castillo?"

"Yeah," Kekoa answered.

That she could do. She took small steps—imperceptible, she hoped—edging closer to a large window overlooking the building's main parking lot. She didn't know where Nicolás was watching from, but something was reassuring in the knowledge that he was out there. She trusted he would do his job if necessary. That's how teams worked.

If only Nicolás would trust her to do hers.

The sound of the metal sliding against steel caused her blood to run cold. All her training at the gun range made the sound very familiar. She swallowed against the fear welling up inside her and forced herself to face the threat.

Dr. Castillo's glazed expression was locked on the gun in his hand.

Her pulse ratcheted up. *One minute.* She prayed Kekoa was right. "What are you doing with a gun, Dr. Castillo?"

"Lyla, get out of there," Nicolás demanded, and from the echo in her ear, she could tell he was moving. Not daring to look out the window again, she kept her gaze trained on the doctor and noticed his face held an eerie expression of calm. Calm was never good. Calm was resolute.

"All this time . . . I'd been fine. No problems. No one asking questions."

"Now, Lyla!" Garcia's voice cut into her ear.

Lyla backed toward the door, but instead of following Nicolás's orders and exiting, which any smart person would do, she turned the lock, trapping herself in the office with Dr. Castillo. Gretchen and Claude were no doubt still talking about Porridge over a cup of coffee. The last thing Lyla needed was Gretchen walking in and catching a bullet or becoming a hostage.

She needed to tread carefully. "I don't know what you're talking about."

"Then you got here . . ." Dr. Castillo blinked several times, and a look of realization darkened his features as his bloodshot eyes narrowed on her. "You."

17

"Got it!"

Kekoa shouted in her ear just as Castillo charged her from behind the desk, faster than she was expecting, the gun aimed at her face. With one smooth movement, her fist found the soft part of his throat, and before his eyes could register the shock of what was happening, the gun fell from his hand and into her free one. Relief flooded her.

Lyla turned the gun over in her hand. HK. Serial number filed off. *Nice.* A Buick trunk special, no doubt. She emptied the chamber before dropping the clip into her hand and met the doctor's wide-eyed gaze.

"Wh—" He choked, grabbing hold of his throat. "Are y-you a Fed?"

"No."

The sound of sirens echoed loudly outside the building. Lights flashed through the window, then the sirens turned off and were replaced with the slamming of doors as the FBI hurried into the building. His wild eyes flashed to the scene unfolding outside and then back to her. "Just leave me the gun . . . and one bullet."

Lyla's stomach clenched. *Suicide.* The coward's way out. No—the hopeless way out. She stared at the doctor. "That's too easy a solution for a man like you. You deserve to rot in a jail cell for the rest of your life."

Rage lit a fire in his eyes. "You're going to pay for this. Just wait. I'll make you pay."

She heard the federal agents' voices in the hallway. Her lips pulled into a smirk. "Give it your best shot."

Castillo snarled, but before he could take a step, Lyla unlocked and opened the door to find three men in suits waiting. One of them gave an imperceptible nod—her cue that her role was done. Time to leave.

Hating goodbyes, Lyla handed the gun to another agent and slipped out the emergency exit and down the stairwell. She would talk to her dad or some of her connections and make sure Gretchen had a job and Claude had someplace he could go to talk about Porridge. She'd see to it that all the veterans Castillo had taken advantage of got the treatment they deserved.

Nicolás met her at the building's exit, his sharp words sucking the relief right out of her. "What were you thinking?"

"What?"

"I told you to leave." Nicolás's hands were fisted at his sides, his chest rising and falling with shallow breaths. "Why didn't you listen?"

"I couldn't leave. He had a gun and could've hurt Gretchen or Claude."

"You could've been shot. Killed. You didn't think your decision through."

Anger twisted her insides into a knot. Why did

19

it always feel like she was disappointing him? Why did it matter? She'd gotten the job done, and yeah, there had been a risk, but it'd been worth it to make sure Castillo didn't hurt anyone else. Grinding her molars, she asked, "Did you get the file, Kekoa?"

"Uh"—Kekoa cleared his throat, a sure sign he'd been caught eavesdropping over the coms— "yeah. You did good, sis."

The muscles in Nicolás's jaw clenched.

Lyla didn't blink. "Am I clean, Kekoa?"

"Spick-and-span."

"And the cameras?"

"Wiped. Bridgette Anderson never existed."

"Then the assignment is done?"

"Yes," Kekoa said, hesitation hanging in the one-syllable word.

"So I guess I *do* know how to do my job."

A flicker of something in Nicolás's eyes . . . Was it concern? No, it was skepticism, and it flooded her cheeks with heat that made her want to cry. She would not cry. Shoving past Nicolás, Lyla let the crisp autumn air cool her down.

Behind her, she heard Castillo's angry voice demanding his lawyer, denying the charges. She turned as the FBI was escorting the doctor away from the building in handcuffs. His furious glare locked on her.

"You're going to pay for this. Just wait. I'll get out and make you pay."

A shudder ran down her spine. It wasn't the first time she'd been threatened, but something in his expression unnerved her. Or maybe it was Nicolás's lack of faith in her.

"That won't happen," a voice behind her said.

Lyla twisted to find Nicolás standing there, chin dipped, eyes full of apology. She couldn't hold on to her own anger. "It's fine. He doesn't scare me."

Nicolás swallowed. "A little fear is healthy, Lyla. Keeps us from making poor decisions."

She narrowed her eyes at him. Her anger wanted to return, but she suddenly felt exhaustion overtaking the adrenaline. "I don't need you telling me what to do. We got the job done, and that's all that matters."

"That's not all that matters." Nicolás's hazel eyes held her. "We got lucky this time, but next time it could end differently."

Lyla watched him walk away, hating that he had the ability to turn the successful ending to their assignment upside down, leaving her feeling inadequate. Just like the Nowak case a few months ago. Nicolás couldn't—wouldn't—trust her to do her job. A soft huff of annoyance escaped her lips. Of all the opinions that mattered to her—his was the one she cared about the most.

2

Squreaaak. Squreaaak. Squreaaak.
Nicolás Garcia shot up in his bed and nailed his elbow against the nightstand, sending a painful sensation through his arm. He ignored it, heart pumping as he homed in on the noise.

Squreaaak. Squreaaak.

He fell back against his pillow when he recognized the sound. There was nothing like waking up to a trash can scraping across the asphalt to start the day. Or the pain radiating from his funny bone. Nic yanked his pillow out from under his head and pressed it over his face. He squeezed his already closed eyes tighter as if that would somehow make the familiar scene unfolding outside his apartment go away.

Ugh. He tossed his pillow and rolled out of bed. Running a hand through his hair, he stared at the dark window. What was he doing out so early?

Squreaaak. Squreaaak.

Gracious. If Nic didn't get out there soon, the whole building would be up. He flipped on a light and grabbed a sweatshirt and pulled it over his bare chest. It wouldn't be enough to keep him warm in the chilly early morning temps that October had brought in, but it would have to do.

He slipped into a pair of boots, then opened the

22

door and saw the hunched form of Louis Brandt in a tug-of-war match with his garbage can. Nic released a long exhale and jogged across the lawn.

"Mr. Brandt, I told you I would take your trash out for you." He called out softly so as not to scare him. The last thing he wanted to do was give his elderly neighbor a heart attack. INFANTRYMAN SURVIVES KOREAN WAR, DIES TAKING TRASH OUT would make a horrible headline.

"Oh, thank you, Nic." The old man let him take the trash can, then tugged on a plaid hat with ear flaps. Nic noticed he was wearing house slippers. "I didn't want to disturb anyone."

Not disturb anyone? Nic's eyes flashed to their building where a few lights were already on. His neighbors had no doubt been woken up by the same noise that had jolted him from sleep.

Several of them had thanked him for intervening in Mr. Brandt's trash day ritual. Nic was usually up before the man began his trek, but the familiar nightmare he'd been having for the last week had kept him tossing and turning all night. He'd finally managed to doze sometime around four and ignored his alarm when it went off this morning.

"It's no bother." Images from the nightmare flashed in his mind. Him standing in front of a window, fists pounding on the glass, screaming

23

but there's no sound, and he watches as Lyla faces off with the gun Castillo has aimed at her. His finger pulls back on the trigger, and then Nic wakes up. Even now, his heart pounded as if the dream were real. "I can take it out in the evenings if that works better for you."

Nic shoved the images out of his mind and placed Mr. Brandt's trash can next to a few others that had been set out the night before.

"Humph." He waved a hand at Nic. "And give those rascally raccoons my personals to ferret through? No thanks."

Nic glanced up at the inky sky still peppered with stars not ready to end their nightly watch. He took a calming breath. In the five years he'd lived here, he hadn't once seen a rascally raccoon in their trash or ever caught sight of one in the wooded area that hedged their property in. Deer, squirrels, rabbits, yes. Raccoons seemed to stay away, but there was no sense in pointing that out to Mr. Brandt, who at the moment eyed said property like he was expecting an assault by raccoon at any moment.

Nic looked down at Mr. Brandt's leather house slippers and shivered. His own sockless toes were numb. "Don't you have some winter boots?"

"Humph." He scrunched his wrinkled face. "When I was stationed in Korea, we had winters so cold it would freeze your nose hair." He started ambling back to their apartment building. "This is practically a tropical heat wave."

Nic looked at the frost stiffening the blades of grass on the lawn they walked past. *Yeah, right.* Mr. Brandt was as tough as they came—the true epitome of a soldier, but also stubborn. Reminded him of someone else Nic knew. He walked Mr. Brandt to his door. "I'll bring your trash can back up when I get home from work."

Mr. Brandt did an about-face and eyed him. "You don't need to be worrying about an old man like me." His cloudy gaze sharpened. "Don't you have a young woman you can pester?"

Nic smiled. "No, sir. No woman I can pester." Lyla's face flashed to mind. Except her. It seemed he was really good at driving her nuts even though it was never his intention.

"Well, get on it, son." A whining noise came from behind the door. Mr. Brandt opened it, and his twelve-year-old lab, Biscuit, wandered out, sniffed Nic's hand, and wagged his tail for a second before going to the grass to do his business. "Life is too short to spend it alone."

Mr. Brandt's statement followed Nic all the way to the Denny's in Arlington, where he sat staring at the tenth verse of 1 Peter. He tried to focus on Chaplain Hahm's voice, his words about the cost of being bold like Elijah, but all Nic could hear was his neighbor's almost predictive declaration.

"Life is too short to spend it alone."

It was like a warning. And if that wasn't troubling enough, the image that followed was extra problematic. Lyla Fox. *Why does my mind go there?* Lyla definitely didn't lack boldness, but he didn't think it was the same kind Elijah had demonstrated. Rather, hers was a dangerous never-thinks-twice-going-to-get-herself-killed boldness that tormented Nic daily.

"You ready?"

The question came from his right, where Jack Hudson was sitting, watching him. Around them the table had begun to clear as the members of the men's bimonthly Bible breakfast headed to work. Most branches of the military were represented, along with several local police and first responders.

Nic had been a bit hesitant when Director Walsh recommended the group, but these gatherings, where each of them could share about the difficulties they faced on the job and in their lives and then pray for one another, had quickly become the highlight of his month.

These men had become like brothers, and none closer than Jack—who was waiting for him to respond.

"Uh, yeah. Sorry." Nic gathered his Bible and pushed his chair back to stand. He pulled out his wallet and laid out some cash for their waitress before turning to find Jack staring at him with those ever-appraising eyes. "What?"

"You all right, brother?"

Nic's muscles stiffened. As close as he and Jack were, it probably wasn't wise to confess where his distracted thoughts were leading him. He headed toward the exit. "Yeah, I didn't get a workout in this morning, so I'm feeling a bit tense."

Outside, the mid-October chill cut through Nic's Carhartt jacket. Anxious to get out from under the stare he could still feel on his back, he pulled his cap out of his back pocket and tugged it over his head before unlocking the door to his truck.

"You sure that tension doesn't have anything to do with what's been going on between you and Lyla over the last week?"

He faced Jack. "That obvious, huh?"

Jack smirked. "There's an old Italian proverb my mama told me after I first met Brynn— l'amore, la tosse e il fumo sono difficili da nascondere—which means love, a cough, and smoke are hard to hide."

Heat flamed across his cheeks. "Dude, I was referring to the Castillo assignment."

"Riiight." Jack nodded, skepticism arching his brow. "What about it?"

Nic gripped the brim of his cap, barely meeting his friend's eyes. His insides coiled tight beneath the weight of that question and the nightmares keeping him awake.

Jack whistled. "This must be more serious than I thought." The playfulness Nic caught in Jack's expression dimmed when Nic remained quiet. "How serious is this?"

Taking a breath, Nic toed his boot across the asphalt. "I'm beginning to doubt myself."

"What do you mean?"

Nic removed his hat and ran a hand through his hair, recalling what had taken place in Dr. Castillo's office a week ago. Replacing his hat, he looked Jack in the eyes. "This isn't the first time I've jumped the gun"—he cringed at the unfortunate pun—"when it comes to Lyla. I nearly blew her cover with the Nowak assignment, and this time, well . . ." He ran a hand down his jaw and along the scruff to his chin. "If I'd made it into Castillo's office before Lyla disarmed him, I'm not sure it would be him sitting in a jail cell right now."

"It was a tense situation—"

"It's more than that, Jack. When it comes to the mission . . . I don't trust my decisions when it comes to her." The words—the fear—slipped from his lips, and Nic wrestled with whether he wanted to take them back. *Too late now.* "The last couple of assignments I thought I knew the right—the safe—way, but Lyla went the opposite direction. She's impulsive and jumps in head-first without thinking." His mind went to the only other person he knew who operated without fear

28

of the consequences. He blew out a breath, the pain of a hundred memories still raw. "It gives her a dangerous confidence that no matter what she gets herself caught up in, she'll figure a way out. But she refuses to believe that one day it might not work, and I don't know if she's ready to live with the fallout."

"Or if you are."

Nic met Jack's intense gaze. In the four years they'd worked together, Jack had never once asked why Nic left the military, but the questions were there. Asked or not, Jack left that part of Nic's life alone, like he was patiently building a bridge of trust and waiting for Nic to cross it.

"There are no second chances when it comes to explosives." He recalled his brief career in the Army Explosives Ordnance Disposal branch. He hadn't been ready for his time there to end so suddenly and shamefully, which is why he needed to have this conversation. He knew too well that one bad decision, one impulsive act, and it could all go wrong. "Lyla's smart and intuitive, and I enjoy working with her, but . . ."

"She's never taken direction well," Jack finished with a chuckle.

"I've worked with people who don't take direction well. It's not just that, Jack." Nic gripped the back of his neck, not sure where he wanted to go with this conversation. "I just know what it's like to make a decision and have it change the whole course of your life. I don't want that for her."

Several long seconds spread between them as Nic searched Jack's face, trying to get a read on his thoughts. His quiet disposition gave nothing away.

"Then explain that to her," Jack finally said. "Sometimes a simple conversation is all it takes to admit you both need each other."

Nic's ears burned. "Pardon?"

Jack gave him an amused look of exasperation and shook his head. "All I'm saying is that I understand where you're coming from. I know the doubt you're contending with. I lived with it for ten years after what happened with Brynn. If you let your emotions control you, you're going to find yourself hiding in the wilderness like Elijah and missing out on the blessing of releasing control back to the Lord."

Releasing control. Nic ground his molars, not liking the sound of that at all. Control was everything when it came to disarming bombs and protecting himself from making another mistake.

"You're a good man, Nic, and I have no doubt the two of you can work it out. Besides, you're going to need to get along sooner rather than later."

"Why's that?"

"You know, just in case I need you to fill in for me."

Worry filled Nic. "Everything okay? Your health?"

Jack smiled. "I'm fine and still cancer-free, which is why Brynn and I thought it would be the perfect time to start trying for a bambino."

"A baby?" Nic smiled. "You serious?"

"Yes, Lord willing." Jack's smile grew, filling his face all the way to his eyes. "So can you do me a solid and figure out how to play nice with Lyla?"

"I don't know, brother," Nic deadpanned. "I think playing with bombs is safer."

Jack tilted his head to the side. "I might actually agree with you on that."

They both shared a laugh just as a familiar silver Volvo pulled into a parking space next to Nic's truck. The passenger-side window rolled down, and Nic and Jack leaned toward it.

Nic pressed a palm on the top of the car. "Morning, sir."

"Bible study's over, sir," Jack said. "You missed a good lesson on Elijah."

"I'm sure I did." Director Tom Walsh gave a genuine smile. "I need to chat with you, Nic, if you have a minute."

Unease coursed through Nic. "Yes, sir."

Jack straightened. "I'll head to work and see you both when you get there."

"Just Nic," Walsh said. "I've got another meeting with the State Department."

Nic didn't know if the displeasure he detected in Walsh's voice was due to the meeting or what he needed to talk with him about. Nic gave a quick nod to Jack as he got into his car and left, then removed his cap before climbing into the passenger seat of the Volvo. "Yes, sir?"

Walsh adjusted the vents in his car, turning the heat down. "I ran into General DeAntona this morning."

Nic's insides squeezed at the name of his old EOD commander. At the time, his boss was a colonel, and now he was a lieutenant general—a rank that didn't surprise Nic in the least. DeAntona was a soldier's soldier through and through. A great leader and one Nic would've appreciated working under for longer than fourteen months. He dropped his gaze to his hands, the shame still weighing on him.

"General DeAntona speaks highly of you and your service as part of the Explosives Ordnance Disposal community."

Nic glanced up, and Walsh's blue eyes held steady on him as if he'd known exactly where Nic's thoughts were. And he did. That day when Nic showed up asking for a job, Walsh didn't ask the questions others had about his past. He made it clear that he knew. Nic didn't ask how, just accepted the chance to redeem himself.

"It was a privilege to work for him."

"He'd like to offer you that privilege again."

Walsh straightened his glasses on his nose. "This morning I was in a briefing with President Lawson, his national security advisor, and the State Department. There's been an uptick in IED bombings in Syria at the announcement of the upcoming election. The most recent one killed a man who dared to challenge the current Syrian president. General DeAntona is taking a group of specialists to Syria at the request of the UN in an operation he's calling Free Vote. The idea behind it is to give the Syrian citizens their best and safest chance to vote independent of influence."

"They want us in Syria?" Nic ran his palm down his thigh to his knee at the memory of his tour in Syria. The devastation caused by the Syrian Civil War. He could still smell the rank odor of burned rubber as displaced families threw tires onto fires to stay warm.

"No," Walsh said. "He'd like you to meet with the FBI this morning and lend your expertise to an IED discovered at the US Embassy in Damascus."

Nic could think of a dozen or more EOD officers, active, whose knowledge would be more relevant. "Why me?"

"DeAntona didn't give me much detail." Walsh reached across his dash and picked up a file, which he handed to Nic. "But he believes you have some personal experience with the particular device in question. He doesn't trust anyone else and wants you on the team. Everything you need to know is in there, including your report date should you choose to go."

Nic took the folder but didn't open it. His brain was trying to wrap around what was happening. He never imagined having another chance to work with the military or DeAntona, but part of him wondered if there was more to this sudden arrangement—especially after his conversation with Jack. Had he mentioned his concern to Walsh?

"Sir, you've always been straight with me." Nic steeled himself. "Am I being fired?"

"What?" Walsh looked genuinely confused. "No. This is a temporary assignment. One I told DeAntona I'd present on the promise he wouldn't try to steal you out from under me. He assured me you'd be released once the mission was complete."

Which could mean weeks. Months. Nic thought about his earlier concerns and the message Chaplain Hahm had given them regarding the prophet Elijah being called to do something new . . . something that would take him away from what he knew. Was this God's answer to his doubts?

"I don't want to add to the pressure of this decision, but the sooner you know, the sooner I can make arrangements with the team." Walsh's words drew Nic's attention. "Nic, I know what happened last week has been weighing on you, but Lyla's behavior is not a reflection on you. I've known her a long time, and I would've been shocked had she done anything different."

If that was supposed to make Nic feel better— it didn't. It was the very thing causing him to question his place with the agency.

"You're a valuable asset, Nic." Walsh looked at his watch, and Nic knew this impromptu visit was done. "I meant it when I made DeAntona promise me he wouldn't try to poach you."

"I appreciate that, sir." He held up the folder. "I'll look through this and have an answer to you ASAP."

Nic exited the car and waited until Walsh drove out of the parking lot. Inside his truck, he started the engine to let it warm up and opened the file. Nic looked at the report date. Six weeks. He glanced out the windshield to the city he'd grown familiar with, and a strange ache filled his middle. Was he ready to leave this? Was he ready to leave . . . her?

3

Chunks of mashed banana splattered Lyla in the face. "Eww, gross, Kekoa!"

Lyla watched Kekoa Young's dark curls bounce across his forehead as he let out a hearty laugh. "Sorry, sis."

She reached across the counter and grabbed a towel to wipe her face. "You don't look sorry."

"What can I say?" Kekoa flexed his tattooed biceps, causing the banana mess in his hands to drip on the floor. "These tanks are too strong for banana guns."

Rolling her eyes, she used the towel to scoop up the mess on the floor of the SNAP Agency kitchen. She didn't need Walsh or Jack or, heaven forbid, Nicolás commenting on the mess. "You wanted me to teach you what I did, so you're going to have to"—she rose, eyeing Kekoa's large hands—"learn how to control your strength, at least while we're using bananas."

The mechanical sound of the lock disengaging turned their attention to Jack as he walked in the door. He stopped, looked at them, and then glanced around. "What?"

"Nothing." Lyla dropped the towel in the sink, ignoring the disappointment that it wasn't Nicolás who had walked through the door. She

36

grabbed another towel from the drawer and handed it to Kekoa.

Jack's brow lifted. "How come it feels like I caught you guys doing something you're not supposed to be doing?"

Kekoa held up his hands. "Lyla's teaching me the move she pulled on Castillo to disarm him."

"We're using bananas." She pointed to the remaining piece of fruit sitting on the island. "It's safer."

"As long as no one steps on one, right?" Jack took off his jacket and gave each of them a pointed look. "Come on. A banana on the floor? Slips . . ." He pressed his lips together. "Never mind."

Kekoa winked at Lyla before they both started laughing.

"Don't quit your day job, brah." Kekoa picked up the last banana and looked at Lyla. "Okay, last time."

"Or maybe"—Lyla took the banana from Kekoa's meaty grip—"we save that for Nicolás's midmorning smoothie. You know he gets cranky without his salad-in-a-cup energy drink." She glanced over Jack's shoulder to the closed door. "Isn't today your, um, Bible meeting club?"

Jack hung his coat on the rack before turning his attention to her with that ever-annoying I-know-what-you're-asking-but-aren't-asking look on his face.

"Yep."

Ugh. He was going to make her ask. Like an annoying brother holding something over her head, just out of reach, making her jump for it. Well, she wouldn't. Her cute leather-heeled booties weren't meant for jumping. *Besides,* she thought with a smile, *two can play at this game.*

"How's that coffee at Denny's?" Lyla walked to her Miele 6800 espresso machine. Her finger glided across the screen, bringing it to life. "Kekoa's dad just sent me a package of premium Kona coffee beans. Aren't those your favorite?"

"Brah," Kekoa half whispered, "she knows your weakness. Just give her the information and nobody's gonna get hurt."

Jack pushed up the sleeves of his sweater like he was ready to square off with her, and Kekoa whistled the tune from *The Good, the Bad and the Ugly*. Jack raised an eyebrow. "If you want to know where Garcia is, all you have to do is ask."

Lyla wasn't going to be intimidated. "I wasn't asking."

Oh, but the heat flashing across her cheeks would tell them she was lying. She began making Jack's Americano. What did it matter if she wanted to know where Nicolás was? She'd ask where either one of the men standing behind her were too. Her curiosity was grounded in concern. That's all.

No, that isn't all. Eyes fixed on the machine,

she replayed the strain of the last eight days over in her mind. Since the Castillo assignment, her easygoing relationship with Nicolás had shifted to uneasy, unsure, and uncomfortable.

The atmosphere wasn't outright hostile, but it also wasn't the amiable, relaxed, sometimes flirtatious—at least on her part—work environment that she loved. In its place was forced conversations that never veered off work-related subjects, and she hated it.

"Garcia seemed a little tense this morning." Jack's brotherly tone echoed behind her, and she clenched her jaw. "Have you two talked about what happened on the Castillo assignment?"

She spun around, caught off guard that Jack had nearly read her mind. "What's there to talk about?"

Jack shifted as Kekoa began taking slow steps backward like he was trying to escape. Normally his humor would've made her laugh, would've defused the aggravation she could feel rising to the surface, but today it was just plain annoying.

"We got the job done." She folded her arms. "I can't help if Nicolás disagrees with how I do the job, but since it gets done, I don't see what the problem is."

"We're a team. If there's a trust issue—"

"That's just it, Jack." Lyla pulled a mug from the cabinet and slammed the door shut. "I'm not the one with a trust issue. For whatever reason,

39

Nicolás doesn't trust *me*."

"Next time it could end differently." Nicolás's words echoed loudly in her head. No, it wasn't just words, it was a warning. Like he knew—or expected—she would screw up at some point. And that hurt, more than she wanted to reveal to him or anyone else on the team.

"It would be nice if I didn't have to face his Spanish inquisition every single time I'm on assignment."

"You know he's only trying to keep you safe."

"And *I* am trained to know what I'm doing." After setting down the mug, she pressed her palms flat against the quartz island countertop and faced Jack, tired of this conversation and of having to explain and defend her actions. *"Redirect. Control. Attack. Take Away.* The hours I spent getting whupped by the Krav Maga instructors at Quantico weren't fun. No one was in that doctor's office but me. I was keeping Gretchen and Claude safe. You didn't see the crazed look in Castillo's eyes. I had to make a split-second decision, and if anyone in this agency thinks I'd run out and leave two innocent people to face a psychopath . . ." She gathered her breath, her gaze moving between Jack and Kekoa. "If it had been either of you or Nicolás making the decision, would we still be talking about this?"

Jack's gaze held steady on her. "I'm not saying

your decision was wrong or that any of us wouldn't have done the same thing, but we must trust that if one of us gives an order, it's for our own good. Just like you said, we couldn't see what was happening in that office with Castillo, and you may not see what's happening outside, in Garcia's perspective. He was running the assignment, and that carries a huge responsibility to ensure the safety of all involved—even if it costs us the mission."

Lyla slid a sideways glance to Kekoa, who was nodding in agreement, and then dropped her gaze to the empty mug in front of her. Jack was mostly right. Nicolás and Kekoa had been her eyes outside of Castillo's office, but her perspective inside mattered too. Trust went both ways. She didn't have military experience or training under the CIA like they did, but she wasn't some inexperienced newbie either. She had defensive training and enough experience to know how to assess a situation. Running out of that office hadn't been an option.

And Nicolás should understand that. Like the rest of his life, he kept the details of his time in the Army close to the chest, guarded, but as an EOD officer, he ran into situations involving explosives. She couldn't imagine him hightailing it out of there when innocent lives were at risk.

The lock on the door sounded once more, and Lyla swung her gaze around and found Nicolás walking in. A few seconds of silence ticked off, leaving him to shift on his feet like he knew they were just talking about him.

"Brah, your timing . . ."

Lyla shook her head at Kekoa's whispered warning. She walked around the island to the closet and pulled out her coat and purse. "I have an appointment this morning. I already let Walsh know that I'll miss the briefing."

Edging past Nicolás, she tried to avoid eye contact, but there was something magnetic in his gaze and she couldn't resist the temptation to meet it. Big mistake. The second her eyes met his, the frustration from the past week and the conversation she just had with Jack curdled the hazelnut mocha she drank earlier.

She quickly slipped out of the SNAP Agency office, unable to take her first deep breath of air until she got to the parking garage. Mistake number two. She coughed on the lingering fumes of gas and oil. Served her right. She had no business letting Jack or Kekoa or Nicolás get to her.

Climbing into her car, she blew out a frustrated breath. She'd been a part of this agency before Nicolás or Kekoa joined, when it was just her, Jack, and Walsh. Neither of them had an issue trusting her to do her job. Okay, that wasn't entirely true. They didn't always voice it, but there were times when she sensed Jack and Walsh wished she'd be a little more conservative in her actions. Still, they let her do her job. Nicolás was the only one who seemed to question her every decision.

Why? She hadn't messed up any missions. In fact, over the last year she thought she'd been pivotal in the bigger assignments, working with Brynn and helping Kekoa keep Elinor safe. She even took down a major cryptocurrency criminal with the FBI. So why was Nicolás so set against her? And why did that hurt so much?

Pulling out of the parking garage of the Acacia Building, Lyla accelerated, wanting to leave that question behind with the man it belonged to. Except it continued to nag her, and she realized that at some point she'd given Nicolás more room in her head than was safe. In the years they'd worked together, she'd come to admire what he brought to the team. But little by little, that admiration had transformed into a craving for his approval. She craved it like Kekoa craved his island favorite, loco moco.

At least Kekoa's craving could be satisfied with a short drive to the Hawaiian restaurant. It didn't seem like she could do anything to prove herself to Nicolás. Even when the assignment ended well, it never seemed to be enough. She wasn't enough.

Lyla shoved the insecurity out of her head. She wasn't that girl anymore. Walsh had helped her find her place in the agency, and she *knew* she was good at her job—whether Nicolás agreed or not.

Twenty minutes later, the self-doubt Lyla had been carrying all her life was humbled silent by her current surroundings.

Lyla watched Dr. Loughridge and her nurse from the comfort of her car, thankful for the blast of heat from the vents. Outside the temps were hovering in the low forties, but the wind-chill made it feel closer to the low thirties. An unwelcome burst of winter weather had most of DC's residents raising the thermostat or throwing more logs on the fire to warm their homes. But not here. Not in this section of the capital.

No, for the residents living southeast of the Anacostia River, a few extra degrees or a couple logs of firewood were considered a luxury, right along with three square meals a day. These were things those residing in the string of run-down row houses in front of her couldn't afford.

Her attention moved back to the home of Jameson Cooper. Lyla had no doubt he would be facing a similar decision—pay for heat to avoid hypothermia or pay for his insulin.

Jameson Cooper was fifty-seven and currently worked as a line chef at the local burger joint two blocks away. As a child he'd dreamed of being a pilot for the Army, but a vision problem had ruled that out . . . or at least that's what she'd been told. Poor eyesight didn't stop Jameson from enlisting in the Army and serving in the conflicts in Kuwait and Afghanistan. It didn't stop him from working in the shipyard after a grenade ended his military career. And it didn't end Jameson's resolute determination to provide for his family—his children—despite his own medical needs.

Despite Castillo's neglect.

Mr. Cooper's door opened to Dr. Loughridge and her nurse, and the poor man was wearing a coat and beanie cap. Lyla grabbed a pen from her car's console and made a note next to his name on a piece of paper. She'd have an HVAC person come out to make sure Mr. Cooper's heater was working properly.

She watched Dr. Loughridge, a friend and family practice doctor, hold out a piece of paper. Mr. Cooper read it and then frowned, no doubt confused. A few more seconds of discussion and he stepped back, allowing the nurse to enter his home. Dr. Loughridge looked back, her gaze connecting with Lyla's. She nodded before she walked into Mr. Cooper's home and closed the door behind her.

Without violating HIPAA, Lyla had given the names of Dr. Castillo's most high-risk patients to Dr. Loughridge. Over the next couple of days she would go to their homes with her nurse and do a full workup—take blood, order labs or tests as necessary, do what Castillo lied about doing in the first place. Then Dr. Loughridge would make sure each patient had a follow-up appointment with a reputable doctor so they could receive continued care.

It was the best Lyla could offer these veterans who'd given so much, and she was grateful for her network of doctors and philanthropic family friends who agreed with her offering financial support and services.

Lyla looked at the list on her lap and put a check mark next to Mr. Cooper's name. She ran a finger over Claude Miller's name. She missed him and his stories about Porridge. Missed Gretchen.

The memory of her confrontation with Dr. Castillo still caused her pulse to thrum with adrenaline.

How many more wolves in sheep's clothing remained?

However many there were, Lyla would continue to do her job and unmask them. It didn't matter what Nicolás thought—she'd make the same choices again.

4

"This wouldn't have just killed Stanburg." Nic looked up from the photos he'd spent several long minutes inspecting. He'd been sitting in the FBI's office in Judiciary Square for the last couple of hours consulting on an IED discovered beneath the car of Deputy Assistant Secretary of State Mark Stanburg in Damascus a week ago. "The amount of pentaerythritol tetranitrate would've scattered pieces of his body more than twelve hundred feet."

The words were rancid on his tongue as ugly images from his past assaulted his brain.

Across from him, FBI Special Agent Kelly Sims shifted in her seat. "Not a pretty image."

"And one we narrowly avoided had it not been for the uneven ground that tripped Stanburg's assistant," Special Agent Jason Reynolds added. "It's a good thing Jered Hollins worked with cars before entering politics."

Nic stared at the photo of the catalytic converter attached to the vehicle's exhaust. A layperson wouldn't have noticed it wasn't in the correct location, but when Jered tripped, he fell near the back of the car and spotted the anomaly immediately. The bomb had been molded and disguised to look like a catalytic converter, and the organic type of explosive material explained why the detection dogs had missed it.

"Does it look familiar?" Agent Sims flipped her blonde braid over her shoulder. "Is it Al-Qaeda?"

Nic's palms grew clammy. *Personal experience.* That's why DeAntona told Walsh he wanted Nic to join them in Syria. He stared at the components of the explosive device, recognizing the similarities . . . except this one was all in one piece. Unlike the pieces of metal, warped and shredded, and the frayed and charred remains of wire stained with the blood of his friend.

Swallowing, Nic set his jaw and focused. "Al-Qaeda in that region typically uses military-grade explosives, like RDX. The PETN in this device isn't commonly used, nor is the method by which it was created."

Agent Reynolds picked up the photo. "You mean creating the IED to look like a piece of the car."

"Yes." Nic leaned forward and pulled a few photos out of the stack and placed them side by side. They were older images that had been taken when he served in the 28th EOD Company during his three deployments to Afghanistan. "Al-Qaeda's main objective has always been to inflict the most amount of damage or casualties, and . . ." He swallowed against the dryness in his throat. "In my experience, their improved methods include ambushes, setting up 'kill zones'

48

with strategically placed IEDs, or double IED traps where they lure attention with a smaller explosion, only to have a larger, deadlier device set to go off when the EOD unit arrives."

Agent Sims studied the photos. "So something like this vehicle-borne IED would be too advanced for Al-Qaeda?"

"It's possible Al-Qaeda's methods have changed or advanced with technology, but they typically stick with what they know works."

"Do you think this VBIED attached to Stanburg's car was an attack meant to kill him or a lure for something else?"

Nic pressed his palms to his thighs. "Thanks to Hollins, you'll never know." He saw Agent Sims narrow her blue eyes on him just like Lyla did when she thought he was being too callous in his honesty. He couldn't help it. There was no room in explosives for emotions. It was precise or it was deadly. "I don't mean that in a harsh way. It *really* is a good thing Hollins discovered the bomb. Countless lives were saved. I'm just pointing out that whatever the plan was for the bomb will remain a mystery."

And for that, Nic found a tiny piece of relief. Mark Stanburg's family would be spared the pain of the alternative.

"Okay." Agent Reynolds leaned forward in his chair, studying Nic for a minute. "You're the expert here. If you don't see this as Al-Qaeda's handiwork, who else should we be looking at?"

Nic didn't know what Agents Reynolds or Sims had been told about his *expertise,* but at least he now knew why DeAntona wanted him on the team. He was getting a second chance. A chance to do what he should've done years ago. It wouldn't change the outcome, but it might bring some resolution to his conflicted soul.

"Based on this bomb . . ." Nic studied the photo again. His eyes traced the wiring, the electronic signal connected to the explosive, and he pondered the effort taken to make it inconspicuous. He met the waiting faces of the special agents. "I think it's reasonable to look outside Al-Qaeda." They waited for more, and he took a breath. "Last time I was in Afghanistan, we encountered several explosives with this kind of detail coming from a group out of Mogadishu. I'd start there."

Agent Sims pushed back from the table. "Thank you, Nic." Her eyes lingered on him. "I can see why General DeAntona recommended you."

Nic picked up his ball cap from the table and placed it on his head before standing. "No problem."

"How much action do you get?" Agent Reynolds asked, gathering the photos.

"Uh . . ." Nic slid an awkward glance to Agent Sims, who bit her lip and smiled. "Action?"

"Yeah." Agent Reynolds looked up. "I admit

I don't know much about the SNAP Agency, but I can't imagine an EOD officer as skilled as yourself sees much action. Or is there some kind of explosives ring you guys bust on the regular that the FBI doesn't know about?"

Nic was relieved to have misunderstood, especially after catching the way Agent Sims was looking at him. He swallowed. "No, no explosives rings." He tugged on the brim of his cap, following both agents out of the conference room. "My EOD experience is primarily used in a consulting capacity like this, I guess."

Agent Sims wrinkled her brow, giving Nic a once-over. "You don't seem like the type to settle into consultation."

Nic thought over the last few assignments the SNAP Agency had worked and smirked. If either agent had the clearance, they would've had access to the many assignments performed in cooperation with the FBI. And even though he wasn't defusing explosives, he never felt like working for SNAP was settling. It was an opportunity he was grateful for, even if it came with a stress level rivaling the peaks and valleys of the Hindu Kush range in Afghanistan.

Especially when it came to Lyla.

Nic thought about the mission file sitting in his desk at the agency. He wasn't sure about the offer, but after walking into Lyla's aggression, the look on her face when she skirted by him was like a punch to his gut. He'd read through the file twice and was left wondering if maybe it would be better for Lyla if he accepted the mission and left the agency. He could see the toll his own doubts and misgivings were taking on her. If he left, then she'd never have to worry about being undermined again.

"Reynolds, if you'll take that file up"—Agent Sims smiled at Nic—"I'll walk Mr. Garcia out if he's ready."

Nic nodded. "Yes, ma'am."

"That makes me sound really old," Agent Sims said as soon as Agent Reynolds left them. She led Nic down the opposite hallway. "You can't be much older than me, right? Thirty-one, two?"

"Thirty-two."

"So we're the same age, and since I don't see a ring on your finger, I'm going to guess you're just as married to your job as I am."

Nic swallowed, seeing the recognizable interest shining bright in Agent Sims's eyes. "The job keeps me busy."

"Oh, I get it." Agent Sims paused by the exit. She reached into her pocket and pulled out a card. "But I do enjoy taking a little break every now and again, and I'm always looking for company if you're ever interested in taking your mind off work."

He accepted the business card, replaying the last couple of hours in his mind. Had he unintentionally flirted with Agent Sims? Given her the impression he was interested in her? She was certainly beautiful and smart—

"Well, uh, if you need anything, my number's on the card. And if we need anything else, Agent Reynolds or I will call you."

The awkwardness in her voice made Nic feel bad. Clearly, she had hoped for a better response than awkward silence. "Oh, yes, sorry." Ugh. He hated lying, but it had to be better than telling her he'd been trying to figure out a reason to accept her flirtation. "I was just thinking about . . . work."

Agent Sims tilted her head, blue eyes sparkling. "Does your *work* think about you as much as you think about her?"

Nic's cheeks warmed. He wanted to argue that she was wrong, but something about the way she was studying him said she'd know he was lying. "It's complicated."

She arched a brow. "I would say forget complicated and let's grab drinks tonight, but I guess someone who handles bombs for a living can handle a little complicated."

The tease in her tone made Nic relax. Agent Sims was funny too. So what was keeping him from asking her out? He knew what. He just wasn't willing to let his mind go there. "How bad is it that I'd choose the bomb?"

Agent Sims laughed and then pointed to the

guard desk. "Just leave your visitor tag in there." She backed away. "Oh, and Romeo, nothing defuses complicated better than flowers and an apology."

Nic arrived at the SNAP office carrying a candle and prepped with the apology he had owed Lyla a week ago. After his confession to Jack earlier that morning about his doubts and after Agent Sims's advice, he wanted nothing more than to settle the tension between him and Lyla as quickly as possible—especially in light of where he was leaning in regard to his decision about the Syria mission.

Lyla, it seemed, had walked in just before him and was talking with Jack, oblivious to his presence, and he was a bit grateful for that. Hanging back in the hallway separating the front living space of the office from the fulcrum, he took advantage of her distraction. He watched her drop her designer purse on the desk and shrug out of the red wool coat that made her look like Carmen Sandiego when her hair was that deep russet brown like it was now.

In six weeks, his work view was going to change drastically. But if his absence took away the pressure she put on herself and *that* kept her safe, he'd travel to other side of the globe.

She turned and caught him staring. Their eyes locked for just a second, but it was enough for him to feel exposed. "Everything okay, Nicolás?"

Lyla was the only one who called him by his full name, and the first time he heard it roll off her lips, he knew he was in trouble. He stepped farther into the room. "Yeah."

Her attention moved to the box in his hand. "What's that?"

Nic looked at the package. "Oh . . . it's, um, for you."

Lyla met him halfway and took the package, confusion pinching her brow as she accepted the box. She opened the flap and squealed. "Mykonos at Sunset." She pulled out the candle, then inhaled deeply, closing her eyes and smiling. "Did you know this is my favorite?"

In the four years he'd spent working next to her, he'd come to recognize the bergamot and citrus scent that clung to her clothing. And at least once a year, when the sunset colored the DC skyline in vibrant shades of yellow and orange, she'd comment about her favorite family vacation to the Greek island. "I've heard you mention it a few times."

"Did I miss her birthday?"

Nic glanced back at Kekoa and felt bad seeing the fear lingering on the Hawaiian's face. "Brother, you don't remember the mustache debacle?"

Kekoa's hand moved to his lip. "Oh, right. *Princess Bride.*"

"I remember that day." Jack laughed, inspecting Kekoa's lip. "I don't think you'll ever grow hair there again."

"Brah, I lost a layer of skin from that fake mustache."

Nic eyed them both. "I'm pretty sure those tight pants she made me wear caused permanent nerve damage to my right leg."

"Okay, okay, I get it." Lyla sighed. "I might have a tendency to go overboard for my parties, but they're always fun."

"The night wasn't so bad."

"See?" Lyla gestured to Jack. "It wasn't *so* bad."

"That's because he got the girl." Kekoa wiggled his hips.

"No thanks to you and your untimely interruptions." Jack shook his head. "It's a wonder I was able to kiss my bride at our wedding."

Nic chuckled at the memory, even as a tinge of jealousy flared within him. He was happy Jack had found Brynn and even happier that Kekoa had found someone to love *all* of him and his hip-shaking quirks, but their relationships only highlighted the emptiness in his own life.

His gaze collided with Lyla's before she quickly glanced back down at the candle.

"So, um, what's the occasion?"

Rocking on his heels, Nic looked between

the group and then back at her. "Can we talk?"

Lyla's blue-green eyes shifted to Jack. Was she nervous? Jack moved to his desk and shut his laptop. "Walsh is at a meeting until one, and I was just heading out to meet Brynn for lunch." He tipped his head at Kekoa. "You wanna try that new place at Union Station?"

Kekoa's brows scrunched. "You're not talking about that salad place, are you?"

Jack rolled his eyes. "Yes, but they also have proteins you can add to the salad. Fish, chicken, steak, and—"

"You think I can ask for a steak salad without the salad?" Kekoa's lips curved into a smile. "Or steak salad, minus the salad, add some chicken?"

"Get your coat." Jack shook his head. "It's like taking a six-foot-four, three-hundred-pound toddler out to eat."

Nic caught Jack's curious look before leaving him and Lyla alone in the office. Lyla set the candle on her desk, then did a slow turn to face Nic.

"Everything okay, Nicolás?"

He tugged the brim of his hat down, giving him a second to assess Lyla like he was assessing an explosive device. Gauging her tone, her posture, her facial expression, the way she was biting the inside of her lip like she did when she was trying to figure something out. His opinion that this fiercely independent woman needed to be

57

approached with caution wasn't an exaggeration. Was she fully charged or—

"I hate it when you look at me like that."

Heat clawed his neck. "Like what?"

She shifted under his watch, tucking her chin to her chest. "The one where I can't tell if you like me or not."

Nic blinked, taking a small step back. He rubbed his neck, caught off guard by her comment and unsure of how to answer.

"Oh my goodness, Nicolás." Lyla met his gaze. "I know we don't always see eye to eye on our assignments, and you think I'm impulsive and I think you're a little uptight, which is funny because you have this whole James Dean meets Matthew McConaughey vibe going on, but I want us to get over it already. We've never let our differences get in the way of our friendship."

Differences? That's how she saw it? Her inclination to face off with danger and his propensity to understand the cost of risk before committing was just a simple variance in how they operated? It was so much more than that, but he didn't think he'd be able to make her understand that in the few weeks before he left.

"No."

"Maybe take a few seconds longer to answer next time." There was a tease in her voice, but uncertainty dimmed her smile. "You had me worried that I'd lost you."

It was the way his heart clung to those last three words that pushed the apology he practiced back to mind. This was why he'd asked her to talk—to set everything straight so there'd be no misunderstandings before he left.

"I want to tell you I'm sorry for the way I reacted after the Castillo assignment. I had no right to speak to you the way I did, and it was unprofessional to question your decision when I wasn't in your position."

Lyla's shoulders relaxed, the planes of her face softening as she met his eyes. "I wasn't professional either. It was your mission, and I shouldn't have assumed you weren't looking out for the safety of all involved. I'm sorry for not heeding your authority."

"Heeding my authority?" Nic's brows rose. "Those are big words. You sure you know what they mean?"

"Har. Har." She gave him a playful side-eye. "I'm just saying that I will try, to the best of my ability, to be more open to your guidance." She lifted a brow. "And not be so stubborn."

Nic forced his lips into a smile. "I doubt that."

"See? This is what I miss. Us." She moved toward him, and before he was ready, she wrapped her arms around his waist, letting her head fall against his chest.

At just a few inches over five feet, she was at the perfect position to hear his pounding heart. He

59

breathed in the crisp, clean scent of her shampoo, letting it form a memory of this moment that he could look back on one day.

Us. One word that meant something different to each of them. Nic took a steadying breath. He needed to tell her about the mission. He opened his eyes, not realizing he'd allowed them to close. "Lyla."

She leaned back, not fully releasing him from the hug, and looked up beneath those dark lashes. "Yeah?"

What was I going to tell her again?

The heavy pounding of footsteps yanked them apart as Kekoa hurried into the office. "Lyla, there's been an incident."

5

I warned you.
I know how to get to you.
You can't hide.
You die next.
—JMM

Lyla's hands shook as she read the words again. A war of emotions twisted her stomach into a nauseating knot of fury.

"You okay?"

Lyla jerked at Nicolás's voice and hated that it revealed only half of what she was feeling. She assessed the damage to her car, and her anger pulsed louder than her fear. "I'm ticked."

"I can see that." The corner of his lip hitched, but there was no humor in the grave expression that had darkened his hazel eyes the second they walked off the elevator and into the Acacia Building's subterranean parking garage. There they found her Audi, the front windshield smashed in with a brick.

Lyla had stared at her car for a full minute before she understood. She wasn't sure if the delay was due to the shock of the vandalism or what took place up in the office with Nicolás.

Jack walked over from the security booth.

"Kekoa's checking our security footage, says he's got video of someone wearing a hooded sweatshirt, but there's no good shot of his face. He's working on every angle to identify who did this."

"We know who did it," Lyla growled.

Jack exchanged a look with Nicolás. "I spoke with Walsh and let him know what's happened. He's certain Jerome Miller is still in prison but was going to reach out to the warden to be sure."

"What about his family?" Nicolás hadn't moved from her side, his steady presence calming the anger pulsing through her. "Friends? Associates?"

"Metro Police are going to look into it." Jack looked at Lyla. "They asked for a list of names to give them a place to start."

"It's nice of them to pretend they care."

Nicolás put a gentle hand on her shoulder. "Lyla."

"I'm not upset about it." She stepped out of his touch and moved to the passenger side of her car. She opened the door, then grabbed her workout bag and a book. "The police have bigger issues to take care of than another one of Jerry Miller's attempts to intimidate me."

"This is more serious than the letters." Nicolás's gravelly voice was low and menacing. "This is a brick in the middle of your windshield. At your place of work."

Lyla closed her car door and then felt silly when, out of habit, she hit the fob to lock it. She marched to the elevator with Nicolás and Jack trailing her and jabbed the button. Her eyes fell to her phone, where she'd taken a photo of the threatening note.

It wasn't Jerry's hatred scrawled on the page that made her uneasy. He was hardly the first to lash out in anger at her. Castillo's threats from the other day came to mind. Caught criminals were desperate and said desperate things, but they were mostly empty threats.

What was unsettling to her was the timing. She'd only been back at the office for maybe twenty minutes, which meant whoever had done this might've been waiting for her. Or following her? It was like Jerry was proving every word of his message was true. At least up until that last line—*You die next*. She shuddered.

"Lyla."

Nicolás stood by the open elevator, his hand holding the door . . . on the eighth floor? Lost in her thoughts, she hadn't realized she'd even gotten on the elevator and ridden up.

She closed the image on her phone and made her way to the office.

"I agree with Garcia." Jack entered the security code and held the door open for them. "This escalation is troubling, and we need to be on alert."

"Oh no." Lyla shook her head and headed straight for her desk. She yanked open the bottom drawer. "I have no doubt that Jerome Michael Miller planned this whole thing to rile me up and set you guys off. I will not allow any of you to run me out of assignments or track my movements, ask for my schedule, run background checks on my friends, or"—she eyed Jack and Nicolás—"crash into a spa."

Kekoa exited his office, head tilted to the side. "I'm sorry, what?"

"Tiny bubbles." Jack whispered the nickname for the mortifying debacle he and Nicolás thought they were so clever to come up with because of the soap bubbles that lingered on their hair as they were shamefully led out of the Selah Day Spa by management. "We unintentionally interrupted Lyla's friend's bachelorette party."

She narrowed her eyes on Nicolás. "Unintentionally?"

One hand gripped the back of his neck, the other tugged down on the brim of his cap. "Jerome Miller was meeting with the parole board that day. We couldn't get ahold of Lyla, so we—"

"Busted in on a bunch of girls," she finished for him. "Heavily armed with champagne and canapés."

Lyla caught Kekoa's lips tipping into a smile and Jack shook his head, but the message wasn't received. He released a belly laugh that nearly shook the room. Nicolás hung his head as Kekoa began singing the Don Ho ballad.

"It's not funny, Kekoa." Lyla frowned. "I haven't been invited to any more spa days with friends since. They're worried about two grown men catching them looking like they've been mud wrestling."

This only made Kekoa roar all the louder. And soon Jack joined in. At least Nicolás had the good sense to look embarrassed. Lyla fought her own smile at the blossom of red coloring his cheeks. It reminded her of the shock on his face when he rushed into a room of women dressed in robes, their faces covered in mud. She didn't know who was more horrified, Nicolás and Jack or the bride and bridesmaids.

"Believe me, Lyla"—Jack's laughter rolled to an end—"Garcia and I don't want that either, but we're going to take this threat seriously."

Jack's tone sobered Kekoa's laughter. "It's true, sis. We got your back."

"And I appreciate that." She dug in her drawer, pulled out a folder, and set it on her desk. "But I don't need you three hovering over me."

"You keep the letters in your desk?"

Lyla caught Nicolás staring at the stack of threatening letters that began arriving randomly after she helped send Jerome Miller to prison for laundering millions of dollars for cybercriminals.

"They're photocopies, and why wouldn't I keep them? Jerry was my assignment." She opened her laptop and quickly found the file on Zane Investments. "Kekoa, can you connect my computer so we can use the screens?"

"Don't you think we should wait for Walsh?" Nicolás glanced back at Jack. "Let the police handle the investigation?"

Lyla's jaw clenched. Were they seriously going to question her on this? "Look, I know the police are going to do their best, but let's be honest, a threatening letter from a man already locked up in prison is low on the list compared to the murder, rape, domestic violence, and child abuse cases that happen every day." Her gaze swung to Jack. "You said the police want a list of names, right? I say we go through the file and earmark anyone we think might still be working with or for Jerry. Once we hear back from Walsh, we can find out if Jerry had any visitors in jail who'd be willing to deliver his recent message and destroy my car." She tapped her lip. "Which reminds me, I need to call my repair shop so I can get my windshield fixed ASAP."

The three men hesitated. She folded her arms, staring each of them down until Jack finally sighed. She grabbed her laptop and moved to the conference table where Kekoa was setting up.

Nicolás pulled her chair out for her and she offered him a smile, but the one she got in return felt forced. *Great.* Was he upset with her again? Was their earlier conversation for nothing? Taking the chair next to her, he remained quiet, focused. She couldn't shake the feeling that things were left unsaid earlier, but right now was not the time to figure it out.

"Since Kekoa wasn't here during this assignment"—Jack's voice pulled Lyla's attention away from Nicolás—"why don't we start from the beginning."

"Okay." Lyla opened several files, their contents popping up on the large screens overhead. "Jerome Michael Miller started Zane Investments, a shell company that laundered money for Eastern European cybercriminals. He recruited and supervised individuals, *money mules,* who hacked into and stole money from corporate and individual American bank accounts, which was then wired overseas." She brought up a series of photos, including one of Jerry. "Just like in the Castillo assignment, I worked undercover as a receptionist for Zane Investments and was able to collect evidence along with the names of those working with Jerry. The FBI was able to move quickly and make several arrests, but I know there are more that we missed."

Kekoa held up a finger. "First, *you* were able to pull the information from the computer? Without moí?" He wiggled his brows. "And second, seems extreme that a white-collar criminal would send violent letters threatening death."

The absence of humor in Kekoa's flat tone revealed his two sides. One, his lighthearted attitude, was often soothing in tense situations. And the other, the one he was showing now, said he wasn't finding anything funny in the threats against her.

"What'd the boss do about this?"

"Walsh demanded the Department of Justice act," she answered Kekoa. "He spoke with attorneys to figure out what kind of charges they could add to Jerry's sentence, but there wasn't a lot that could be done to stop them."

"Walsh also hired a security team to watch over her," Jack added. "When Garcia and I couldn't."

"Day and night." She gave them a mocking glare. "Jack and Nicolás here ran lead on every assignment in a sweet attempt to keep me tucked away safely in the office. It was smothering."

"We were looking out for you," Nicolás grumbled next to her.

"And that was reassuring." The memory of those days still flustered her. "Until I began to jump at every creak and shadow. Afraid that the barista or mail carrier or any driver in a nearby car might be someone hired to carry out Jerry's threats against me. It made my life hard, which is exactly what I think Jerry's intentions were. And why we're not going to let him do that again. Right?"

Lyla looked at each of them, waiting for their agreement. Kekoa's was quick, but Jack and Nicolás took a little longer, their eyes meeting before they finally nodded. She bit back the retort of annoyance that wanted to come out of her lips, fearing that if she spoke, they'd change their minds and make her wait until they heard back from Walsh.

Clicking the first name, she forced her voice to be light. "Let's get started."

By the time Jack dropped Lyla off at her Alexandria townhome, she was ready to crawl into bed with a bowl of ice cream and a rom-com. Inside, Lyla punched in the code to her alarm, dropped her keys into the basket in her mudroom, and stepped into the kitchen. She paused, backtracked to the door, and twisted the bolt, locking it.

"Your life is over."

"Don't stop looking over your shoulder."

"You're going to pay."

Those were the nicest of Jerry's threats to her. Lyla had forced herself to forget the more vulgar and frightening ones. But after spending the rest of the workday going over the Zane Investments file, it was all fresh in her head. That they still hadn't heard from Walsh made the situation all the more unnerving.

Lyla dropped onto her couch, tugged the zipper

down on each of her booties, and kicked them off. She sank back against the cushions and looked around her townhome. The effects of Jerry's threats were everywhere. Her windows and doors were protected with a security system that alerted not only the police but also Walsh and her team for their immediate response. Which, according to Nicolás, wasn't fast enough, so he began taking her to the gun range. Taught her how to use a gun and then, when she felt confidently trained, she bought Cupcake, her Smith & Wesson revolver. She carried it with her for nearly six months before finally accepting Jerry's threats were just that—threats from an angry man who was caught and taken from his life of privilege to rot in prison. Until now.

Lyla shuddered and rose to her feet, needing a distraction. Back in her kitchen, she checked her fridge and wrinkled her nose at the lack of consumable contents. She closed the door and flipped through the menus clipped to a magnet. What sounded good?

She stopped on a menu for Nightlight Cookies. Yes. Lyla smiled. Fresh-baked cookies sounded like the perfect dinner for a day like today. Using her phone, she quickly ordered a dozen, which would give her enough leftovers to take to work the next day, and then walked upstairs to change out of her jeans and into a pair of joggers.

The smart home tablet on her counter lit up just

as her doorbell rang. The security video from her front porch showed her who was at her door.

"What in the world?" Seeing the smiling faces, Lyla hurried to the door with a new energy. She opened it, and Brynn and Elinor stood there with covered aluminum trays in their hands. "What are you doing here?"

"We brought dinner!" Brynn raised her tray. "Jack's mom made baked ziti."

"And the boys are bringing the salad and breadsticks."

Lyla looked past Elinor. "Boys?"

Brynn raised a brow. "Jack and Kekoa told me to tell you they're checking tire pressure."

"Which means they're doing a security check around my house." Lyla stepped aside, letting Brynn and Elinor in. "I told Jack I was fine."

"Garcia insisted," Elinor said, setting down the tray of ziti. She was the newest addition to the friend group, but her sweet disposition and penchant for nerdy science jokes made it feel like she was the missing link—especially to Kekoa's happiness. "Can I please ask you to explain once more why the two of you are not a thing?"

Lyla paused and then quickly busied herself setting the trays in the oven. "We're friends."

"Friends, like *eww-la-la?*" Elinor asked as soon as she turned around. "Or friends like *ooh-la-la?*"

Immediately, Lyla was reliving the hug, the

71

way her body seemed to tuck so perfectly against Nicolás. She felt silly even thinking about it in the first place. *Friends hug.* So what?

"For the record," Elinor whispered, bringing Lyla out of her daydream. "I think you and Garcia are like copper and tellurium."

"Huh?"

Elinor winked at Lyla. "Cu-Te. From the periodic table."

Brynn looked at Lyla and giggled just as Jack, Kekoa, and Nicolás stepped into the kitchen.

"Are we ready to eat?" Kekoa wrapped his arms around Elinor from behind. "I'm feeling swoony."

"Ugh." Jack made a face. "Losing my appetite over here."

"Swoony?" Lyla arched a brow at Kekoa.

"Elinor and I have been watching a PBS series on the Victorian era, and apparently swooning was a thing, but honestly I'm not really sure I believe it was over the men. The poor wahine in those lacy stomach traps were just starving."

The kitchen was quiet for several seconds before everyone busted into laughter. The kind that filled the room and brought back a few minutes of peace. Her mother always told her God's blessings came in unexpected ways, and it was easy to consider the friends around her as her favorite blessings.

Brynn handed Lyla a basket filled with sliced

72

garlic bread. She turned to take it to the table and ran into Nicolás, who was carrying a jug of tea and a jug of lemonade from Chick-fil-A. *My favorite.*

She was about to thank Nicolás for remembering when she caught the dismay on his face pinpointed on her.

"You left your door unlocked."

"Sorry." She swallowed. "I got distracted when the girls came in with all the food."

He stepped closer, his arm reaching around her so that his chest brushed against her arm as he set the jugs down. "Distraction can be dangerous."

From the corner of her eye, she caught Brynn and Elinor giving her silly looks and mouthing "ooh-la-la" while they fanned themselves.

"We should eat." Lyla held up the basket of breadsticks between her and Nicolás. "Wouldn't want Kekoa to swoon from starvation."

Over the next hour and a half, the six of them consumed one and a half pans of Mama Hudson's delicious ziti while Jack shared childhood stories about his Italian-American family. The distraction of their presence had been just what she needed.

When dinner was cleaned up and the leftovers were wrapped for Kekoa, Brynn set out the cookies that had been delivered. Lyla was making a pot of coffee when her doorbell rang.

The house grew silent, then the smart home screen showed Director Walsh standing outside her door.

"He always knows when dessert is about to be served." Lyla's laugh sounded nervous, and she could feel their stares following her when she went to answer the door.

She twisted the bolt, then opened the door. "You missed dinner."

"It's a bad habit, I know." Tom Walsh had been her father's best friend since childhood, and as she grew up, he had filled the role of honorary uncle who sometimes seemed to understand her better than her own parents. He'd had a way of guiding her adolescent impulsivity into productive activities like sports or serving the community. Sometimes their personal relationship blurred the lines of their professional one, but she appreciated that, for the most part, Walsh didn't give her any special treatment. "Everyone here?"

"Yes." She led him into the kitchen, where he greeted everyone. "There's some leftover ziti. I can make you a plate."

"No, I'm good. Thanks." Walsh's brows lifted, his blue eyes deepening with a fatherly affection she'd come to lean on throughout her life. "Are you okay?"

Everyone in the kitchen was watching her, and she slid onto one of the kitchen stools. "Yeah, of course. Just another one of Jerry's stupid letters."

Walsh exhaled. "I don't have a lot of details, but I spoke with Jim Tolusky, the warden at Paterson Correctional Facility." Something in the way he looked at her caused a shudder to snake down her spine. "Jerome Michael Miller died two nights ago."

Lyla's stomach heaved. This was not what she'd expected to hear at all, and it left her feeling shaky. "What?"

"They found him in the laundry room where he had night detail. Apparent suicide."

He's dead.

The room dimmed as she blinked, trying to wrap her head around what she'd heard. Dead? The threats Jerry Miller had been sending her for the last three years had haunted her, and now it was . . . over.

"I guess I should feel some kind of relief, but"—she met Walsh's blue eyes—"I don't."

"That's understandable." The lines on his face deepened. "If I'd known he was going to target you—"

"No one knew," Lyla said, releasing her grip from the edge of the stool. Her eyes met the concerned looks from her friends until they landed back on Walsh. "Jerry was a whacko who was ticked off that we sent him to prison. He blamed me and wanted to make my life as miserable as his was, but . . ." She swallowed, not wanting to voice the disturbing question giving her chicken skin. "But if he died two nights ago, why was his death threat delivered today?"

6

"here are two basic motivating forces: fear and love."

Tom Walsh drove away from Lyla's townhome with John Lennon's words circling his brain. Not because he was a huge Beatles fan, but because he knew Lyla well enough to know that familiar glint of ire in her eyes. It wasn't fear that drove her to take risks so much as it was her innate sense of making sure justice was served.

I wonder who she gets that from?

Taking the ramp onto 95, Tom felt a hollowness in his chest that he hadn't experienced in a long time. Lyla was like a daughter to him. His best friend, Keith Fox, and his wife, Catherine, had raised her well. Even when she tested every boundary they'd set in unconditional love, forgiveness, and mercy. They were great parents, and if the cards dealt to him and Samantha had been different, he hoped he would've been like them.

There were plenty of times as agency director when he felt like he had to parent her in some ways. He thought about the Castillo case. Poor Garcia. The man never stood a chance of wrangling his feelings for Lyla, but would his doubts cause him to leave the agency? He wasn't sure.

77

The speakers in Tom's car announced an incoming call and he answered. "This is Walsh."

"Tom, hey, it's Jim up at Paterson. Uh, do you have a minute to chat?"

The traffic on 95 was moderate but not so bad that Tom couldn't focus on a conversation with the prison warden he'd spoken to just an hour ago. "Sure, Jim. Just headed home. Everything okay?"

Their earlier conversation had revolved around the unexpected news of Jerome Michael Miller's unfortunate death. It wasn't atypical for a prisoner to end his life, but just like Lyla, Tom was left wondering why he would threaten her posthumously.

"Well, I'm not sure. After your call, I started digging into Jerome Miller's death and his time here at Paterson. I pulled in all the corrections officers from D Block and asked them about Miller. Most said he was an ideal inmate— quiet, polite, and respectful—and they seemed surprised at his decision to take his life. I asked about the letters, and none of them ever witnessed him writing letters. However, one of the officers, Darryl Holcomb, has only been here a few months and seemed nervous when he came into my office, so I pressed him. Appears we had a visitor the day after Jerome Miller killed himself." Jim's West Virginia accent filled the car, and Tom was laser-focused on every word.

"Someone from the DOJ stopped by. Wanted all the information regarding Mr. Miller's death and his time here at Paterson. It's protocol for us to do an internal investigation when an inmate dies of unnatural causes, but we'd barely even started."

Tom frowned. He thought back to his demands for the Department of Justice to charge Miller for his threats against Lyla. It was like talking to a wall, which made their interest in Jerry's death that much more interesting. "You didn't tell me the DOJ was involved."

"I didn't know," Jim said, nothing defensive in his answer. "Holcomb was on duty that morning and failed to follow procedure. Allowed a Mister . . ." There was the sound of papers shuffling, then Jim spoke again. "Mister Jordan Kemp flashed his badge, and the rookie allowed him free passage into Jerry's cell and let him go through Jerry's belongings. Kemp asked Holcomb about Jerry's family, visitors, wanted to see the visitor log. Holcomb confessed to me that he started getting nervous about the DOJ being there, but before he could involve a supervisor, Kemp concluded his inquiry and made like the wind." Jim gave a long exhale. "Holcomb is on administrative leave until we get to the bottom of this, but I thought you should know."

Tom's nerves thrummed. It wasn't typical for the Department of Justice to get involved in a situation like this unless something was suspicious about the death. Was there?

"I appreciate the call, Jim. Did Holcomb recall if this Kemp character mentioned why he was there on behalf of the DOJ?"

"No, but he said it seemed like Kemp was looking for something, and he was asking about Jerome Miller's visitors and who he had communicated with while in prison."

"You said Jerry was visited by his lawyers and his sister, right?"

"That's correct, but like we talked about earlier, Miller hadn't had a visitor in about four months."

"Right," Tom said. He checked the time. A little after eight. Not too late to make another call. "Jim, will you keep me posted about any new information you get on this? I'd like to make a trip up to visit with you and Officer Holcomb, maybe get a look at the surveillance tapes, if you don't mind."

"Sure thing."

Tom ended the call after confirming that he'd make it up to Paterson first thing in the morning. Then he dialed another number.

"Calling a little late, Walsh."

"My apologies, Bill. I hope I'm not interrupting anything."

"Just catching up on some work." Bill Darne was the DOJ's deputy attorney general. "What can I do for you?"

"You know I don't have a favorable reputation with Director Goldman, but I need to find out if he sent someone named Jordan Kemp out to Paterson Correctional Facility to inquire into the death of an inmate."

"Give me a second." The phone went silent, like Bill had put him on mute. Tom flipped on his blinker and took the exit toward his home in Alexandria. "Okay, sorry. What was the name again?"

"Jordan Kemp. I'm assuming he's under the Bureau of Prisons."

"Nope."

A buzzing noise started at the base of Tom's skull. "Pardon?"

"I've pulled up our employee database, and we don't have anyone named Jordan Kemp under BOP or anywhere in the DOJ. You said he was investigating the death of an inmate?"

Tom's nerves lit with a current of anxiousness he didn't care for. If Jordan Kemp didn't exist in the DOJ, did he exist at all? Tom had been in this line of work long enough, had experience in the world of pretense when he worked in the CIA, and had handled enough assignments within SNAP to recognize the warning in his gut.

"Maybe I misheard the name," Tom said. "I'll reach out to Jim and double-check and get back to you. Have a good night, Bill."

When the call ended, Tom was left with the

quiet hum of his car as he accelerated down North Washington to his home. Lyla's iron-willed expression flashed to mind. The second she caught wind of this information, she'd be unstoppable in her quest to find out who and what was behind the threat against her. Tom needed to get ahead of this ASAP.

7

Never had a dead man caused Nic so much grief.

Nic's palms ached with the pressure of his fingers curling into fists. Rising from his desk, he stretched and moved toward the wide window with the panoramic view of the Capitol and DC's busy landscape. His gaze zeroed in on the streets outside the Acacia Building, Lyla's question from the night before circling his mind again.

If Jerry was dead . . . who was threatening Lyla's life?

Was this Jerry's idea of a sick joke?

Nic tensed. It hadn't been lost on him that not only had the person who smashed the brick into Lyla's windshield known she'd just gotten back to the office, but that meant it was possible Nic might've seen him. Crossed paths with him in the parking garage . . .

He dragged a hand down his face, agitation tightening the muscles he'd worked out for two hours earlier that morning.

Jack walked up next to Nic. "You okay, brother?"

"Lyla should be back by now." He pulled off his hat and ran a hand through his hair before replacing it. "Does Kekoa really need to eat three breakfasts?"

"First breakfast, second breakfast, elevenses!"

Kekoa called out from his office. "Good enough for hobbits, good enough for me."

Nic blew out a breath. "Does he realize he's the size of ten hobbits?"

"That's why he needs five meals a day."

"Seven!"

Nic and Jack exchanged smirks.

Jack's attention moved back to the street outside the Acacia Building. "You think he'd be crazy enough to show up here again?"

Kekoa still hadn't identified the hooded figure they'd caught on their cameras, but it wasn't a stretch to assume the person was male. "Part of me is hoping he does show up, then I'd—"

At the sound of footsteps, Nic spun around to find Lyla standing there carrying a tray with baked breakfast croissants on one side and a mixed fruit bowl on the other. She arched a brow at Nic, a spark in her eye. "You'd what?"

"I'd call the police." Nic tipped the brim of his hat down. "After my fists confirmed his identity."

Lyla's amused laughter caused Nic to let his guard down, and it was a sweet release.

"Well, let me save you the trouble of a fistfight that might damage that handsome mug of yours." She winked. "I'd hate for you to be unable to eat healthy—hold the bacon—rabbit food."

Kekoa strutted out of his office. "Someone say handsome?"

Lyla smiled, and Nic didn't detect an ounce of

84

tension in it. Unlike what he'd been feeling the last twenty-ish hours. She set the food on the conference table, then went to the kitchen and returned a few minutes later with another tray of plates, napkins, three cups of coffee, and one bright green drink that he knew was meant just for him.

Jack's cell phone rang, and he stepped into Walsh's office to answer it.

"You didn't have to go out of your way," Nic said when she handed him his favorite pineapple-kale smoothie from the café down the street. "I'd have been fine with water."

"I know, but I also know you really like these salads in a cup, so . . ." She shrugged and took her usual seat at the conference table.

Nothing in her posture or expression hinted at the seriousness of what had taken place yesterday. She set out the sandwiches and unwrapped her own, taking a bite and closing her eyes as if it was the best thing she'd ever eaten. It defied reason as to how Lyla ate that amount of artery-clogging cheese and bacon squeezed between a buttery croissant and still stayed fit. Especially because she was allergic to working out . . . or so she told him.

"You gonna eat, brah?" Kekoa took a hearty bite of his own sandwich, chewing before he smiled. "Or is that how you keep that handsome mug of yours so trim?"

"Sit down, Nicolás, and eat. You can't defend my honor if you don't have any food in your body."

Defend her honor? Lyla was fully capable of doing that all on her own, but it didn't stop the comment from warming his cheeks.

"See?" Kekoa flexed. "That's what I tell Elinor all the time."

Nic sat next to Lyla just as Kekoa began wiggling in his chair like a toddler. "Brother, do your hips ever stop moving?"

Kekoa's left brow shot up. "This is my food dance."

"Food dance?" Nic took a sip of his smoothie.

"Ono grindz makes me happy." Kekoa winked at Nic. "Your hips would move too if you ate something other than lettuce in a cup."

"New mission," Lyla said around a bite. She shimmied her shoulders. "Find out what kind of food will make Nicolás dance."

"This looks great, Lyla." Jack grabbed a sandwich and dropped in his chair. "Walsh is on his way up."

Nic tugged his brim, grateful for that conversation to come to an end.

"Good morning," Walsh said, walking in. At the conference table, he paused. "I apologize for my tardiness, but I wanted to pay a quick visit up to Paterson."

"Any new information?" Nic asked.

Walsh's gaze flickered to him for a second before looking away. "No new information about the letter."

"So the brick was just a final kick-in-the-shins gift to me?" Lyla sat back, folding her arms across her chest. "What a jerk."

Lyla's name for Jerry was a lot tamer than the ones running through Nic's head.

"Did he leave a note?"

"Not that I'm aware of." Walsh sat and removed his glasses. "Why?"

Lyla shrugged. "Just trying to decide if I should be flattered that I was the last thing on Jerry's mind before he offed himself."

The muscles in Nic's shoulders bunched at Lyla's grim humor. Or maybe it was her cool composure that had him stressed. Three years ago, when Jerry's threats first arrived in the mail, the words written on those pages nearly drove him to pay Jerry Miller a visit in jail, but Lyla never blinked. Never shuddered, at least that he could tell, at the man's attempt to terrorize her. Even after yesterday's tangible threat, she was chill. Just like she'd been while facing the barrel of Castillo's gun.

"There's still someone out there who did Jerry's bidding." Nic looked at Walsh. "We can't dismiss the possibility that he may have set up more threats or attacks."

Lyla frowned. "Or maybe whoever Jerry paid

to send me this last message didn't get the memo that he was dead." She shrugged. "I have to believe that if Jerry really wanted to hurt me, he would've done it before now and certainly would've lived to see it." She got up and went to the acrylic board, where she pulled down a copy of the threatening note taped there. "This was nothing more than his final, lame attempt to scare me."

The logic behind Lyla's argument made sense, but Nic didn't think his apprehension would go away until whoever threw the brick was caught and questioned.

Director Walsh slipped his glasses back on, and Nic caught the familiar worry weighing down his features. The man was like a second father to Lyla, and even though he treated her just as professionally as the rest of them, there was always an added element of concern when it came to her.

"Garcia's right." Walsh held up a hand as Lyla's posture stiffened, her lips parting to protest. "But so are you. I'd like to believe Jerry's threats died with him, but until the police collar the person responsible for the vandalism, I want you to be vigilant."

Jack turned to Kekoa. "Where are we on identifying the hooded character outside our building?"

Kekoa tapped on his silicone keyboard. "With

the help of the police, I got permission to pull CCTV footage for a six-block radius from here." The screens overhead came to life with video. "Two cameras caught the same person . . . here." He paused a video, and Nic zeroed in on the hooded figure walking around the corner of the Acacia Building near West Wing Café on the corner of D Street. "Unfortunately, he keeps his head down, so I can't get a clear shot of his face. But the timing matches. Metro PD gave me access to their traffic cams to track the individual. Hopefully we'll see him get into a vehicle or at least be able to track the general direction he headed. Get an image of his face."

Nic studied the hooded figure. Based on the newspaper stand next to him, he wasn't very tall and probably not very heavy either, though it was hard to tell with the baggy clothes. Young? Throwing a brick through someone's windshield was a juvenile approach.

"What about Miller's son?" All eyes turned on Nic. He folded his arms across his chest. "In his file, last night"—he looked at Lyla—"you said Jerry had a son and a daughter, right?" She nodded. "Old enough to be in high school? Might fit the physical description of the unsub in the footage."

Lyla chewed her thumbnail. "You think Jerry's son would come after me?"

Nic scrubbed a hand over the scruff along his

jawline. "His dad killed himself. He might be looking for someone to blame."

He regretted the words when he saw the impact they had on Lyla. She dipped her chin to her chest, gaze falling to her hands.

"Jerry should have paid for what he did, but I never wanted him dead."

"We know, Lyla." Walsh's cell phone rang and he pulled it out, exhaustion coloring his expression before he silenced it. "Kekoa, assist the police in any way you can. Otherwise, I think Jerry Miller's only purpose behind those letters was psychological, and I'm happy to officially put his case to rest." His forehead wrinkled. "Didn't mean it like that, but you know what I'm saying." He checked his watch. "We have a growing list of assignments that require our attention. If you need me, I'm going to be in and out all day today."

Walsh disappeared into his office. Nic helped Jack clean up second breakfast, or—he looked at his watch—elevenses. Lyla had moved to her desk, and Nic couldn't help the surprise he'd felt when she so readily accepted Walsh calling Jerry's case closed.

Maybe she was going to follow through on her assurance to heed authority and be less stubborn. Of course that would happen when he was on his way out . . . but not gone forever. *Right?* It was a question he'd wrestled with since Walsh presented him with the opportunity. He knew DeAntona would keep his word and allow Nic to return to SNAP, but would that be for the best?

His gaze moved back to Lyla, who was twisting her hair around a finger as she worked on her laptop. The woman's personality was as vibrant as the hair color choices she liked surprising them with during certain assignments. Nic had never met anyone who so fully and completely embraced their job. It was like her identity was inextricably wrapped up in the success of each and every assignment. Which wasn't far from accurate. Without her extensive network of connections across the globe in every facet of business, politics, and society, their work would be a lot harder to complete. But with her mesmerizing personality that made resisting her requests next to impossible and her innate— albeit often impulsive—intuition, Nic credited many of SNAP's successful assignments to her.

So why did she approach the job with such recklessness? What was driving her to take unnecessary risks? It wasn't just the Castillo assignment. He put himself in her shoes, and he would've done the same thing she did, though that didn't make him feel better. But in other assignments, when lives weren't in immediate danger, Lyla still seemed too comfortable stepping into the line of fire.

"Did they sneak something in your smoothie, Nicolás?"

Lyla was staring at him, and he had no idea why. "Sorry?"

"My mom wants to know who all is riding in the drag hunt so we have enough horses available."

Kekoa stepped out of his office and shook his head vigorously. "Not me." He jumped into a surf stance. "I ride the waves, not the horses."

Lyla gave him an exaggerated eye roll. "What about Elinor?"

"Oh, she's riding." Kekoa headed toward the kitchen, probably for twelvses. "She's been so excited, she's read two books and three equestrian magazines to make sure she knows the right lingo."

"Please tell her that's not necessary." Lyla wrinkled her nose at Nic as if they shared a secret. "The drag hunt is just an informal fox hunt, but no foxes and just for fun. What about you, Jack?"

"Brynn and I will be there."

"And you, Nicolás?"

"I'll be there."

"Good." She wrote a note and passed him a smile before answering her ringing cell phone.

Nic hadn't been on a horse in years, but he'd grown up riding and he missed it. And with his pending departure, he wanted to enjoy as much time with her *and his team* as possible. Just in case.

"I'm really beginning to think that health nut slipped something into your smoothie."

Nic blinked at Lyla, who was staring at him again. "What?"

"I think you need some sleep, Nicolás." She picked up her purse. "My rental car is ready. Can you drop me off?"

"Sure." Ears warming, Nic tugged his brim down, embarrassed how easy it was to become distracted by her. This was what he'd been trying to convey to Jack the day before. When it came to Lyla, his perspective had become skewed. Distracted. Which meant his mind wasn't focused on the job. Like he'd told her last night, distraction was dangerous.

Nic did a quick scan of the parking garage when they walked out of the elevator. He unlocked his truck and opened the door for Lyla.

"Thanks for doing this," Lyla said after he climbed into the driver's seat. "I know you're busy."

"I don't mind." He started the engine and did another quick scan of the parking garage before pulling out. "Where to?"

She gave him directions, then bit her lip. "I guess it's not really that far. I could've walked—"

"No," Nic said far louder than he'd meant to. He ran his palms over the steering wheel, embarrassed. What was wrong with him today? "We're following Jack's directive to remain vigilant, remember?"

She nodded, pointing to the tight smile on her face. "See? This is me cooperating."

He raised his eyebrows, opening his eyes wide. "This is me looking shocked."

"Whatever." She playfully smacked his arm, laughing. "Oh, so I'm heading to my parents tonight for dinner, but I was thinking of asking Walsh if I could leave a little early. I was going to ride the hunt trail with Hank, my grandfather's stable master, and make sure it's ready for the drag hunt." She faced him. "Do you want to go with me?"

"Tonight?"

"Yeah. We could do a quick ride, have dinner with my parents, and we should be done in time for you to drive back before it gets too late."

He swallowed. "I have, um, plans tonight."

"Oh, with the guys?"

Nic wished it were with Jack and Kekoa. *Just tell her.* This was the perfect opportunity to let her know he was accepting the mission in Syria.

"Is it a date?"

"What? No. It's work."

Lyla quirked a brow. "I bet I can talk Walsh into letting you leave early. I'll ask him—"

"It's not work for the agency." Nic pulled into the parking lot of the rental car office and parked.

He turned to Lyla, knowing full well he'd stepped on a land mine. "I'm meeting Captain Isaac at the range tonight."

"Naomi?"

The way Lyla said her name made Nic want to lie. Made him want to take it back, find a reason to cancel with Naomi, but he wasn't a liar and he kept his word. He needed to make sure he was qualified on his weapons before heading to Syria, but explaining that to Lyla right now felt risky.

"Oh, that's . . . that's good." Lyla fumbled for the strap of her purse, and then it got tangled in the seat belt she was trying to take off. "Thanks for the ride. I'll—"

"Lyla." Nic reached for her arm just as her other hand grabbed the door handle. She looked back at him. "I can cancel tonight if—"

"Oh no. Don't do that." She gave a tight laugh. "I just thought if you didn't have plans, it might be something fun to do. It's no big deal. I'll see you back at the office, okay?"

Without waiting for his response, Lyla pulled the handle, slid out of his truck, and closed the door. Nic watched her walk into the rental car office, assessing the blast radius of his oversight. Exhaling, he bounced his fist against the steering wheel.

He didn't know what to make of Lyla's reaction. Was she jealous? Why? She knew he and Captain Isaac were friends. And only friends, because Nic didn't do one-night stands and didn't care for superficial relationships. He dated with marriage in mind.

Nic shifted his truck into drive and accelerated out of the parking lot, desperate to get away from the images and memories he hadn't allowed himself to think about in six years. He didn't need to think about her to know he couldn't entertain a single thought about dating Lyla.

8

Naomi Isaac. Lyla wrinkled her nose as she steered her rental car onto I-295. During a quick stop back at the office, she'd asked Walsh if she could take the rest of the day's work and head up to her parents' property early. He'd agreed, but she'd sensed some concern in his agreement. Pasting on a smile, she'd assured Walsh she was fine and thanked him. Then she'd avoided all eye contact with Nicolás, who, per his usual self, had watched her from beneath the brim of his worn ball cap, and collected her laptop and left.

Agitation clawed up her spine because she couldn't quite identify what was bugging her about Nicolás's plans with his old Army buddy. *Old* and *buddy* didn't seem fitting for the picture Lyla was imagining. No, in her head, Naomi Isaac either looked like Fiona the ogre from *Shrek* or Angelina Jolie as Lara Croft from *Tomb Raider*. She doubted either was accurate but feared the latter was the closest possibility.

Captain Naomi Isaac. Ugh. Even her name sounded beautiful.

Lyla's shoulders sank against her seat. Why did it feel like Nicolás had dropped a bomb on her? Wasn't *Naomi* supposed to be overseas? When did she get back? Nicolás confirmed it wasn't a date, which she believed. Over the years, she hadn't known Nicolás to date, which was weird, because on more than one assignment with him, she'd overheard women express their interest in him and his good looks. But nothing ever went anywhere, and she never really bothered to investigate why.

So why had she invited him to her parents' and grandparents' houses anyway?

Why not? It wasn't like she was asking him out on a date. It was a friendly invitation. If she'd been at the office, she would've extended it to Jack or Kekoa.

Ugh. Arguing with herself was giving her a headache.

What was the point? Just because Elinor thought they'd be c-u-t-e together didn't mean it was realistic. *Nicolás struggles to trust me.* She saw the sincerity in his apology, but she also felt the hesitancy when she tried to assure him she would do better. That hurt her more than she cared to admit.

A noise of frustration escaped her lips. She bet Nicolás probably had no problem trusting *Naomi.* How could he not? From what little Lyla knew, the woman had been part of his unit just before he got out. And working with the SNAP team for nearly a decade, she'd experienced firsthand how tense situations drew people closer. Maybe Naomi had the insight to the kind of deeper friendship Lyla wanted with Nicolás. Was that it?

"He can have more than one friend. Doesn't matter."

Lyla's words echoed back at her, and the sound of them was just as ridiculous as the reason why she should care. Her eyes flashed to her reflection in the rearview mirror, and it was like catching someone in a lie.

It mattered because in the four years she'd worked with Nicolás, she'd grown close to the cautious, quiet, reliable man who sometimes let his guard down, giving her a glimpse of his humor and thoughtfulness, and it had left her impatient to know more.

Lyla started to take the exit toward Rock Hill, the town where her parents lived, and noticed for the third time a red car behind her change lanes when she did. She'd spotted the conspicuous vehicle as it followed when she left the Acacia Building in DC, but her concern had felt silly. Commuters had few choices as far as routes to leave the city, leading most to choose I-295. If the driver in the car was tailing her, he wasn't trying to hide it. Which made her think it was just coincidence. Until now.

The odds of someone leaving from the same place in DC and changing lanes when she did and taking the same exit were slim. And even if all that was by chance, even if the driver in the red car did live in Rock Hill, he would've taken the first exit and not the one that bypassed most of the neighborhoods. The only people who took the back road to Rock Hill Terrace were residents.

Too coincidental to be chance.

Changing lanes, Lyla let her thoughts about Nicolás fade in light of her concern about the red car. When the red car did the same, Lyla's evasive driving training kicked in. *Don't lead them to your home.*

Accelerating, she weaved her way between cars and put some distance between her and her tail. She took the next exit that would lead them back into Rock Hill's historic downtown. The city was designed in a grid pattern, but if a driver wasn't familiar with the layout, they wouldn't know that one wrong turn would lead to a dead end or a one-way street. Tourists were constantly getting caught up in them, and Lyla knew she could lose the person following her . . . except part of her wanted to know who it was.

Was it the person who threw a brick through her windshield? Was that only a warning, and now they were back to finish fulfilling Jerry's final wishes?

She eyed the car in her rearview mirror, her adrenaline spiking. "You picked the wrong day."

After turning right onto Carrington, she changed lanes and took another right, catching sight of the red car just as it entered the street.

Lyla slowed enough to be sure the driver would see her turn.

Ahead of her was a white SUV. Lyla sped up. It was a Lexus, and her rental was a white Mazda CX-5—close enough to work. She changed lanes, using the mirror to keep the red car in view, and then changed lanes again, putting her back behind the Lexus. Lyla sent up another quick prayer, and when the Lexus driver flipped their blinker to turn right onto Pickett, she laughed. "Thank you, Lord."

"There are no what-ifs, only God." Her mother's voice repeated the words of Corrie ten Boom, words she'd offered to Lyla whenever life seemed to shift on her. Good or bad. A gentle reminder that God was always in control no matter the circumstances.

The Lexus turned left, and Lyla turned right, in the opposite direction down Barrows. She smiled. *Barrows the narrows.* When Lyla's father was teaching her how to drive, he made up rhymes to help her remember the nuances of the street layouts. This was a one-way with a narrow alley on one side. Most people missed it unless they were looking for it or managed to get stuck down the road and needed to use it to turn around.

Lyla slowed and then quickly threw her rental into reverse, backing into the alley. The tall buildings on either side of her provided just enough shadow to give her cover. She turned off her driving lights and held her breath, waiting for the red car. If they had followed the Lexus, then she'd lost them. But if—

The red car passed in front of her and Lyla smiled. Ha!

Waiting a few seconds, Lyla edged out of the side alley, glancing to her right to see the red car's brake lights as the driver realized his mistake.

"Leave. Get out of there." Nicolás's voice echoed in her ear. Leaving was the smart choice. Probably the right choice. But if she left now, she wouldn't know who was following her or why.

Lyla peered at the back of the car again, trying to make out the license plate number. She wouldn't leave without that, at least. Kekoa could look up the car's owner. The driver's-side door opened, and Lyla's pulse picked up. A woman stepped out and looked directly at Lyla. *Move, Lyla. Get out of there.*

Before Lyla could heed her own internal voice, the woman raised both hands in the air as if to surrender. Or maybe to show she was unarmed? Her lips moved, but Lyla couldn't hear her, so she rolled down the passenger window.

"Please, I just need to talk to you for a second."

"Who are you and why were you following me?"

"I need to give you something," the woman yelled back.

Lyla frowned. "What?"

102

"Um, can I . . ." The woman looked around her. "Can I come over there?"

Not a good idea, but curiosity was thumping almost as loudly as the warning to leave. Lyla eyed the woman. She was wearing a pair of jeans, worn tennis shoes, and a thin leather jacket. Her hair was tousled but not in a way that said it was purposeful, more like the hasty way Lyla's looked when she was in a hurry.

"Tell me who you are first."

"Genevieve. Genevieve Miller." The woman dropped her hands to her side. "I'm Jerry Miller's sister."

Lyla was out of there. She twisted the steering wheel to leave when the woman shouted again.

"No, wait! Please!" Genevieve ran a few feet toward Lyla's car and then stopped. "I have something for you."

Another brick? Lyla eyed the woman again. She easily could have a gun tucked into the back of her jeans. *Leave, Lyla.*

"My brother was guilty and deserved to be in jail."

Genevieve's words halted Lyla from speeding out of there. "What did you say?"

"I said that I know my brother was guilty of stealing money, and he deserved to be in jail."

"Don't come any closer," Lyla said when the woman started to walk forward again. Her gaze drifted to the glove box, where she would've kept

Cupcake if she'd been in her car and not a rental. She met Genevieve's eyes. "You have something for me?"

"Yes." Genevieve nodded and then started to reach for her pocket but paused. "It's in my pocket. A flash drive."

Lyla tipped her chin, holding her breath that she wasn't about to get shot. Relief flooded through her when Genevieve held a tiny flash drive in her hand. "What's on it?"

"My brother was in trouble."

"That's why he was in jail."

Genevieve shook her head. "No. I mean, he had a gambling problem and made a deal with the wrong people. He was a smart man."

Lyla blew out a breath. Where was this going? "Apparently not smart enough to not get caught."

"That's just it." Genevieve's shoulders rolled forward. "I think he was, but he was scared of something. Something outside of jail made going to jail safer. We hired the best attorneys, but he wouldn't cooperate."

Lyla thought she remembered Walsh saying something about that, but she'd assumed he wasn't willing to accept a plea deal in the hope he could convince a jury he was innocent.

"He told me he had an insurance policy, but that it might run out."

"What does that have to do with me?"

"Do you know what happened to my sister-in-law, Tiffany, four days ago?"

"I don't make it a point to keep tabs on the families of criminals."

Genevieve's brows dipped, the edge of her lips drawing down. "She was in a car accident. Nearly killed her. And if my niece or nephew had been in the car, it would've killed them."

Lyla regretted her insensitive words. No matter how she felt about Jerry, his wife and kids were secondary victims to his crimes. "I'm sorry to hear that."

"There are two things I'd bet my life on, Miss Fox. My brother would protect his family over his own life." Genevieve's voice wavered. "And he would never kill himself."

Lyla wasn't sure she agreed. Jerry Miller committed crimes for criminals across the world, thus putting his family in danger. And according to the medical examiner's report, he had hung himself.

Genevieve held up the flash drive, then tossed it so that it landed on Lyla's passenger seat. Then she started to back away toward her own car.

"What's on it?"

"I don't know." Genevieve shook her head. "Jerry asked me to visit and gave me that. Didn't tell me anything else, but my gut tells me it's safer that way. I'm not a conspiracy theorist, but the mechanic who looked over Tiffany's car said it had a faulty brake line." She opened her car door. "She bought the car, brand new, a week ago."

With that, Jerry Miller's sister got into her car and Lyla pulled out of the alley. She'd expected Genevieve to back out after her, but in her rearview mirror, she watched as the red car remained there. Not wasting another second, Lyla pressed heavy on the gas, anxious to get away from Genevieve—but more importantly, anxious to find out what was on the flash drive.

After thirteen minutes going fifteen over the speed limit and two double-back maneuvers to make sure she wasn't being followed, Lyla pulled up in front of the stately home she'd grown up in, a beacon of comfort that would normally loosen the twist of knots filling her stomach.

Except now.

Sitting in her car, Lyla brushed her hair off her face as she stared at her laptop, which held the flash drive, feeling like she'd been duped.

Counterfeiting ring.

In Lebanon.

Two years ago?

Was this another twisted joke concocted by Jerry? Her jaw ached with frustration over the expectancy that there was something valuable on the flash drive. But a two-year-old news article did not explain the harrowed look on Genevieve's face, the way her eyes kept darting around like *she* was afraid someone was following *her*. Why—

"Yoo-hoo!"

Lyla jumped at the shrill voice, jerking her head to the left, where only a piece of glass separated her from her parents' neighbor Elizabeth Davenport.

Heart pounding, she glanced around Elizabeth's face pressed against her car window and saw her mother, Catherine, standing on the veranda giving her an apologetic shrug.

"Lyla! Hellooo!" Elizabeth's coral-colored fingernails tappity-tapped against the glass. "Are you coming inside?"

For a fraction of a second, Lyla considered throwing her car into gear and zooming off, even at the risk of potentially running over Mrs. Davenport's toes. But she wouldn't embarrass her mom by behaving rudely.

Instead, she reluctantly closed her laptop, set it on the passenger seat, and pasted a smile on her face before opening her door.

"Hellooo, my dear." Elizabeth Davenport didn't wait until Lyla was out of the car before she came in for a hug. One that left a haze of sweet, floral perfume behind when she let Lyla go. "Were you going to sit out here all day?"

"Lyla, I wasn't expecting you until later this evening." Her mother walked over and hugged her like she hadn't just seen her a few days ago. "Everything okay?"

"Yeah. Director Walsh let me bring my work up here so I could help you with the hunt."

"Mrs. Davenport just dropped by to ask about our caterer for the drag hunt." Her mom smiled politely. "I told her we were trying something new this year and using food trucks, but that I would save her generous suggestions for another time."

Mrs. Davenport grinned. "And perfect timing because I get to see you."

"I can't think of anyone luckier than me." Lyla's mom shot her an *almost* indecipherable look. "Luckier than I?"

Behind Mrs. Davenport and out of her line of sight, Lyla's mom rolled her eyes. Catherine Fox was nothing if not tactful. A product of her gentry lineage that seemed to have skipped a generation.

"Will you be joining the hunt, Mrs. Davenport?"

Mrs. Davenport's high chirp of a laugh caused Lyla to cringe a little. "Oh, no, dear. I've left my riding days behind, but do you know who will be in attendance?"

Please don't say it. Please don't say it. It was clear from the look on her face that she really wasn't waiting for Lyla to answer. *Please don't say it.*

"Mason!" Mrs. Davenport's excitement came out a near squawk. "He's down from New York City for a bit. Isn't that nice?"

Lyla's disdain for Mrs. Davenport did not

extend to her son. They grew up together and were close friends until going their separate ways for college and work. But in those thirteen years of friendship, Mason's mom never hid her desire to see the two of them date and then marry. Thankfully, Mason was a lot like Lyla and not one to conform to his mother's expectations. But given the way Mrs. Davenport was eyeing Lyla expectantly, the woman did not give up easily.

"Oh, Elizabeth, if Mason is in town, I don't want to take you and Frank away from him. We have plenty of volunteers for Saturday if the two of you want to spend the weekend with him doing something else."

Lyla flashed her mom an appreciative smile, but it was short-lived when Mrs. Davenport tsked.

"Certainly not." Mrs. Davenport ran a hand over her coiffed hair—a style that hadn't changed in all the years Lyla had known her. "The Davenports have always participated in the Whitlock Estate Hunt. It's been a tradition for years." Her hazel eyes looked Lyla over and she smiled. "Besides, I know Mason is anxious to catch up with Lyla." Mrs. Davenport stepped closer. "Did I mention he's interviewing for a position at the *Post*?"

Lyla stopped her fake smiling, her aching cheeks grateful. "*New York Post*?"

"*Washington Post*."

Oh, she did not like the way Mrs. Davenport was eyeing her. "I, uh, I thought Mason liked New York City?"

Mrs. Davenport waved her hand as if she were brushing away such a silly notion. "You know Rock Hill has always had a piece of his heart. Or maybe *someone* has." A look settled into the overpowdered features of Mrs. Davenport's face, and Lyla's stomach clenched. "You know, Mason isn't seeing anyone, and aren't you—"

"I'm dating someone," Lyla blurted out.

The shock on Mrs. Davenport's face matched the look lighting Lyla's mom's eyes. "You are?" She rounded on Lyla's mom. "You didn't mention that."

"Oh, um, well, I think it's a *new* relationship."

Guilt pummeled Lyla for putting her mom on the spot, but she didn't know what else to do. Left to Mason's mother, they'd have been married years ago, with a brood of Davenports in tow by now. Lyla shuddered internally at the thought.

"Yes." Lyla stepped in front of Mrs. Davenport, shielding her mom from the questioning stare. "It's new."

"Well, does the lucky young man have a name?"

Name? She hadn't thought up a name. Why couldn't she think of a name? How many times did she have to come up with a story in a pinch to do her job? But right now, staring into the determined eyes of a mother hell-bent on marrying off her son, Lyla couldn't think of a single name.

"Nicolás." Her throat went dry. Why had she said that? Her mother's eyes widened, and heat clawed at Lyla's neck.

"Nicolás?" There was suspicion in Mrs. Davenport's tone. "Well, I sure look forward to meeting him. Will he be attending the hunt?"

Oh no. Oh no, no, no, no. What had she done? Swallowing, she couldn't think of any way to get out of this. "He will." *And he's going to kill me.*

9

The blast of the gunshot rattled his bones. Nic's shoulder ached with the impact of the rifle's recoil, but he ignored it and leveled the scope on the target. The paper silhouette in the form of a body was riddled with holes, but Nic had three more shots. He adjusted his aim as he focused on the reticle. After slowing his breath, he held it and pulled the trigger three times.

Pop. Pop. Pop.

The echo of the shots was muted through his ear protection, but the sound was as satisfying as the shells flying out of the chamber and landing with a *clink, clink, clink* on the cement floor of the gun range.

A soft tap on his shoulder drew his gaze back. Naomi smiled and thumbed to the soundproof viewing room behind them. Nic nodded.

Checking that his rifle was empty, he popped the clip out, set the safety, and laid the rifle on the high-top counter preventing shooters from going downrange. He pressed a button on the side of his cubby, and the electronic pulley system began moving his target to him.

Stiffness moved through his shoulders as he secured his weapon into its case and locked it.

His muscles were still aching from his morning workout, and he knew he'd be swallowing some pain medicine after this, but coming to the range earlier than planned had been a good decision.

Especially after the situation with Lyla.

Situation.

Is that what it was between him and Lyla? *Again.*

The hurt in her eyes when he turned down her invitation was undeniable, but the way it deepened when he mentioned Naomi had struck him to the core. He didn't think he could feel like a bigger putz—that is, until she returned to the office and spoke to Walsh before she went to her desk, grabbed her belongings, and left. Not looking at him once.

He wasn't a complete idiot. Anyone else and he'd assume it was jealousy, but this was Lyla. She never expressed jealousy when it came to him. However, heat flooded his cheeks as he thought of the times he'd allowed annoyance—that's what he was calling it—to flare through him whenever Lyla casually brought up her suitors. It was annoying because he thought she could do better. Thankfully, Lyla was nothing if not smart, and she usually figured it out quickly, allowing his annoyance to be short-lived. So then why was he picking up the vibe that Lyla was having similar feelings? It didn't make sense.

The whirring mechanism stopped, and Nic

glanced up at the target. A tight circle of shots cleared center mass, and the only evidence of the last three shots was a single hole in the silhouette's head. Kill shots. All of them.

"Based off that target, I don't really think you came here to qualify," Naomi said when Nic walked into the lounge. She handed him a bottled water. "Aggression or frustration?"

Naomi Isaac's frayed jeans and Zeppelin T-shirt gave her a youthful appearance that belied the maturity she carried for a twenty-nine-year-old explosives officer. She didn't wear much makeup and didn't need to, because her light black skin always seemed to glow with a confidence Nic rarely found in women her age. *Like Lyla.*

Nic's previous thoughts tumbled around his head as they exited the range and walked through the parking structure toward their vehicles. It wasn't aggression he was feeling—maybe frustration or confusion. But he held back.

It wasn't that he didn't trust Naomi. He did. Her steady bearing made her a reliable teammate in the field, one he'd want by his side facing an IED. But talking about Lyla to another woman felt a little bit like he was betraying her.

"Wow." She stopped at the back of her car. "Must be serious."

"It's not." At least he didn't think so. "I appreciate you meeting up with me this afternoon."

After dropping Lyla off to get her rental, he had called Naomi to see if they could adjust their range time, hoping he could let Lyla know he was free to accept her invitation. But he never got the chance.

"Sure." She opened her trunk, but before she could set her rifle bag inside, Nic reached for it. "Something in your voice told me you needed this." She gestured back to the building. "And from the way you were shooting, I was right. You sure you don't want to talk about it?"

"Just some work stuff." He felt safe admitting that as he set her rifle bag in the trunk and closed the door.

She leaned against her car. "I thought you liked working for SNAP."

"I do." Working for Walsh, with the team, had been a blessing after his time in the Army. An answered prayer. So why was he leaving? What did it say about him that he couldn't get a grip on his emotions when it came to Lyla? He caught Naomi watching him and somehow felt like she could read his thoughts. He averted his eyes and squinted at the ring he hadn't noticed before on Naomi's left hand. He glanced up, and she was beaming. "When?"

"Two nights ago!" She wiggled her newly adorned hand in front of her face. "I won't bore you with the details, but there were roses everywhere, soft music—he hired a cellist, can you believe that? Our families were there, and it was just magical."

He smiled. "I thought you weren't going to bore me with the details?"

Naomi rolled her dark-brown eyes at him. "Whatever. I know you're a romantic. You just keep it buried deep, deep, waaay deep down, but the right woman will bring it out of you." She clamped her lips shut, the spark of excitement from a second ago replaced with remorse. "Garcia—"

"It's fine." But the heat warming his cheeks said otherwise. "I'm happy Will finally proposed."

"Me too." She gave her left hand an admiring glance before meeting his eyes. "Have you talked with Chad recently?"

"Yeah." He opened the back door of his truck and put his rifle bag away. Shame filled him at his admission. Chad Johnson was another Army officer in the EOD unit and the closest friend Nic had in the Army, but their conversations barely numbered a couple times a year.

"You going to his birthday party next April? The big three-five, and what does the brother want to do? Jump out of a plane." Naomi laughed. "He's crazy, but I think it's kind of cool that even after everything, he won't let anything hold him back."

Nic's jaw tightened. It was easy to admire Chad when you didn't have the whole story. Chad

116

wasn't crazy, and if he'd only held back . . . Nic couldn't help but think of how different everything in his life would be.

He closed his door and faced her. "Depends on my schedule, I guess."

Naomi opened the driver's-side door of her car and sat in the seat and looked up at him. "One of these days, I hope you'll see that the loss was hers and not yours. And in case my instinct is right and the reason you killed a paper target isn't just about work but maybe the five-foot-something firecracker *at* work"—her expression told him he wasn't going to like what was coming next—"I think you need to recognize she's not Brittany."

Nic knew Naomi wasn't trying to be cruel bringing her name up, but it didn't stop him from feeling like that paper target he'd shot holes through. "I know that." Lyla was nothing like Brittany. Polar opposites, actually. Lyla loved risk, thrived on the unknown, and Brittany . . . she hadn't been able to accept the risk of what his job in the EOD entailed. "I'll try to make it work for Chad's birthday."

"Good." Naomi smiled at him like she knew why he added that last part. "Because it won't be the same without you. You're the other half of the dynamic duo."

He shook his head and met her fist bump with one of his own before he closed her car door. He waited until she pulled out, then got into his truck. Starting the engine, he took a deep breath. He needed to make it work with Lyla too, but he wasn't sure a candle would work this time.

Nic walked into the SNAP office and felt the charge of electricity that vibrated his nerves, telling him something was wrong. The second he stepped into the fulcrum, his instincts were confirmed when he found Jack with his arms crossed, stance rigid, and gaze zeroed in on what was happening in Walsh's office.

The glass-and-steel grid wall allowed Nic to see Lyla sitting with Walsh, looking frustrated, and his stomach pitched. What had she gotten herself into this time?

"What's happened?"

Before Jack could respond, Kekoa let out a frustrated growl that turned them around. Inside his office, Kekoa was hunched over his computer. Normally Nic would be baffled by how fast the Hawaiian's mitts could fly over the keyboard, but the fury behind their speed right now told him something was *really* wrong.

"Jack—"

The door opened, and Nic turned back as Lyla walked out, her gaze meeting his before dropping to the floor in front of her. Walsh followed, threading his arms through his wool coat. He looked between Nic and Jack. "I don't know what

Jerome Miller had planned or who he put up to this, but I want them caught and prosecuted."

"Yes, sir." Jack's hands dropped to his side. "Kekoa is working to remotely wipe all information from Lyla's laptop. He's confident the safeguards he's set up on our work computers should be enough, but just in case, he's also running a tracking program to trace back any attempts to breach the system. He'll keep an eye on that as well."

Nic's head was spinning. Someone tried to hack into Lyla's laptop? When? Where? She didn't look up, but he saw the scowl etched in her forehead.

"I've got a meeting at the Pentagon. If anything pops up, send someone to find me."

"Yes, sir," Jack said.

Walsh was not one for dramatics, which meant the strain in his words wasn't for nothing. It wasn't until Walsh walked out of the fulcrum that Lyla's posture shifted. Eyes up, she headed straight to the conference table, pulled out a chair, and sat.

"I'll be right back." Jack passed Nic, sending him a proceed-with-caution look before he stepped into Kekoa's office.

Nic shoved his keys into his jacket pocket and took a slow stroll toward Lyla. She was moving some papers around on the table as a distraction to avoid him. Was she still mad about earlier, or was this about what just took place in Walsh's office?

"Okay." Jack walked over, pausing to grab his laptop from his desk before joining Lyla. "Why don't you fill Garcia in on what happened, and then we can go over all the information we have on Genevieve Miller."

Nic took the seat next to her and noticed the way she wrinkled her nose like she'd rather do anything but fill him in. *Stay calm.*

"Earlier when I left the office, I noticed a vehicle was following me." She straightened her shoulders and tipped her chin up like she was posturing for a fight. "I used some evasive driving techniques to be sure, and when they stayed on me, I figured it might be the same person who put the brick through my windshield. I didn't want to lose them, so I pulled down Barrows because there's an alley most people don't know about where I could catch them in a dead end. It worked." The pride in her voice dimmed when she met Nic's tight expression. "I was going to get the license plate for Kekoa, but then Genevieve Miller got out and told me she had something for me. A flash drive that came from her brother, but there was just some article on it about a counterfeit ring—"

"And malware," Jack said, "that Kekoa is currently battling before it steals our agency's classified information."

Lyla frowned at Jack. "And I have all the faith that Kekoa will win the battle."

Nic clenched his jaw to keep from saying the words he wanted to unleash on Lyla's optimism. He didn't doubt Kekoa's ability to defend their systems, but he wouldn't have had to if Lyla hadn't put herself into the situation. And his opinion wasn't likely to make a difference. She was so determined to go her own way.

Lyla continued explaining her run-in with Genevieve Miller like the encounter was totally normal and *not* driving Nic's blood pressure through the roof, and by the time she was done, he was ready to head back to the range and kill another paper target.

When Jack stepped away to answer his cell phone, Nic stretched his neck muscles, tilting his head to one side and then the other in a vain attempt to release the knots caused by a dead man.

Or his sister.

Or Lyla.

"I know I should've called the agency right away, but—"

"But nothing, Lyla." His tone darkened her eyes, but he wanted so badly to get through to her. "Did you consider that your run in with Jerry's sister might've been another part of his plan? A trap?"

"I did," Lyla snapped. "I got it. I messed up

and my computer was compromised, but all I was thinking about was what had Genevieve so scared."

"Maybe that was the bait? Use your concern to get to you, infiltrate our files. Who knows what kind of damage the malware is doing. You have no idea what her intention was, and you could've led her or someone else straight to your family. Did you think about that?"

Lyla didn't move, didn't speak, just absorbed his words as a glint of fear smothered the fire in her eyes.

"Nicolás."

Normally his name rolled off her tongue with a tease or tension. This time it was vulnerability, and it caught him off guard. "All I'm saying is that we need to consider that Genevieve was another pawn in Jerry's game."

"We ran a cursory check into her when we first took on the Zane Investments assignment." Lyla's posture softened. "And on the rest of Jerry's family, and nothing alerted us they were involved in Jerry's crimes."

"*Then,*" Nic said. "It's been three years since Jerry's address changed to Paterson. It's possible his sister may have picked up where he left off."

"Got him," Kekoa said, interrupting their conversation with an energy that made Nic sit up. Kekoa unfurled his silicone keyboard on the table and brought one of the screens to life. "Connor Baldwin."

Jack rejoined them. "Who?"

"The lolo who smashed Lyla's windshield," Kekoa said. "Surveillance footage pulled from a convenience store four blocks away shows a man fitting the description of the one we pulled from our cameras. Metro picked him up, and it didn't take much pressure before he confessed to the crime. But says he was paid to do it by his uncle."

"Who's his uncle?" Lyla asked.

"Terrel Baldwin. Convicted of mail fraud and served five years at Paterson Correctional Facility." Kekoa looked at them, his eyebrows wiggling like they did whenever he had the goods. "His cellmate was Jerry Miller, and I sent a copy of Terrel's parole papers to Jack's hand-writing friend at the FBI. They're a match."

"Nice catch, brother." Jack fist-bumped Kekoa. "Has Metro picked up Terrel?"

"He missed his check-in with his PO this morning, but I did a little recon and learned Terrel Baldwin, while a criminal, is at least a loyal lover." Nic about choked on his spit, and Kekoa laughed. "Before he went to prison, he had a girlfriend, Shondra Jackson. According to the visitor log at Paterson, she was a regular visitor. So, I checked out Ms. Jackson's social media, and she just posted this."

123

He pulled up a photo of a nice-looking woman wearing a bright turquoise bowling shirt that matched the rest of the smiling women around her.

"You think Terrel blew off meeting his parole officer to go bowling with his girlfriend?"

Nic's skepticism stole a bit of Kekoa's moment until he pointed at an overhead screen behind the group with the bowler lineup. Terrel was bowler number four.

"Yes." Lyla stood. "Let's go get him."

"Hold on." Nic held up a hand. "Kekoa, contact Metro and let them know you have a lead on Terrel's location."

"No, don't, Kekoa." She turned those blue-green eyes on them, and Nic recognized the single-minded look. "You heard Walsh. If you believe Genevieve is a pawn, then Terrel is another piece on the board. We don't know why he didn't check in with his PO, but if you send the police over there he might run, and we lose our chance to find out why Jerry is still coming after me when he's six feet under."

Nic blew out a frustrated breath. She was right, and from the look on Kekoa's face, he agreed with her. Nic rubbed his forehead, trying to find an argument he could win to keep Lyla from diving headfirst into this—but from the look on her face, she was all in.

"If something seems off, if *you* decide it's too

dangerous . . . I'll trust your decision. We can leave and call the police."

Lyla prepared to leave as if her assurance was enough to silence all the doubt and questions roaring in Nic's head about his ability to work with her. But what choice did he have? Lyla wasn't going to sit back and let Jerry get away with whatever postmortem plan he'd set in motion.

And someone needed to keep Terrel Baldwin safe from Lyla.

10

Lyla pressed the button on the espresso machine inside the SNAP Agency kitchen. The sound of the grinding beans soothed her frazzled nerves but did nothing to calm the shaky feeling inside. She didn't need any caffeine, but if she was going to survive the drive with Nicolás, she needed liquid courage.

His agreeing to talk to Terrel hadn't come easily, even after her promises. The wariness she caught in those hazel eyes of his made her feel terrible. Could she blame him? She was surprised Walsh hadn't fired her on the spot.

When she had finally escaped Mrs. Davenport's matchmaking, Lyla had grabbed her laptop out of the rental car to get some work done, only to find her computer wouldn't turn on. At all. Not even plugged in. Panic kicked in after she'd called Kekoa and heard the alarm in his voice when he told her to get back to the office.

How could she have been so stupid? Why hadn't she turned around in the alley and left? Why hadn't she called one of the guys when she saw the car? Why had she opened that flash drive?

There was only one answer to these questions, and it proved Nicolás was right—her impulsivity

126

was not just a risk to herself. She'd now put the agency and potentially her family at risk too.

After pulling a travel mug out of the cabinet, she made quick work of her vanilla latte—extra cinnamon—and grabbed another mug and filled it with plain black coffee. She'd meant what she said. If Nicolás gave her any direction, she would listen. Follow through. Because more than anything, she wanted to prove to him that she could be trusted. All she had to do was control her impulsive, stubborn, sometimes reckless nature and be who he wanted her to be.

Tears stung the back of her eyes. *Fearfully and wonderfully made*—except when it didn't fit someone else's definition.

"How you doin', sis?"

"Good." Lyla quickly wiped at her eyes, then busied herself twisting the lids onto the mugs. "Fine."

He raised an eyebrow. "Do you need a little Hawaiian aloha?"

"No." She held up her hands, shaking her head. "I'm good."

"Aw, come on, sis." Kekoa closed in on her in two strides and wrapped her in a hug that smushed her face against his chest. "Now, see?" He petted her head. "Everything is better."

"Vrthing's dahk." Lyla tried pulling her head back, but like a python of love, Kekoa's grip tightened gently. She opened her mouth, eating her own hair as she tried again. "Ke-ko . . . can't breev."

A rumble echoed in his chest, vibrating against her cheek as he started laughing. The movement caused his muscular arms to contract, crushing Lyla with every breath. This was not the way she imagined dying.

She managed to wriggle an arm free and with a deep breath of readiness, she reached up and tickled him beneath his arm.

"Bahh!" Kekoa half screamed and half laughed, his arms unwinding instantly, but the relief was short-lived as he pushed her away with such force that she stumbled back into the couch and nearly lost her balance before he caught her. "Sis," he wheezed, "why you gotta go for the tickle?"

"Me?" She yanked her arm from his grasp and began smoothing the rat's nest he'd turned her hair into. "You were suffocating me."

Kekoa's eyebrows danced. "With aloha."

Lyla rolled her eyes. "Homicide is still homicide, even if it's hiding behind a hula skirt."

"Kane wear malo, not hula skirts."

"What's a malo?"

The corners of his lips lifted in a snicker. "A loincloth."

"Oof." Lyla cringed, closing her eyes. "Not the image I needed."

Kekoa's laughter drew her gaze back to him, and his goofy smile soon had her smiling and laughing with him. It was a nice relief to the tension that had gripped her all day.

"Thanks." She took a deep breath. "I needed that."

"Garcia was less grateful." Kekoa pulled a bottle of water out of the fridge. "Was like hugging a barracuda."

"You tried to hug Nicolás?" She could only imagine how that looked, and she pressed her lips together to suppress the giggle. "Why would you do that?"

Kekoa wiped his mouth after taking a swig of water. She didn't need him to say what was clearly readable in the arch of his brow.

"Just to drive him nuts, huh?"

"You know it."

Lyla sighed. "I know he's upset with me and this entire situation, but it feels like something else is going on."

"You can always"—Kekoa sucked in a breath of air, eyes wide with fake shock—"ask him."

A voice cleared behind Kekoa. He twisted, revealing Nicolás standing in the hallway. "Ready?"

"Yeah." She grabbed the coffees and ignored Kekoa, who was giving her a double thumbs-up as she followed Nicolás out. *Such a dork.*

Dork or not, Kekoa's intel took Lyla and Nicolás toward the Galaxy Bowl-O-Rama in Prince George's County, where Terrel and

Shondra were supposed to be. The sky had darkened and the wind was picking up, but Nicolás had made sure the temperature in his truck was comfortable. A John Mellencamp song played softly in the background.

"Thank you." She hoped her gratitude didn't sound shallow. "I know it's been a long day and you had plans this evening." Her mind went immediately to Naomi. "Maybe Terrel won't be there, and we can call it an early night."

"I hope he's there." It sounded like a growl. He looked over at Lyla. "My only plans are to make sure you and your family are safe."

"Um"—she cleared her throat—"if you want to bring Naomi to the drag hunt, I can make sure we have an extra horse."

"Lyla." Nicolás shut off the radio. "Naomi is a friend." He looked over at her. "A friend who showed me the stunning ring her boyfriend put on her finger when he proposed and she happily, eagerly said yes."

"She did?" There was far too much enthusiasm in her voice. "That's exciting. Wait . . ." She was confused. "When did you see her?"

"I rearranged our time at the range so I could accept your invitation if it was still available."

Lyla suddenly felt hot. Really hot. She reached for the vent and adjusted it away from her face. "I'm sorry, Nicolás. I didn't mean to make you

130

change your plans. I shouldn't have assumed you didn't have plans and put you on the spot like that."

"You didn't make me change my plans." He sent her a sideways glance. "I was hoping your father could regale me with more of your childhood stories, Stinkerbell."

Lyla tried to look appalled at Nicolás's use of her childhood nickname, but one tilt of his lips and she couldn't resist the giggle that erupted. "I still haven't forgiven him for revealing my secret identity."

"Secret identity?" Nicolás chuckled. "Not sure the DC mayor is going to be sending up a signal for the fairy on wheels."

"Hey!" She shot him her fiercest look, which only made him snicker more. "I was one of the toughest girls on my roller derby team. Other teams were scared of me." She lowered her voice. "My teammates wanted to be me."

Nicolás held his laughter in for a solid three seconds before letting loose, and Lyla relished the sound of it. It was the best sound. It instantly wiped away all the tension she'd been carrying since she drove up to her parents'—*Oh no*.

She'd completely forgotten about the lie she told Mrs. Davenport about Nicolás. Ugh. "Nic—"

"We're here."

A giant neon sign in the shape of a pin and a bowling ball glowed brightly from a pastel

131

building, welcoming them to the Galaxy Bowl-O-Rama and postponing her confession.

Nicolás found a parking spot in the nearly full lot and shut off the engine. "I didn't realize bowling was still a thing."

"This place looks amazing." Lyla unbuckled her seat belt. "I'm booking it for my next birthday. Eighties themed. Or maybe yours since it's the next one up."

"Lyla . . ."

She faced him, and beneath the neon-pink light shining on his face, she could read the hesitation—or was it doubt?—in his eyes.

"First sign, if you see anything that sets you off, we're out of there."

The skin between his brows tugged together. Definitely doubt.

Turning in the passenger seat so she was looking him straight on, she had to swallow against the earlier feeling of disappointing him. "If you say leave, I'll leave. No pushback."

A second passed before Nicolás gave his nod and Lyla exhaled.

"Okay, let's do this."

Nicolás led the way to the glass door and held it open for her, and the inside of Galaxy Bowl-O-Rama was everything Lyla had imagined it to be. The walls were painted in wide stripes of turquoise, pumpkin orange, and chartreuse, circa the 1960s or '70s. It reminded Lyla of an old cartoon she used to watch with her grandfather, *The Jetsons*.

"Stay on my left."

She barely heard Nicolás over the sounds of falling pins, voices laughing and cheering, and the blaring disco music that was interrupted by a man with long hair and a goatee behind the shoe counter on a crackling microphone.

Nicolás put himself between her and the bowlers sitting on semicircle benches covered in turquoise pleather. They walked past a wall of tiny orange and white lockers and a snack bar offering a special on nachos and beer.

"Do you see him?" Lyla yelled over the noise.

"Not yet." But then Nicolás paused. "There."

Ahead of her was the group of women in their turquoise bowling shirts from the picture. Two men were sitting in the back at a picnic-style table, enjoying the snack bar special. One was facing them, but he had a gray beard and wore glasses, which didn't match the most recent photo Terrel's parole officer sent over. That left the man with his back to them.

Nicolás started forward, but Lyla quickly grabbed his arm. "Wait." Suddenly she wasn't so sure this was a good idea. "What are we going to say? What if he has a weapon of some sort?"

"Lyla." Nicolás looked adequately offended, and it was the most Kekoa thing she'd ever witnessed from him. "I'm just going to talk to him."

At the table, Nicolás's imposing six-foot-two frame towered over Terrel Baldwin and the man sitting across from him. Both of them looked her and Nicolás over, no attempt to hide their suspicious assessment.

"Terrel Baldwin."

Terrel moved a toothpick between his lips. "Who are you?"

Lyla blinked before sending Nicolás a frown. She stepped forward. "I'd think you'd recognize the woman you've been sending threatening letters to for the last three years. Or maybe you should ask your nephew Connor what I look like since he's the one you paid to smash my windshield."

The toothpick fell out of Terrel's mouth, his eyes bulging for a second before he tried to recover. Scooping up the toothpick, he narrowed his eyes on them. "I don't know what you're talking about."

Nicolás straddled the bench next to him. "Why don't we try this again? Right now, your nephew is sitting in a jail cell for throwing a brick through my friend's windshield. The brick was wrapped in a note that a forensic hand-writing specialist from the FBI has matched to your probation paperwork. And by the way"—Nicolás pulled out his cell phone—"your PO is wondering why you missed your check-in today."

134

Terrel cursed. "Man, I told Jerry we was gonna get caught."

The woman Lyla recognized from the photo walked over and put a protective hand on Terrel's shoulder. "Baby, what's going on?"

"Nothing, Shondra." He kissed her palm. "Go bowl and have a good time."

She didn't move right away, but the man sitting across from Terrel stood and walked her back to the group. Lyla heard him mention something about fixing a mess.

Lyla took the vacated spot and leaned her elbows on the table. This was more than fixing a mess. "Why are you sending me threatening letters?"

Terrel eyed Nicolás. "You gonna turn me in to my PO?"

"Yes." Nicolás didn't hesitate. "But not before you answer our questions."

Blowing out a breath, Terrel let his head fall into his hands. "I needed the money. Jerry promised me fifteen large if I did him a favor. Another ten for the last letter, to make sure she got it."

Where would Jerry get twenty-five thousand dollars? As far as Lyla knew, all his assets had been used for restitution.

"Why did Jerry pay you to send the letters?"

Terrel shrugged. "I guess he didn't want to get his hands dirty. But I figured what's the harm."

He locked eyes with Lyla. "Sticks and stones but words never hurt."

"I wouldn't be so sure," Nicolás growled. His posture shifted forward, causing Terrel to shrink back. "Jerry had to have had a reason why he wanted to send those letters. You look like the curious sort, so why don't you tell us what he told you."

Terrel swallowed. He used the napkin to wipe his forehead. "Look, I don't want no trouble. I only did what he asked. He never told me why he wanted to send the letters to her." He tilted his head in Lyla's direction. "Only that he had to—every third month, no exceptions. Jerry was easygoing about a lot of things, but not that."

"Why was he obsessed with me?"

Terrel ran his palms over the Formica tabletop. Lyla noticed he was glancing around the bowling alley similar to the way Genevieve had in the alleyway.

"Was Genevieve always a part of the plan?"

"Who's Genevieve?"

"Jerry's sister." Lyla caught the quick shift in Terrel's gaze, revealing he knew exactly who Genevieve was. "Did you send her to give me the flash drive? What were you trying to steal?"

"I don't know what you're talking about. I don't know Jerry's sister, and I ain't stealing any-thing."

His frustration looked genuine, and so far the man seemed forthright in his answers.

Nicolás frowned. "You don't know about the flash drive?"

"Look, I already told you I sent those letters, but you ain't gonna pin no theft on me. Go ahead and call my PO." He chewed on his toothpick. "I'm ready to go in. Safer in jail anyway."

Lyla sat forward. "What did you say?"

Terrel eyed her. "What?"

Her heart began pounding faster. "You said you're safer in jail. Why did you say that?"

"I don't know. I heard it."

"From who?" Lyla watched him press his lips together, and her frustration grew. "From who? Jerry?" His eyes widened a fraction. "Why was Jerry safer in jail? Did he tell you?"

"Look, I'm done." Terrel started to stand. "Call the police or don't."

"Jerry Miller is dead," Lyla blurted out.

Terrel froze. "What?"

"Two nights ago," she said. "Killed himself."

"Nah." Terrel shook his head. "Nah, that's not right."

"Why not?" Nicolás asked.

"I don't know what you've been told, but Jerry didn't kill himself—he was murdered."

11

Nic watched the color drain from Lyla's face. He turned on Terrel and asked, "What do you mean Jerry was murdered?"

"Man!" Terrel's breathing grew rapid, his eyes darting around the bowling alley. He was becoming agitated. "I thought the guy was blowing smoke, but you two come in here and now I got to be worried about my girl."

This coming from the same man who sent his nephew to bust Lyla's windshield with a brick. Nic wasn't buying it. "What makes you think Jerry was murdered?"

"Look, I don't want no trouble, but Jerry was scared, man. I'd been in two years already, and you have to get tough, ya know what I'm saying? Can't come in looking like an appetizer. Tax evasion, fraud, or murder—brothers will eat you up. Not Jerry. Man waltzed in like he was checking into the Ritz. Set himself up real nice, and I thought, *Man, this guy knows how to do it*. 'Cept he gets a visit from his lawyer, and Jerry's on edge, like he's taken a hit on the good stuff, know what I'm saying?"

Nic was beginning to wonder if Terrel had taken his own hit from the way his knees were bouncing beneath the table. It was starting to make Nic nervous. Across the table, Lyla appeared calm, but the way she was worrying her lower lip told him it was a façade.

"Anyway, he asks me to write some letters." Terrel looked at Lyla. "To you. Never told me what to say, just to make it scary. I asked him what his beef was with you, but he wouldn't say. Just wanted you to know he was still there. I never thought much about it until I was about to get out. Jerry asked me to write one more letter, 'cept this time he told me exactly what to say." Terrel gave a nervous chuckle. "I thought maybe I'd taught him well, but there was something different about him. Brother was scared. First time I seen him like that. Asked him if he was okay, said I could keep writing the letters if he was willin' to pay, but he said this would be the last letter and he wanted to make sure you didn't miss this one. He called me a couple days ago and told me to deliver it. I paid my sister's kid to deliver it, but"—his nervous gaze flickered to Nic—"I didn't tell him how to deliver it."

"Why was this letter so important?"

His attention back on Lyla, Terrel rolled the toothpick between his lips. "He wanted you to know they'd killed him."

"Who? Who killed him?"

"I don't know, and I ain't sticking around to find out." This time Terrel slid his legs out from under the table and stood. "Shondra, come on, we're leaving."

"Wait." Lyla stood. "Did Jerry tell you anything else? Mention an insurance policy or the flash drive?"

The frown lines cutting into Terrel's forehead were his answer. "Honey, I already told you I don't know nothing about no flash drive." He helped Shondra put on her coat. "And the only insurance policies inmates carry are the ones that get 'em outta jail or . . . keep 'em alive." Terrel's shoulders sank. "Looks like Jerry's policy ran out."

Lyla came around the table and Nic rose, putting himself within arm's length of knocking Terrel out if he tried anything. "Who do you think killed Jerry?"

Through narrowed eyes, Terrel seemed to be checking out his surroundings. "No idea. Good thing too. I ain't about to follow Jerry to the grave. Ain't safe outside, ain't even safe inside."

Terrel ushered Shondra away from the group, leaving Nic and Lyla standing out like sore thumbs among the bowlers, who appeared less friendly now.

"We can't let him leave."

"We're not." Nic pointed in the direction of the exit, where four police officers had just stepped through the door. "We should go and let them do their job."

Nic escorted Lyla away from Terrel's friends and out a side door he'd seen a couple of smokers

140

use. Outside, Lyla gripped the collar of her coat against the cold October night, and Nic used his key fob to start his truck.

"How did the police know Terrel was here?"

"I sent his PO our location when we arrived." Nic opened the door for her. "He sent the cops."

"Okay, hear me out, Nicolás," she started as soon as he got into the truck. "Genevieve told me she didn't believe Jerry would kill himself, and now his cellmate, a man who could've lied but for whatever reason was like 'yeah, I sent you the letters, what of it,' and—"

Nic choked on a laugh.

Lyla's eyes narrowed on him. "What?"

"Nothing." He pulled out of the parking lot. "I was just admiring your spot-on impersonation."

"Spot-on?" Lyla wrinkled her nose at him. "Spot-on. Is it spot-on, Nicolás?" she repeated in a British accent. "Are you watching those Victorian shows with Kekoa and Elinor too?"

"No." Nic relaxed in his seat. Enjoying this brief respite of playfulness was like a balm to his frayed nerves. "I prefer Westerns."

"Why does that not surprise me?" She giggled. "Anyway, what was I saying again?"

"That Terrel didn't believe Jerry killed himself."

"Right, and he was scared about something, which matches what Genevieve said, except he didn't know why she gave me the flash

141

drive or anything about an insurance policy."

An unsettling revelation struck. "He wanted you to know they killed him." Nic's grip on the steering wheel tightened as he whispered Terrel's words.

"What?"

"The letters are the insurance policy." Nic stared at the road, the brake lights ahead of him flashing like the warning in his head. "When I was in SWAT, we were called to a scene where a guy had barricaded himself in his home with a bomb. He'd kidnapped a girl and was demanding a ransom, but when the FBI asked for proof of life, he couldn't provide it because he'd already killed the girl."

"That's horrible." Lyla shuddered. "But what does that have to do with Jerry sending me letters?"

"I think they might've been his proof of life. If we believe what Terrel and Genevieve are suggesting, then the insurance policy might not have been an actual monetary policy, but like Terrel said, one that keeps inmates alive." He looked over at her. "The letters Jerry sent you may have been the insurance policy letting you know he was still alive."

She wrinkled her face. "He couldn't just send me a nice letter? 'Hey, I'm alive! Hope you're well. Thanks for putting me in jail. How 'bout them Yankees?' "

There was a slight waver to Lyla's sarcasm that made Nic think all this was starting to affect her. "Maybe he couldn't risk giving you details in the letter in case it got intercepted. He had Terrel write them for a reason. Someone could've been watching Jerry."

"So why me? Why not let the FBI know? Send the letters to them? Or tell his lawyer?"

Nic stopped at a red light. He was wondering the same thing. Why wouldn't Jerry report a threat against his life? Most people had a natural inclination for self-preservation. Fear being a motivating factor. His eyes slid to Lyla. Reality throbbed heavy in his chest as he recognized that part of his own fear was directly related to his feelings for Lyla. Or rather the idea that he could make a mistake with her. He wasn't worried about preserving his life as much as he was about preserving *hers*.

What scared her—and then it hit him.

The first time he'd seen fear flicker in those sea-colored eyes of hers was when he mentioned she may have put her family in danger by engaging with Genevieve.

"Family." He looked over at her. "What was the one thing Genevieve said Jerry would do?"

"Protect his family." Lyla swiveled in her seat, her hand landing on his arm. "We need to talk to Genevieve, find out what she knows about the trouble Jerry was in and what she was so afraid

143

of and what the article was about on the flash drive. I don't think she meant to send a virus into our system, Nicolás, but maybe whatever was on there had some sort of a fail-safe to hijack the information she was trying to give me." He stopped at another light and looked over and saw the alarm in her eyes. Then she continued, "His wife, Tiffany. What if her car accident wasn't an accident?"

"Lyla, breathe." He raised a brow at her stubborn countenance until she finally inhaled deeply, which from the curve of her lips he could tell she was doing just to appease him. "We'll check into all of that . . . Monday."

"Monday? No way, Nicolás. We need to head back to the office and contact the warden at Paterson and get access to the surveillance cameras to find out who was with Jerry the morning he died. Talk to his lawyers and—"

"Monday," he cut in, needing to get ahead of her. "It's after five, and I'd bet his lawyers don't work past five on a Friday."

"Okay, then tomorrow. The warden might be working on a Saturday, and we can at least try to get in touch with Genevieve." She glanced around as if suddenly realizing he wasn't on the road back to HQ. "Where are we going?"

"I'm taking you up to your parents' place like you had planned." Nic took a left. "You have plans tomorrow, remember?"

A second passed before he heard her sigh. "The drag hunt." She blew out a frustrated breath. "I can back out of it. Tell my parents it's work."

"Are you really thinking about disappointing Elinor?" Nic hoped this was going to work. "You heard Kekoa, she's read books and magazines in preparation for tomorrow."

"She can still go. Or we can do it another time. I'll make it up to her, to all of you."

"Lyla, Jerry's dead. If he was killed, then it was because he got into something he shouldn't have and faced the consequences." He cringed a little at the similarity this had to how Lyla operated. Had she caught it too? She was facing away from him, so he couldn't tell. "I know Walsh wants us to find out who's behind the malware, but you've made a commitment to your family to be there tomorrow, and we're all looking forward to it."

This turned her to face him. "You are?"

The eagerness in her question squeezed his heart. He was speaking on behalf of the team, but more so for himself. He'd come to enjoy Lyla's crazy antics *outside* of work, so long as tight pants and fake mustaches weren't part of the equation. He was going to miss them—her.

"Sure." He stretched his arm along the back of the bench, his fingers close enough to brush her hair from her face. He pulled his arm back. "This might be the only time I can win an argument with you."

Her brows puckered. "What argument?"

"The one that's about to happen when I tell you that I'll be crossing that finish line tomorrow before you."

"Ha!" She lifted her chin defiantly. "You have no idea who you're challenging."

He tilted his head. "Oh, I think I do."

"Fine. I suppose we can wait until Monday."

"How much did that hurt?"

"This much." She spread her thumb and forefinger apart by a few centimeters before moving both hands wide apart. "But it's going to feel really good when I show you up."

Nic breathed a sigh of relief. Facing off with Lyla on a horse seemed a lot easier than trying to convince her to pause her determined interest in Genevieve and Jerry Miller.

"Are you scared of anything?"

"What?"

The shock in Lyla's voice made him regret asking. He didn't want to get into an argument when things were going his way.

"I'm just trying to gauge the best path to a win. If it's spiders, I know a place I can get a few plastic ones to toss at you tomorrow."

Lyla gave him a playful punch. "I never took you for a cheat, Nicolás."

"It's not cheating . . . it's finding your competitor's weakness and exploiting it."

Her laughter paused, and when he glanced over,

he found her looking at him with an expression that made him wish every moment with her was as easygoing as this.

"Etta used to scare me."

"Pardon?" Etta was a lovely eighty-something woman he'd met briefly, but in no way would he consider her a threat. "You were scared of your grandmother?"

"Yep. Etta is the epitome of refinement. Her home is meticulous, she expected manners, dresses, and pantyhose." Lyla scratched the top of her legs as if feeling the memory. "I was not a pantyhose kind of girl. Torn jeans and scraped knees were my outfit of choice. I'm not sure how old I was, maybe four or five, when I knew I didn't belong."

Nic's heart ached at her quiet confession. "What do you mean?"

Lyla sighed. "I think my grandparents and my parents expected certain things of me. As a Whitlock, I'd act according to some of their assumptions, but it wasn't me. The more they pushed, the more I pushed back."

"You and your family seem so close."

"Oh, we are now." She smiled to herself. "But it took years of me testing the boundaries of their love until I began to trust that they did, in fact, love me for me."

Without thinking, Nic reached over and took Lyla's hand, appreciating the way her soft skin felt in his calloused palm. The touch spread warmth through him, waking up a part of his heart that had been lying dormant since . . . Brittany.

Nic pulled up to the stately home of Lyla's parents and put his truck in park. Then he turned to her. In the moonlight, the color of her eyes looked like the depths of the ocean, and he knew he'd get caught in the current if he wasn't careful.

Good grief. Kekoa would mock this moment for all eternity if he were here right now.

"Nicolás." Her fingers moved between his, and the intimacy of the touch made him hold his breath. "Something tells me this situation with Jerry and his vendetta against me is bigger than we think." She gently squeezed his hand. "I need you on my side. I promise I'll do whatever you say. Just like at the bowling alley. If you think it's getting too dangerous, I'll pull back, but you can't let Walsh or Jack keep me from this assignment. Please promise me."

Nic ground his molars. He stared straight ahead as the warning battled the beating inside his chest. After hearing what Terrel had to say, he agreed the situation had taken a turn, and he knew Jack and Walsh would be concerned. He was too. So then why in the world wasn't he refusing? *Because if I refuse, she'll do it anyway.*

As he looked down at her hand in his, the touch no longer felt light and intimate but weighted with the promise she was asking him to make.

He lifted his gaze to meet hers. "Do not make me regret this."

"Thank you, Nicolás." Lyla nodded and squeezed his hand once more before she released it to unbuckle her seat belt. "Do you want to come in? I bet there are leftovers I could warm up for us."

"I think I'd better call it a night. I want to get back and ask if Mr. Brandt will be my date for tomorrow."

"I'm looking forward to meeting him." He thought he saw a flicker of disappointment in the smile she forced to her lips. She opened the door. "You have Etta and Tully's address, right?"

"I do."

"Okay, well, I'll see you tomorrow, Nicolás."

"Think you can stay out of trouble that long?"

This time her smile reached her eyes, and the sight of it loosened the breath he'd been holding. She ran a finger across her chest. "Cross my heart." She raised a brow. "Besides, my rental is back at the office, which I don't think was a coincidence."

Nicolás gave an innocent shrug. "We'll get you to work on *Monday*. Don't worry."

Her lips twitched into a smile before she closed the door, jogged up the front porch, and gave a quick wave before disappearing inside. Looking up at the luxurious home Lyla grew up in, he found it hard to reconcile the down-to-earth woman she'd grown into, especially given the insight she'd just shared with him. He had no doubt the little girl who'd pushed boundaries inside those walls was fiercely loved.

He wasn't imagining the hope he heard in her voice. And he didn't know if it was due to Naomi's earlier comment or Lyla's touch that still vibrated his soul, but the boundaries he'd carefully set up when it came to Lyla were blowing up, and that was dangerous. Boundaries were there for a reason—to protect.

12

"L ord, thank you for the meal we are about to eat and the dirty little hands that made it." Giggles erupted, and he peeked one eyelid open to see the faces seated around the table. Eyes were pinched closed, the older ones' hands were folded nicely in front of them, but the littles had theirs tucked up under their tiny, round faces. A rainbow of skin colors that made the backs of his eyes burn with tears.

I have so much to be grateful for.

"Brooks, honey."

Across the table he caught Lydia using her eyes to indicate patience was waning. He smiled at his wife before closing his eyes and continuing. "Thank you for my amazing family who's going to let me see the Cowboys beat the Chiefs tonight instead of watching their silly movie. Amen."

"No!"

"Daddy, no!"

"We already picked *Cars*."

"No, *Planes!*"

Brooks opened his eyes to find his little cherubs squabbling about their movie choices over slices of pizza. He smiled at Lydia, who tried for exasperation, but she was smiling too. Their two

151

oldest, sitting on his left, were rolling their eyes at their siblings.

"Tori, have you been working on your college applications?"

"Yes, sir." Tori bit her lip. "I've already applied to a few of the local community colleges, but I talked with my counselor and she thinks I have the grades to get into William and Mary." Tori's eyes dashed between him and Lydia. "I know it's not cheap, but my counselor said I might be eligible for scholarships, and there are even some work-study programs I can apply for too."

Brooks finished chewing and wiped his mouth. "I belonged to the Tribe."

Tori's dark-brown eyes twinkled. "I want to go there because it was your school."

His heart heaved in his chest. Tori, eighteen, had grown into a well-rounded young woman. Straight A's, a member of the National Honor Society, captain of her volleyball team, and now she wanted to go to his alma mater.

The odds hadn't been in her favor when he and Lydia got a call from the social worker about a two-year-old girl whose mother put drugs in her bottle to put her to sleep. The second he and Lydia took Tori into their arms, they knew she belonged with them. They took turns at the hospital rocking her as her little body went through the violent withdrawal process, crying and praying over her until they were able to bring her home. And as soon as they could, they began the paperwork to adopt her.

"Look," ten-year-old Thomas shouted. "Daddy's crying."

Brooks blinked, feeling a tear slip down his cheek. He wiped his face and realized he was in fact crying.

"Are you sad, Daddy?"

He met six-year-old Angelina's dark-brown eyes, the same as those of her twin brother, Anthony, sitting next to her. Both had an awareness in their face that spoke of the many times they'd likely seen their biological mother crying after their stepfather came home drunk.

"No, honey." He reached out to her, sliding a hand along her cheek, remembering a time when she would cower anytime he came close to her. "These are happy tears. I'm happy."

"Oh." She ate a bite of her pizza. "Like Michael's 'mojis."

Brooks looked at their sixteen-year-old son, who dipped his chin and pushed up his glasses. "I let her use my phone. Showed her the emojis. She likes the smiley face with the tears. I told her it was like when I tickle her and she laughs so hard she almost cries. Happy tears."

Anthony held up his hand. "I like the poop 'moji."

Bursts of laughter broke out around the table, which led Anthony to keep saying *poop* until they all looked like the happy-tears emoji.

"So," Tori said above the noise, "what do you think about William and Mary? Can I please try to get in? See if I get any scholarships? And if it's still too expensive, then I'll just go to one of the community colleges as planned."

"No." Brooks looked at his wife sitting at the other end of the table. She gave him a subtle nod, and he turned to Tori. "If you get accepted into William and Mary, then we'll make it happen. No matter what."

"Really?" Tori squealed before shooting out of her seat and racing around the table to his chair. She wrapped her arms around him and hugged tightly. "Thank you, thank you, Daddy. I promise I'll get as many scholarships as I can and work two jobs if I have to."

Then Tori ran to her mother and repeated the same thing.

"We still get to watch *Planes*, right?" Anthony said.

"No, *Cars*," Angelina cried out.

"It's Friday night, and I think we have a reason to celebrate." Brooks knew Lydia was going to tan his hide after this, but he didn't care. "Let's watch both movies!"

As expected, Lydia's eyes went round and Brooks held up his glass of soda, leading the kids to do the same.

"To Tori and her acceptance to the Tribe."

• • •

An hour later, dinner was cleaned up and the kids were draped all over the family room floor watching Dusty Crophopper earn his wings. More popcorn was on the floor than in the bowls, and he'd been kicked in the shin twice by a squirming Anthony, but Brooks couldn't imagine a better way to spend a Friday evening.

A vibrating noise rattled from the side table and the littles groaned.

Thomas looked up at him. "No calls during family night, Dad."

"I know, buddy." Brooks wriggled out from under Angelina and reached for his phone. He hesitated when he saw *Unknown* on the screen. It vibrated again. He stood and mouthed to Lydia that he'd be back. Thankfully the kids were too invested in the movie to notice him step into his office and close the door.

"Hello?"

"Enjoying a nice evening with your family?"

The voice on the other end caused Brooks's skin to crawl. He moved to his window, peeking through the blinds at his quiet neighborhood. Was he out there? Watching him and his family? It was an invasion of his privacy, and it made him feel vulnerable. "What do you want?"

"The flash drive is gone."

He took a calming breath. "Why are you calling me about this?"

155

"Because you answered, and I need to know what you want me to do with the woman."

"What woman?" Brooks whispered harshly. He looked back at his office door and listened to the sounds of the movie playing on the other side. He moved deeper into his office. "What are you talking about?"

"The sister," he said impatiently. "She got rid of the flash drive, and now I need to know what I'm supposed to do with her."

His pulse pounded loudly in his ears. "You weren't supposed to do anything with her." Brooks closed his eyes and rubbed his temples. "All we asked for was the flash drive."

Silence filled the phone, and Brooks felt his heart beating much too fast.

"Miscommunication, I guess. You asked for the drive, and that required a little up-close-and-personal conversation. She was resistant at first but eventually told me she gave it to someone named Lyla. Worked with her brother, I think."

Brooks ran a hand over his head. Not sure his legs would keep him standing, he grabbed his desk chair and dropped into it. He forced himself to ask the question. "Is she . . ." His throat was dry. "Did you . . ."

"Dead? Not yet. Just waiting for the word."

"No." He said it too loudly and quickly covered his mouth, his eyes darting to the door. "That was never part of the plan."

156

"Plans change. We can't just let her go."

How did I let it get this far? The wall of his accolades mocked him. Meaningless pieces of paper compared to what was sitting in his family room. It was never supposed to last this long. A single decision and—

"Tick. Tock."

"Shut up." Spittle flew from his lips. "Just give me a minute." He gripped the back of his neck in frustration. "I sent you to retrieve the flash drive. Nothing else. You want to know what to do—you know who to call."

With courage he didn't feel, Brooks ended the call and turned his phone off. He slapped his cheeks and inhaled deeply before sliding the phone into his back pocket. When he stepped out of his office, he was met with Rascal Flatts belting the theme song for *Cars*.

"Where's your mom?" he whispered over Tori's shoulder.

"In the kitchen making more popcorn."

He eyed the mess on the floor and shook his head. The microwave hummed in the kitchen, where he found Lydia with her back to him, facing the window over the sink.

"I think we can make another bowl just by scooping the popcorn off the—" Lydia's shoulders shook, and Brooks rushed to her side. "Honey, what's the—" She faced him, her eyes rimmed red and her cheeks wet. "You're crying."

She leaned into his chest and cried. "They're h-happy tears."

He kissed his wife's head and rubbed her back. "Are you sure?"

Sniffling, she pulled back and smiled up at him. "Yes. I was sitting there watching a silly plane who dreamed of being a racer and thinking how ridiculous it was, but then he does it." She wiped her nose. "And it made me think about the dream I had as a little girl." She gestured around the kitchen. "For this. A family. A home. A Friday night watching a cartoon movie with a popcorn mess and . . . and I got it."

"You dreamed of popcorn messes?"

Lydia slapped his chest playfully before walking to the microwave just as it beeped. She grabbed the bag of popcorn with her fingertips and emptied it into a bowl. When she faced him, a tear slid down her cheek. "Thank you."

He took her into his arms again. "For what, honey?"

"For all of this. Our kids will never know what it was like for me. Because of you, they'll never know what it's like to clean up their mother because she's so drunk she can't make it to the bathroom. Or learn the best hiding spots to avoid the carousel of *new daddies* brought home to replace the one locked up in prison."

Lydia's voice murmured against his chest, and hearing her relive the painful memories

158

of her childhood made him hug her tighter.

"Tori and Angelina will never have to do . . ." Lydia looked up at him. "They'll never have to live the life I did before meeting you. Because of you, our children will have a better life than I ever could've dreamed of for us."

Brooks wiped the tears from her cheeks before kissing her lips. A deep kiss, which he hoped conveyed how much he loved her. When he pulled back, he found her blushing. He tilted his head in the direction of the family room. "Everything good about those five blessings sitting in there is because of you. You're a wonderful mother, and they're lucky to have you. I am too."

"Six."

"Sorry?"

"Brenda called. They have a little boy. Eight. Autistic like Michael. She thinks our family would be perfect, but I said I'd have to talk to you first."

Unbridled hope sparkled in her eyes. She was an advocate for the weak, abandoned, and suffering. And he couldn't tell her no.

"I think I saw someone in the neighborhood selling a twin bed on the Facebook page. I'll check to see if they sold it."

Lydia beamed and wrapped her arms around his neck, rewarding him with a kiss so passionate he was afraid one of the kids might walk in on them.

He was about to warn of this possibility when the house phone rang.

Separating, she shook her head and grabbed the bowl of popcorn. "If it's Robbie from next door, please tell him Thomas is not allowed to talk after eight, even on a Friday."

"Okay." They were probably one of the last families in the country who maintained a landline, but the adoption proceedings for the twins had been volatile, and he wanted a surefire way for his family to get help if they needed it. He picked up the receiver and answered. "Hello?"

"Imagine the looks I received when I interrupted my own dinner party to answer a phone call that could've been taken by you."

Brooks turned on the sink faucet and started the dishwasher to create a noise barrier. "He wanted to know what to do."

"So you tell him."

The scathing tone caused the hairs on the back of his neck to rise. "No. I want no part in it."

"No part in it? There's not a single part that doesn't have you irrevocably tied to it. Look around you, Brooks. You have a good life. A wife who adores you and children who are growing into well-adjusted adults despite where they'd be without you. I hear you've even got one considering William and Mary." Brooks's eyes flashed around him. *Is my home bugged?* Anger unfurled within him. "It's a good school. I'd hate to see her application get derailed."

"Please don't do that." His reflection stared back at him from the window. *How did I let it get this far?* He could hear his children laughing. His wife's words weighed heavily on him. *"Because of you, our children will have a better life than I ever could've dreamed of for us."* "What do you want me to do?"

"Nothing. I've taken care of it, but don't you think for one minute that your hands aren't as bloody as mine. You've got a lot to lose. Remember that the next time a decision needs to be made."

The line went dead—and not for the first time in his life, Brooks wished he were too.

13

The Whitlock property bustled with activity. It was a brisk morning, but the sun rose in a cloudless blue sky. Energy grew in Lyla as she listened to the dogs yipping with excitement as the huntsman and his assistants managed them. Behind her, at the stables, field masters were already directing riders into their groups.

The wide lawn was covered by a white tent, where party staff and florists had decorated tables with crystal, bronze chargers, and the most stunning arrangements of sunflowers, dahlias, and roses. Set up on the side of the tent was the newest addition to the Whitlock Estate Hunt—a BBQ food truck with a full-size smoker filling the air with an aroma that had her mouth watering. Next to the smoker was a hot chocolate and mini-donut stand.

Kekoa is going to lose his mind.

Excusing herself after another round of welcoming guests, Lyla watched for her friends and kept an eye out for Mrs. Davenport, who she shamefully prayed would wake up with a head cold. It was wrong, and she really didn't wish ill will toward Mason's mom, but she had to figure out a way to keep her away from Nicolás.

Lyla pressed a hand to her stomach. Why had

she lied? Why had she given Mrs. Davenport Nicolás's name? Her anxiousness was going to keep her from enjoying the mini donuts, which would be a shame but also maybe a rightful punishment for her hasty lie.

"Looking for your boyfriend?" Lyla's mom walked up next to her. "I thought it was a joke, but you took off back to work before I could ask. Then you drove up in his truck. You rushed into the house, grabbed a Pop-Tart and an apple, and then raced to your room. The last time you did that was after Brian Pierce kissed you in the seventh grade." Her mother's blue eyes twinkled. "So when did this happen?"

Lyla closed her eyes. "We're just friends, Mom. I shouldn't have lied, but that woman is . . . is . . ."

"Incorrigible? Loud? Determined?" Her father walked over and raised his eyebrows. "Did I mention *loud?*"

"Shush." Her mother playfully slapped her dad's arm. "She just wants the best for Mason, and I have to say, you two have always gotten along nicely."

"Not sure getting along nicely makes for the perfect pairing." Lyla searched the crowd. No sign of either Nicolás or Mason's mom. "Shouldn't there be some kind of, I don't know, feeling in my gut that tells me he's the one?"

"The va-va-voom." Her dad wrapped his arms

163

around her mom. "Felt it the second I saw your mother."

"See? Dad gets it."

"Fine, fine," her mom said and kissed his cheek. "Does Nic have the va-va-voom?"

"Motherrrrr."

Her exasperation made both her parents laugh, and she rolled her eyes. A couple waved them over, and Lyla breathed a sigh of relief. Her mom wasn't as bad as Mrs. Davenport, but on more than one occasion she expressed a hope that Lyla would find the right one. She knew it wasn't Mason, because he definitely didn't give her the va-va-vooms.

Did Nicolás? Or was what she felt for him a kinship forged in the dangerous work they did for SNAP, like the military brotherhood he and Kekoa talked about?

"Lyla!"

Elinor waved excitedly from the lot where the valet was directing cars to park. Lyla blinked as she watched Elinor, Kekoa, Jack, and Brynn walking like one of those million-dollar shots from an action movie—only they looked like models for a Ralph Lauren ad.

Lyla hurried to meet them. "You guys look amazing!"

"So do you!" Elinor squealed, grabbing Lyla's hands. "This is so exciting."

"I'm so glad you guys came." Lyla hugged

164

Brynn and looked around. *Nicolás isn't with them?* An odd combination of disappointment and relief settled over her. If he wasn't here, she wouldn't have to worry about Mrs. Davenport or Mason. But why wouldn't he come? Had he changed his mind?

"He's helping Mr. Brandt out of the car," Brynn whispered over Lyla's shoulder. "See?"

Lyla looked in the direction Brynn was pointing and saw Nicolás walking at a slow pace with an older gentleman at his side. Their eyes met and he smiled.

Her chest unexpectedly squeezed at the sight of him. It wasn't like this was the first time she'd seen him out of his usual uniform of jeans, flannel, and boots, but today . . .

Today, he wore a green plaid shirt complemented by a dark-green tie and gray vest under a chestnut-brown jacket. It wasn't the typical riding attire, but, man, he looked good. *Really good.*

"Lyla, I'd like to introduce you to my neighbor, Mr. Brandt."

"It's nice to meet you." Lyla shook the man's extended hand. "Thank you for joining us today."

"Young man"—Mr. Brandt eyed Nicolás—"you didn't tell me you'd be introducing me to a Hollywood starlet."

A blossom of pink colored Nicolás's cheeks, and his hand instinctively searched for the ball cap that wasn't there. He ran a hand through his hair to cover the move, but Kekoa snickered.

"Well, now, aren't you a dapper-looking group." Lyla's grandfather walked over with her grandmother and great-aunt. "It's nice to have some young blood on the course."

"Blood?" Elinor squeaked.

"He's just teasing, dear." Lyla's grandmother smiled. "We just love seeing young people enjoying the sport."

"Etta, Tully, these are my colleagues." Lyla introduced her friends. "And this is my grand-father and grandmother, and"—she hugged the woman next to Etta—"my great-aunt Effie."

"You didn't tell me I was going to be among such beauty." Mr. Brandt stepped forward and extended his hand to Effie. "May I say what a privilege it is to be here today."

When Mr. Brandt lifted Effie's hand to his lips to kiss her knuckles, she giggled. Lyla shot her grandmother a look and she shrugged.

"Mr. Brandt, would you care to keep me company?" Effie asked him.

"It would be an honor."

"Brah's got game," Kekoa whispered as they watched Mr. Brandt escort Effie away.

"Hank is bringing out your horses," Tully said before he placed a hand on Lyla's shoulder. "Ride safe, my dear."

Lyla kissed his cheek and squeezed Etta's hand before they walked away. "Always."

Elinor sighed. "You have the cutest family."

"Thanks." Lyla couldn't deny it. Her family was special, and it meant a lot that her team was here to meet them.

"Yoo-hoo!"

Noooo.

Lyla cringed and avoided looking at Nicolás as she turned to face—"Mrs. Davenport . . . you made it."

"Of course! We wouldn't miss it," she said and gestured to Mason at her side. "You remember Mason."

"We've been friends for twenty years, Mother. I think she remembers me." He wrapped Lyla in a hug as if it was the most natural thing in the world even though she felt her own stiffness at his touch. He whispered, "I've been home less than twenty-four hours, and my mom is going to drive me nuts."

Lyla smothered her giggle as Mason stepped back. "That's a record, I think."

"So, which one of these young men has captured your"—Mrs. Davenport's gaze moved up Kekoa, eyes widening a bit—"heart?"

Lyla's cheeks burned at the curious, amused, and confused expressions her friends were giving her. Quickly introducing them, she paused at Nicolás, eyes pleading that he would forgive her for what she was about to do. "And this is Nicolás." Lyla readied herself. "My boyfriend."

The gasps, snorts, and chuckling coming from her friends were not helping to sell her story. Neither was the stunned expression lining Nicolás's face, but it shifted when his gaze moved to Mason. She quickly reached for his hand at the same time he lifted it up like he was going to put it around her shoulder, but instead their failed attempt at fake affection ended with him accidentally hitting her on the chin and knocking her a few steps backward.

Nicolás swiftly took her hand and gently guided her back toward him, their eyes meeting for one, two, maybe three pulse-pounding moments. Then her attention snagged on Kekoa, who was having a laughing fit, hand on his stomach as Elinor helplessly swatted at him.

"Nicolás." Mason reached out his hand, which required Nicolás to extricate his fingers from Lyla's clammy grip. "Pleasure to meet you."

"Same," Nicolás said quietly and then stepped back, shooting a glare at Kekoa before he wrapped his arm around her waist with a bit more finesse. Lyla relaxed into the position all too naturally.

"Must be a fairly new relationship."

The suspicion in Mrs. Davenport's countenance worried Lyla. If the woman caught even a whisper that there was a chance of hope for Lyla and Mason, she'd be on it like the barking foxhounds around her.

"How long have you two been a couple?"

"Awhile."

"Not long." Lyla shot Nicolás a look. "We've been friends for a while."

"I can see why our little Stinkerbell is smitten. You're handsome in an exotic way," Mrs. Davenport chittered. "I had a Spanish boyfriend once. *Rodrigo*. And when he would kiss me"—she closed her eyes—"he would say 'que sabroso.' "

Yummy?! Why can't the ground open right now and swallow me?

"Mom!" Mason hung his head.

"What? Nothing wrong with a little Spanish love, am I right, Lyla?"

"Tell them your nicknames for each other." Kekoa tilted his chin, eyes dancing with mischief.

I'm going to kill him.

He smiled at Mrs. Davenport. "They're so cute."

"Ms. Lyla."

She spun to find Hank, the stable master, holding the leads on two sorrels with beautiful red coats. Behind him another groom led a chestnut quarter horse, and her horse, Sir Winston, a black Dutch Warmblood gelding.

Perfect timing, Hank. She took Sir Winston's lead. "Maybe we can catch up after?"

Mason nodded and took his mom's arm. "It was nice meeting everyone."

169

"Hank, I'll help Elinor and Brynn, if you can get Jack and Nicolás ready."

"Yes, ma'am."

The second Lyla led them to one of the paddocks, leaving the guys with Hank, Brynn and Elinor rounded on her.

"What in the world was that?" Brynn whispered. "I don't think I've ever seen Garcia's head spin."

Lyla groaned, looking over her shoulder to where Hank was tightening the cinch for Jack. "I know." She turned back. "I panicked and told her I was dating Nicolás. Mrs. Davenport has been trying for years to marry me off to Mason. She can't get it through her shellacked hair that we're just friends."

"Are you sure about that?" Elinor slipped on her helmet. "I'm not certain, but it seems like there was some sizing up between him and Garcia."

"Yeah," Brynn agreed. She stepped into the groom's hand, and he lifted her to the saddle. "Garcia seemed really comfortable putting his arm around you."

"Nicolás and I are total opposites." Lyla tightened the cinch on her horse. "He needs someone who—" *He can trust.* It hurt that trust was the first thing that came to mind, but it was better to admit that painful truth to herself now than to let her emotions get the better of her.

"Someone who doesn't stress him out, which is pretty much all I seem to do."

"Lyla . . ."

"You ladies ready?" Jack asked, interrupting whatever Brynn was going to say next. He and Nicolás led their horses over to the paddock. Kekoa followed, giving the horses a wide berth.

"So how does this work, exactly?" Elinor gripped her reins. "We're not actually hunting foxes, right?"

"No." Lyla smiled. "This is a drag hunt, which means no foxes or animals are being hunted. A drag man has already gone out on the trail laying a scent the dogs will pick up on. And then he'll give what we like to call 'hound music,' a little cry or howl, and then we're off to follow them. But this year we're also hunting the clean boot, which means a human quarry's out there and the first team to track their hounds to him wins."

Brynn's gaze flashed to Jack. "Wins what?"

"Bragging rights." Lyla laughed, knowing she and Jack were highly competitive.

"I'll take bragging rights." Brynn smiled wolfishly.

"It's a good thing I'm on her team." Jack laughed.

The dogs' excited yips had grown louder. They knew the hunt was getting close as riders mounted. Lyla slipped her booted foot into Hank's laced fingers, and with a quick lift, he helped her up onto Sir Winston. "Thanks, Hank."

"I can't believe how calm the horses are with all the noise." Jack patted Storm's neck.

"They're used to this chaos." Lyla did a quick visual check of her friends—making sure their helmets were buckled and cinches were snug against the horses—looking anywhere and everywhere except at Nicolás, who had brought his horse next to hers.

"You coordinated your outfit with your horse?"

"What?" Lyla glanced down at her hunter-green coat and tan breeches tucked into her riding boots. He leaned over and reached for the end of her braid and gave the red ribbon a little tug. "Oh, you mean the ribbon?" Lyla pointed to the green ribbon tied to the tails of their horses. "Green means the rider is inexperienced. But don't worry," she quickly added, seeing Elinor's eyes widen. "Hank put you all on the most experienced horses. The green ribbon will let other riders know to watch out for you."

"And red?" Jack asked.

"Red means my horse likes to kick."

"Like rider, like horse." Nicolás smiled, looking at the ribbon in her hair. "Fitting."

His teasing words made her smile. Lyla searched his face for any hint that he was upset with her. She needed to apologize for catching him off guard like that.

But before she could, the hunt master called

for everyone's attention. "Anyone in a red coat is a field master, and you don't pass him," Lyla quickly explained as they walked their horses forward. "We're divided into three groups. Those with riding experience will ride with the first flight. Then our group, the second flight, will go out. It's a moderate ride with no jumping. And if you want to slow your pace, you can join the Hilltoppers, or third flight."

"I'm just gonna stay over here." Kekoa backed away as more riders and horses started to fill in the space. "But I'm sending you a cheehoo, baby!" Kekoa made a heart with his hands and then sent Elinor a shaka.

"Good luck, everyone." Brynn leaned sideways, meeting Jack as he leaned toward her. "Be careful out there."

Jack kissed the tip of her nose. "I will."

For the first time, Lyla felt a jarring pang of discontentment. It wasn't that she hated being single. She liked her independence, but she was beginning to feel like maybe she was missing out.

Mason moved into her field of vision and waved. She waved back until she caught Nicolás watching her. The field master gave the signal to move and the dogs were set loose, their barks echoing as they led the first flight and Mason into the field.

Jack and Elinor walked their horses forward.

Lyla ran her hand along the reins, feeling that familiar jitter of nerves she always got before a ride.

"So, are we going to talk about this?"

Lyla exhaled. "Nicolás, I want to apologize for earlier. I didn't mean to lie. Well, actually, I did mean to lie, but I didn't mean to make you a part of that lie. I know how uncomfortable that made you, and I'm sorry."

Nicolás's brows lowered. "Oh, you're talking about that thing with Memphis."

"Mason," Lyla corrected, but she could see from the glint in his eyes that Nicolás knew his name. "What were you talking about?"

Nicolás lifted a brow. "You put me on *Buttercup?*"

Lyla laughed at his unamused expression. She leaned down to pat Nicolás's horse a few times. "Ah, Buttercup, you're a sweet girl, aren't you?"

"You know Jack and Kekoa laughed for a full five minutes."

"Buttercup is one of our best mares. She could run this trail with her eyes closed." Lyla watched the field master for the second flight move forward. "She has only one weakness."

"What's that?"

Lyla leaned over her saddle and hugged her horse. "She always lets Sir Winston lead."

"Exploiting my weakness. Well played."

174

Nicolás set his jaw, the edge of his lip tweaking up. "You better hold on, Stinkerbell."

The field master gave the signal, and the horses took off. Nicolás winked and gave a quick kick of his heel in Buttercup's flanks, and the horse responded instantly.

Lyla smiled. *Oh, the hunt is on.*

14

Nic's pulse raced nearly as hard as Buttercup's, the steady beat of her hooves pounding the ground the only thing loud enough to silence the beating of his heart. He could still feel Lyla's body against his side, and if his head hadn't been so turned around trying to figure out what was going on, he might've enjoyed it more.

He glanced over his shoulder. Lyla's tiny frame was tucked close to Sir Winston, his long, muscular legs quickly catching up. There was a fire in Lyla's eyes that matched the smile lighting her face, revealing how much she loved this. The adrenaline. The competition. The risk.

Facing forward, Nic let Buttercup go a bit farther before pulling the reins just enough to slow her down to a canter.

Lyla pulled Sir Winston up beside him, and Buttercup gave a snort. "You're slowing down already?"

Her cheeks were pink, and the wind had freed a few pieces of hair that framed her face beneath her helmet. She was breathless . . . and breathtaking.

"Why are you smiling?"

As they let their horses slow to a walk, he

turned a serious gaze on her. "I didn't want you to feel bad because I was winning."

"Pshh." Lyla patted Sir Winston's neck. "We were holding back, huh, boy?"

Nic chuckled, but the way she was riding told him that if she'd given it her all, she would've smoked him—racing and jumping her horse like the polished equestrian she was.

"I thought you said you've only ridden Western?"

"That's right."

"Rodeo?"

"Herding cattle." Nic leaned back in the saddle.

Lyla's head tilted to the side. "You never told me you worked on a cattle farm."

"My father did, but I helped him out. Learned to ride early and discovered I had a knack for making wayward cows do what I say."

"You said that with a bit of twang just now." Lyla giggled. "I didn't think Arizonans had a drawl."

"They don't. We don't." He listened to his voice. "I don't think."

Lyla's laughter spilled around her. Nic breathed in the cool morning air and took in the wooded property of Tully and Etta Whitlock's estate. It was stunning, the trees hanging on to the last vestiges of fall color before winter set in. The sound of the hounds could be heard even though the animals couldn't be seen.

In the solitude of this moment, in God's handiwork, Nic allowed himself to imagine his future. And no matter how many times he saw it, the woman riding next to him was by his side. Did that mean in a professional manner or more? Was God revealing a reason to stay at the agency?

"Maybe it's just being back in the saddle." Lyla squinted against the sun. "Brings out the real you."

Nic swallowed. The real him was leagues beneath Lyla and her family. He didn't need to see the Whitlock family crest or Lyla's initials monogrammed on all her livery to know that. The sight of her in her riding outfit and the way her body moved so effortlessly with her horse made him a bit jealous. "You seem to enjoy it too."

"Yeah?"

Nic lifted his brow. Her disbelief was surprising, but after their conversation last night about her not feeling like she fit into this life—maybe it shouldn't be. He didn't understand it, though. What would make her think she didn't belong? "You don't think you do?"

Lyla shrugged. "I guess maybe out here I do." She smiled, her gaze drifting to the winding trail ahead. "My mom and dad put me into lessons when I was little, but my instructor was b-o-r-i-n-g and insisted I learn all the fundamentals before I could jump."

"And you couldn't wait."

178

"Don't act like you know me, Nicolás." She sent him a side-eye. "But, yes. Unfortunately, my parents were of the same mind as my instructor, but not Tully. I think he sensed my restlessness, so he'd take me out and we'd run and race, and then he'd point out a hedge or small ravine and tell me to jump."

Nic could see the whole thing in his mind. This rambunctious little girl, braids flapping in the wind, charging ahead without a single fear holding her back. He dipped his chin. Fear was healthy. It was God's alert system to warn of danger, keep us safe . . . sometimes from ourselves.

For some reason, Lyla's alert system seemed to be muted.

"How do you think the others are doing?"

He smirked. "If Brynn has her way, I bet she's already at the front of the pack. I'm sure Jack has told her to slow down at least a dozen times in the last hour."

"I can see that." Lyla smiled. "How many donuts do you think Kekoa's eaten?"

"Too many, I'm sure. My attempts to get him to eat healthier are about thirty percent effective."

Lyla brought Sir Winston to a stop and let him graze. "He *has* started adding lettuce to his burgers."

"That's true." He loosened Buttercup's reins so she could reach the grass. "If we can get him to eat a salad once in a while, it'll be a miracle."

"Mac salad *is* salad," Lyla said in a low voice pretending to sound like Kekoa. "Elinor's been good for him, though, and I think he might be getting ready to ask her to marry him. Has he told you anything?"

Nic started to reach for his hat but remembered he was wearing a helmet. "No."

"Nicolás!" Her eyes—bluer today—rounded. "Do you know something?"

"I really don't." Nic raised his right hand in an oath. "But I imagine the day is coming soon."

Lyla sighed. "I'm so happy for them."

"Me too." Nic studied the reins in his hand. He was very happy for Kekoa and Elinor and Naomi and Will, but the energy it took not to let it remind him of what he almost had, and then lost, with Brittany was more than he expected. And now . . . he slid a sideways glance to Lyla. "So, um, you and Memphis?"

"Mason." Lyla met his gaze, cheeks turning red. "I'm really sorry. I never should've involved you in that horribly awkward situation."

His thoughts went back to the way Lyla fit next to him. "I've been in worse."

"Worse than reminding Mrs. Davenport of her Spanish lover?"

Nic screwed up his face. "That was a first."

"Again, I am so sorry." Lyla shook her head. "Mrs. Davenport has been trying forever to arrange for *Mason* and me to be together. I had no idea innocent playdates of peanut butter and jelly sandwiches were a lure." She gave a nervous laugh. "Yesterday, she put me on the spot when she mentioned Mason was back in town. I knew where she was headed. I told her I had a boyfriend. When she asked for his name, yours was the first one that popped into my head. I am so, so sorry."

It was ridiculous to feel any kind of gratification that his name was the first she thought of or that he was found worthy over Memphis.

"I promise I'll tell them the truth as soon as we get back." She sent him a sly smile. "Or we can hang out here and wait them out."

"Oh, and here I thought you just wanted to enjoy the beautiful scenery with me and Buttercup."

Lyla smirked, then looked around. A breeze sent some oak leaves raining down between them. "It is beautiful, isn't it?"

Not compared to you. The rogue thought didn't feel so uncommon anymore, and it scared him. This was why he needed to take the Syrian mission. Give him some time to figure out if his desire to keep her safe was going to continue to impede his ability to work with her and SNAP.

"We've played the part before during a few of our assignments." He shrugged, hoping it came off noncommittal. "We'll just pretend this is

181

an assignment. Operation Keep Lyla Single."

Lyla looked up at him from beneath dark lashes. "Are you sure?"

"His mom used PB and Js as a lure." He scoffed. "What kind of person does that?"

"A very dedicated moth—"

Crack!

Lyla's eyes went wide just as her horse reared back. "Was that—"

Crack! Crack!

They both hunched over their horses. Nic whipped his head around, looking for the source of the gunshots when another one rang out. "I thought you said there was no hunting."

"There's not." Another shot rang out, and Sir Winston's ears pinned back. "Hunting season doesn't start for another two weeks, but nobody should be shooting near the property."

Crack!

Bark splintered over Lyla's shoulder.

"Move!" Nic tugged on Buttercup's reins, directing his horse so they were now in front of Lyla, his line of sight on the dense Virginia landscape a couple hundred yards away. The perfect spot for a shooter. He looked back. "Into the trees, Lyla!"

"Nicolás, we've got riders on the trails." Her expression darkened as she tightened her hold on the reins, causing her horse to do a little side trot of defiance. "Where are the shots coming from?"

Crack!

Nic's gaze swung to his ten o'clock, where a forty-foot rock face protruded through the trees. Something glinted in the sun. Scope?

Lyla clicked her tongue, and he turned in time to catch her tap her heels into Sir Winston's side before bolting in the direction he was looking.

"Lyla!" *What is she doing?* Nic knew the answer and didn't like it. He gave a quick kick, and Buttercup raced after them.

Lyla charged ahead, and with the distance growing between them, he was certain she'd been holding back earlier. He followed her as she went right and ducked, narrowly missing a branch. Even though he dropped low, the branch snagged the back of his coat and he heard it rip. He couldn't tell whether they were on a trail, but from the way Lyla surged forward, she knew it well.

Now would be a great time to unmute her fear, Lord.

"Lyla!" His scream flew back in his face, and he gritted his teeth. "Why do you have to be so stubborn?"

They exited a canopy of trees into an open field just about fifty yards from the rock outcropping that would give a shooter a clear line of sight— to Lyla. He remembered the shot that hit the tree near her. His blood ran cold. *Is someone hunting Lyla?*

Nic urged Buttercup to go faster despite her already rapid pace and labored breathing. Would the horse make it to Lyla before it was too late?

"You've got to be kidding me." Nic raised up a bit, his eyes tracking the narrow creek hidden by shrubs and tall grass. Except the closer he got, he realized it wasn't as narrow as he'd thought. "No way."

It had to be five feet wide, and Lyla was heading straight for it at full speed. Nic searched for another way around, but the terrain got steeper in both directions. *She's gonna jump.* As if she'd heard his thought, Lyla tucked her elbows in, bringing her chest close to Sir Winston's back, her body moving in rhythm with her horse's long strides until—air.

Nic watched as Lyla and her horse seemed suspended over the creek until they landed on the other side with enough grace to make a ballet dancer jealous. He released a breath, annoyed by the awe trying to overtake the frustration of knowing he wouldn't be able to follow.

At least not fast enough to catch up with her.

Slowing Buttercup into a trot, he led her down the creek bank, through the water, and back up again. "Let's catch 'em, girl."

Buttercup started her race again, but she'd never be able to make up the distance. Nic tried to slow his breathing so he could hear over the pounding in his ears. There hadn't been any more shots. Was it a hunter? Or was it someone lying in wait as Lyla drew closer?

Nic brought his fingers to his mouth and let out a whistle that startled Buttercup, but it worked. Lyla looked over her shoulder at him.

Crack!

Lyla's horse jerked backward, the momentum catching her off guard. Nic watched in horror as Lyla scrambled for the reins, but it was too late. Sir Winston reared, his front legs coming up and tossing Lyla backward like a rag doll sailing through the air.

Nic raced toward her but was helpless to do anything as her body dropped to the ground with a sickening thud. Not waiting for Buttercup to stop, he swung his leg over and jumped to the ground, his arches aching with the hard drop. He ignored the pain and ran to Lyla, grateful to find her eyes wide open, looking stunned.

"Lyla, are you hurt?"

"I . . ." she gasped, her wild gaze looking over his face. "Okay. Knocked . . . my . . . breath out. Sh . . . shooter?"

The sound of the gunshots had gone silent. Had it been seconds? Minutes? Time seemed to stall when he watched Lyla fall. "I think it's stopped for now." He hoped.

"Winston?"

Nic looked over to where both horses had tucked themselves against some brush. "He's fine, but you need to stay still. You might've broken something."

"Don't . . . worry," Lyla said, her chest still rising and falling quickly. "Give me . . . a minute. Nothing's broken."

He was skeptical. "You're not moving until we get some help out here to check you out."

"Don't give me that look, Nicolás, I'm fine. I've fallen dozens of times."

"Are you seriously going to argue with me right now?" Nic looked her over. "I'm going to check you real quick, and then we need to figure out how to get you back."

"I told you not to worry." Lyla pulled up the cuff of her jacket to show him a thick black bracelet that looked like a smartwatch. A red light was flashing on the screen. "It's a tracking device. Sends an alert to Hank if it detects . . ." She took a breath. "A hard fall. They'll be here soon." She tried to get up but winced before resting her head back on the ground. "Maybe I'll just wait another minute."

"Until they do, I'm going to check you out." She raised her eyebrows at him, and he rolled his eyes. "For injury, which means I have to touch you."

Lyla smiled up at him. *"Nicolás."*

She wasn't going to make this easy. Nic, worried about a concussion, looked at her pupils. He was grateful for the helmet on her

186

head. "How does your head feel? Are you dizzy?"

"I did a somersault in the air, Nicolás. What do you think?"

"Well, the sarcasm didn't get knocked out of you." Nic ignored her eye roll and began a quick check, running his hands over her legs and arms, asking if anything hurt. She shook her head with each question. When he was sure there was nothing broken, he looked around. Both horses stood by steadfast, grazing as if nothing out of the ordinary had taken place.

Only something had.

"What did you think you were doing, Lyla? You don't run toward the shooter."

The soft lines of her face hardened. "Says the man who used to run toward bombs."

Nic exhaled slowly. "We never run toward an explosive. We act swiftly after a careful assessment."

"This is my family's property. Their friends, *our* friends, are on these trails, and someone is shooting at them." Something shifted in Lyla's expression, exposing a vulnerability he didn't normally see. "I have a responsibility to keep everyone safe."

Nic brushed his thumb over her brow. "Lyla, they were shooting at you."

15

"They were shooting at you."

If Lyla hadn't been stunned by her fall from Sir Winston, the ominous words Nicolás had delivered while she was flat on her back would've done it. After the mini tracker attached to her wrist had detected her fall, a signal led Hank and his team to her and Nicolás. They arrived on all-terrain vehicles and brought a medic who did another quick assessment before allowing her to ride back to Etta and Tully's house. She'd never, ever felt unsafe at her grandparents' home, but now the cold, hard possibility was that she had led trouble straight to their doorstep.

She walked to the window overlooking the front lawn. The last of the guests were leaving, and party staff were cleaning up what was left of the Whitlock annual event her mother and Etta had seamlessly concluded without too many guests realizing what had happened.

Thankfully most of the riders from the first two groups had finished the hunt. The last group had safely been on the opposite side of the property from the shooting, and those close enough to hear the shots over the barking hounds seemed to dismiss it with the simple explanation that it had been a hunter on a nearby property—not an entirely unusual occurrence for this area.

Except Tully and her father confirmed deer hunting season didn't start for another two weeks.

Now Nicolás was with them, the sheriff, and a few of his deputies, searching the area for the shooter while she had been ordered to stay back with Jack, Brynn, Kekoa, and Elinor. She'd been ready to argue, but a single look from Nicolás had kept her quiet. And here. Waiting and worrying. Wondering.

"They were shooting at you."

Lyla bit the inside of her lower lip. Who? Was this another one of Jerry's parting gifts? She blew out a breath. If it was, it was just brilliant enough to get her respect. Arranging to have her killed but doing it after he killed himself so he couldn't be charged was next-level evil. It also didn't fit the profile of someone like Jerry.

So, why? What had she done to him to deserve such hostility? Surely her role in his arrest didn't warrant this level of vindictiveness, and even if it did—he was dead. What was the point? And who was his point man now? Terrel was taken into custody last night . . . had he been released? But again, nothing about his personality made her believe he wanted to harm her. He just wanted the money.

"Lyla," Brynn said softly behind her. "You need to stay away from the window."

She looked over her shoulder. "What?"

189

"Standing in front of a window probably isn't a great idea right now."

"Oh." Lyla stepped away but glanced outside again. The only people she could see out there were Etta, her mom, the staff, and her great-aunt Effie, who was sitting at a table with a teacup and saucer in hand, clueless about the danger lurking nearby. Panic cinched her chest. "We need to get them. It's not safe out there."

"Lyla." Jack walked over, his voice commanding but gentle. "Your father already had plainclothes security on-site. The sheriff called in more officers who are monitoring the perimeter and searching the area closest to your grandparents' property."

She wished Jack's reassurance made her feel better, but it only reiterated his belief that someone out there had tried to use her for target practice.

"It's a precaution," Brynn said, her quiet tone steady as she stated the fact. Sometimes Lyla forgot Brynn had had her own fair share of close calls working for the CIA. "Until we figure out what's going on."

"Would you like some more water? Something to eat?" Elinor looked out of place and scared. Kekoa put a hand on her shoulder, and she leaned into his touch. "Can I get you something?"

Lyla wasn't really in the mood to eat, but she wasn't going to tell Elinor that. It was clear the woman was looking for something to do or a way to step away from her own memories of danger not too long ago. "Sure, that would be nice. Thank you."

Kekoa started to escort Elinor out of the house, but Brynn stepped in and gave him a reassuring look before he kissed Elinor's forehead and then returned to the couch.

Lyla felt horrible. This was her fault, but she didn't know why.

The front door opened, and the sheriff walked in with Walsh. Nicolás came in behind them, his eyes flashing to her for a moment before the men paused in the foyer where they held a quiet discussion. A flicker of annoyance started in her middle at their hushed tones, as if she was some vulnerable victim to protect.

This was exactly what she had wanted to avoid when she asked Nicolás to have her back. She wasn't a victim, and if she *had* been the intended target, someone had just made a huge mistake endangering her family.

Lyla marched toward them, the muscles in her backside aching from the fall. "Did you find anything?"

"We didn't locate the shooter." The sheriff faced her. "But we've got officers canvassing the property, and Mr. Fox, uh, your father, and Tully are talking with the closest neighbors. So far, all of them have denied firing any weapons or giving permission to anyone to hunt on their properties, but that doesn't mean hunters didn't trespass."

That was true. Etta and Tully's thirty-plus acres were mostly unfenced. On occasion during hunting season, hunters had trespassed, but it was rare. Now it was a little too coincidental, given Jerry's final threat and the direction of the shots.

"In my experience, deer tend to scatter when they hear the hounds, so my gut tells me there's more to this than an illegal hunter. We searched the general area looking for any shell casings, but without a tighter search perimeter it might take a couple of days or longer before we find anything." The sheriff slipped on his hat and exchanged a look with Walsh. "I'd like to get out there and chat with the Feds. Given the status of some of the guests, I'm surprised they're not pulling rank. But they're willing to allow us to determine criminal intention before stepping in. You'll keep us updated on your end?"

"We will." Walsh shook the man's hand. "Thank you."

Lyla watched the sheriff leave. He might've been surprised by the FBI's cooperation, but no one else in this room was. She was certain Walsh had something to do with the two agents who arrived quietly and were discreetly handling their part in this investigation.

Walsh stalked into the living room. "Kekoa, I need you to get with Keith and Catherine Fox, maybe Mrs. Whitlock too, and get a complete list of everyone who was in attendance today. Those who showed up and anyone who didn't. The FBI is going to run their own investigation, but their focus will be centered on the high-priority guests. I don't want anything or anyone overlooked."

Kekoa nodded. "Yes, sir."

Glancing back out the window, Lyla remembered welcoming a senator and a federal judge with her parents. Her dad introduced her to a few wealthy investors in the tech industry and the secretary of defense, whom he'd met at the space defense gala a few months ago. There were several other less prominent guests who may have had unintentional consequences associated with their work, like Mason's father and grandfather—both commonwealth attorneys who were well-known for not being lenient on criminals. However, what was the likelihood they had an active threat against them?

She stole another look at Nicolás pacing a rut into the polished oak floors of her grandparents' home. The frustration etching a scowl between his brows told her he didn't believe in coincidences either.

"Jack, I want you running point with the FBI," Walsh said. "If they pick up anything that indicates a new direction, I want you ready to offer any assistance if they ask."

"Yes, sir."

"Sir." Nicolás stopped pacing. His dark gaze moved from Lyla to Walsh. "What about Genevieve Miller?"

Lyla frowned. "You think Genevieve Miller tried to shoot me?"

"She did infect your computer." Nicolás's tone was sharp. "We have to consider every possibility."

"If we're going to consider every possibility, we'd better start making a list."

"This isn't a joke, Lyla."

"I'm not trying to be funny. We've helped put some really bad people away, so it's not unthinkable to suggest that what happened today might not be connected to Jerry. The list of people who could have a grudge against me . . . or us . . . is long."

"And you don't think Genevieve Miller might be on that list?"

Lyla looked at Jack, then at Kekoa and Walsh. "I can't say for sure, but after what Terrel told us last night . . ." This time she did meet Nicolás's sober expression. "It doesn't make sense. If Genevieve wanted to shoot me, she could've done it in the alley. She gave me a flash drive. She was scared. She said her brother wouldn't kill himself, which matches what Terrel told us last night. And I got the feeling Terrel was scared too. We might need to look at this from a different angle and find out what or who they're scared of."

"The report you sent us last night said Terrel was taken into custody." Walsh looked at Nicolás, who nodded. "Let's find out if he's still behind bars. And I'd also like to bring in Ms. Miller for a chat about what she believes happened to her brother and why she tried to hack into our system."

The worry she saw in Walsh's eyes made her anxious he was about to let their familial relationship interfere with the investigation. She didn't want to be pulled from this. "I can work on the lists of those who might have a vendetta against me, but I'll need to go back to the office to access the files. I just need someone to run me by my parents' house so I can change first."

"I'll take you."

Nicolás's lips barely moved, his brow furrowed deeply, and Lyla suddenly hoped Walsh would say no, would insist on taking her home himself, because the idea of riding alone with Nicolás when he was in one of his moods was . . . well, she'd almost rather face the shooter.

"That works," Walsh said, dashing her hopes. He grabbed his corduroy jacket from the back of the couch. "Tomorrow's Sunday, and I know we could all use the rest—"

"We'll be there, sir," Jack said.

Everyone nodded in agreement, and it was like

a double heaping of guilt on Lyla's head. This wasn't the first Sunday they would work on an assignment, but it stung knowing she was the cause.

"Be safe, Lyla."

"Yes, sir." She met Walsh's eyes, and the fatherly look in his expression told her he was struggling. It caused her throat to swell with emotion. He loved her as much as her own parents did. And if it were up to them, she wouldn't be working for SNAP. There had been a few times, like now, when it seemed Walsh agreed with them, but he knew asking her to do anything else wouldn't fit with who she was, so he gave a quick nod and headed out the front door with Jack and Kekoa just as her parents and grandparents walked in. After a brief exchange with Walsh, they came over and checked on her. Lyla quickly reassured them she was fine and then briefly explained that Nicolás would run her to their home to collect her belongings before they headed back to DC to work on an *unexpected* assignment.

Lyla could tell from the look on her parents' faces that they knew she wasn't giving them the whole truth, but they kept quiet for Etta's and Tully's sakes.

"Honey"—Etta's soft hand reached for Lyla—"are you okay?"

A rush of emotion filled Lyla's chest, bringing

with it an urge to cry in Etta's arms, hug her fiercely, and tell her it was going to be okay. If Jerry had wanted to hurt her, he'd done it by bringing her family into his sick game.

Forcing her voice to work, Lyla took her grandmother's face in her palms. "Etta, I'm okay. I don't want you or Tully to worry."

"Our girl is strong, Etta." Tully wrapped an arm around Lyla's shoulders and squeezed her. Lyla had never known the patriarch of the Whitlock family to be emotional. Feisty, yes, much like her, but he believed emotions were best kept private. Yet there was a waver to his voice that kept Lyla from meeting his eyes. She needed to leave before her emotions got the better of her.

Nicolás cleared his throat. "We should head out."

Lyla hugged everyone again and quickly slipped out the back door with Nicolás. They were a few miles down the road before she finally took a full breath. She checked the sideview mirror, no longer able to see the Whitlock estate. *Lord, please keep them safe.*

"We should've looked into Terrel's story last night. Located Genevieve." Her head began to throb. "If I'd done that instead of coming to the hunt, maybe whoever Jerry sent after me wouldn't have come to my grandparents' house." She blew out a shaky breath. "I need a Bible verse."

Nicolás looked at her, confused. "What?"

"Something to make me feel better." She bit her thumbnail. "You have one of those?"

Running his hand over the steering wheel, Nicolás let two breaths pass before swallowing. "Even though I walk through the valley of the shadow of death, I will fear no evil." He looked over at her. "For you are with me; your rod and your staff, they comfort me."

The familiar words were soothing. Or maybe it was hearing Nicolás speak them with the same confidence he had when giving details about a bomb or weapon—like he knew what he was talking about on a level that went deeper than just recitation.

"How many Bible verses do you have memorized?"

"A few." He reached down and opened a coin tray and picked up a coin and handed it to her.

She immediately recognized it. *Non timebo mala.* The words inscribed on the coin Director Walsh handed to them right before their first assignment as a team. *I will fear no evil.* She ran her thumb over their agency shield. Psalm 23.

I will fear no evil.

"I'm sorry I took off toward the shooter, Nicolás. I-I wasn't thinking about the danger for myself. Just my family and the other riders, and I just . . . reacted."

She waited for him to say more, to spill what

had likely been building in him, but for the rest of the drive he stayed quiet, and that was worse than if he had yelled at her. At least she could argue her side—there was no arguing with silence.

When Nicolás pulled up to her house, Lyla couldn't take it anymore. "Are we doing the silent treatment again? Because I know you're probably chalking this up to me being reckless, but all I could think about was my family." Her voice wavered as she remembered the fear she'd seen in their eyes when she left. "They're scared now, and it's my fault."

"Lyla, can you not see it?"

"What?"

"Your grandparents, your parents . . ." He blew out a breath as if the frustration level was making it impossible to talk to her. She could feel her defenses rising. "Lyla, they're scared for *you*."

Her guard dropped. "What?"

"I saw the same fear you did, only it wasn't for themselves." He looked over, and there was pain she couldn't understand radiating from the depths of his hazel eyes. "It was for you. I've only known you a few years, but I cannot imagine loving you your whole life and knowing it's not enough."

"Nicolás, we're all in a dangerous profession. You, me, Kekoa, Jack. Brynn. Our families' love for us can't keep us from doing the hard things. It should be what drives us to make the world better." She started to reach for his hand and then stopped short, afraid of his rejection. "I'm not trying to hurt them. Or anyone. Please believe me."

Nicolás took a slow breath and pressed his lips together before finally saying, "You're not making it easy."

It wasn't the reassurance she was hoping for, but she was desperate to ease the tension between them. "I'm going to run in and change."

"If you don't mind, I'll walk you in and wait downstairs."

"Oh, yeah. Sure, that's fine." Lyla led him up to the house. Her eyes darted to the landscaped hedges that lined her parents' home. Was someone waiting there, ready to try again? "I'll be quick."

Lyla unlocked the door and stepped inside. Nicolás followed, but his steps slowed as his gaze moved around the space, taking in her family home. It made her feel a little self-conscious. She knew he didn't come from wealth, and while her family home was grand, it wasn't the most extravagant show of wealth she or Nicolás had witnessed in their line of work.

"I'll be right back." She started to turn, then stopped. Something wasn't right. She took two steps back and looked around.

"What's wrong?"

Lyla bit the inside of her cheek. "I don't know."

Nicolás was at her side, his posture as tense as the look in his eyes. "Go outside."

"What? I'm not—"

"Lyla." There was a softness to his exasperation. "Go outside and come back in, slowly. Take your time and see what it is that doesn't feel right."

"Oh." She stepped out with Nicolás shadowing her. "The shooting probably has me imagining things." Lyla exhaled at Nicolás's silence and pulled the door shut. This was silly. After a beat, she opened the door and stepped in and looked around. "See, it's—"

Lyla spun to her left to the alarm panel that was silent.

"The alarm. It wasn't set."

Nicolás walked past her to the alarm panel. "It's working. Do you remember if you or your parents set it when you left?"

"I don't remember." She touched her head. While her helmet had done its job, her brain was still aching. "I don't think my parents ever leave the house without setting the alarm. Even if they forget to do it on the panel, they can activate it with their phones." She surveyed the living room again. Her mother's taste was simple, the décor focused on a few select pieces of art. A few were quite valuable, but nothing was out of place. "We were running late this morning. Maybe they forgot."

"Is it okay if I go with you to your room?"

To her room? Her childhood bedroom that still had posters of teenage crushes, her stuffed otter sitting on her bed? Had she left her pajamas on the floor? Made her bed? It looked the same as it did when she was a teenager. What would Nicolás think when he saw it?

"As a precaution, Lyla."

"Uh, yeah, sure."

On the way up, Lyla prayed silently that the most embarrassing thing Nicolás would find in her room would be her obsession with Justin Timberlake. She held her breath when she pushed open her door.

And then the blood drained from her face. She didn't need to worry about what Nicolás thought of her boy-band crushes, because he'd be too distracted by the torn pillows, overthrown drawers, ripped mattress, and pain from her fingertips digging into his arm.

"Nicolás."

"Lyla, call the police."

16

A few hours later, the team was back in DC at their office and Nic was staring at the list of a dozen or so names Jack had written down on the acrylic board. Lyla was surprisingly calm, but his anger hadn't stopped burning since the second he realized someone had broken into the Fox family home and ransacked Lyla's bedroom.

After a thorough search, neither the police nor Lyla's parents found anything else disturbed or stolen. Nic knew there were plenty of valuable items that easily could have been taken.

Except one.

Nic glanced at Lyla and saw the dark circles beneath her eyes. Her normally bright complexion had dulled from the fear she was trying to hide.

"Sis, I'm glad we're on the same team." Kekoa stared up at the list. "I think I'd rather face a barracuda than you."

"Funny, brah." Lyla playfully kicked Kekoa's chair. "I admit not everyone loves me, but I assure you that everyone is dealing with the consequences they deserve. Some of these people might want me hurt, but I can't think of a single reason why anyone would come to my parents' home and destroy my room when I'm not there."

She tugged at the hem of the pale blue sweater that normally made the blue in her eyes sparkle. *But not today*. "What do you think, Nicolás?"

Nic squeezed the brim of his ball cap, thankful he'd been able to shed the stuffy riding attire for the extra set of clothes he kept at the office. Jack, Kekoa, and Lyla had done the same, making a clear distinction between their lives outside the agency and their work within.

Which made her question to him all the more unusual. Nic wasn't used to Lyla asking for his opinion without first stating what his opinion ought to be, but he'd sensed something had shifted in her after they left her parents' home. "It looked like someone was looking for something. Since nothing of value was stolen, my gut is telling me we need to consider that it can't be coincidence that the day after Genevieve gives you a flash drive, you're shot at and your parents' home is broken into."

"But the only thing on it was an old article and a virus," Lyla grumbled. "Last time I checked, most people aren't anxious to catch a virus or read the news."

Lyla's sarcasm nearly brought a smile to his lips. "So maybe something else was on the flash drive."

They all looked at Kekoa, who shook his head, curls bouncing. "Brah, that flash drive was too corrupt to pull anything from. However, in my infinite wisdom, I did pull up every article I could find on anyone named Ammar El-Din, and let me tell you that name isn't as unique as you think it is."

The screens overhead lit up with dozens of articles in various languages, including several photos of different men, but then Kekoa began to type and soon the images shifted to several articles still in different languages but all with photos of the same man.

"This is Ammar El-Din, thirty-seven. He was arrested at Istanbul Airport two years ago with a forged passport and a double-layered suitcase he used to regularly smuggle fake money in and out of the country. He was convicted of running a major counterfeiting network in Lebanon, and his arrest led to ten additional arrests, the discovery of three printing houses, and billions of bogus US dollars, deutsche marks, Saudi riyals, and French francs that had been circulating since the nineties."

Jack folded his arms. "Any connection to Jerry or Zane Investments?"

"Here's where it gets interesting." Kekoa pulled up a magazine cover. "This was published in an online magazine called *UYB*, which stands for Use Your Brain. They focus on stories that range from the satirical to the conspiratorial, with the occasional piece that has caused some in the intelligence world to be highly concerned."

"Concerned about what?"

Kekoa gave Nic a pointed look. "What they get right."

Nic read the article titles listed on the cover. "Not sure I believe the NSA is concerned about Elvis's twin being in the CIA or the possibility Nixon stole nuclear plans from China."

"I mean, that last one might be concerning." Lyla tipped her head, a tease in her eyes. "But then again, if Elvis's twin is half as good as he was, the world's been missing out on epic music."

"Agreed." Kekoa held up a fist, and Lyla bumped it with her own.

Nic looked at Jack, who shook his head at the pair. It was silly, but sometimes, like now, he felt a bit jealous of their easy friendship. It also reminded him of what could be lost if he pursued a relationship with Lyla. Would their friendship survive if their relationship didn't?

"Anyway, in this article, Ammar El-Din claims he was moving money on behalf of the United States government."

Nic leaned forward, resting his elbows on the table. "For who?"

Kekoa swiped at a curl. "No names. Just initials. J.M.M."

"Jerome Michael Miller," Lyla whispered. "He outed Jerry."

"Or paid him back."

Jack looked at Nic. "What do you mean?"

"Jerry was arrested three years ago and El-Din two years ago. We know not everyone connected to the Zane case was caught. What if Jerry gave up Ammar El-Din? Told someone about the counterfeiting operation to secure some kind of deal for a shorter sentence?" He looked at Lyla. "Genevieve said he would do anything for his family, right?"

"Yeah. And Ammar had him killed for it." Lyla chewed her thumbnail. "That fits with Genevieve and Terrel's theory that Jerry may have been murdered."

"It also means someone got to Jerry inside a federal prison." Nic didn't like the unsettling feeling in his gut. "If this was retribution, then it should've ended with Jerry. If we can't figure out what's on that flash drive, then we need to talk to the people who might know or want it."

"Where's Ammar El-Din, Kekoa?"

"Central Prison in Roumieh, Lebanon," he answered Jack. "Still awaiting trial."

Lyla's eyes rounded. "For two years?"

"Speedy trials aren't a global right, which may give Ammar motive to come after whatever he thinks is on that flash drive," Jack said. "Maybe names or evidence that support his claim that the United States is involved in his counterfeiting operation, giving him leverage to get out of jail."

"Or killed." Nic roughed a hand over his chin. "We don't know for sure that it was Ammar who got to Jerry, but whoever it was made it past barbed-wire fences, steel bars, and armed guards, at least figuratively, to get to him. Even if they paid someone to do it on the inside, that shows how far they're willing to go."

"I'm starting to worry that Genevieve might have gone into hiding. We should check on Jerry's wife and family too."

"I agree, Lyla." Jack pulled out his cell phone. "I'm going to update Walsh." He pointed to the list on the acrylic board. "I think we should run through these names. Cover all the bases."

Jack walked off to call Walsh, and Kekoa returned to his office, leaving Nic with Lyla. She rubbed her temples.

"When was the last time you took pain medicine?"

She blinked up at him, and he noticed the smudge of mascara beneath her lower lashes. "I can't remember."

Nic offered her a gentle smile, controlling the urge to scoop her into his arms. "I'll be right back."

In the agency kitchen, he grabbed the bottle of pills and poured Lyla a glass of juice. He was about to take it back to her but paused. *What am I doing?* He pressed his hands on the counter and closed his eyes. The details of the case whirled in his head, but all he wanted to do was take Lyla back to her family. Keep her away from this investigation. He wondered what it would do to him if something else happened to her. It was a selfish attitude and one Lyla would not appreciate if she could read his thoughts.

"You okay?"

Nic opened his eyes to Jack putting on his coat. "I'm good. Something happen?"

"Walsh wants me to meet with someone at Secret Service to go over what we found on Ammar El-Din. Depending on how long that takes, I'll probably just head home from there. It's been a long day." He eyed the Tylenol. "If you don't find anything in the next two hours or so, I want you to call it. We can start fresh tomorrow."

"Got it. Please thank Brynn again for driving Mr. Brandt home." Nic felt terrible for abandoning his neighbor, but the veteran seemed to understand something was amiss. His easy agreement might have had something to do with Ms. Effie's offer to send him home with plenty of BBQ leftovers.

Walking back into the fulcrum, he found Lyla standing by his desk. "Pain meds and a side of orange ginger juice with matcha for an extra energy boost."

"You know I'm a coffee girl, Nicolás. I've already had two cups." Her halfhearted attempt to smile told him the caffeine wasn't helping.

"Try this. It'll help your immune system too. Keep you feisty."

"Do you really think I need help in that department?" She took the drink, sniffed it, and slowly took a small sip. Her tired eyes met his. "It's not horrible."

"I'll take that."

Lyla swallowed the pills, then tucked a chunk of loose hair behind her ear and looked over the map sitting on his desk. "Is that my grandparents' property?"

"I was hoping I could tighten the perimeter to give the sheriff and his deputies the best place to look." Nic pointed at the map's topography and the areas he circled with an orange highlighter. "These spots have a higher elevation, giving the shooter the best vantage point—"

"To target me," she said, her voice void of emotion. "Do they teach you how to figure that out in the military?"

"Yes."

"You never really talk about your time in the Army. Why?"

The knots in his shoulders tightened. "I don't know." But he did. Talking about that part of his life would inevitably lead to its conclusion, and he was ashamed. He didn't know what Lyla thought of him most days, but the fear of what she might think of him if she knew about his past . . . well, he couldn't handle another woman looking at him the way Brittany had.

"Have you spoken to your family?"

"Yes. Talked with my dad." Her shoulders drooped. "He convinced Etta and Tully to stay at the house since my parents' property isn't as big as theirs, and the private security team he's hired can protect it and . . . . them better." Her voice caught, and she wiped at a tear. "My parents have a general idea of what we do here. Dad more so than Mom, but that's probably because Tom, er, Walsh, shares more with him. Tully and Etta have no idea. What happened today . . ."

The guilt was eating away at her, and for the first time, Nic could relate to the burden she was carrying. Without thinking, he reached for her hand and intertwined his fingers with hers, squeezing to reassure her but unable to find the right words.

This isn't smart. Nic looked down at her fingers and noticed the red scrapes across her ivory skin. An urge to kiss away the pain overwhelmed him, and he slowly released her hand. The absence of her touch left his skin cold. She glanced up at him, and there was a question hanging in the depths of her gaze that he couldn't decipher. *I'm leaving.* He reminded himself of the plan. Except he hadn't confirmed his decision with Walsh yet.

"I overheard Jack say we have two hours." Lyla went back to her desk. "Let's see who can find something first."

Nic accepted her challenge, letting it keep him from having to address that the reason he hadn't told Walsh his decision was because he was afraid to tell the woman in front of him.

Nearly three hours later and having made little progress, they decided to call it a night. Inside his truck, Nic hit the GPS for directions to Lyla's parents' home and pulled out of the Acacia Building parking garage.

"I'm not going back to my parents'," Lyla said from the passenger seat.

Nic swallowed his frustration, counted to ten, and braced himself for the battle. "You can't stay at your place tonight. I don't care if you somehow convinced Walsh your security system is state-of-the-art or you've got blast-resistant windows or if you never want to speak to me again, I am not driving you home to stay by yourself, Lyla. It's not safe."

"You finished?"

His fingers ached from clenching the steering wheel. Nic kept his eyes on the road, afraid that if he looked over at her, she'd wield her inner Jedi and convince him she'd be just fine. Maybe she would. Maybe she'd get a good night's sleep, but he would not.

"I just got you talking to me again," she teased. "You can take me to Jack and Brynn's. I spoke to her earlier, and she said I could stay with them for a few days—if necessary—until we get a better understanding of what's going on."

His shoulders relaxed. Just like that? No argument? He peeked over and found her watching him, her lips twisted into a pert pout.

"So you got all worked up for nothing."

Had he? A throbbing began at the base of his neck, a symptom he recognized from his time in the Army that happened when the adrenaline controlling his exhaustion and stress began to taper off and reminded him he was human.

"I'm sorry." He took the I-495 ramp south. "I was just—"

"Expecting me to put up a fight."

He hated the sound of surrender in her voice. "Making sure you take care of yourself. On top of everything else, you were thrown off a horse today. As much as you want to hide it, I can tell you're hurting."

"I'm okay."

He glanced over. "You keep shifting your position to get comfortable, which means you've probably got some bruising and stiffness. Maybe even cracked ribs. You should've listened—" He caught himself before he said "to your parents." "You should listen to your body. Let it rest."

For several minutes, the only thing filling the silence between them was the hum of his truck, the heater, and a song playing quietly from the radio. He took the exit for Jack's place and felt Lyla's eyes on him.

213

"I wish there were an answer I could give you that would take away that look of hesitation in your eyes, make you believe I'm not so self-absorbed that I'm oblivious to the risks to those around me—"

"Lyla." He made sure she was looking at him before he continued. "Self-absorbed is the last thing I would ever call you."

She gave him a half smile. "I appreciate that, but ten minutes with my parents and they'll give you a lifetime of stories in which I play the starring role of defiance. I like to say it was bold independence, but"—she exhaled—"I know it's gotten me in trouble a time or two." His eyes flashed to hers, and she smiled—a real one. "Fine. Five times, tops."

"Just this month."

"Your exaggeration is interrupting my attempt to apologize. I know you asked me to be more cautious, and I promise I'm trying, but when I heard the shots . . ." Her voice wavered, and he reached over and took her hand in his in an all-too-comfortable way. "Nicolás, today the four people I love most in the world are basically under lockdown with armed guards patrolling our home because of me. Not to mention endangering a senator, a federal judge, and a few key members of the Defense Department. Those people mean nothing to me compared to my family and to Walsh, Jack, Brynn, Kekoa, Elinor, and you."

Nic tried not to read into the way her voice dipped at the end. She really did feel bad, but would it be enough to make her change? To consider the risks before engaging? He wasn't so sure. Lyla's self-preservation revolved solely around those she wanted to protect. And at her own admittance, she would do anything to keep them safe.

He sighed. And he would do anything to keep her safe.

Fifteen quiet minutes later, Nic pulled up in front of Jack and Brynn's home, and the front porch light turned on. "We're going to find out who's behind this, Lyla."

Lyla squeezed his hand with a nod before releasing it. "So, tomorrow you'll pick me up and we'll go by the hospital to see Jerry's wife?"

The porch light revealed her apprehension. Like she was already expecting him to go back on his word. He wouldn't do that. "Yes, but I can swing by midmorning if you want a few extra hours of sleep."

"Visitor hours start at nine." She grabbed her purse and opened the door. "I'll be ready by then. Good night, Nicolás."

"Night, Lyla."

Jack walked over, and Nic rolled his window down. "She'll be fine, brother. We've got alarms, we're armed, and whether or not she likes it, Walsh has some friends from the police

215

department patrolling the area." He gave Nic a reassuring smile. "We are officially the safest neighborhood in NoVA."

Nic watched Brynn welcome Lyla into the house. "That's the best news I've heard all night."

"I don't know how you talked her into staying with us."

"That was all her doing." Nic held up his hands. "But I'm grateful. Means I'll be able to sleep tonight." His body reacted to his words, feeling heavy at the weight of the day. One day, and it felt like a week. He imagined Lyla felt the same way—maybe worse, considering the fall she took. "Will you make sure she eats and takes pain medicine? And sleeps?"

Jack's lip tweaked. "I can do that."

"Don't give me that look, Jack." Nic sighed. "I'd be reminding you and Kekoa to do the same thing."

Jack laughed. "You wouldn't have to remind Kekoa to eat—ever."

"Did you find out anything about Ammar?"

"Secret Service is working a counterfeit investigation that might be connected. Walsh said the FBI is going to try and get an agent into Roumieh to visit Ammar, but they're probably not going to roll out the welcome mat, if you know what I mean."

Nic exhaled again. "We're going to swing by the hospital and check on Tiffany Miller.

See if she knows anything or can tell us where Genevieve is."

"I hope she can answer that last one. My gut's giving me a bad feeling."

"Mine too."

"It's good to know we haven't lost you yet."

Nic's attention swung on Jack. "What?"

"Walsh mentioned you're considering an outside mission." Jack waited a beat. "Have you told her?"

Nic watched Lyla cross the front window. She was smiling, and he took another deep breath, recognizing his breathing had come easier over the last few minutes knowing Lyla was safe. It felt cowardly to admit that he hadn't told her yet. "I'm trying to figure out the best way to do it. Sometimes she takes things personally."

"Is your decision to leave personal?"

That grabbed Nic's attention, and he dipped his chin.

"Brother, I've thought about what you said the other morning about doubting yourself, but if you think leaving the agency is going to give you some kind of control over your feelings for her, I can tell you right now you're making a mistake. I understand the fear you feel when it comes to her and the way she handles the job, but believe it or not, she's the best version of herself when you're around."

Nic blew out a breath. "Around me? The

woman owns real estate on the edge of risk, and next to her I look like Mr. Rogers."

Jack laughed. "No one is confusing you for Mr. Rogers, Garcia. You know there's always going to be risk involved in our jobs and in our lives. Loving and caring for people is risky. You have to decide which risk you're willing to accept. Walk away and you're risking a chance with Lyla. Stay with her and you risk losing your heart to a woman with the middle name Chance." Jack tapped his hand on the truck before backing up the drive. "Now go get some sleep so you can keep up with her tomorrow."

17

Lyla finished tying her shoes and glanced out the second-story window of Jack and Brynn's home. The neighborhood was quiet for a Sunday morning, families readying themselves for church or tucked warmly into their homes enjoying brunch. Safe.

Did her parents and grandparents feel the same way waking up this morning? Her chest burned with the emotion she'd been holding back. Fear for her family, anger at Jerry, and guilt. *Lord, forgive me for endangering them. Please keep them safe.*

She swallowed. When was the last time she prayed over her family? Their safety? It wasn't like she avoided prayer . . . she just didn't do it. So why now?

Because I'm desperate to keep my family safe.

On the dresser, her cell phone vibrated. She glanced upward as if God could see her smirk. Then answered her phone.

"Hey, Mom."

"Lyla, honey, how are you? Are you okay? How are you feeling?" Her mother's questions came out in a rush of concern that caused her throat to burn. "How's your head? Do you know the signs of a concussion? I told Tom—"

"I'm okay, Mom." Lyla grabbed a bottle of pain medicine from her overnight bag. She shook out two pills and swallowed them without water. "How are you?"

"We're, uh . . . we're fine."

Something was wrong. "What is it, Mom? What's wrong?"

"It's nothing." Her voice grew quiet. "Everything is fine now."

Lyla dropped the bottle of pills back in her bag. "What do you mean everything is fine *now?*"

Her mother's exhale filled the phone. "Etta was having some chest pain, but her doctor came by and checked her out. She's fine but needs to rest."

"What?" Lyla sat on the edge of the bed. Etta had a massive heart attack a year ago and another mild heart attack earlier this year. "What did her doctor say? Shouldn't she be in the hospital where they can monitor her?"

"Dr. Korsh said she's fine to stay with us so long as we keep her rested and calm."

Lyla twisted her lips to the side to keep the emotion brimming at bay. This was her fault. All of it. "Mom, I'm so sorry. I never meant for this to happen and—"

"Honey, it's not your fault." Her mother's soothing tone barely touched the surface of Lyla's guilt. "I told Etta to let me handle the hunt, but she insisted and it was too much."

She sniffled. "Mom, it's more than that."

Several seconds ticked off, and Lyla wondered if her mom's attempt to allay her guilt was out of matriarchal duty. If something happened to Etta, would her mom hold her responsible? Would that be the thing that pushed her mom to stop loving her? To be reminded that Lyla was just *too* much. A tingle began at the back of her throat at how quickly the insecurities of her youth came flooding back. It didn't help that she'd shared some of her childhood uncertainty with Nicolás. She ran her fingers against her palm, the memory of him reaching for her hand, reassuring her without saying a word.

"Honey." Her mother's voice drew her back to the conversation. "I know you and your father and Tom want to believe I'm in the dark about what you do for a living, but they forget that I got the call from your camp counselor because you paddled across the lake by yourself, and from your fourth-grade teacher when you decided to walk on the second-floor handrail at the art museum after seeing the Wilhelm Simmler painting of the tightrope walker, and that I picked up your car from outside a brothel the night you convinced Tom to hire you." She sighed. "I might not know specific details about your work, but I know you. While I don't want to imagine what kind of circumstances led to the events yesterday, I can only pray that God will hem you in when your instincts tell you otherwise."

"You sound like Nicolás." Lyla sighed.

"Next to your father and Tom, I don't think I've seen a man more scared about what happened, Lyla. Are you sure that young man knows your act was for Mrs. Davenport's sake?"

Lyla cringed, closing her eyes at the memory of the awkward situation. "Nicolás was as shocked as everyone else to learn about our fake relationship."

"Mm-hmm."

She opened her eyes. "Mm-hmm—what?"

"Well, he certainly knew how to play the part."

"What do you mean?" Lyla straightened. "Did you see how uncomfortable he was?"

"What I saw was a man who looks at you the way Daddy looks at me. I didn't see discomfort, I saw longing."

The last thing Lyla needed was her mom to lean into the imaginations of a romance that didn't exist between her and Nicolás the way Elinor and Brynn did. "Mom—"

"Lyla Anne," her mom said. "I am not Elizabeth Davenport. I have never pushed you into a relationship or voiced my opinion about your dating life—and believe me, you have dated some real *winners*."

Her lips pressed into a smile to suppress her laugh. "I dated half the guys just to annoy you and Dad."

"We know." Her mom laughed. "But of all the

guys you've talked about, none of them light your eyes the way Nic does. And from the way his eyes sparkled around you, I'd say that young man has a case of the va-va-vooms."

An uninvited tickle started in Lyla's middle. She pressed a hand to her stomach, but it didn't stop her mind from going to the single memory from the day before that stuck with her more than the chaos of the shooting. When Nicolás walked up after he arrived, the way he looked at her, there was something about it that made her feel more than beautiful—it filled her with confidence.

"Honey?"

"Oh, hey. Yeah, still here. I'm just . . ."

"Daydreaming about a handsome Spaniard?"

"Okay. Well, now you sound just like Mrs. Davenport," Lyla teased, but her cheeks were burning at her mother's intuition. She rose from the bed and grabbed her jacket, avoiding the question. "I need to get ready to go. Please give Etta a big hug for me. Dad and Tully too. And promise me you'll call if anything changes with Etta."

"I will, honey. Stay safe."

Lyla headed downstairs, pausing outside Brynn and Jack's kitchen to let her cheeks cool. Her mom was right, she was not like Mrs. Davenport pushing a relationship. But her comment about Nicolás and the va-va-vooms was making her dizzier than her fall from Sir

223

Winston. Heat flooded her cheeks again. What in the world had her mom done to her? If she thought facing Mrs. Davenport was awkward, spending the day working with Nicolás while her mom's words about the va-va-vooms danced in her head was going to be more awkward than the bangs she gave herself in the seventh grade.

Because it isn't true . . . right? Her mom was confusing Nicolás's agitated concern with her for taking off toward the shooting with romantic concern. Two very different feelings.

When Lyla finally walked into the kitchen, Brynn looked over from where she was pouring a cup of coffee into a to-go mug. "See, now you walk in looking like one of Charlie's Angels. That jacket makes me want to rethink my decision not to work for SNAP." Her gaze drifted down to Lyla's shoes, and she squeaked. "Tennis shoes? That's it. I'm putting in my notice first thing tomorrow morning."

Lyla glanced down at her high-waisted jeans, graphic tee, and leather jacket. Her Vans were a comfort choice more than anything else, but compared to the low, chunky heels that seemed to be the dress code for women in the intelligence field *and* looked like the kind she'd find in Etta's closet—she understood Brynn's discontentment.

"Babe, the CIA needs you." Jack walked in behind Lyla and over to Brynn and kissed her temple. "And SNAP needs you in the CIA. You're our in."

Brynn handed Jack his coffee. "One of many, I'm sure."

Jack set the coffee on the counter and reached for Brynn's waist and pulled her toward him. "The only one who makes my heart sing."

Brynn squished Jack's cheeks, pushing his lips into a fishy face, and kissed him. "That's my man."

Lyla wrinkled her nose at the silly affection. *Va-va-vooms.* She didn't know if her mom was right about Nicolás's feelings, but her comments had certainly stirred something inside that made her curious—and had her heart thumping a little harder against her ribs. *Thanks, Mom.*

Jack reached for his coffee and his keys, eyes meeting Lyla's. He paused like he had forgotten she was standing there witnessing the strangest yet most endearing display of affection. *Had my thoughts not been back on Nicolás.* He cleared his throat. "Uh, so Garcia's picking you up?"

"Yeah, we're going to the hospital to talk with Tiffany Miller and then heading to the office. You?"

"Walsh wants me to join him for a meeting with the DOJ."

Through the kitchen window, Lyla saw Nicolás pull into the driveway. She grabbed her purse, and Brynn held out a to-go mug for her. "Thanks."

"No problem." Brynn tugged her robe tighter when Jack opened the door. "Go, be safe, and save the world."

Lyla lifted her mug of coffee in a salute to Brynn's departing instructions, then quickly walked past Jack when he went in for another kiss. *Goodness.* She rolled her eyes but secretly adored the affection between them.

Nicolás exited his truck and met her at the front, bringing with him the soft scent of pine and sandalwood. The smell perfectly matched the man wearing worn jeans, faded flannel, and a wool-collared jacket—and it made her feel swooshy inside. Was that a thing? Swooshy? Because there was no other way to describe it. And even though this wasn't the first time Lyla recognized the rugged style that enhanced Nicolás's good looks, she blamed Jack and Brynn for putting her in a mood she suddenly identified with the word *swooshy*. Her mom too.

"Morning, Lyla."

Did he always have that soft twang in his voice when he greeted her? Yikes. This was going to be bad.

"Good morning." She quickly climbed into the truck and found a paper bag sitting between them. She sniffed the familiar scent and smiled. *Bacon.*

When he opened the door, she pointed at the bag. "You got me real bacon."

"As opposed to fake bacon?"

"AKA turkey bacon."

Nicolás started the truck and backed out. "I like turkey bacon, but yes, I got you real bacon. And eggs, cheese, and an everything bagel to go with it. They're all kind of smushed together, like a breakfast sandwich."

"Har-har." Lyla unwrapped her sandwich and took a bite. "Mm-hmm. Rwel . . . con . . . ishus."

"I have no idea what you just said." He looked over with a blank stare.

"Real bacon is—" Lyla tried again around a bite, but she inhaled and a piece of egg or bacon went down the wrong pipe and she began coughing.

"Please don't choke. I can't give you the Heimlich while I'm driving." Nicolás looked annoyed, and then his expression shifted to concern when he realized she wasn't faking. He reached over and began patting her back, waking up her injuries from the day before. "Hold on, I'll pull over."

She coughed some more and then held up a hand, finally catching her breath. Wiping her watering eyes, she took several slow breaths before sipping some of her coffee. Then she began to laugh, and that earned her a scowl from Nicolás. "Good thing we're already headed to the hospital then, huh?"

Nicolás rolled his eyes at her joke but didn't

stop stroking her back. Even though his fingers were grazing the bruises from the day before, she didn't move. "Are you okay?"

"Yes, thank you." She was a bit disappointed when he withdrew his hand, and she half considered faking another choking spell. *Time to move to a safer thought.* "Death by bacon. Kekoa's dream."

Nicolás groaned but then tilted his head in a way that said he agreed before he laughed. Lyla smiled and exhaled. Maybe today wouldn't be as bad as seventh-grade bangs after all.

"What do you mean Tiffany Miller is gone?"

"Mrs. Miller is no longer here." The nurse looked up from the computer at Lyla like she couldn't believe she had to repeat herself. "She checked out yesterday. Against medical advice."

Lyla repositioned the bouquet of flowers they'd grabbed on the way to the hospital. "Why would she do that?"

The nurse gestured around her. Nurses, techs, and hospital staff hustled back and forth as the phones rang, patient call bells demanded attention, and someone down the hall screamed for pain meds. "I'm nearing the end of a twelve-hour shift that turned into fourteen because two of my nurses called in sick and someone decided to celebrate their twenty-first birthday by going drunk ice skating. You'll have to excuse me if I don't demand a reason from a woman ready to check herself out early."

"Her injuries from the car accident must not have been too bad." Nicolás leaned his elbows on the nurses' station and earned himself a hard stare. He straightened. "To just walk out of here."

"She was rolled out by a family member, and I can't tell you about her injuries except to say she likely needed another week here." Another alarm went off, and the nurse shook her head before pinning Lyla with a stare. "If that's all, I need to go."

Lyla set the flowers on the counter. "Keep these."

The hard lines of exhaustion marking the nurse's face softened. She pressed her lips together and gave a nod before hurrying away to help a patient.

"That woman deserves a vacation."

"And a medal," Lyla agreed with Nicolás as they skirted two nurses jogging toward a patient's room. She pulled out her cell phone. "I have Jerry's address. It's about twenty minutes north of here."

"Let's go."

Twenty-five minutes later, they pulled up in front of a two-story colonial. Unease swirled in Lyla's stomach. This was Jerry Miller's home. Where he lived in comfort while stealing millions of dollars from innocent people—maybe even from some of his neighbors—for criminals.

Walking up, Lyla kept close to Nicolás's side. It was silly. Jerry was dead, but it didn't ease the anxiousness coursing through her. "It's weird."

"What?"

She pointed at the driveway, where a single car was parked. "Jerry died a few days ago, and there's no one here to console his wife and children."

Nicolás continued up the walk. "Maybe he burned too many bridges."

"Doesn't mean his wife and children aren't devastated." The unwilling victims.

Nicolás rang the bell. A dog barked from inside before the door was opened by an older woman with frizzy white hair escaping a messy chignon. She pulled her sweater tighter over her chest and eyed them suspiciously. "Yes?"

Nicolás removed his ball cap. "We're looking for Tiffany Miller."

"Why?" The woman's eyes kept sweeping back to Lyla. "Who are you?"

"We're with the SNAP Agency and—"

"It's you." Recognition lit the woman's eyes with a fire. She pointed a finger at Lyla and stepped toward her. Nicolás blocked her advance with a single step. She looked him over before her hard gaze landed back on Lyla. "You're the one who put my Jerry in jail."

"Ma'am, you're mistaken." Nicolás's tone was

friendly but held an edge of warning. "Your Jerry put himself in jail. We're only here to make sure his wife is doing okay after her accident."

"She's not here," the woman snapped, taking a step backward. She wiped at her eyes, then wrapped her arms around her waist. Lyla saw the toll of her suffering. The frailty wearing her down, a helplessness to do anything except love her son the way only a mother can—unconditionally. "Tiffany took the kids and left."

"Do you know where?"

"No," Jerry's mom answered Nicolás. "And I wouldn't tell you even if I did."

She stepped back inside and started to shut the door, but Lyla stepped around Nicolás and put her hand on it. "What about Genevieve?"

The woman's expression tightened for a few seconds before exhaustion drew her features downward. "I haven't heard from Ginny since she called me a few days ago to say she couldn't handle this and was leaving. Gone. Both of my kids and now my grandkids. Thanks to you."

"Ma'am—"

Lyla put a hand on Nicolás's arm, feeling his muscles tense beneath her touch. She gave it a gentle squeeze. Jerry's mom was hurting, probably more than she was angry. Right now she wanted to blame someone, and Lyla would accept it.

"Mrs. Miller, I know you might not believe

me, but I am truly sorry for what you're going through. Thank you for your time."

With a gentle tug, Lyla urged Nicolás back to his vehicle. Behind her she heard Jerry's mom suck in a sob before closing the door. Lyla quickly got into the truck, feeling her own emotions building in her chest. It wasn't fair. Jerry wasn't the only one who had to pay for his crime. Crime was selfish. No matter what reason a criminal came up with—it was always self-serving.

18

Nic followed Lyla into the fulcrum, disappointed that Mrs. Miller's misguided blame had had the power to ruin Lyla's mood. And steal her smile. Even worse was the feeling that no matter how he tried to defuse the harmful words, it didn't seem to help.

"We're back, Kekoa!" Lyla called out as she shed her jacket and grabbed her new laptop. "We need to find Genevieve."

"I'm on it, sis." Kekoa joined them at the conference table. "Working with her cell service to see if we can get a last location for her."

Nic sat. "Mrs. Miller said she left town."

Lyla raised her brows. "Without her cell?"

"You said she was acting nervous, like she was being followed. Maybe she got a new one."

"You're right, Nicolás." Lyla nodded. "Is there a way we can find that out?" She looked at Kekoa, whose mouth was slightly ajar, his confused gaze moving between her and Nic.

Nic sent his friend a look that he hoped warned him to let whatever immature thought he was having go. "Kekoa?"

"Sorry. I just got confused by Lyla's admission that you were right." Kekoa smiled. "But to answer your question, if Genevieve used a credit card, yes, but as of right now she hasn't accessed her bank accounts or credit cards for the last two weeks."

"Someone hiding would use cash for everything, right?"

"Yes," Nic answered Lyla, and they shared the same expression. *This is not looking good.* "What about running her image through one of our CCTV programs like you did for Terrel's nephew? If she went to an airport, train station, passed by a street camera or toll road, we could find her location."

"I'm trying, but so far—bah. I got nothing." Kekoa typed on his silicone keyboard. "But I do have this." Once again the screens overhead filled with news articles, but this time they weren't about Ammar El-Din. "That article yesterday made me curious, especially when I started fact-checking some of the information in it. I fell into a rabbit hole of government conspiracy, which was as funny as it was scary. But there were several like this one." Kekoa highlighted an article: US RUNNING WEAPONS FOR MONOPOLY MONEY. "Aside from the clickbait title, this one mixes a bit of fact with theory surrounding the investigation of a man named Roger Colthorpe, a financial advisor in Florida, who confessed to being a gunrunner, smuggling guns out of America to Ireland for five years."

Nic's jaw tightened. His short time in the military had exposed him to a handful of situations in which military-grade weapons had landed in the wrong hands. There were always rumors or theories about how it happened that seemed to revolve around the "enemy of our enemy is our friend" proverb, but that didn't sit well with him. "*Which* pieces are fact?"

"Roger Colthorpe does live in Florida. He was a financial advisor. *And . . .*" Kekoa hesitated. "I pulled some records from certain departments that indicate Mr. Colthorpe was given immunity from the US for information about those involved in the gunrunning."

"Which part of that is theory?"

Kekoa looked at Lyla. "He claims the United States paid him to run the guns into Ireland but doesn't have a name or proof."

"Or won't give it." Nic leaned his elbows on the table, reading the article again. "Wait." He sat back. "The Police Service of Northern Ireland reopened this investigation ten years ago. How is this connected to our case now?"

"Thank you for asking." Kekoa typed again. "Brynn helped me with this. The PSNI was able to connect the weapons Mr. Colthorpe smuggled in with weapons used by the Real Irish Republican Army, a paramilitary group focused on ending British rule in Northern Ireland. They used terrorist methods to attack British military and Irish police forces, killing almost two thousand people."

"And Mr. Colthorpe claims America is behind arming this terrorist group?" Lyla's skepticism matched what Nic was feeling.

"Not in those exact words. According to this article and the theory of the author, Mr. Colthorpe was paid to smuggle the weapons into the country but denies knowing who they were going to. Says he was paid in US dollars. Dollars"—Kekoa raised his brows—"that were bogus."

Nic locked eyes with Kekoa. "From Ammar El-Din?"

Kekoa smiled. "One and the same."

"Okay." Lyla pushed out of her seat and began pacing. She wrapped her long hair up in her hand and twisted it into a bun. "So, we have a gunrunner in Florida who took guns to a terrorist group in Ireland and was paid with fake cash by Ammar El-Din, who also claimed he was moving money for the US and gave Jerry's name to the journalist who interviewed him. Now Jerry's dead. Is that where we're at now?"

"Oh, you're about to lose your mind at what I'm going to tell you next."

Nic blew out a breath. "Do you need a spotlight?"

Kekoa raised a dark brow. "Do you have one?"

Lyla stifled a giggle. "Keep going, Kekoa."

"Okay, so when I dug into these articles, I came

236

across another one printed in Veritas Esquire, an investigative column in the *London Telegraph*." Kekoa pulled up the article: TRUTH BEHIND OMAGH—US INVOLVED. "Pay attention, because this is going to get crazy."

Nic and Lyla watched as the screens above them split into different images—Ammar El-Din, the article with Roger Colthorpe, and a final one that tightened Nic's muscles. He easily identified the charred and mangled explosion that had taken out one side of a city street.

"In 1998, there was a bombing in Omagh, Ireland, that killed almost two dozen people who were unintentionally misdirected toward the bomb threat instead of away from it. The Real IRA was behind the attack. According to reports, it might have been prevented except for an intel miscommunication between British, Irish, and US agencies. During the investigation, a cache of US military-grade weapons was found along with large amounts of money—some real, some fake—inside double-layered suitcases similar to the ones discovered at the print houses in Lebanon after Ammar El-Din's arrest."

"The same money used to pay the gunrunner in Florida who supplied the material that was used to kill innocent people." Lyla exhaled. "Do you think Jerry had any idea what the money he was stealing was being used for?"

"Possibly." Kekoa brushed a curl off his forehead. "With permission from the DOJ and Paterson's warden, I was able to access Jerry's prison email account and found two emails of interest. One from Ammar El-Din two months after he was arrested and one *to* R.D. Leto. Two weeks before he died."

"What?" Lyla's gaze zeroed in on Kekoa. "Who's R.D. Leto?"

"The journalist behind these articles."

Lyla pressed her hands on the table. "Please tell me you have his contact information."

"Well . . ." Kekoa looked apologetic. "That's proving to be a bit difficult."

"Says the man who never fails to remind us that he hacked the NSA." Lyla smirked, then realized Kekoa wasn't playing humble. "Wait, you're serious? You can't find him?"

"I'm good. Really good." Kekoa shrugged. "But journalists like this who focus on political and government conspiracy usually live on the left side of paranoia. Their theories, when published, can lead to unwanted attention from law enforcement, particularly if they get a little too close to the truth."

Nic tipped his chin. "Like these articles."

"Just like these," Kekoa agreed. "Their entire lives can be flipped upside down as they're intimidated to stop investigating, which leads them to go dark and take themselves off the grid for fear of retaliation against them or their families. I wouldn't be surprised if this R.D. Leto isn't even the journalist's real name."

"So how do we find him?" Lyla said. "He's the last person to have contact with Jerry that we know of. He may know what Jerry had or why he was killed."

"*If* he was killed," Nic corrected. "Jerry's death is still ruled a suicide."

"And you don't think it's suspicious that the cameras inside the laundry room weren't working?" Lyla looked to Kekoa. "Right?"

"They were working, but the angle is blocked so you can't see anything."

"See?" Lyla said. "I'm not a conspiracy person, but that seems suspicious to me. Especially with everything we're learning."

"I'm not disagreeing, but we have to approach this without prejudice to make sure we're not forming this investigation into what we want it to be." He waited for Lyla's argument, but she simply exhaled and nodded. Nic didn't want to focus too hard on her assent in case she was just trying to come up with an argument she could win. He turned to Kekoa. "Can we contact the editor for the *London Telegraph* and get R.D.'s contact information?"

"We'd never get it," Kekoa said. "The media protects their journalists, especially the ones whose stories drive attention. Articles by R.D. Leto are very popular."

"I have an idea." Lyla straightened. "What about Mason? He's a journalist in New York. I'm sure he has connections that might help us find R.D. Leto. Or at least he might be able to get a message to Leto's publisher that could get us into contact with him. What do you think, Nicolás?"

Nic turned to Lyla. She was waiting with hesitation lingering in the depths of her blue-green gaze like she was afraid of his answer. He frowned. "What do *I* think?"

"Yes." The timidity in her answer was unusual. "Do you think reaching out to Mason for help is a good idea? I don't want to put anyone else in danger."

Nic hesitated, which had nothing to do with the assignment but everything to do with the prospect of Lyla turning to Mason for help. Kekoa cleared his throat and Nic blinked. "I think he's the right choice."

"I won't tell him anything he doesn't need to know." She picked up her cell phone from the table. "And I trust him to keep everything confidential."

"I trust you." Nic saw a flicker of something turn the edges of her lips upward. She stepped away to make the call.

"Brah, you don't got to worry about that high maka maka braddah. You know Lyla isn't into that."

Nic stared at Kekoa. "Brother, I have no idea what you just said."

"Lyla doesn't like Mason." Kekoa spoke without a single hint of his island accent. "She's not into men from uppity families, so you do not have to worry."

"I'm not worried." Nic folded his arms but couldn't resist looking over to where Lyla was talking on the cell phone—smiling. Even in the middle of all the stress and fear, her smile always showed off her confidence. The self-assurance and poise that defined her character was even more radiant than her beauty.

Nic didn't know if she realized that sharing the small glimpses into her childhood with him had revealed a seesaw of insecurity, but it was becoming clear that Lyla's personality was defined by the faith others had in her. And he'd been robbing her of that every single time he questioned or doubted her.

Maybe this was the nudge he needed to solidify his decision. Leaving SNAP might not be what he wanted, but if it allowed Lyla to thrive and smile . . . he'd do it.

"Brahhh," Kekoa whispered. "You've got it bad."

Nic swiveled in his chair. "Brah, you need to stick—" He frowned. What was that? "Um, I think there's an alarm going off in your office."

Kekoa shot out of his chair, sending it rolling

241

backward, and jogged to his office. Nic righted the chair and caught Lyla watching him. He shrugged, then followed Kekoa.

"What's going on?" Lyla came up behind Nic.

"I don't know."

They watched Kekoa quickly tapping on his keyboard, humming the theme song to *Mission: Impossible*.

"Gotcha!" Kekoa leaned back in his chair and flexed his fingers. "Genevieve's cell phone came back online, and I have a location."

"You do?" Lyla pushed in closer and put her hand on Nic's back. He sucked in a breath at the totally innocent touch. "Where?"

"Falls Church." Kekoa frowned. "Maybe near her home . . . maybe not."

"What does that mean?" Nic leaned over Kekoa's shoulder to look at the map on the screen where a little dot was highlighted. "You have the address, don't you?"

"I have a location." Kekoa tapped the screen. "It's near her home address, so she's probably there. But this doesn't give me an exact location. She could be in her car. In her backyard. Borrowing sugar from her neighbor." Lyla gave Kekoa a playful punch in the arm. "All I'm saying is that right now, she's there, and if you want to talk to her before she shuts off her phone, you need to go right now."

19

As Lyla and Nicolás drove to Genevieve's home in Falls Church, Lyla prayed Jerry's sister was all right. Kekoa would let them know of any movement or if she turned off the phone.

"It's got to be a good sign, right?" Lyla looked over to Nicolás. "Genevieve turning on her phone."

"Depends on the reason."

"That's one of the things I love about you, Nicolás." She caught her words the second he glanced over. "You never mince words. Just tell it how it is." Even when she didn't always want to hear it. "But I need a little sunshine and ponies here."

"I'm more of a partly cloudy and armadillo kind of guy."

Her jaw went slack. "I'm sorry, what?"

Nicolás tugged on his cap and gave her a quick side-eye. "I'm not really the guy you come to for sunshine and ponies."

"No, I get the partly cloudy. Makes sense because you're a bit moody, but armadillo? I'm going to need an explanation on that."

"Actually, I'm partly cloudy because it's the perfect balance of weather—sun on your face but the shade to cool you down. You learn to

243

appreciate partly cloudy days when you're out in the field all day. And an armadillo because of its built-in Kevlar."

Several beats passed between them before Lyla laughed.

"Of course you'd pick an animal because of its armor. But, Nicolás, you realize you could've picked a crocodile or a rhino for the same reason?"

"True." Nicolás's lip twitched with a smirk. "But can they roll into a ball like a Transformer?"

He was so serious about his reasoning, Lyla couldn't help but laugh again, and this time Nicolás obliged with a few quick chuckles that reminded her of what she loved most about their relationship.

Lyla's eyes had moved along the planes of his face as she listened to him explain. The hard lines of his jaw were softened by the scruff he allowed to grow there. His dark lashes were long and covered the kind of hazel eyes that had flecks of gold along their edges. They might be her favorite feature if they weren't always hidden in the shadow of his ball cap, and if she wasn't such a sucker for his smile. His smiles were rare, which made them all the more special. Lyla swallowed. That tickle was back, and it made her think of her mom's va-va-voom comment. This was not that. Maybe it was a *va,* but it definitely was not a full-fledged va-va-voom.

244

She quickly shifted her thoughts back to work.

"So, um, Mason said he would see what he could find out about R.D. Leto. He did an internship in Germany and thinks one of his colleagues did one for the *London Telegraph*. But don't worry. I told Mason our interest in R.D. was out of concern for his safety, which wasn't a lie, exactly. He seemed eager to help."

"He seems like a nice guy."

Lyla noticed the muscle in Nicolás's jaw pop like it did when he was upset or . . . holding back. "He is. Although we didn't keep in touch much after we left home. Only during the holidays when he's home and his mother is Molly Matchmaker."

"How come it never worked out between you?"

She let out a soft laugh, but the quick look he sent her way said his question wasn't a simple inquiry. "There wasn't anything to work out. We were friends. And I think dating someone like Mason would come with expectations I couldn't meet. I mean, do you see me hosting dinner parties? Hosting soirees?"

Nicolás's top lip edged upward. "I don't even know what a soiree is."

"Me either." She glanced out at the neighborhood they were driving through. "I missed that day at the debutante academy."

"There's an academy?"

The bewilderment in his tone made her laugh.

"No. At least I don't think so." She pointed at a ranch house with a carport, where Genevieve's red car was parked. "That's the house."

Nicolás pulled into the driveway and cut the engine. Checking out the house, Lyla unbuckled her seat belt. It was cute. Redbrick, blue shutters, simple landscaping that a single woman could manage. That gave her pause. "I can't remember if Genevieve had a boyfriend back when Jerry was arrested. Do you?"

"No."

Getting out of the truck, Lyla paused by the car. She looked through the windows and saw nothing out of the ordinary. A few crumpled receipts in the cupholder. A shirt or sweatshirt in the back seat. Nothing that looked like she had just returned from a trip. Or was getting ready to take off.

A chill scuttled down Lyla's spine. "Do you think she's here, Nicolás?"

"I'm not sure."

His straight answer didn't assuage her worry, and she shouldn't have expected it to. Nicolás was probably assessing the situation the same way she was. Why had Genevieve dropped from the radar after handing off the flash drive, and what had made her return?

Lyla continued toward the quiet house. The sheer curtains were drawn over the window near the porch, and she fought the urge to peek in. If

Genevieve was anxious the night they met, she'd probably be shocked to find Lyla on her porch peering through her window.

Nicolás pressed the doorbell. A minute passed, and no sounds came from inside the house to indicate someone was inside. He pulled out his cell phone and hit a button.

"Kekoa, is she still here?" Nicolás glanced over his shoulder. "Okay, keep us posted." He put his phone in his back pocket and knocked on the door. "He says the phone is still on and pinging to this location."

Lyla walked back over to the front window, deciding it was worth the risk of scaring Genevieve. Cupping her eyes, she peered into the front room of the home. It was hard to tell, but— Lyla's stomach clenched. "Nicolás, I think we have a problem."

"What?"

"Either Genevieve is a slob or her house has been ransacked."

Nicolás flipped his ball cap around and pressed his hands and face to the window. He moved around, trying to get a better look before he shook his head. "I can't tell. I have a flashlight in my truck. You call the police and let them know we need them to do a welfare check."

Lyla pulled out her phone and dialed 911 as Nicolás ran to his truck. She gave the emergency operator a brief explanation and the reason behind their concern. Nicolás ran back up. "They're sending a patrol out, but it's not a priority." She rolled her eyes. "And they told me we're not allowed to enter the house because this isn't the movies."

"Okay, I'm going to walk around the house. You stay up here and wait for the police."

She sent him a look that told him exactly how she felt about his instruction. "How about we both walk the house, you in one direction and I'll go the other way. It'll be faster."

He exhaled, and she could see the argument in his eyes. "If you see anything, call for me. Immediately."

"Do not pass go. Do not collect two hundred dollars. Yes, sir." She saluted, then wrinkled her nose at him, which earned her a half smile. She'd take it. "See you at the back."

Twisting on her heel, she headed down the porch steps and started around the house, not wanting to give him another second to change his mind. There was a side window that looked into the front room. Peeking in, she saw the same disarray. Cushions overthrown. Shelves emptied. Not the way she'd leave her place if she were going on a trip.

Lyla moved to the next window but had to climb through a rosebush to get to it. The blinds were open, revealing a bed and dresser.

Maybe Genevieve's return hadn't been planned.

248

Maybe she came back for something and was rushing to pack what she could and leave again. Was that what Jerry's wife and kids had done? Were they meeting up? But that didn't explain why Jerry's mom would be left out of the loop. If they were in some kind of danger, they would've taken her with them, right?

Unless she was like Mrs. Davenport . . . Lyla shoved that unkind thought from her mind and returned her focus to what was in front of her. Overturned drawers and clothes on the floor—just like her bedroom.

Goose bumps prickled her skin.

Genevieve's home had been searched, and Lyla's instinct told her it was for the same reason her own bedroom was—for the flash drive.

A rustling noise caused Lyla to jump and spin around. Thorns caught against her clothes, reaching her skin in painful scrapes. Behind her a squirrel eyed her for several seconds before scampering into the neighbor's yard.

Stupid squirrels.

Lyla checked out the neighbor's home. No more than twenty feet separated the houses. Maybe they knew Genevieve or had heard something, but another look at the window that mirrored the one Lyla was standing next to revealed the interior of the home was gutted. Cans of paint and lumber were stacked on the unfinished floor.

No help there.

Walking between the houses, Lyla checked Genevieve's next window, but the blinds were closed. She rapped on the glass, just in case. "Genevieve?"

Nothing.

Ahead of her, Genevieve's wooden fence separated her yard from the neighbor's, but the ground was overturned and muddy where the fence protecting the neighboring home had been removed to give the backhoe parked there access to the yard.

Lyla froze when she heard a clattering noise nearby. What was that? Another squirrel? She jerked when a branch snapped, her gaze darting to movement in the trees edging the fence line between Genevieve's yard and her neighbor's property.

She took slow steps forward and readied herself to call for Nicolás in case it wasn't a squirrel. Taking another step, she blew out a breath. Not a squirrel but a little boy, maybe nine or ten, watching her from a tree branch.

"Hello." Lyla crossed the rest of the lawn, having to step around construction debris. She gestured to the house whose yard they were in. "Do you live here?"

He shook his head.

"Do you know the lady who lives next door?"

Another shake of the head.

"Are you supposed to be back here?"

Hesitation, then finally a slow shake of the head. The little boy moved his hand, and Lyla saw what he was holding. "Is that your phone?"

The little boy hopped down from the branch, looking a bit guilty. "I didn't steal it."

Lyla offered a gentle smile. "Did you find it?"

"Mm-hmm."

She held out her hand. "May I see it?"

"The screen is cracked." He handed it to her. "I didn't do that."

"I believe you." Lyla tapped the screen and an image of Genevieve and two teenagers, a girl and a boy, popped up. Jerry's kids. Her stomach twisted. She met the little boy's big brown eyes. "Where did you find this?"

He bit his lip, looking around like he was ready to dart.

"I promise you're not in trouble. I'm just looking for this lady right here." Lyla pointed to Genevieve's face. "She lives in that house over there. Have you seen her?"

He shook his head.

"Did you find the phone at her house?"

Again another head shake.

Taking a deep breath, Lyla smiled. "Can you point to where you found it?"

Lifting his arm, he extended his index finger in the direction of the renovated house. An ugly feeling settled in her gut. Turning to the little boy, she tried to give him a reassuring smile.

"Is it okay if I keep this so I can give it back to the lady who lost it?" He nodded, looking relieved he wasn't going to get in trouble. "And I need you to go back to your house, okay? It's dangerous back here with all this equipment."

Another quick nod, and the boy ran out of the backyard and down the street. Lyla stared at the phone in her hand. This was certainly not a good sign.

Lyla walked to where the little boy said he'd found the phone. There was a first-floor deck that covered a sliding door to the basement, but the glass was protected with a plastic tarp that had traces of paint on it. Next to it was another door with a small window that wasn't covered.

Her foot slipped in the mud left from the hole being dug for a pool and she groaned. Gross. She moved to a small pad of concrete and started to scrape her heel but stopped when her eyes caught on something sticking out of the pile of sodden leaves.

Lord, please don't let it be . . . Lyla edged closer, hoping her eyes were playing tricks on her, but they weren't. It was a shoe. A pink Nike about her size. With her pulse pounding in her ears, Lyla used her toe to tap the shoe, closing her eyes in expectation she would meet resistance from a foot connected to a leg, connected to a body . . .

The shoe moved easily, and Lyla released an

audible breath of relief that left her feeling shaky. She opened her eyes, grateful there was no body, but it didn't stop the weight of alarm warning her that the shoe, just like the phone, belonged to Genevieve.

"Nicolás!" Lyla called out as she started for the back door to look through the window. "I'm around back. Next door."

The inside of the basement was too dark from the windows being covered to see anything. She reached for the doorknob and twisted it. Unlocked. Lyla swallowed, looking toward Genevieve's house. "Nicolás?"

Was he coming?

Lyla pushed open the door just a few inches and instantly covered her face at the wretched smell. Her eyes watered, and she clamped her jaw down, hoping to keep her gag reflex from reacting.

Only one thing could smell that bad. *A body*. Lyla backed away, anxious to find Nicolás. *See, not running into danger*. He'd be prou—

The hit came fast and hard, knocking Lyla against the door and into the basement. There wasn't time to brace herself from slamming against the concrete floor. She screamed on impact, a sharp pain shooting up the side of her face and head. Her vision blurred, and a painful ringing sensation filled her ears.

Lyla heard the door close and scrambled to get

up, but whoever was behind her grabbed her feet and yanked her onto her back, straddling her legs.

"No!" she screamed, kicking with everything she had to get out of his grip and off the ground. Her self-defense training told her it was the most dangerous and vulnerable place to be, and she needed to get up if she had any chance of fighting back. Twisting back and forth, she kept moving to free her legs until finally she did it. With her left leg loose, she bent her knee and kicked out as hard as she could in the darkness, hoping to connect with her assailant. But she missed. "Nicolás! In the house—"

She choked on her breath when a punch landed in the side of her ribs. Gasping for breath, she tried to use her adrenaline to overcome the temporary incapacitation caused by the blow. *Fight!*

Nicolás? Lyla's head felt woozy. Moving her arms along the ground, she searched with her hands for anything she could use to defend herself and nearly thanked God aloud when her fingers felt a piece of wood. Gripping it with all her might, she prayed for strength. She took a deep breath, curled upward, and swung.

There was a satisfactory crack of wood on bone as the weight holding her leg eased. She didn't wait. She crab crawled backward to get away, but something hard behind her stopped her escape.

A bit of light from the window showed the

shadow of her attacker coming toward her. She tried to roll to the side, but he caught her hair and yanked her onto her back. A slap cranked her head sideways, and a cry escaped her lips as sharp pain seared through the side of her face. Her mouth filled with blood and she spat it out, afraid of choking on it.

"Try that again and I'll kill you. Give me what I want and I'll let you live."

Lyla forced her eyes open. She wanted to see the face of the person making a promise she didn't believe he'd keep, but he was shadowed in the darkness.

"Tell me where it is."

Her jaw ached as she opened her lips. "Where. What. Is?"

A low chuckle rumbled from the man whose weight was crushing her chest, and in the darkness, she didn't see the next hit coming until it connected with her face. Tears streamed from her eyes, but she wouldn't cry in front of him.

"Where is it?"

The angry whisper hovering near her ear made her want to recoil. Instead, she allowed her body to go limp, relaxed against the cold, damp ground like she was giving up. A second passed, and she felt the grip on her arms loosen just enough. With a burst of speed she didn't know she had, she twisted her elbow, breaking the man's hold, and struck straight up with the palm of her hand, hoping for the nose but landing close to his eye. His head reared back a bit but not enough to give her time to break free of his hold.

"Nicolás!" she screamed before her head was slammed to the ground and everything just disappeared. The silence overwhelmed her senses. Was she dead? No, because she could still feel the man on top of her.

Lyla blinked, trying to clear her vision. A mirror. She was staring at a mirror. Weird. She blinked again. Her reflection wasn't blinking back. Why? It hurt her brain to figure it out. It hurt everywhere. Her head pounded.

Lyla! Nicolás's voice echoed in her mind— *No!* Lyla blinked, her senses waking up. That wasn't a voice in her head. That was Nicolás. He was here.

"Nicolás!" She choked out his name and winced, preparing for another hit, but all she felt was a sudden lightness to her body. She curled into a fetal position as nausea climbed her throat.

The sound of wood breaking caused her to flinch. She squinted, trying to adjust to the brightness, and that's when she saw the mirror. Except it wasn't her hair splayed out on the ground next to boxes of tile. Or her eyes staring back at her. It was Genevieve's.

The horrific odor of decay washed over Lyla and she gagged.

"Lyla, hang on." Nicolás was at her side. "The ambulance is on its way."

"Go." Her demand came out strangled and weak. She tried to get up, but dizziness anchored her to the ground. They couldn't let him get away. "Go. I'll be fine."

"Lyla—" Her name came out scratchy as he brushed the hair out of her eyes. "I'm not leaving you."

20

Raging crazy. Was that a thing? It felt like a thing. Should be a thing. Because it perfectly described the minefield of emotions Nic was trying to navigate. He looked down at his hands, which were still red and raw from scrubbing her blood off in the sink. He shook them, trying to get rid of the tingling sensation he hoped was from fear. Or rage.

Listening to Lyla give an account of what took place, from finding the cell phone to being shoved into the house by the jerk who ran off when Nic got to the door, had been difficult. If only he'd gotten there sooner. The blood on his hands wouldn't have been Lyla's.

Nic lifted his gaze to the closed blinds inside Walsh's office, giving Lyla and the physician tending her wounds some privacy. *She should be at the hospital.* But when he'd refused a trip to the hospital, so did she—against the EMT's advice—choosing instead to bring in Dr. Patel to look them over.

Kekoa held out an ice pack. "What'd the doc say?"

"Likely a concussion." Nic gently pressed the ice pack to the throbbing goose egg at the back of his head. He'd been coming around the back of Genevieve's house when someone smashed a brick against his skull. He didn't know how long he was unconscious, but when he opened his eyes, it was to Lyla's scream. His stomach rolled at the memory of it and finding her on the floor, her face battered and bloodied. "She got the worst of it."

"Don't do it, brah."

Nic sat his hips against his desk. "What?"

"Don't start beating yourself up for what was beyond your control. It's a path that leads to nowhere. Trust me on this."

He knew Kekoa wasn't trying to make him feel better. Nic had witnessed the helplessness his friend experienced firsthand when Elinor was attacked a few months ago under their watch. They all bore the weight of that, but none more than Kekoa. It almost drove him to walk away from the team.

And now Nic faced a similar decision. *Leave or stay.*

"Have you heard from Jack or Walsh?"

"No." Kekoa folded his arms across his chest. "Jack updated the boss on what we found on Ammar and that gunrunner in Florida. Secret Service is involved now. I think that's where they're at, but I know they mentioned meeting up with DOD too. I've never seen Walsh so angry. I think Jack went with him just to keep him from strangling someone."

Nic understood exactly how Walsh felt. He dropped the ice pack on his desk. "Kekoa, you ever thought about working outside the office?"

"What do you mean? Like remotely?"

"No, like what Jack and I do. Running leads on assignments like you did with Elinor."

Kekoa tucked his hair behind his ear. "In case you don't remember, I was set up." He looked at Nic, then shrugged. "You guys are better at that than I am."

"That's not true, brother." Nic curled his fingers into a fist and then stretched them again. "That assignment was successful because of what you did outside of your genius behind the computer."

Kekoa slapped his forehead. "Brah."

"What?"

"You finally admit I'm a genius." Kekoa spread his hands around him to the empty room. "And no one was here to hear it."

Nic started to shake his head, but the painful throbbing stopped him.

"You sure you're okay?"

"I should be, according to Dr. Patel." Nic looked down at his open palms and fingers. "I've got this tingling sensation she said could be a side effect from the concussion but that it should go away." He ran his hands down the front of his pants, anxious to get rid of the weird feeling.

"Maybe you should take your own advice and go to the hospital."

Nic folded his arms over his chest. "I'm good."

"Is that why you're asking about me going into the field? In case you're not *good?*"

Inhaling slowly, Nic turned to Kekoa. "I'm asking because I might be leaving for a bit. Taking a temporary assignment overseas, and I—"

"What are you talking about, you're leaving?" Kekoa frowned. "That ain't funny."

"I'm not being funny, brother." He looked back at Walsh's office. "I think it's time, and I need you to remind her she's not invincible. Keep her from going all gung ho on the bad guys."

Kekoa snorted. "You think she's going to listen to me?"

Nic sighed and looked at his friend. "You guys are close. Somehow you've managed to hack into her defenses like you do with computer systems. She trusts you."

"Nice analogy, but Lyla trusts you too." Kekoa tucked a curl behind his ear. "She's all tough on the outside, but brah, she's like a pineapple. Or maybe a coconut." He shook his head. "No matter. What I'm trying to say is that underneath that rough exterior, she's just a softie desperate for your approval."

Nic dipped his chin. That Jack and Kekoa both saw how Lyla needed his approval reinforced his feeling that maybe it would be better if he left.

Then Lyla wouldn't feel the need to seek what was already hers.

Kekoa rounded on him. "Have you told her you're thinking about leaving?"

The door to Walsh's office opened and Nic stood, his heart leapfrogging into his throat as Lyla came out with Dr. Patel behind her. His fingers curled into his palms as he watched her take slow and steady steps, being cautious of the injuries he couldn't see.

The left side of Lyla's face had taken the brunt of the attack. There was a cut above her eyebrow, angry red scrapes and purple bruising along her cheek and near her chin. It wasn't as bad as he'd allowed himself to imagine when blood caked the side of her face, but it still made him want to punch something. Or someone.

"I'm to inform you," Dr. Patel said as she put her coat on, "that her injuries look worse than they are. And while I have my own opinion about what I would tell my daughter in this situation, I'm to assure you boys that Lyla is still fit to work."

Nic shot Lyla a look, but her attention was on Dr. Patel, who sighed.

"And she doesn't want any special treatment unless it comes in the form of coffee, chocolate, or a spa day to make up for the tiny bubbles episode—whatever that is." She zipped up her coat, and Lyla cleared her throat, indicating there was more. Dr. Patel heaved a sigh but continued. "And those are doctor's orders."

This time Lyla met Nic's eyes. "I'm going to walk Dr. Patel out so we can get started."

Dr. Patel paused next to Nic and eyed his balled fists. "Be sure to schedule an appointment if you have any persistent side effects."

"Yes, ma'am." Nic relaxed his fingers and offered a tight-lipped smile to mitigate the concern on Lyla's face as she led Dr. Patel down the hall to leave.

"You knew she was going to be raring to go as soon as she got the okay." Kekoa chuckled and pulled out a chair at the conference table and sat. "You're lolo if you think anything *I* say will get that wahine to back down."

"I know." Nic grabbed his paperwork and joined Kekoa. "I'd just hoped Dr. Patel would lean in our favor."

"Fat chance, brah."

"What's a fat chance?" Lyla walked into the fulcrum with a bit more energy, but Nic could see the strain in her eyes. He pulled out her chair. "Thanks."

"Lyla, are you sure—"

"You heard Dr. Patel." She glanced up beneath dark lashes, and even with a battered face, she was beautiful. She shrugged. "Besides, I've taken worse hits from Maddie 'Mad Dog' McGinnis."

Kekoa paused his typing. "Mad Dog McGinnis?

I'd hate to know what crimes she committed."

"She wasn't a criminal. She was ninety-seven pounds of muscle at ten years old and the lead jammer for the No Good Novas, my roller derby team. She had a mean bite. Gave me this scar on my chin."

Kekoa's eyes rounded. "She bit you?"

"Nah, she slung me across the track, and I hit a post."

Kekoa's eyes moved to Nic, his lip curling. "Brah, and you thought five-foot-nothing Dr. Patel was going to be able to take—" He looked at Lyla. "What was your nickname?"

"Stinkerbell," Nic answered without thinking. He went to tug down his cap, but he'd left it off because of the knot on his head.

"No way Dr. Patel is going to take down Stinkerbell." Kekoa reached out to Lyla for a fist bump. "My girl takes a lickin' and keeps on tickin'."

"Speaking of ticking." Lyla glanced up at Nic, her eyes soft with worry. "How are you? What kind of side effects was Dr. Patel talking about? Do you need to go home and rest?"

"I'm fine, Lyla."

Her shimmering gaze hesitated on him. "You're sure?"

"Just a bump on the head. That's all."

"Okay, but concussions are serious, and I *do* listen to the doctor." She narrowed her eyes on

Kekoa and tucked her hair behind her ear, but it fell right back in her frustrated face. "If we feel dizzy or nauseated, we're supposed to go to the hospital. In the meantime, let's work on finding out why Genevieve was killed."

Nic exhaled. He had to pick his battles. There was no way he'd be able to convince Lyla to go home and get the rest she needed. And honestly, at least with her here, next to him, she was protected. If only he could figure out how to keep her here.

Fat chance.

"The medical examiner could only give us his initial thoughts. Genevieve was shot but did have visual signs of injury on her face and arms." Lyla's voice lowered. She moved her hair from her face again, but the wayward strands slipped through her fingers once more. "He also said it appears she'd been dead about forty-eight hours. He won't know the exact time of death until the autopsy is complete."

"Which means the shooter at your grandparents' property could be the same person," Kekoa said.

Lyla nodded and attempted to pull her hair back but stopped, cringing. Nic saw the agitation on her face at not being able to do a simple task.

"Give me your hair thingy." Nic held out his hand, but Lyla just stared at him. "I'll help you."

"You want to do my hair?"

Lyla glanced at Kekoa like he was the better

265

choice—what with those Hawaiian curls he always bragged about.

Kekoa turned to the screens. "I'll just keep working on the timeline."

"Okay." Lyla handed Nic her hair thing. "Just a ponytail, please."

"Sure." A ponytail should be easy. Right? He stood and walked behind her. Taking a breath, he gently began scooping her hair into his hand and immediately realized he'd been overconfident in his ability. Especially since the buzzy feeling in his fingertips made it hard to stop her hair from slipping through his fingers. *"Just a temporary side effect of a concussion. It should go away."* Nic hoped Dr. Patel's diagnosis was correct.

"Ow."

"Sorry." Nic swallowed, and from the corner of his eye he saw Kekoa watching him, his lip twitching. He tried again, being careful not to pull. When he had most of her hair in his hand, he worked the band thing around it, twisting until his arm got tangled and he had to adjust his grip. "Sorry."

"That's . . . okay."

Was he hurting her? It sounded like he was hurting her. Why didn't he just ask Kekoa to do it? *Stick to your lane, Nic.* He tried one more twist and then, holding his breath, let go.

When it stayed together, he smiled. *It stayed!*

It wasn't as nice as Lyla could do, and he was

certain Kekoa could've done it better, but hey, it looked natural—like one of those messy buns. Except it was a messy ponytail.

He stepped back. "How's that?"

Lyla reached back and ran her fingers over his work. "Good job, Nicolás."

Man, he was grateful she couldn't see it. Sitting down, she tried to smile, but it was lopsided as she tried to protect the skin pulling against the abrasion on her cheek. Even lopsided, it still caused his heart to skip a beat.

"I really hope Mason can get us in touch with R.D. Leto," Lyla said. "I feel like there's a good chance he might know what was on the flash drive."

Nic pointed to the copies of the articles written by Leto that they had printed and taped to an acrylic board. "Or maybe we go straight to the sources. It might be easier to get ahold of Roger Colthorpe and find out if he knew Jerry."

"That sounds like a good angle to look into." Lyla stood, and for a second Nic thought she looked like she had to steady herself, but then she met his eyes. "I'm going to make myself a coffee. Do you guys want anything?"

Nic said no and Kekoa shook his head.

"See, brah," Kekoa said when Lyla disappeared down the hall. "I don't think Lyla would've given in that easily to me or Jack or Walsh. If you leave—"

"You're leaving?"

Nic whipped his head around, sending his brain rattling against his skull. He focused on Lyla and not the aching pain. "Um, yeah, it's an assignment—"

"I'm going to check on that thing we were looking into on Leto." Kekoa popped to his feet and backstepped to his office. He sent Nic an apologetic grimace before closing the door.

"What's the assignment?"

"There have been some bombings in Syria. They need someone familiar with the type of IED used and asked if I'd be willing to go."

"Oh." Lyla blinked. "Okay. It's temporary, then."

"That mission is, but I'm considering going contract." Nic remained still. "Work with explosive teams around the world."

Lyla's face paled. "You're leaving SNAP? For good?" She started to shake her head but winced and stopped. "I don't understand. Does Walsh know you want to leave?" Her eyes rounded on him. "Wait, Kekoa knows. Does Jack?"

Nic felt sick to his stomach. "I wanted to be sure about my decision before I told you."

"But everyone else knows?" She rubbed her head and winced when her fingers hit a sore spot. "And you've made your decision?"

He took a step toward her, and she backed up a step. "About Syria, I think so, yes. I'm just not sure about what happens after."

Lyla bit the inside of her lip, eyes shining. She folded her arms over her chest. "Okay, so, um . . ." She sniffled. "When do you leave?"

"In about five weeks."

She dropped her arms to her sides, and her gaze sharpened on him. "Fine." Her posture straightened. "That means I have five weeks to convince you you're coming back to SNAP after Syria."

21

Tom removed his glasses, set them on his desk, and rubbed his eyes. Exhaustion weighed on him, but not nearly as heavily as the anguish when he got the call from Jack about the attack on Lyla and Nic. He was beyond grateful they were okay, but his stomach still hadn't settled and now . . . he exhaled slowly.

He opened his eyes and watched Nic offer a wave before he left the office for the night. The man was all integrity and had waited until after eight for Tom to arrive to let him know of his decision to join the Syrian mission.

The deep creases at the edges of Nic's brows told Tom the decision hadn't come lightly, but it was what Nic said afterward that had him concerned. *"I'm considering leaving the agency."*

Nic didn't offer much explanation, but Tom knew the young man was carrying regret and looking for closure that likely wouldn't come without some meaningful conversations with the Lord. *And then there's Lyla.*

Tom recognized that Nic's attentiveness to Lyla went beyond that of a teammate, but he maintained a professionalism that Tom both respected and appreciated. Unfortunately, the last couple of assignments seemed to push the young

man to confront what was beyond his control—
Lyla.

Tom's phone chirped, and when he saw who
the incoming email was from, he sat up. His
exhaustion was replaced with an anxiousness
he hadn't felt in a long time. He put his glasses
back on and read the encrypted email from the
secretary of defense.

Tom,

I apologize for not being able to get
back to you earlier, but I wanted to
look into a few of your questions before
responding. As you already know,
Jordan Kemp is working an investigation on behalf of the Secret Service,
not the Department of Justice. It has
come to my attention that Mr. Kemp's
team has uncovered several counterfeit
rings that have direct links to weapons
sales involving the Department of
Defense and that the discovery of
weapons procured through government
contracts have been illegally smuggled
and sold to countries, rebel groups,
and individuals, some of whom are not
friendly to the US or our allies. It also
appears these unauthorized violations
occurred as far back as twenty years,
maybe longer.

I've informed Under Secretary of Defense for Acquisitions and Sustainment Christine León of your inquiries. She has offered her full cooperation on the matter and has put her chief of staff, Richard Vale, as the point person to further assist you.

I recognize this breach is a potential threat to our nation's security, and as such, you have my assurance that my office is taking this very seriously. If you need anything else, my door is always open.

Carl Rosch

Tom read the email once more and sat back in his chair. Weapons illegally smuggled . . . rebel groups . . . as far back as twenty years. Maybe longer.

Longer.

Opening the middle drawer of his desk, Tom pulled out a photo taken twenty-five years ago of him and his friend. *"Stop 'em, Tom . . . get truth . . . make the world better."*

The final words his friend spoke before he died had haunted him for nearly three decades. And even now, they took him right back to the hardest day of his life and to the single question Tom had never been able to answer: Was someone in the US involved?

Tom read the secretary of defense's words again and felt like his friend was speaking from the grave, reminding him of the promise he made that fateful day.

22

The next day, Lyla hurried down M Street, dodging a group of college-aged women juggling their cell phones and Starbucks cups on their way toward the Georgetown campus. She was headed in the opposite direction to meet up with Mason.

His phone call an hour ago had come out of the blue. The nervousness in his voice when he asked her to breakfast had made her anxious. She wondered if his mom was still trying to orchestrate a love connection, but he quickly squashed that fear when he said R.D. Leto was in town and she had agreed to meet.

She. Lyla wasn't sure why she'd assumed the conspiracy journalist was a man, but it had been a lot easier to convince Nicolás to let her accept Mason's terms that she come alone, knowing R.D. was a woman. Especially after what happened at Genevieve's the day before. She shuddered, and it caused the bruising in her body to ache. Lifeless eyes had haunted her all night. If Mason hadn't been her childhood friend, Lyla wasn't sure she'd have agreed either.

Crossing the street, she tugged her scarf against the harsh October wind biting at her cheeks and causing her eyes to sting with tears. The dark, bitter weather suited her mood.

Her brain circled back to the thoughts she hadn't been able to escape all night. Nicolás was leaving. No matter how many times Lyla repeated the words to herself, she couldn't believe them. Nicolás was leaving. *And he doesn't know if he's coming back?*

Why was she taking this so hard? Nicolás explained that his old Army boss had requested him personally because of his expertise with the specific explosive being used to kill innocent people in Syria. A quick Google search after she got back to Brynn's last night, and Lyla saw the horrifying effects of the death and destruction at the hands of terrorists determined to keep the Syrian people from having the democracy they wanted so badly.

Nicolás had to go. She knew that. He was just as much an advocate for the innocent as she was. A protector. His uncompromising determination to keep his team safe wasn't reserved just for SNAP . . . so why was she angry?

"You okay?"

Lyla jumped at Nicolás's steady voice echoing through the piece in her ear. "Yeah, I'm good." She casually glanced over to the laundromat where he was positioned across from Dexter's Donut Shop, watching her. "Mason inside?"

"Yes, but he's alone."

"Maybe R.D. hasn't arrived yet." Lyla paused and pulled out her phone as if she was checking a message, but she really surveyed the busy street. "Or maybe she entered through the back."

"Kekoa's monitoring all entry and exit points."

"Okay." Lyla put her phone away and reached for the door. Her other hand rested on the inconspicuous bulge in her purse where Cupcake was secure but within quick reach should she need it. "I'm going in."

Inside, the smell of grease and sweet icing welcomed her straight into a line of customers waiting to pick up donuts. A shorter line waited to be seated in the dining area to her left. Lyla rose on her toes searching for Mason and found him at a table near the back, reading a newspaper.

She weaved through the busy dining area and past waitresses carrying trays of chicken and gourmet donuts instead of waffles. Her stomach growled.

"Was Dexter's ever this busy when we were kids?"

Mason looked up from the paper, his gaze widening. "Good grief, Lyla. Is that from your fall? Are you okay?"

"What?" It took her a second to realize he was referring to her fall from Sir Winston at the hunt. Her fingers went to the bruises and scrapes she thought she'd masterfully covered up with makeup. "Oh, yeah. I'm okay."

Lyla held her breath when Mason stood to hug her. The bruising and aches in the areas that couldn't be seen weren't as easy to hide with foundation. And nothing covered up the distress that came when she found out Nicolás had been struck in the head by a brick. It was her first concern this morning when she called to check on him, and as expected, he assured her he was fine.

"Are you sure?"

Mason's question pulled her out of her thoughts. She offered the best smile she could with her bruised lip. "Yes." She let Mason help her out of her coat, then took a seat in the chair across from him. "So, Leto. Is she late?"

"She's here."

Lyla sat forward. "Where?"

Mason waved a waitress down and ordered a coffee and waited for Lyla. She wasn't here for coffee, but she ordered a vanilla latte just to get the waitress to leave. When she did, Lyla pinned a stare on Mason.

"So where is she?"

"Keep talking to Mason like he's the most interesting person you know," a female voice said from behind her.

Lyla started to turn, but Mason reached across the table and took her hand with a gentle squeeze, his eyes warning her even as he smiled.

"There are only two reasons why I'm here," the voice said.

Lyla checked the window, but the woman was

positioned so there was no way to catch her reflection. She scanned the ceiling and spotted a camera, but it was angled away from the corner where the table behind her was positioned. Why hadn't she paid better attention to who was sitting around Mason? *Because I was checking out the donuts.* Ugh. Kekoa would understand—Nicolás would not.

"First, I owe Mason. And second, Ms. Fox, you're going to owe me."

The snort that slipped out of Lyla's mouth caused Mason's face to light up the way it had when they were kids. Only this time, there was no humor behind Lyla's reaction. Her second attempt to face off with R.D. was stopped once more when Mason gave her hand a gentle tug and shook his head.

Ugh. Lyla gave him a dirty look that made him shrug as if there was nothing he could do.

"You realize that look is more enchanting than it is hostile?" Nicolás spoke softly, and it nearly drove her to look in the direction of the laundromat. "Just hear her out. And if Mason doesn't take his hands off you in—"

Lyla quickly pulled her hand free of Mason's, dropping it in her lap. His eyes shifted subtly around them like he was keeping watch, but with the kind of finesse that would make anyone paying attention think he had eyes for only her. It didn't make her uncomfortable because there was

278

nothing meaningful lingering in Mason's blue eyes. *Unlike what I thought I saw in Nicolás's hazel ones.* Or was that some distorted image she'd made up because of her mom's va-va-voom comment compounded with the panic he'd set in motion when he said he was leaving?

Lyla refocused herself. "What do you think I'm going to owe you, *Ms. Leto?*"

"I know you didn't come alone. That would make you stupid." R.D.'s voice was barely loud enough to hear over the din of the nearby customers. "Especially in light of what you've been through, which is why I'm going to explain what you're going to owe me first."

Lyla's pulse spiked. The question of how R.D. knew what she'd been through was trumped by Lyla's annoyance that this woman thought she could demand something from her. Genevieve's killer was out there somewhere, and she didn't have time for games.

"Her posture suggests she's nervous," Nicolás said. "Kekoa is pulling audio from the cameras inside the restaurant. Let her talk, Lyla."

This time she casually narrowed her eyes as though she was squinting to look outside, then she rolled her eyes before looking back at Mason.

"I saw that."

Nicolás's whisper made Lyla grin, causing Mason to look confused before smiling back. *Oops.* "What do I owe you?"

"After this conversation, I'm heading out of town, and I need your Hawaiian friend to make me disappear."

Lyla spun in her chair, this time pulling her hands back before Mason could take hold. She thought she'd catch R.D. by surprise, but the woman had turned to face Lyla like she'd expected it. She was a lot younger than Lyla had anticipated. Maybe mid to late twenties, with long, dirty-blonde hair that hung in waves across her forehead, hiding one of her light-brown eyes. Her brow was double pierced with two gold hoops that matched the one in her nose.

They sized each other up for a second before Lyla narrowed her eyes. "What are you talking about?"

"Your cryptologist, Kekoa Young." R.D. pinned Lyla with a knowing look. "I know he's been working those tattooed muscles pretty hard to figure me out. You can let him know I appreciate the interest, but I'm already spoken for."

Lyla's cheeks burned with indignation, wanting to defend both Kekoa and Elinor, but Nicolás was already talking in her ear.

"Ask her what she wants Kekoa to do."

"Why do you want to disappear?"

"Because you found me." She looked over her shoulder, and Mason picked up the newspaper but didn't read it. His eyes moved a slow circle around them.

280

"You mean, you found us." Lyla eyed Mason. "I didn't arrange this meeting, which means you must need us more than we need you."

R.D. pursed her lips and sighed. "You've read my articles, so you understand that my job doesn't exactly win me favor with the people I'm investigating. I've managed to stay under the radar . . . mostly. But a week ago my water and electricity were shut off. The companies said I was delinquent in payment." Her jaw tightened. "I wasn't. I pay ahead because I never know if I'm going to have access to the internet to make payments when I'm on assignment. And then my bank called and said I've been bouncing checks and they're closing my account. Nearly thirty-seven thousand dollars"—she snapped her fingers—"gone."

"Kekoa's checking," Nicolás said. "Her name is Randy Darryl. She's telling you the truth. He said it looks suspicious."

"You think someone is coming after you?"

R.D. checked her watch. "I know someone is."

When the woman looked back up, Lyla saw worry hanging in her features. Real worry. The kind Lyla had seen in her own reflection recently.

"They want the information I have, the information I'm willing to give to you if you help me disappear. The second I get on that plane, I want my name removed from the passenger manifest, all video footage from the cameras your Hawaiian friend is likely watching me on erased. I need to fall off the grid until you guys do what you do."

There wasn't any hesitation in R.D.'s request. Only confidence to suggest she'd done her homework on their agency and expectation that she'd get what she wanted.

"Tell her Kekoa will help her."

"Not until I know what she has," Lyla slipped, answering Nicolás. R.D.'s brow lifted in a way that said she knew. *Nice, Lyla.* "My friend will help you, but I need some assurance that the information is worth our time."

R.D. looked around them, and Lyla did as well. No one seemed to be paying any attention to them. Most were enjoying private conversations and their meals. But that didn't mean anything.

"Kekoa's running the customers through his program. Everyone is clean so far."

The sound of Nicolás's unshakable composure always had a way of reinforcing her confidence—like he could read her mind and know what she was thinking. Proving he was always right there for her. What would it be like when that was gone? When *he* was gone?

"Mason said you're looking into my article on Ammar El-Din, right?"

R.D.'s question pulled Lyla back to their conversation. "Yes."

"Well, if you're hoping to find him, you're too late. He's gone."

Lyla frowned. "What do you mean he's gone? He's in a prison in Lebanon."

R.D. shook her head. "Not anymore. I reached out to a source before I arranged this meeting with you, and they said El-Din was transferred out of Roumieh two days ago."

How did they not know this? "To where?"

"I don't know, but we can assume it wasn't an early release for good behavior. Men like him, men claiming to know scandalous details about the United States' role in criminal activity, only disappear for one reason."

Lyla's heart dropped to her stomach. Had someone gotten to him like they had Jerry? Two seconds passed, and Nicolás came through.

"Kekoa's working to confirm."

"Who's your source?"

Irritation colored R.D.'s expression. "Did you not hear me when I said someone is coming after me? You think I'm going to give up my source so they become the next target?"

"The next target?" Lyla gritted her teeth. "A woman was killed. My colleague and I were attacked. You might think it's honorable to protect your source, but I'm trying to protect someone else from being killed, which, from the sound of it, could be you."

R.D. clenched her jaw, but Lyla could see she was working something out in her mind. Finally, she swallowed. "I can't give you my source,

283

and I know you think that's stupid of me, but if you're right, then I'm not going to be the one responsible for endangering their life." She blinked. "And I'm sorry to hear about Genevieve."

Lyla's nerves hummed with adrenaline. "What do you know of Genevieve?"

"Jerry told me he was worried about her. About his family. It's why he wouldn't give me any information." R.D. paused, looked around, and then leaned in. "El-Din didn't have names but suggested Jerry might. But Jerry wouldn't confirm anything that supported El-Din's claim that someone in the US government was involved in his counterfeit operation."

"There are always conspiracies floating around about the US being involved in sketchy operations. Unless you have proof, or a name, it's nothing more than a theory."

"But I do have a name." She checked her watch, then began pulling on her coat. "Barún an bháis, Irish for Baron of Death."

"Who's that?"

"Look him up for yourself. He's got quite a reputation in the United States. Particularly with the CIA." She rose from her chair, and Mason stood to meet her. They embraced, and she kissed him on the cheek with whispered words Lyla couldn't hear. The scene made her curious. How close were Mason and R.D.? She faced Lyla. "If I come across more information, I'll try to get it to you if I can."

Lyla was momentarily dumbstruck, caught off guard by this bizarre meeting that left her with nothing more than some supervillain name. She quickly refocused. "What if we need to get ahold of you? How do we find you?"

"You won't."

Lyla stood, meeting R.D. eye to eye. "You really think we're going to just let you walk away?"

Taking a step back, R.D. nodded. "I do." And then she offered a tight-lipped smile. "Because you said you were trying to protect someone else from being killed. I might be that someone, so I'm going to trust you and your agency to do just that."

Turning on her heel, R.D. weaved through the tables without another look back. Did she really think she could just waltz out of there and Kekoa wouldn't have her every move tracked? If she was trusting Kekoa to make her disappear, then she had to know he could also make her reappear. *"I'm going to trust you and your agency . . ."*

"Nic—"

"Kekoa's got eyes on her," Nicolás answered. "He's found at least three airline tickets booked in her name."

Lyla reached for her coat. "We can't lose her."

"Is what you said true?" Mason's question and

the touch of his hand at the small of her back jerked her attention to him. His gaze moved to the cut above her brow before he searched her face. "You were attacked?"

Mason's pained expression toyed with her emotions. She saw the reflection of the teenage boy she remembered. Kind, generous. He had always loved a good adventure, which made him the perfect companion to whatever scheme she talked him into. There were moments, like this, throughout their friendship when Lyla wondered if her childhood friend didn't maybe share some of the hope his mom had for something more than friendship. Unfortunately, the kind of chemistry Mason's mother hoped for just wasn't there. No va-va-vooms.

"I'm okay, Mace."

"I don't know why I figured you'd have some kind of desk job. I should've known better."

"I've never been one for a desk."

Mason smiled, then it melted away. He reached over and gently brushed the hair away from her eye. "Lyla, I don't know everything that's going on, but I've never known R.D. to be nervous. She's a lot like you, willing to toe the line, cross it even if the story is worth it. But the fact that she's backing off . . . ." Mason's hand slipped to her shoulder and moved down the back of her arm. "I want you to be careful."

"I'll be okay." Lyla's heart pounded in her

chest. Not because there was anything between her and Mason but because across the street, Nicolás was likely interpreting the intimate concern in Mason's body language and tone. "Thank you for setting up this meeting, Mason. I can't tell you how helpful this will be, and I promise I'll be careful."

Mason stepped forward and drew her into an embrace. His breath whispered softly next to her ear. "I know better than to trust that promise, Ly. The difference between you and R.D. is that she has someone she loves enough to know when not to cross that line. I hope you do too."

23

She has someone she loves enough to know when not to cross that line."

Mason's whispered words meant for Lyla had landed with a punch to Nic's gut. As did the hug they shared before parting ways. It lingered longer than Nic was comfortable with, long enough that he began to read more into the words spoken in Lyla's ear.

From his vantage point, Mason's mom wasn't the only one who desired a future with Lyla in it. And in the time it took Nic to follow Lyla's rental car back to SNAP HQ, that thought had settled in his gut with all the weight of an M-1 tank.

Worse was the fact that in the elevator ride up from the parking garage to their office, Lyla didn't ramble on about her meeting with R.D. like he'd expected her to. She was quiet and pensive and went straight to Kekoa's office to make sure R.D. Leto was being tracked, leaving him to dwell on the unsettling reason she was avoiding eye contact or . . . He stared at his computer—the *Baron of Death*.

Which is worse?

Nic's eyes moved to where Lyla was hovering over Kekoa's shoulder, biting her thumbnail as she watched whatever he was doing. Frustration tightened the soft planes of her face like they had last night when Kekoa spilled the beans about the Syria mission. Lyla had taken it better than he'd expected. *"I have five weeks to convince you you're coming back."*

She had no idea how those words had impacted him. Where they landed deep within his chest. Or the way they led him back to the painful memories with Brittany.

After rubbing his eyes, Nic refocused on his computer screen. It was better to stay on task than to let his mind wander where it didn't need to go.

Why does facing the Baron of Death seem safer?

It wasn't. At least not when he looked over what he found on the man the Irish called Barún an bháis. It wasn't R.D.'s article that had him on edge but rather the facts weaved into the narrative that matched multiple news sources. The worst of it was what Nic was staring at now.

"She's gone."

Nic glanced up to find Lyla stalking out of Kekoa's office. "What?"

"R.D. or Randy Darryl." Lyla waved her hand in the air. "Or whatever fake name she gave us is gone. Ghosted us."

"She didn't ghost us," Kekoa said, coming up behind her. "Technically, someone who ghosts you doesn't tell you they're going off the grid. They just disappear. Like a ghost."

Lyla shot daggers at Kekoa, and the man had either all the courage of a bull or the awareness of a fly, because he smiled.

"I know what ghosting is," she said through gritted teeth. "What I don't know is how you, our cyber genius, allowed her to disappear."

The sting of her comment drew Kekoa's brows together. He turned on his heel and went back to his office.

Lyla blew out a breath and sat. "Ugh, I wasn't trying to be short."

"Have you taken any more pain medicine?"

"Have you?"

Nic looked down at his hands. The numbness had gotten better in his left hand but not in the right, and pain medicine didn't help. "I'm fine." He met Lyla's aquamarine gaze. "Your goodies helped."

"They did?" A deep smile wiped away the fatigue for a few seconds. "Do you know how hard it is to find things with armadillos on them in DC?"

He chuckled, thinking about the stuffed armadillo and armadillo socks that had been waiting for him in a basket with protein bars and a note from Lyla about his head being as tough as an armadillo shell. He was trying really hard not to read into the gesture, but he'd be lying to himself if he didn't admit it only stoked the flame he was feeling for her.

"Are you sure you're okay?"

"Yeah." She took a deep breath. "Just frustrated."

And likely exhausted and in pain, no matter what you say.

"Here." Emerging from his office, Kekoa slid a handful of Dove chocolates across the table. "I've got more if you need it."

Lyla looked down at the offering, then burst into a mixture of laughter and groaning as she clutched her side.

Kekoa looked confused. "What?"

A tear trickled down Lyla's cheek as she reached for a piece, her laughter softening. "You can't just throw chocolate at women to calm them down."

"Dr. Patel said chocolate or coffee or spa day. I'm not touching your machine, and I wasn't here for tiny bubbles." Kekoa returned to his seat. "I had chocolate."

"Good chocolate too." Lyla gave a sigh of contentment. "Thank you."

Nic shifted in his chair, hating that he was once more envious of Kekoa and Lyla's friendship. Or that he hadn't thought to offer Lyla something more than pain meds.

"You good?" Kekoa asked Lyla. She unwrapped another piece of chocolate, ate it, and nodded. "R.D. was smart and knew what she was doing. Randy Darryl Leto is a unique name, and at least

291

three flights were booked under that name, but she never made it past TSA or to her gate."

"Where'd she go?"

"Ghosted, Nicolás." Lyla chewed another piece of chocolate. "Disappeared."

Kekoa rolled his eyes. "Using the airport cameras, I tracked her to a women's restroom near the baggage claim." He let out a sigh, and Nic could see he was trying to hide his frustration. Lyla didn't make it easy to disappoint, and Kekoa didn't like to disappoint. "Four domestic and two international flights arrived within minutes of each other. There were at least several hundred people, women who went into the same bathroom. I never saw R.D. come out, or if she did, she didn't look the way she did when she entered. I've got my program running facial recognition, but—"

"She's gone." Lyla blew out a breath. "She knows you're good, Kekoa, and she was ready."

"It's not over, sis." Kekoa pulled his shoulder-length curls back into a man bun that always made Nic cringe. "She has no idea who she's messing with. I'll find her."

"Maybe we don't," Nic said, and both Lyla and Kekoa frowned at him. "I know R.D. probably thought she was helping, and she did give us new information, but based on the trouble she went to, knowing we'd be watching, I think we have good reason to let her hide—for now."

"I hope your suggestion means you have something on our Duke of Death." Hope lingered in Lyla's eyes and voice.

"Nothing says good morning better than Duke of Death." Jack walked in. "I take it that's not the name of Lyla's newest coffee creation."

Lyla speared him with a glance. "Okay, you know what, no more fancy coffee for you."

Kekoa flicked a piece of chocolate across the table, and Lyla caught it with a quick hand. She unwrapped it and eyed Jack, who cautiously took his seat. "You're on warning, Hudson."

"Noted." Jack looked between Nic and Kekoa, clearly confused as to what was happening. "Is the Duke of Death Lyla's latest date or—" A piece of chocolate flew at Jack's head, and he ducked before smiling at Lyla. "Nice aim, but you're too slow, Fox."

Nic gave a soft chuckle, joining Lyla and Kekoa, and it made him appreciate the friendship rather than envy it. If he left, he knew they'd be okay. He swallowed. If he left, he'd miss this.

"Baron of Death," Nic corrected as he tapped a few keys, giving his laptop access to the overhead screens. "The man the Irish call Barún an bháis is Narek Grigoryan. Armenian-Syrian, he was born and raised in Istanbul, where he joined the French Army out of school. There he became proficient in weaponry. Once he left the military, he married and moved to Lebanon, where he used his knowledge to procure weapons and sell them to militias in Eastern Europe. He was arrested by the United States for illegal arms deals during the Iran-Iraq War and Lebanese Civil War, and for arming smaller revolutions in other countries."

"Is he connected to our gunrunner in Florida?" Jack looked at the names listed on the acrylic board. "Roger Colthorpe?"

"Nothing directly connects him," Nic answered. "However, just like Colthorpe, after Grigoryan was arrested, he started claiming top American officials were involved in the transactions and was suddenly released and began working *with* the CIA. But a man like that is loyal to only one thing—money. I guess the CIA didn't pay enough, because it didn't take long before he opened operations in Jordan and France until he was arrested for bank fraud." At this Nic raised a brow to Lyla. "Want to guess who he banked with?"

"Zane Investments." Lyla stated it as fact.

Nic nodded. "I also found this article from the *Irish Independent*. An Irish man identifying himself as Michael O'Sullivan claims he tipped off British and American intelligence agencies to Narek Grigoryan's role in supplying weapons to the Real IRA. O'Sullivan was a member of the Official Irish Republican Army but later became an informant until his identity was exposed shortly after he identified IRA leader Eamon

Flannery. He's fled Belfast, fearing for his safety, and he blames the US Secret Service and British police for failing to protect him."

"Wait." Lyla frowned. "Why would the Secret Service be involved?"

"I might have the answer to that." Kekoa popped his knuckles. "I did some further digging into Roger Colthorpe. The weapons he was smuggling into Ireland were connected to the bombing in Omagh, and an arrest was made a few years after. When Eamon Flannery was arrested, they found him in possession of a package containing supernotes that he had smuggled in from Moscow."

"I'm sorry," Lyla said. "What are supernotes?"

"They're fake one-hundred-dollar bills that are so perfect even Secret Service experts have a hard time telling the fake ones from the real ones."

Nic stared at Jack, waiting for him to continue, but all he got was a tight-lipped side glance. Weird. Was this why Jack was meeting with the Secret Service? It didn't look like this information was entirely new to him.

"Right." Kekoa pulled up another article. "R.D. Leto wrote this article about an incident in London a few weeks after the bombing. Apparently a deal was made to deliver a cache of weapons to a member of the Real IRA, but supernotes were used and the deal went south, ending with a shoot-out that killed two members of the Real IRA. Rònán O'Hagan and Connor Murphy. Read the last line of the article."

Nic gestured for Lyla to read it aloud.

"Though no one from Britain's Security Service or American Central Intelligence Agency will confirm, rumours continue to circulate that Connor Murphy may have been a member of American intelligence and defected to the Real IRA before being killed." Lyla swung her gaze to Jack. "Do you think Brynn can help us find out if Connor Murphy was in the CIA?"

"I wouldn't count on it." Jack pushed back in his chair. "True or not, the CIA isn't going to reveal the identity of one of their officers."

"Even if they defected?" Lyla asked. "Or died?"

"Yes, Lyla, even then." Jack's tone shifted, and he stood. "I think we need to hold off on moving forward on this information until we pass it by Walsh."

Nic studied Jack. It wasn't like him to pull the reins on an assignment. He was usually the first to suggest they keep digging so they'd have all the information needed to present to Walsh.

"Hold off?" Lyla looked as confused as Nic was by Jack's decision. "We need to move forward. We should get to Florida and talk with Roger Colthorpe before he suddenly disappears like Ammar El-Din. And if Brynn can't give us

296

information about Connor Murphy, maybe she can help us reach out to Eamon Flannery or this Baron of Death guy."

"Lyla—"

"Jack." Her voice was hoarse. "All these men claim someone in the United States has been orchestrating a gun-smuggling and counterfeiting scheme that may be connected to Jerry's death, or at the very least to Genevieve's death, which has led to the threat against me. *Nicolás and I were attacked.* It's put my own family in danger. We can't hold off."

A shimmer of emotion filled Lyla's eyes again, and Nic's heart hurt for her and the guilt she loaded onto herself. He swung his attention to Jack. "There has to be something we can do while we wait for Walsh. I agree with Lyla. We can't afford to lose time if it means more people are going to be killed. Someone came after Lyla and—"

"And that's exactly why I'm asking you to stand down." Jack's gaze landed hard on Nic. He exhaled and rubbed the side of his temple. "Look, I want the person who killed Genevieve and attacked the two of you to pay severely for what he did, but for now we sit on this until Walsh gives us the all clear to continue our investigation."

Something in Jack's tone didn't sit well with Nic. Their team leader looked . . . rattled. Why?

297

It took Nic back to his earlier reservations that maybe Jack knew more about what they'd uncovered—maybe knew it before they did.

"No." Lyla put her hands on her hips. "Make me understand, Jack. We just got valuable information, timely information that we can't sit on. R.D. took great risks to speak to me, and I'm not going to let any more leads die. I owe that to Genevieve."

Jack raised his hands. "It's above my pay grade."

"Walsh, then?" Lyla pursed her lips and narrowed her eyes before she marched to her desk and grabbed her cell phone from her purse. Spinning on her heel, she faced them. "Excuse me, but I have a phone call to make."

The three of them watched Lyla stalk into Walsh's office and slam the door shut behind her.

Kekoa's chair squeaked as he got up. "Um, I'm just gonna hide back in my lair, away from the shrapnel about to hit da roof. You guys call me when it's safe."

Nic heaved a sigh and looked at Jack. "How's this going to turn out, man?"

Jack gave Nic a sympathetic look. "Walsh is in a secure meeting. Won't answer her call. And even if he could, she's not going to change his mind."

There was an undercurrent of meaning, and Nic locked eyes with him. "This directive have something to do with the meetings you've been attending?"

Jack gave a nod.

Nic looked to where Lyla was pacing in Walsh's office, her cell phone pressed to her ear. Her agitation was growing, and he knew she was a ticking time bomb. "When's he supposed to be back?"

"A couple of hours." Jack's shoulders stiffened when the door to Walsh's office opened. "Why?"

"Mind if I get her out of the office for a bit?"

"Brother, if you can defuse that situation before Walsh gets back, I'll buy you a steak dinner."

"He's not answering," Lyla fumed. "And. I. Could. Spit. Nails."

Nic smiled at Lyla's colloquialism. "Come on, Lyla, let's find a place to spit those nails."

24

Whatever frustration, anger, and annoyance were pulsing through Lyla fifteen minutes ago had been replaced with confusion, then curiosity, and now amusement.

Lyla stood in a commercial warehouse with walls covered in graffiti and stickers. Music played loudly over the speakers in an attempt, she believed, to cover the violent banging happening behind the corrugated metal wall separating the Make Rage, Not War front desk from the destructive but therapeutic rooms, where—according to one sign—"relief is just a sledgehammer away."

"I can't believe you brought me to a rage room." Lyla zipped up the white coverall over her clothes. "I've always wanted to go to one. Did you know that?"

"I've heard you mention it a time or two."

Lyla let that sink in, realizing Nicolás did listen to her. He wasn't showy like she was in her emotional expression, but in his own way, these little gestures—like when he gave her the candle—proved he cared. And that sent her heart racing.

Or was that caused by the way Nicolás was filling out the hideous, bulky white coveralls they were required to wear over their own clothing? Unlike hers, his fit his form without any extra material ballooning in all the wrong places. "How come you don't look like you're about to clean up a chemical spill?"

Nicolás looked down at himself. "We look the same."

"No, I look like an Oompa Loompa when they try to save Mike Teavee, and you look like one of those muscly guys the mob brings in to clean up a crime scene."

The rage room employee, Rob, turned at that exact moment, his eyes widening a fraction as he walked over with two chest protectors. "The outfit is meant to keep you safe." The handlebar mustache that gave him biker vibes bristled. "There are steel toe caps lined up by size, and there's a welding helmet that you must wear at all times—even if it messes up your hair."

Lyla narrowed her eyes on Rob before tucking her hair up into a bun. She grabbed a pair of ugly steel toe protectors and a helmet. "You know, people don't come here because they're having a good day."

Rob eyed the wounds on her face. "I can see that."

Lifting her chin, Lyla eyed him right back. "You should see the other guy."

With a smirk, Rob lifted a shoulder. "The only customers who scare me are the wives who discover their husbands have been cheating." He slid a look at Nicolás before meeting her eyes again. "That the case here?"

"We're coworkers."

Lyla's cheeks warmed at Nicolás's quick response. It was the truth, so why did it bother her? Her earlier awareness came roaring back to mind. They weren't just coworkers. They were friends. And if the strange sensation that had been tickling her midsection was to be acknowledged . . . a small part of her maybe *wanted more?*

Nicolás's arm bumped hers—completely inno-cently—but she wouldn't know it if the thumping in her chest was to be believed. What was happening to her?

"You signed up for rage machine." Rob's voice drew her back to their walk down a hallway. "Which means you get an hour in the Room of Destruction."

As they passed other rooms, the ear-shattering noise of destruction was barely muted by the loud music echoing from each room. She paused by one door and listened to the familiar country song by Carrie Underwood about a cheating man.

"Let me guess, caught her husband cheating?"

Rob kept walking. "With two women from her yoga class."

It was concerning how much personal infor-mation had been shared with Rob that he then shared with them, and also the amount of glass shattering and cursing that was coming from the room.

"This is your room." Rob wrote their names on a small whiteboard hanging on the door while she and Nicolás put the steel tips over their shoes and slipped on the welding helmets. "Choices of tools are inside, and everything is fair game to destroy. There's a panic button near the door for your safety." He handed them each a pair of gloves and opened the door. "Get your rage on."

Lyla walked into the room the size of a two-car garage. In fact, an old car, spray-painted and missing a door, was parked on one side, with enough space on the other side for another car if it weren't for the piles of glass dishes, bottles, old computer software, small appliances, and a big screen television circa the eighties.

"What's your rage weapon of choice? We have baseball bats, golf clubs . . ." Nicolás pulled out a crowbar. "This looks like it could do some damage."

She couldn't see his face because of the helmet, but there was a sound of excitement in his voice that made her smile. "I'll take the bat, please."

Nicolás handed her the bat and then pointed at a screen on the wall protected by plastic. "We can pick a song. Do you have a preference?"

"Surprise me."

He nodded, pressed a button, and soon the speakers blasted with guitar riffs and chest-pounding drumbeats that instantly got her adrenaline pumping. Stepping aside, Nicolás gestured for her to begin.

Lyla eyed the possibilities and suddenly felt nervous, vulnerable with him watching. She didn't know if he sensed her hesitation, but she felt him come up beside her, his steady presence making her extra warm beneath the coveralls.

"Imagine Becky 'the Basher' Benning just took out your lead skater, and you're one point away from roller derby world domination." His fingers went to the back of her shoulders, and the encouraging touch sent a shudder through her middle. "Show 'em what you got, Stinkerbell."

Thank goodness the mask covered the blush his words had brought to her cheeks. She didn't know if it was his touch or that he remembered the name of her roller derby nemesis or the crazy fluctuation of feelings pumping from her chest and spreading through every part of her, but she lifted the bat, eyed her target, and swung with powerful energy.

The second her bat connected with the side-view mirror, her ears rang with a shattering sound that was deliciously satisfying.

"Whoop!" She swung again, this time connecting with the car's headlights. Her adrenaline spiked, and she let out another war cry as she continued to beat dents into the car's hood and fenders.

For several minutes, she focused on nothing else but the jarring ache vibrating through her still-tender muscles as she swung over and over. Her breathing came hard, and she could feel the sweat dripping down her back, but she didn't care. This was fun. When she knocked the mirror off the car, she turned and looked at Nicolás, who was standing back, arms folded, and though she couldn't see it, she imagined his expression was probably both amused and slightly terrified. It made her laugh. A deep, belly-aching laughter that made her double over to catch her breath.

Nicolás stepped toward her. "Are you okay?"

"Y-yes." She wheezed through more laughter. "I think my adrenaline is in overdrive."

"I don't think I've ever witnessed anything like that in my life." His voice was muffled by the mask. "I'm actually worried about Becky now."

"Don't worry." Lyla straightened, her lungs still hungry for air. She took a deep breath. "Becky's a correctional officer at a maximum security prison." She tried to wipe at the sweat beading on her forehead but forgot she had a mask on. "Are you going to try?"

"I'm enjoying watching you get your rage on."

"Nicolás, you didn't put on that silly outfit just to stand there and watch." Swinging the bat to her shoulder, she put a hand on her hip. "Imagine

305

your worst enemy." He stood there, and she imagined the frown tugging his brows together. "Saturated fats."

"They are the silent killer." Nicolás chuckled. "Okay, let's do this."

A new song came on. He lifted his crowbar and she lifted her bat, a toast before they spent the next thirty or so minutes demolishing everything they could in that room. By the time they were done, Lyla was a hot mess of sweat, exhaustion, and peace. *Definitely therapeutic.*

Outside their rage room, Lyla removed her helmet and set it in a bucket to be cleaned. She caught her reflection in a window. Ew. Half her hair was matted to her forehead and the other half was sticking out all over the place. She pulled her hair free of the elastic band in an attempt to fix it but stopped when she saw Nicolás.

Seriously? She watched him step out of his coveralls, shirt damp with perspiration as it stretched over his broad shoulders. He ran a hand through his hair, which was mussed up just perfectly, before covering it with his baseball cap. His eyes met hers and a warmth slid through her, leaving her feeling a bit heady.

"Everything okay?"

"Yeah." Lyla walked to the water cooler in the hallway and grabbed a paper cone cup. She filled it with cold water, drank, and filled it again. "I was just, um, thinking it wasn't fair that I came out of there looking like Clifford the Big Red Dog licked my head. And you pop a baseball cap on your head and suddenly you're MLB's poster boy."

Lyla dropped the cup into the trash can and started to fix her hair, but those sore muscles she'd ignored were now having their own rage party. She winced.

Nicolás closed the distance between them, his gaze tracking the movements of her hand as she attempted to pull her hair back. He reached for a piece near her ear, his fingertips tickling her skin, and helped her brush it back.

"Ponytails are my specialty."

Lyla handed him her ponytail holder and let him work his hands through her hair, gathering it back like he had the night before. Except this time, the feel of his touch, the closeness of his body behind hers caused a chill to skirt over her skin and brought the thudding in her chest to her ears. An awareness fired up inside of her at the intimacy of the moment, and she was left with the sudden realization that his tenderness was filling a space in her heart that hadn't been filled before.

Nicolás stepped back when he was done, and when he walked around to face her, she noticed the worry in his eyes.

"What?" She looked at his hands as he stretched out his fingers. "Is it your hand? Are you still feeling numbness?" Without thinking, she grabbed his hands in hers and began massaging his fingers and the palms of his hands. "How's that?"

His Adam's apple moved a few times before he answered. "Um, yeah, thanks." His thumbs traced lightly over her knuckles before he tipped his head to the side and his eyes moved to her hair. "I may have overstated my expertise."

"I'm sure it's fine." Lyla laughed. Reaching back, she felt the bumps of his attempt, but at least no loose pieces were hanging out. "Thank you for trying."

Nicolás pulled off his cap, adjusted the back, and then carefully slid it on her head. "Better."

It was. Not the hat, but the way Nicolás's attention seemed to shift everything inside her, causing what she thought she knew about her feelings for the man standing inches away from her to blur. Somehow the way he was tending to her, watching her, didn't feel like an annoyed attempt to cage her in. It was more.

Her heart continued thundering in her chest. *How much more?*

Lyla let that question simmer in her mind until they were walking out the doors of Make Rage, Not War. She paused outside his truck. "Thanks for doing this, Nicolás."

"It was fun." He half smiled, but it looked like he was holding back.

His silent struggle with whatever was on his

mind was making her nervous. "Why are you leaving?"

"That was the other reason I suggested we leave the office—so we could talk."

Lyla narrowed her eyes on him. "You brought me to a rage room to talk?"

"I figured that if I ticked you off, I'd pay for another hour so you could hit something else." He shrugged. "Seemed like a smart idea until I saw what you could do with that bat."

Ugh. Did he realize how charming his modesty was? And why hadn't she paid attention to that before? Why had she waited until he announced he was leaving to see Nicolás for who he was? *Because I thought he'd always be there.*

Lyla silenced the painful truth and asked him again when they were back in the truck. "Why *are* you leaving?"

Nicolás didn't speak for a few minutes until they were back on the road. "When I joined the Army, it was the first time I'd ever seen my father cry. He was so proud, and I realized that it was as important to him as it was to me, and I threw it all away because I dropped my guard and didn't consider the risks of my choices."

Lyla shifted in her seat, his words feeling like a chastisement. From the set of his jaw, she knew they weren't directed at her, though. "What happened?"

"My last deployment to Afghanistan, my buddy

309

Chad and I were on the same explosives team. Chad is charismatic, adventurous, fun, the life of the party, and like you, never shied away from risks. We got called out to a convoy that had gotten ensnared between IEDs. I took the rear one, and Chad took the front one. I knew right away something on the device was different, including a single wire that, if clipped, would set it off. But before I could get the message to Chad—it was too late."

Emotion balled in Lyla's chest. Her hand reached for his forearm, her fingers wrapping around the muscles bunching there for several seconds. She wanted to take away the pain she could see him struggling to control, but words weren't strong enough to convey how much she was hurting for him and with him.

After a few minutes, Nicolás cleared his throat. "Chad came home a double amputee, and I came home riddled with guilt. Chad returned to his wife, Tara, and a life of rehabilitation. I returned to . . ." He swallowed. "A woman I had hoped to marry."

An undeniable zing of jealousy wrapped itself around her heart and yanked it to the pit of her stomach. She pulled her hand back, pretending to wipe a nonexistent piece of fuzz off her jeans. It wasn't that Lyla thought Nicolás hadn't had girlfriends. He was pretty much the whole package. His quiet thoughtfulness and unexpected acts of kindness often revealed how much he knew about someone and about what they needed. It also didn't hurt that he was attractive. But it stung to hear that he'd been ready to marry.

"How come it didn't work out?" Lyla hoped her question didn't come off as nosy. She wasn't necessarily excited to hear the details of his relationship, but the evolving feelings swirling in her heart demanded she understand whether her growing affection was born out of fear for his decision to leave or was something deeper she'd been refusing to acknowledge.

"When I returned home from the deployment, I could tell something was off. I expected some distance. Deployments are hard, but so is the readjustment period. After a few weeks, nothing was getting better. One night Brittany explained that after witnessing what Tara had gone through when Chad came home, she couldn't do it. Couldn't accept the risks that came with the job—with me."

Lyla wanted to say something rude about Brittany for her stupidity, but a small voice echoed that if Brittany had been smart, Nicolás wouldn't be here. "Wait, did you leave the Army because of her?" A plot to meet this girl and give her a piece of her mind was already forming in her head until Nicolás shook his head and answered with a quiet no.

311

"After we broke up, I buried myself in the job. I volunteered for a training exercise about a year later, stayed up almost forty-eight hours in the field. The promotion list came out, and when I got back, a couple of my friends and I went out to celebrate." Nicolás stared out the windshield. "I was still upset about Brittany and decided a couple of beers might help numb the pain. It didn't and I drove home, but a block in I could feel the effects of the fatigue and alcohol, so I pulled over to sleep it off. Woke up an hour later to a police officer at my window. I received a DUI that was reported to my commander. I had just finished my obligation to the Army, so he gave me the option to leave, or I could stay and take the Article XV that would've ended my time as an EOD officer immediately and haunted me the rest of my career."

Lyla's heart squeezed in her chest. "I'm so sorry."

Nicolás backed into a parking spot in the Acacia Building parking garage and shut off the engine. "I admire Chad's boldness." He faced her. "Yours too, but it's hard for me not to assess the consequences of risk and decide which risks are worth it."

Which risks are worth it? Those words reminded her of what Mason had said, *She has someone she loves enough to know when not to cross that line.* Lyla looked up into Nicolás's bright hazel gaze and her heart pounded. New feelings were muddling a line she'd set up between her and him, and now . . . *Now* her pulse was pounding in her ears, her breath caught somewhere in an exhale she wasn't willing to release because the risk of exploring what she was feeling for Nicolás felt like a line she shouldn't cross—but wanted to.

Honk!

Their attention jerked to the car idling in front of them and Jack's goofy grin. Lyla was going to kill him. She caught Nicolás sending him a look that said the same thing. Nicolás slid out of the truck, and Lyla grumbled as she got out too.

Jack rolled down the driver's-side window. "Walsh is upstairs, waiting for you both."

"Thanks, man." Nicolás shoved his keys into his jeans pocket. "You good?"

"Birthday dinner for Nonna." Jack looked over at Lyla. "You feeling better?"

"I *was*."

Jack winked and started to drive toward the exit. "Stay out of trouble, you two."

Lyla's cheeks flamed with heat. She had no idea what the situation must've looked like to Jack, but now she'd be contending with his teasing, and if he told Brynn . . . She sighed. There would definitely be a phone call in her future that would require an explanation Lyla wasn't sure how to give. Maybe talking out these feelings with Brynn would be good. She probably understood better than most, but for now Lyla needed to convince Walsh to let them continue their investigation.

25

Nic had hoped his pulse would've slowed by the time he and Lyla reached the office, but a new kind of nervousness washed over him as he prepared to face his boss, the man who was like a second father to Lyla.

Something had shifted between him and Lyla today. He couldn't exactly name it, but he felt it. And for half a second, while sitting in the truck together, he'd actually considered kissing her. It was an action he'd normally consider extremely risky, if it hadn't been for the look in her eyes that made him believe she wasn't thinking of the consequences either.

The heat of that moment was still radiating heavily in his chest as they entered the office. He didn't have time to address his feelings or what happened before Lyla was halfway through Walsh's door.

"Sir, Nicolás and I wanted to brief you on new information we discovered about what Jerry Miller might've been involved with—information that could possibly support his sister's suspicion that he didn't kill himself."

"Jack informed me of your findings." Walsh gestured to the chairs in front of his desk and they both sat. "I'll tell you what I told him. The assignment is on hold."

Lyla's hands flexed over the edge of her seat, and Nic could nearly feel the shuddering tension moving between her and Walsh. "Why?"

Walsh leaned back in his chair, and Nic was surprised by his relaxed state. Did he not know he was poking the bear? Nic almost considered excusing himself to grab some chocolate from Kekoa's office just in case.

"I understand the information you're gathering seems"—Walsh's brow furrowed as he searched for the right words—"indicative of a larger plot involving Jerome Miller, but I've spoken with the warden, and Jerry killed himself. There's no question. As far as what this reporter is telling you . . ." He took off his glasses and rubbed the bridge of his nose. "She's a conspiracist. Her stories sell because she takes bits and pieces of the headlines and fills in the blanks with her own version of the truth."

"Not her version," Lyla said. "We've looked into her articles and compared them to facts Kekoa pulled up on Ammar El-Din, Colthorpe, and Narek Grigoryan. All of them are claiming the same thing—someone in the US is connected to the gun smuggling, counterfeiting, and money laundering. It goes back several decades. Jerry might not have been murdered, but I believe it's all connected. If we want to prove it's not conspiracy, then we need to keep digging."

Walsh's posture shifted, barely noticeable, but

Nic caught the tightening near his eyes, the way his Adam's apple moved, and the downward tilt of his chin as his neck muscles stiffened. "It's not our job to investigate conspiracy theories."

"Are you serious?" Lyla's shoulders bunched. "Half of what we investigate is based on suspicion of unlawful plots against people, companies, and the government. This is no different."

"It is, Lyla. We look into every request before we accept any assignments." He slipped his glasses back on, his posture stiff. "All this started with Jerome Miller. He's dead. Whatever connections he may or may not have had with these other individuals are of no consequence."

"No consequence?" Lyla looked at Nic. "There's been a consequence at every turn. First Jerry, then Genevieve. Nicolás and I were attacked. Someone took shots at me on my grandparents' property. All this because of a flash drive that could've compromised our agency's computer network but led us to Ammar El-Din. A man who was smuggling counterfeit money and is also connected somehow to a shoot-out in London where an American named Connor Murphy was killed. A man who might've been CIA."

Walsh's gaze cut to him. "Connor Murphy."

Was he asking a question? Or asking for confirmation that he'd heard Lyla correctly? Something told Nic the name wasn't unfamiliar to Walsh, and a quick glance at Lyla said she was waiting for him to have her back. "Sir, an Irishman named Eamon Flannery, a member of the Real IRA, began working as an informant for MI5, providing information about the weapons and cash being smuggled in and out of Ireland. There was a shoot-out in London that he claims killed two members of the Real IRA."

"And he's saying one of them is CIA?"

Nic slid a look at Lyla and exhaled. "No, R.D. Leto's article claims that."

Walsh's hardened gaze turned slowly to Lyla, and Nic instantly grew uncomfortable. "There's no longer reason for you or anyone else"—his eyes flickered to Nic and then back to Lyla—"in this agency to continue moving forward on this matter. This journalist has found someone else to feed her conspiracies to, and it's time we move on to other assignments that need our attention. Let the police do their job, Lyla."

"And what if I decide to keep following the leads?" Lyla folded her arms, chin up. "I'm not willing to so easily dismiss Genevieve's death or the threat against my life just because the source of our information doesn't suit you."

Walsh didn't back down from Lyla's threat. "You'll find yourself behind a desk and your security clearances revoked. There are rules and procedures in place for the protection of the agency, the team, and our clients. If you have difficulty controlling your impulsivity, there will be no leniency."

The tension was crackling in the air around them. Nic knew he needed to get Lyla out of there before she said something she would regret.

"Thank you for your time, sir." Nic stood, and he was glad when Lyla did too. Maybe she was going to accept the directive—but she didn't move when he started for the door. "Lyla—"

"If this had been Jack or Kekoa or Nicolás, would you be pulling them from the assignment?"

Walsh rubbed his forehead. "What?"

"I'm not a child, Tom. I've been doing this job for nearly as long as Jack, and I'm standing here with information to support the theory that Jerry's death is related to a larger plot involving the United States, yet suddenly it's not enough. Or maybe it's me? Maybe I'm not good enough to be trusted."

"That's enough."

Nic had never heard Walsh raise his voice like that. Especially not to Lyla. There was concern in the severity coloring Walsh's eyes, but it was the shadow of fear lingering beneath it that had Nic concerned there was something more. Something Lyla was missing because of her own defiance, even though he noticed her rigid posture had softened, her arms dropping to her sides.

"You believe you're treated differently from the rest of the team, and that's true," Walsh said.

"I've given you more chances than I would any of them when it comes to the way you do your job. Your instincts are good, Lyla, but there's no denying the risk you take when you disobey instructions."

Nic swallowed. A strange desire to step in and protect Lyla, defend her, came over him, but he didn't know why. Walsh wasn't saying anything that wasn't true or that she didn't need to hear, but he wanted to shield her from the painful truth for some reason.

Walsh's gaze suddenly looked tired. He inhaled slowly and released the breath. "There comes a time when the Lord directs us to stand still and trust even when our instincts—even when the crisis—lures us to act." He looked at Lyla. "I'm asking you not to become impatient. And don't let fear trick you into retreating. Stand firm." His gaze landed on Nic. "Don't presume that being still means nothing is happening. God didn't call his people to step into the Red Sea until it was parted."

A second or two passed before Lyla swiveled on her heel, barely meeting Nic's eyes before marching out. Nic gave Walsh a quick nod before he followed after her. He caught Kekoa peeking up from his desk, a look of worry passing between him and Lyla as he watched her leaving the fulcrum.

Nic jogged to catch up. "Lyla, are you okay?"

"He used God, Nicolás." She stormed out of the office and jammed her finger on the elevator button. "How am I supposed to argue against God?"

"You don't." The doors opened and Lyla stepped in, with him following behind her. "You wouldn't win anyways."

Lyla let out a soft huff of a laugh before leaning back against the elevator as it took them to the garage. She looked up, and a single tear rolled down her cheek.

Without thinking, Nic brushed his thumb against the curve of her face, and she turned into his touch, pressing into his palm. Beneath long lashes, the emotion of what had taken place turned her eyes greener and appealed to his senses to bring back the light missing in them.

"Chocolate."

Lyla blinked, straightening. "What?"

"You need chocolate. Yes?"

She half smiled and sniffled, wiping beneath her eyes. "Does anyone say no to chocolate?"

Nic started to open his mouth, but Lyla put a finger to his lips.

"Nope." The elevator door opened. "You don't get to be a health freak tonight, Nicolás. Tonight you're going to tap into your inner teenager and consume copious amounts of chocolate with me."

Nic smiled against her finger, and Lyla arched a brow. "My inner teenager didn't eat chocolate."

"Copious. Amounts." Lyla exited the elevator and called back over her shoulder, "I will not wallow in my defeat all by myself tonight."

Nic swirled another strawberry into the pot of chocolate, caramel, and pecans before setting it on the plate in front of Lyla. He groaned when she set a skewer holding a marshmallow and a banana chunk covered in dark chocolate on his plate.

"Just because there's a banana doesn't mean it's healthy."

Lyla forked the strawberry into her mouth. "We're not talking about healthy eating, Nicolás. And if we are, dark chocolate is supposed to be good for you."

Nic bypassed the marshmallow and cut the piece of banana in half before he ate it. The fondue restaurant was nearly full of families and couples enjoying the interactive dining experience. He hoped the fun atmosphere was easing Lyla's frustration from the meeting with Walsh.

"How are you feeling?"

"My muscles are sore." Lyla rolled her neck, massaging the back of it with her hand. "And I'm still frustrated with Walsh."

Nic rubbed his hands down his legs, trying to rid them of the tingling sensation. Lyla watched him as he lifted his hands and set them on the table.

"Are you still having numbness from the concussion?"

"It's getting better."

Lyla took his hands in hers and massaged them, her touch triggering an awareness in his middle. "Have you gone back to see Dr. Patel?"

"When would I have done that?"

She released his hands with a laugh. "I don't know. I'm sure there's been like two minutes when you haven't been watching me like a hawk so I don't get into trouble."

"Keeping you from that desk job you love so much."

"Ugh. The worst." She popped another strawberry into her mouth. "Is that why you're really leaving? Not enough action, have to get in the field and get your hands all tangled up in wires?"

She was teasing, but there was a glimmer of emotion in her eyes that tickled the back of his throat. "I think it's time for me to move on."

"You say that, but I thought you loved working for the agency. I mean, who else is going to force leafy greens down Kekoa's throat?"

The sentiment building in his chest was getting hard to avoid, especially when she looked at him the way she was now.

"There's more to it, Nicolás. I can see it in your eyes. Why are you really leaving? Why now?"

The answer—the truthful answer—was lodged in his throat. Telling Lyla he was leaving because

323

working with her was more than his heart could handle would be like lighting a short fuse, and he wasn't willing to leave Walsh, Jack, or Kekoa there to clean up the mess.

"Working here was an answered prayer, but it's beginning to feel like I need to move on."

"Move on to where?" Her voice cracked. "We need you here. I . . . I know Jack and Kekoa feel the same way. Our team won't be the same. What you do is—"

"Isn't working," Nic finished for her. "Not anymore. I'm no longer confident in what I can offer the agency, and that becomes a liability to what we do here."

Lyla reached across the table and placed her hand back on his. "Nicolás, you don't really believe that, do you?"

He wanted to avoid her eyes, the way they seemed to find that space in his heart that at some point had reserved itself for her, but he couldn't. They pulled at him with magnetic force, and it made him want to lie . . . or maybe tell her the truth. Instead, he went with what was easier.

"There's no room for doubt in our field, Lyla. You were right to call me out on it. I needed to trust you, but I let doubt cloud my judgment. That can be just as deadly."

"But we talked about that, remember? We said we were both going to work on working together. You trusting me more and me not running into risk like the Lone Ranger." She smiled. "Remember?"

He did. But that didn't stop the doubts from continuing to linger, especially after everything that had happened since that conversation. Lyla was trying, but was he setting her up to meet expectations beyond who she was? Was that fair? Risk was the name of the game in their career, and he wanted to trust that she'd consider the dangers before she made a decision. But if she didn't—then what? Would he care for her any less? Hurt any less if something went bad?

"Is it me?"

Her words made him refocus, and he swallowed over the dryness in his throat. "What?"

Lyla pulled back her hand. "The reason you're leaving. The reason you doubt yourself. It's me. You don't trust yourself because of me. I'm the reason?"

A single second of hesitation on his part, and her eyes filled with so much hurt it felt like a knife through his chest. *Tell her she's wrong.* But he couldn't. Because she wasn't. Not entirely.

26

Tom pulled out of the Acacia Building's sub-terrane garage and onto M Street. Frustration laced with growing concern had his stomach clenched in a twisted knot of anger. He wasn't angry at Lyla. She was right. Under ordinary circumstances, they would most definitely continue the investigation into the claims being made by Ammar El-Din and Roger Colthorpe. And most certainly by Eamon Flannery.

But these aren't ordinary circumstances.

And he couldn't have her looking into something he'd been protecting for decades.

Tom dialed the number and prayed he could stay one step ahead of Lyla. The fire in her eyes when he told her to drop the assignment was a mixture of confusion and hurt. But there was also that familiar spark, reminding him she wasn't one to back down. He hoped sharing the message his pastor had delivered on Sunday would reach Lyla, or at least give Garcia a fighting chance to convince her to be still—trust.

"Answer the call." His voice echoed back to him as the ringing sound continued. "Come on, Bob."

Tom didn't know if this was the right call to make, but he needed to know if what Lyla had found was . . . intentional.

He drove past the National Mall, normally his favorite part of leaving work, but this evening the streetlights filled his car with an ominous flickering glow. Maybe he should've called the FBI, found out what they were doing to find the person responsible for Genevieve's murder and the attack on Lyla and Garcia. Or pressed Kekoa harder to find the journalist behind the articles— stirring the pot.

Connor Murphy.

Hearing his name come out of Lyla's mouth had nearly stopped his heart. It took every ounce of self-control not to react, because if she saw it, even caught the slightest hint that the name meant anything to him . . . everything would be for nothing.

The call clicked, and Tom glanced down to see that it had been answered.

"I had a feeling this call was coming." Bob Perkins's voice cut into the car and jarred Tom from his thoughts. "Should've known it wouldn't come during office hours."

Tom snickered. "Office hours are for bankers."

Bob sighed. "I should've chosen my profession more carefully."

Bob Perkins was division chief for the CIA, but Tom knew him when they were lowly intel analysts. At least until their assignment in Ireland went south and decisions were made and lives were changed.

Tom circled back to Bob's words. "You were expecting a call from me?"

"I just got off the phone with the station chief in Belarus who informed me that they discovered the dismembered body of a Lebanese man. A man who was in prison a week ago. A man who has suddenly garnered a lot of attention for a conversation he was recorded having with an American journalist a few weeks ago."

Tom clenched his teeth. "Ammar El-Din."

"When we learned your team was looking into him, I figured you'd call. My question is why were you looking into him, and what do you know about his unexpected death?"

"What makes you think we know anything?"

"Come on, Tom." Bob laughed, but there was no humor in it. "Your team is good, but their work doesn't go unnoticed no matter what your cyber techie thinks. From the second he proved NSA was weak, those guys won't let him step out of the house without someone keeping tabs on him."

Agitation clawed across Tom's skin. "Are you telling me we're under surveillance?"

"No. I'm telling you that your agency, while beneficial to the overall welfare and security of the American people, doesn't get to probe into characters like this El-Din and not expect red flags to pop up. We're all working toward the same goal here."

"We can agree on that." Tom was still rattled by Bob's off-the-cuff remark that his team might be being monitored. He'd check into that, but right now he needed different answers. "But I'm not calling about Ammar El-Din. I figured his life span became limited when he gave that interview to R.D. Leto." He flipped on his blinker. "What do you know about Eamon Flannery?"

The sound of a keyboard clicking filled the car, followed by Bob's familiar humming that he did when he was reading. "Eamon Flannery was arrested in Belfast for his role— Tom, what's this about?"

"Eamon Flannery was running the Real IRA when we were there, Bob. He was arrested for the Omagh bombing, and his name came up in an investigation my team was running."

"What kind of investigation?"

"Oh, you know, just weapons trafficking, money laundering, smuggling counterfeit super-notes."

"Bah." Bob snorted. "That all?"

"A journalist published an article after interviewing a man identifying himself as Michael O'Sullivan, who says he was an informant for the CIA. I was there and I know who our informants were, but this guy has details about what took place in London with Connor. I need to know if our assignment back in Omagh has come back to life."

"*My* assignment in Omagh was put to bed." Bob sighed. "You left the light on when you went back of your own accord."

"I had no choice."

"I know you believe that, and I wish the outcome had turned out better, but that wasn't a sanctioned CIA operation."

Tom's chest ached with the painful memory as if he were back there all over again. The stench of smoke and gasoline filling his lungs as his friend's blood stained his hands.

Flexing his fingers over the steering wheel, he had to keep his promise. "I'm not asking you to break any rules, Bob. I know everything is black and white to you." Tom pressed his lips closed, hating the bitterness in his tone. "I just need to make sure the file on what happened in London . . . *doesn't exist.*"

A few seconds passed until Bob muttered something Tom wasn't sure he wanted to decipher. "It's a redacted file—no names, no details. If this O'Sullivan guy has something, it's because he was there."

"Can we find that out?"

"You said your team is investigating this?"

Tom exhaled. "You mentioned my team is being watched."

"Tom, you know every inquiry made into our nation's security is going to be monitored. I know your agency has the ability to skirt around the red tape that hems most of us in because we have rules to follow and congressional boards to answer to. If your team has looked into any person or group the rest of us have eyes on, it's going to get attention."

"Which is why I'm giving you our intel." *And keeping my team safe.* Flashing orange lights warned Tom of road construction ahead, and he slowed down. "I've asked my team to stop their investigation, and I can send you our file."

"And why would you do that?"

"To make the CIA look good." Tom smiled to himself. "And because it's personal."

Bob groaned. "You know this quid-pro-quo thing never works in my favor. Always adds more work to my life."

"If you didn't love it, you'd already be on that boat of yours."

"My wife points that out every morning when I roll out of bed."

The GPS suggested an alternate route, and Tom took the exit to avoid a construction zone on the turnpike. A beep echoed, indicating an incoming call from Special Agent Bailey Hutchins with the Secret Service. "Bob, I have to take a call, but I appreciate your help on this."

"Capitals tickets. Two."

Intel always had a price. "I'll see what I can do."

"Tell Lyla they're for my grandson's sixteenth birthday."

"Good night, Bob." Tom ended the call and knew Lyla didn't need to be coerced into getting tickets to a hockey game for Bob. He answered the incoming call. "Hey, Bailey."

"Hello, sir," the young man answered. "I'm sorry to call so late, but I have the information you asked for."

"Go ahead."

"The details around Eamon Flannery's arrest are correct. He was caught at the Belfast airport carrying a bag with more than a hundred thousand in supernotes. He claims he didn't know they were fake, but Interpol was tipped off when Flannery was tracked entering the North Korean embassy.

"What's interesting is that three men were arrested this morning at the Miami airport after they were stopped by Homeland Security agents. The agents discovered nearly half a million dollars in supernotes hidden across four suitcases."

"Coming into the country or leaving?"

"Heading to Colombia, but the men are Venezuelan and claim they are humanitarians bringing money to help the Venezuelan and Colombian citizens caught in the violence at the border."

"Where'd they get the money from?"

"They don't have a name." Bailey's frustration was evident in his tone. "They flew to America from Bogotá, were given directions to a hotel and a room key. They arrived to find the suitcases already packed with clothes and toiletries, along with instructions to head to Arauca once they returned home."

"Let me guess—no name, just a location, right?"

"Yes. I've been told the CIA has field officers heading to the location and will be running aerial surveillance as well. They're also looking into all American travelers who've entered the country in the last forty-eight hours."

Tom frowned. "American travelers?"

"All three men said it was an American man who sought them out. Paid them cash, provided them with their passports and tickets to Miami."

"All of them are claiming the same thing— someone in the US is connected to the gun smuggling, counterfeiting, and money laundering."

Lyla's words rang loudly in his ears. Tom needed to make another phone call to Bob. Military weapons trafficking, money laundering, counterfeit supernotes . . . if someone in the US was connected to this, they had a broad reach. Especially if they were securing passports for foreigners.

Tom pulled up to a light. "Bailey, keep me updated on this. I'm going to have Kekoa pull surveillance footage from the airports, and I'll get in touch with Richard Vale."

"I've already spoken with him, sir," Bailey said. "About an hour and a half ago. I got caught in a meeting, which is why I didn't call you with the information right away."

"That's no problem. I'll reach out to Bob Perkins and update him."

Ending the call, Tom drummed his thumb against the steering wheel. He hated to do it, but he pressed Bob's number again.

This time Bob answered after the second ring. "I would like to go home, Tom."

"It might be a long night." Tom hit another red light at the next intersection and groaned. Maybe he should head back to the office himself. He didn't imagine he'd be getting any sleep anyway. "I just got off the phone with Special Agent Hutchins, and I think there's a bigger issue we're facing."

Tom looked over to his left to see if he could change lanes when the light turned green, but a car pulled up. The driver made eye contact, and a vise tightened around Tom's gut. Before he could hit the gas, the man pulled out a gun and fired.

27

"Nicolás, say something."

He dragged his hand down the side of his face, trying to find the words, but all he could think of was the truth. She at least deserved that. "Yes, Lyla, it's partly because of you, but not in the way you're thinking." The hurt on her face was devastating. "Over the last four years, I've come to admire your relentless desire to fight the atrocities of the world, but sometimes I wonder if you do it at the detriment of your safety because you don't realize"—he took a breath—"what it would do to those who love you if something happened to you."

Her brow dipped into a *v* as she took in his words. Nervous energy bounced through him. He rewound the words in his mind . . . had he said he loved her? Sort of? Not clearly, but—

"I don't think I've ever considered that."

Nic smiled. "Because that's not who you are, Lyla."

"But I'm trying to be different, so you don't have to worry and then you don't have to leave."

"That's the thing. Who you are is what makes you stand out above everyone else, Lyla. I've realized that I care way too much about you to stifle your pluckiness."

Lyla's lips tipped into a smile. "You think I'm plucky?"

"Among other things, yes."

Lyla's cell phone rang, and Nic's cheeks burned when he saw Mason's name and face appear on the caller ID.

"He's just a friend, Nicolás," Lyla whispered before she answered the call.

The reassurance should've made his peek at her phone less awkward, but it only caused his cheeks to flame hotter. Nic pulled out his wallet and paid for their dinner of chocolate and forced himself not to listen in no matter how much he found himself wanting to. He was not *that* guy. Then again, he never guessed himself to be the guy to confess feelings over a vat of molten chocolate either.

Nic peered into the nearly empty pot. What'd they put in there? Secret confession sauce?

Lyla's grip on his arm pulled his attention from the chocolate to the worry lines creasing her forehead. "Okay, yes. We'll meet you there."

"What's wrong? Is your family okay?"

The lines at the corners of her eyes softened. "My family is fine. That was R.D." Lyla was sliding out of the booth but caught the concern on Nic's face. "She's fine too but wants to meet us."

Relief washed through him, but it was momentary. "I thought she left?"

"So did I, but I guess she's still in town, and she used Mason's phone to call me. Told me she has something that can prove the US is involved in the weapons and counterfeiting."

Nic's internal alarm system was ringing loudly. "Lyla, Walsh directed us to stand down."

Outside the restaurant, Lyla put on her coat while walking to his truck. "Okay, so then take me home."

He didn't need to see the daring look on her face to know she was being facetious. "I thought you're staying at Jack and Brynn's?"

"Now, why would I need to stay there?" She climbed into his truck when he opened the door for her. "Walsh says the assignment is over, which basically means the threat against me and my family is over too. I can go home now because there's no reason to keep investigating into the person or persons who attacked us . . . right?"

Nic's hand fisted over the brim of his cap. How did he counter that? And there was no way he was dropping her off anywhere, because the second he did, he knew she'd head straight out to meet R.D. anyway.

"What if this is a trap?"

Lyla pulled out her phone. "Call the number back and talk to R.D. yourself. If you think she's being used and it's a trap, then we won't go."

The muscles in his neck bunched because he'd walked right into the trick. He palmed her phone, and she hit the button to call Mason back. It rang. And rang. After the fifth one, it went to voice mail.

He handed the phone back. "No answer."

If he thought that would prove his point, the arch in Lyla's brow said otherwise. "Maybe she's in trouble."

"Maybe she *is* trouble." Walsh's words about presumption leading them to jump in when they should wait played through Nic's mind. "Lyla, we don't know why Walsh asked us to stop looking into this, but I think we can safely assume he wouldn't do that without good reason."

"And I think *we* have good reason to assume we should at least check this out. Think about it, Nicolás, R.D. was skittish just like Genevieve was, and now Genevieve is dead. We can't let that happen to R.D. She asked us to help her disappear and then ghosted us, which means she didn't even want us to know where she was. And now suddenly she's calling me to come meet her? With proof that might help us convince Walsh to keep investigating? Don't you want to be able to head to Syria without worrying about someone coming after me?"

Nic eyed her and curled his lip. "Low blow, Fox."

Lyla's lips tipped up. "But it's the truth, right?"

Blowing out his frustration, Nic rolled his head back and stared up at the inky sky. *A plague of locusts right now would be awesome, God.* He waited. Looked around. No locusts.

Settling his attention back on Lyla and her relaxed posture that said she could wait him out all night if she had to was both aggravating and bewitching. Worst of all—she knew it.

"Call Mason."

Lyla's posture stiffened. "What?"

"Call Mason and make sure R.D. has his phone. If they're together, then we can assume she's safe for now, which will give us time to call Walsh before we meet her."

"How am I going to do that if R.D. has his phone and she's not answering?"

"Call his house."

"I don't have his number." Then Lyla's face drained of color. "Please don't make me call the Davenports."

Nic worked to control the laughter that wanted to escape at the exaggerated horror on her face. "I'm not going in blind to meet up with a woman we barely know." The humor bubbling in his chest died down as his gaze roamed the healing wounds on her face. "I'm going to call Walsh, but I want you to confirm how R.D. got ahold of Mason's phone."

"Fine."

Nic left Lyla and her disgruntled mood to call Walsh, having no idea how he was going to convince him to let them meet up with R.D.

A quick glance back at Lyla made him smirk. She was rubbing her temple with her eyes closed, looking pretty miserable. He shouldn't take so much delight, but if she was going to get her way, he'd at least make her work for it.

The call to Walsh went to voice mail. Nic tried the office. Maybe he was still there. No answer. Should he try his home number? Nic checked his watch. It was barely after eight. He hated disturbing Walsh and his wife, Sam, at home, but he figured Walsh would want to at least know what Lyla was up to.

He hit the call button and listened to it ring several times. *No answer. Great.*

"I don't have good news," Lyla said when he came back. "Mason did give his phone to R.D. this afternoon when she had a friend from New York call him and they met up at the mall. Mason said she was scared but wouldn't tell him anything else."

Nic looked down at his phone. He really needed Walsh to pick up.

"Nicolás, I'm worried. I think we need to go meet her."

He was worried too. About R.D. Lyla. What Walsh would do when he found out. *Desk jobs.* Might not be such a bad thing for Lyla . . . if they could keep her behind one.

"Okay, let's go." Nic shut the door and went

around his truck. "Lord, the Red Sea needs parting."

Thirty minutes later, Nic and Lyla were riding the escalator down to the L'Enfant Metro Station. A burst of warmer air greeted them, along with the smell of burned electrical wiring and oil. The squeal of brakes echoed from below as the Silver Line pulled in. Nic scanned the passengers riding the escalator up—the ones impatiently passing him on the left, the others who were in no rush whatsoever.

"Where are we supposed to meet her?"

"I don't know." Lyla's eyes were searching the faces around them. "She just said to meet here."

"What's she wearing?"

"I don't know."

"Did she give you a time?"

"Nicolás"—Lyla faced him, worried—"I don't know. She just said to come here and that she had something to prove her theory."

He put a hand on Lyla's back, and she leaned in so that her body was pressed against his. When he inhaled, he picked up the subtle scent of her shampoo and his heart reacted. Whether or not she returned his feelings, at least she knew the truth. He could leave knowing he'd been completely honest.

At the bottom of the escalator, they looked around. The Metro security booth was empty.

Passengers were moving through the turnstiles or purchasing tickets. Lyla looked around but shook her head. She pulled out two Metro cards from her wallet and handed one to Nic. They scanned them through the turnstile and headed toward the train platforms.

There weren't a lot of people down here, so it shouldn't be hard to spot her, except no one waiting for their train looked like R.D.

"Excuse me." A girl with bright purple hair shaved on one side, an earful of piercings, and dark lipstick tapped on Lyla's shoulder. "Can you tell me what time the next train is coming in?"

Nic eyed the girl's ripped jeans, combat boots, and green military fatigue jacket circa Vietnam and guessed her to be in her early twenties. Was she a threat? A distraction? Working IEDs in Afghanistan, that was the game. His attention moved to those around them, assessing anyone who might be the real threat.

Lyla pointed to the electronic sign. "Orange Line is coming in two minutes. Yellow in four."

"Thanks." The girl reached into her pocket, and Nic was already moving in front of Lyla when she withdrew a folded piece of paper. She gave Nic a dirty look. "I was told to give this to you."

Lyla took the piece of paper. "From who?"

The girl threw up a peace sign and walked away. "Peace."

"Was that R.D.?" Nic tracked the girl, who

had stuck an AirPod in her ear and was already halfway up the escalator. "Do we need to follow her?"

"No, that's not her." Lyla glanced around for a few moments before opening the paper. "It's a copy of a photo."

Nic glanced over her shoulder at a grainy image of three people—two men, one woman—talking outside of what looked like a large building. The photo was taken at a distance and there was something about it, the clothes or something, that made it look like it wasn't a recent shot.

Nic's phone vibrated in his pocket. He pulled it out, hoping it was Walsh. *Jack*. He answered but could barely hear Jack's voice before the call cut out. The bars on his phone indicated his service was bad.

"Do you know what the photo is?"

"No." Lyla shook her head and turned the page over. "Wait, she wrote something. 'Photo taken September '98, Tottenham, London.' Wasn't that where Connor Murphy was killed? The CIA officer?"

Nic's phone vibrated again. Jack. "Let's head back up. Jack's trying to call, but I can't hear anything he's saying."

"Okay." Lyla moved with him, only glancing up to look around again. "Do you think R.D. sent that girl just to deliver this to us?"

"Who knows." Nic was just grateful they were

leaving without an incident. He checked his phone again and answered the call as they rode the escalator up. "Hello? Jack?" But Nic couldn't make sense of the garbled, staticky words. "I'll call you back in one minute."

Nic hoped Jack had heard that and ended the call. He led Lyla off the escalator and heard his phone ping with a message. He opened it and felt the blood drain from his face. He looked over at Lyla, a knot in his throat. "It's Walsh."

Lyla nodded, not lifting her eyes from the photo in her hand. "Yeah, I know."

He frowned. How'd she know? And then he realized she was referring to the man she was pointing to in the photo. One of the men standing near the scene where a CIA officer was killed was their boss, Tom Walsh.

"Lyla." Nic swallowed and placed a gentle hand on Lyla's shoulder, causing her to look up. "It's Walsh. He's been shot."

28

"This is my fault." Lyla's voice was near frantic. "I did this."

Nicolás took her hand, his strong grip holding her shaking fingers steady as he sped toward the hospital where Tom was. What happened? Shot? By who? Why?

"This is why we shouldn't have stopped our investigation. This is why we needed to keep digging. There's no way he's going to convince me to back down now. He's—" Lyla sucked in a sob.

"He's in good hands, Lyla. Jack said the doctors here are some of the best."

Lyla nodded, wishing Nicolás's assurance would relieve the twisting pain inside her chest. She wiped beneath her eyes with the edge of her sweatshirt. "Tell me what they said again."

"Your mom or Jack?"

"Either." The shock of the news had overwhelmed her senses, and she couldn't remember what they'd said. Only the heartbreak in her mother's voice when she said to hurry. "Tell me what they said."

"Walsh was on his way home. The police think someone pulled up next to him and fired a single shot that entered his chest."

Lyla cringed at the image. The shock and confusion on Walsh's face. How long did he sit there before help arrived? Dying. *Lord, please don't let him die.* "This is my fault."

"Stop saying that, Lyla. It's not your fault. The police have no idea who did this or why. It could be completely random."

"Do you really believe that?" Nic's jaw muscle popped, and she had her answer. "Me either."

Nic pulled up to the front of the emergency room. "Do you want me to drop you off here or find a parking spot and walk in with you?"

Lyla squeezed his hand and didn't want to let go. "My parents are already in there with Sam." Her throat ached. "I'll meet you inside."

He nodded, and she opened the door to get out.

"Wait." Nicolás threw his truck into park and jumped out and came around the front. Before she knew what was happening, his arms were wrapped around her waist, drawing her to his chest. Her body heaved with emotion, causing tears to spill down her cheeks again. He massaged her back, then leaned down to whisper in her ear. "It's going to be okay, Lyla."

She hugged him tightly back, feeling like everything would be okay so long as she was here in his arms. The world was right. Tom was okay and Nicolás wasn't leaving. Sniffling, she backed out of his touch. She ran her hand down the side of his cheek.

"I'll see you inside."

Lyla entered through the emergency room and focused on the bank of elevator doors ahead of her. The sounds of machines beeping, children crying, and too-loud television sets made her skin crawl. She checked the map on the wall and located the ICU.

Inside the elevator she caught a glimpse of her reflection and the teary mess. She wiped at her eyes, wanting to be as strong as she could for her parents and Sam. Lyla's heart twisted at the agony Tom's wife must be going through.

The doors opened on the second floor, and two nurses stepped in. *Hurry up.* Lyla looked up at the digital numbers. When the doors finally slid open on the ICU floor, she nearly shoved past them to get to the nurses' station.

"I'm here for—"

"Lyla."

She turned to find her mom walking toward her, eyes rimmed red, arms open, and Lyla fell into them. For several minutes she let her mom comfort her the way only a mom could—by allowing her to cry and offering soothing tones that slowly calmed the storm raging in Lyla's chest.

"Where's Sam?" Lyla looked around her mom's shoulder to the small waiting room that was filled with other distraught family members. "Dad? How's he doing? What have the doctors said?"

"Shh, shh, honey." Her mother led her to a couch, where a pair of coats were hung on the back. "Sam and Dad are back with the doctor right now. Tom's in surgery to stop the internal bleeding."

Lyla took a shuddering breath and focused on the television, hoping to stay the tears at the edge of her lashes. After several deep breaths, she swallowed and looked at her mom. "How could this happen?"

"I don't know, honey, but the Lord is watching over him."

Nicolás's familiar form appeared in the hallway. Lyla started to wave him over when four more familiar faces stepped off the elevator. Jack, Brynn, Kekoa, and Elinor had showed up, and their presence filled her with so much gratitude that it made her start crying all over again.

Brynn and Elinor rushed over and hugged her. Mom hugged everyone else and gave them the same update she'd given Lyla.

Jack settled in a seat next to her mom. "Is there anything we can do, Mrs. Fox?"

"Just having you all here." Catherine dabbed at her eyes with a tissue. "It means so much to us and to Sam, and Tom. You all have really become the children they could never have."

The words couldn't have been any truer. Lyla knew how much Tom loved his job, but it was in large part due to the team he'd handpicked. Each of them—Jack, Kekoa, and Nicolás—meant something to him, and now Elinor and Brynn were part of that family.

Footsteps sounded behind them, and they turned to find her dad walking with his arm around Sam. Lyla ran to embrace them.

"What did the doctor say?"

"Lyla"—her father released her from a hug and put his hands on her shoulders—"Tom is a fighter. He's going to pull through this."

Sam's normally gentle features tightened. "The doctors are doing everything they can. They need to stop the internal bleeding and repair the damage from the bullet." She wrapped her arms around herself, and Lyla's mom gave her a side hug. "All we can do is pray."

"What about the doctors?" Lyla wiped her nose. "Who's the surgeon? Can we call—"

"Honey." Her father walked her toward the nurses' station. "I've called in every favor I can, and Tom has the very best working on him. Sam needs you to be strong, to pray, and to let the staff here at Mercy General do what they do best."

Lyla's gaze dropped to the linoleum floor. "I hate feeling helpless."

"Me too, honey." He kissed the top of her head before nudging her to look up. "I think Jack needs you."

Jack was standing next to Nicolás, a stern look on his face. She joined them.

"What's wrong?"

"I just got a call from Bob Perkins. He's the division chief of intelligence and foreign affairs for the CIA. He was on the phone with Walsh when he was shot. Said Walsh asked him to look into our investigation, specifically Eamon Flannery."

Lyla felt nauseated. Her eyes met Nicolás's, and she could tell he was thinking the same thing she was—*Walsh was working on the investigation.* Except . . . she remembered the face she recognized from the photo in her pocket. It was Walsh.

Someone in the United States is behind the weapons deals. Smuggling. Counterfeit money.

Certainly not Walsh. But then why was he in that photo? Who was he with? From the corner of her eye she saw Kekoa feeding dollar bills into a vending machine.

"Does he think the shooting might be related to the case?"

"Perkins received a phone call from Secret Service Agent Bailey Hutchins from the counterfeit division. He didn't give me all the details but said there was a recent development involving some men from Venezuela smuggling money into Colombia. CIA field officers set up a fake drop-off and tracked the money to an exchange point where a cache of US military-grade weapons was being purchased for the rebel forces."

Numbness washed over Lyla. "Just like in Ireland."

Nicolás raised his brows at her. He wanted her to tell Jack about the photo, but . . . she couldn't. She needed to think.

"I'm going to help Kekoa." She walked over to where Kekoa was gathering the salty and sweet treats he'd purchased. "Did you buy out the entire machine?"

"I didn't know what everyone might like." His answer came out bashful, but it was the stress weighing him down. "I can run out and get something better."

"Kekoa, this is really thoughtful of you." She scooped up the bags of M&M's and a bag of Cheetos Puffs and walked with him back to the sitting area. They set everything on the table, and Kekoa generously offered the items to a few of the other waiting families. "I'm going to get some coffee. Mom, Dad, Sam?"

Her mom nodded. "Thanks, honey."

"I'll help," Nicolás spoke up behind her.

There was a small room down the hall with coffee and tea available for family members. Lyla wrinkled her nose at the burnt smell and lost any hope that the coffee would taste good. She prayed it would at least be hot.

"Are you going to tell him?"

She started pulling Styrofoam cups out and filling them with coffee that steamed against the chilly hospital air. "Not until we know the context behind that photo."

"Lyla—"

"Tom—Walsh—our boss, was shot tonight. It feels like a nightmare I can't wrap my head around, and I have a photo in my pocket that might put Walsh at the scene of an arms deal gone bad. I can't." She released a shaky breath. "I just need a minute to process everything."

"I agree."

She frowned. "You do?"

"Lyla, I'm on your side." Nicolás took the cup of coffee out of her hand and set it on the table. Then he took her hands in his. "But I think we need to proceed with caution. We don't know why R.D. gave us that photo. The first thing we need to do is authenticate it and then identify the other people in it. I'm not saying we have to hand this over to the CIA, but we certainly need to let Jack know."

"I like that plan." Lyla breathed in deeply. "Thank you, Nicolás."

They stood there, unmoving, and a feeling she couldn't immediately identify pushed her to step forward. Her hands trailed up his arms to his biceps. Her breathing slowed as she met his eyes again before allowing them to move to his lips for just a second—but long enough for her to clearly recognize that the feeling blossoming inside her chest was more than attraction.

Movement outside the room stole Lyla's attention from Nicolás. Her father, Sam, and a woman with red hair walked by in a hurry. Was Tom out of surgery?

"Nicolás, I'll be right back."

"Go. I'll get the coffee."

Lyla stepped into the hallway and headed in the same direction she'd seen them walking. Ahead was a double door that required an authorized badge to enter. Had they gone in there? She heard her father's voice echo from a room off to the side. The sign on the door that was cracked open identified the room as the Nurses' Lounge. She edged closer and paused when she heard her name.

"Do you think they're coming after Lyla?"

Sam's question clearly wasn't for a doctor or nurse, but it didn't make sense for her to ask Lyla's dad. Her father worked with a few defense companies, but . . . Lyla edged closer but couldn't get a clear view of the redheaded woman.

"I don't know." Lyla cocked her head to the side at the sound of the female voice with a British accent. "But we can't rule it out."

"Why would they come after her now?" Her father's tone was sharper than she'd ever heard. "It's been twenty-five years!"

Twenty-five years? Who was coming after her?

"I don't know," the redhead answered. "My best guess is they're not, that all this is coincidence.

353

So long as we can keep her from finding out who Connor is—*was*—I know that's what Tom was trying to do."

"That's what we've all been trying to do," her father replied, and Lyla didn't like the sadness she detected. "All these years, and there's not a single second when I don't see her as my daughter."

Lyla stepped backward. *See me as his daughter?* Pushing the door open, she stared at her father, who lost the color in his face. Sam covered her mouth, eyes watering. The redheaded woman stood there, unflinching.

"What do you mean, not a second goes by when you don't see me as your daughter?"

"Lyla . . ." Her dad headed toward her, and she took one step back. He glanced at Sam, then to the redhead.

"Am I not your daughter?"

A tear streamed down her father's cheek. "You have always been my daughter."

His resolute answer unhinged something inside her, bolstering her to ask again. "Are you my biological father?"

A second ticked by, and he gave a tiny shake of his head. Everything in Lyla collapsed. She fought the tears, forcing herself to ask one more question.

"Mom?"

Her father wiped at his cheek. "No."

His voice came out in a hoarse whisper and Lyla backed up, moving down the hallway several steps before she turned, nearly running into Nicolás carrying two cups of coffee.

"Lyla, what's wrong?"

She shook her head, couldn't talk. She ran to the elevator and began pressing the button over and over again.

"Lyla, honey?"

She turned her head to see her mom—*no, not my mom*—coming toward her, and there must've been something in Lyla's expression that caused her mom to bring both hands to her mouth and shake her head as she began to cry.

Lyla couldn't take it. She spotted the exit sign leading to the stairs and ran toward it. Nicolás reached out, but she ignored his attempt to stop her. She had to get out of there, had to get away, had to breathe, had to figure out how her whole life had been a giant lie.

29

Nic walked into the SNAP HQ and breathed a sigh of relief when he found Lyla at her desk. Her back was hunched forward, her gaze intent on whatever was on the computer screen in front of her, and from the muted music, he guessed she had her earbuds in.

He didn't know what had happened at the hospital to run her off, but Jack had stopped him from chasing after her. Their work cell phones could be tracked, and Kekoa monitored her as she caught an Uber back to their office. It didn't stop Nic from being scared out of his mind that somewhere on the way someone might try to shoot her too.

And then Lyla's father explained briefly that Lyla had learned the truth that they were not her parents. At least not biologically—and that's all that was said.

But it was enough to crush the woman he'd fallen for.

Not wanting to scare her, Nic walked around the edge of the room. He was within a foot when she lifted her head.

"You don't have to skirt around me, Nicolás." She pointed at the security screen in the corner of the room without looking up. "You know the

356

monitor over there alerts us when someone walks through the door."

His shoulders relaxed but only for a second, because when she finally turned, he caught the sadness rimming her eyes.

"I can't find a single thing on Connor Murphy." She sniffled. "It's like he never existed outside of the report about his death."

"Is that . . . is he . . ."

"My father?" Lyla swiveled in her chair and stared at her screen. "I didn't stick around for that detail, but from what I overheard, my guess is yes. Connor Murphy—maybe CIA officer, killed at the scene of a botched arms deal, traitor to America—might be my father."

He proceeded with caution to make sure the words he spoke next reflected his respect for her feelings. The last thing he wanted was for her to think he was trying to excuse a situation he didn't fully grasp or explain away how she was feeling in this moment.

"I'm so sorry." He rolled his desk chair next to her and sat. "What can I do to help?"

"Help me find out who my parents are." She ran her hands over her head and released an exasperated cry. "You know, I had this feeling while growing up that I was too different—that something was wrong with me because I wasn't this calm, obedient child. Other people noticed it too." She shook her head. "Once when I was little, I overheard a woman say something to my grandmother about not being able to choose me. I had no idea at the time what she meant. Etta was quick to put that woman in her place and reassure me I was loved—but it stuck, ya know?"

The crack in Lyla's voice about did him in. He scooted his chair closer and swiveled her chair so their knees were touching, and he reached for her hands. "I have no idea what that woman was talking about, and I'm not trying to diminish your feelings, but I want you to know that over the years I've known you, hearing the way you talk about your parents and Etta and Tully, they adore you. Every part of you . . ." He swallowed, holding back.

"At least that explains my rebellious nature." She gestured to the photo R.D. had given to her. "I'm the child of a traitor. It's in my nature, I suppose."

There wasn't an ounce of self-pity in her tone. Just anger.

"Do you think that's why I'm so careless? Taking risks? Because I'm fighting my own DNA by trying to help people, fighting the bad guys when my own father was one of the bad guys." She blinked. "Or maybe I'm here as some sort of penance. Right the wrongs of my family tree."

"Lyla, we don't know anything about the man in that photograph, but I know you. Yes, you have a rebellious streak, but it's not necessarily a bad thing."

She sniffled. "Says the man denying he's leaving because of me."

Nic moved in, his fingers brushing her hair behind her ear before letting them trace her jawline to her chin, which he tipped up so their eyes met. "A rebellious nature is good when it's combating evil. When it goes against the Lord and his will, then it's not good. I have no idea why your parents didn't tell you the truth or how this involves Walsh, but can you sit here and tell me the devastated couple sitting back at the hospital doesn't love you with their whole hearts?"

Lyla's lips twisted into a silent no, and her eyes filled with tears.

"If you want my advice"—he raised a brow at her, and she offered a sad smile—"let Walsh and your parents explain before deciding to go antihero on us."

"Will Walsh . . ." She bit her lip, and Nic read the question in her anxious expression.

"They stopped the bleeding and are optimistic, but the next twenty-four hours are critical."

Lyla looked away, and Nic rose to his feet and pulled her up to him. She pressed herself against his chest, threading her arms around his waist in a desperate grip, like she was lost and needed something to anchor her. So he held her. Her body trembled with her crying, and it was almost more than he could bear. He pressed his lips to her head and prayed. For her. For Walsh. For her parents. For reconciliation. And for Lyla to believe she was loved—wholly and completely.

Lyla's crying slowed until it was just sniffles. Her voice vibrated against his chest. "I'd make a terrible antihero."

He smiled. "Yes, you would."

An alert echoed from the screen. Nic glanced up and saw that Jack, Kekoa, and the British woman had entered the office. He felt Lyla's body go rigid.

"Hey"—he tipped Lyla's chin up again—"she might have answers."

Lyla's jaw clenched, but she gave a nod before releasing her hands from his waist and wiping her eyes. She stepped back just as the others walked into the fulcrum.

"Walsh is resting," Jack said. "He's in a medically induced coma to give his body a chance to recover, and the doctors are hopeful."

"Thank you," Lyla said quietly.

"Hello, Lyla." The redhead took a tentative step forward. "My name is Sophie Bridges, and I'm with MI5. I'd like to explain why I'm here and maybe answer a few questions I'm sure you have."

Lyla walked to her seat at the conference table and sat. Kekoa grabbed his silicone keyboard from his office and took his seat as the rest of them followed suit. Ms. Bridges sat between Jack and Kekoa, opposite from Lyla.

"I'm very sorry for what's taken place tonight and for the way you've come upon information that I know Tom would've preferred you found out differently." The woman tucked her hair behind her ear, giving Nic a closer look at her. She was older than he'd first guessed, lines creasing her skin with age and likely stress from the years of working intelligence. "I've been given permission from MI5 to read you in on the 3 September mission that killed Connor Murphy."

Ms. Bridges continued to speak, and Kekoa's fingers tapped furiously on the keyboard to bring up the information she was talking about, but the woman's attention was locked on Lyla.

"Connor Murphy was the alias for an American named Sean Murphy. He had a wife, Annie, and was working undercover as a member of the Real Irish Republican Army, gathering intel about the violence being perpetuated by the paramilitary group. On 15 August 1998, a bomb killed innocent people in Omagh, Ireland. A fact"—she looked around the table—"you all probably already know. Annie was one of the victims."

Lyla reached under the table and took hold of Nic's hand. He gave it a reassuring squeeze.

"She was also pregnant." Ms. Bridges looked at Lyla. "With you. You were delivered safely, and one of the nurses, an informant for the CIA, was able to get you to safety and back to your father. I don't know what happened regarding the CIA's actions immediately following the bombing, but a few weeks later I ran into Tom in London. He was looking for your father and stubbornly interfering in an MI5 mission."

"Sounds about right," Jack mumbled, and Nic saw Lyla's lip curve upward for a second.

"Again, I don't have all the details about the CIA's role at that time or what it had to do with Tom and Sean, but my mission was to find out how the Real IRA was obtaining weapons, specifically US military-grade weapons. That day in London, Sean led us to a man named Rònán O'Hagan, who had organized the arms deal. But it was a setup—a fatal one. I don't know what Tom can tell you about Sean or if the CIA will give you any information. They're not usually forthcoming. But I'm here to tell you that without Sean's work and sacrifice, we would not have found Eamon Flannery, the leader giving the orders for the attacks against Irish and British forces, and many, many more lives would have been lost."

Ms. Bridges stayed still, apparently giving Lyla all she could, but would it be enough? Would Lyla see that her assumption—R.D.'s assumption—

was wrong? Sean wasn't a traitor. He sacrificed his life . . .

The truth hit him. Lyla was right. Her biological father's DNA was alive in her, only it wasn't in the rebellious, obstinate way that she'd imagined it to be. When she ran into danger, sacrificing her own safety for others, it was because that is exactly who God created her to be.

Nic felt her hand in his, and a cold realization washed over him. He was doing the same thing Brittany did. Leaving because he was afraid of Lyla's innate drive to protect at all costs. He'd called Brittany selfish for being unwilling to accept his calling to serve in the military. And while he wasn't asking Lyla to quit, he was expecting her to change—and that was selfish too. He didn't want her to be anything else. And the truth, the heart-pounding truth, was that he didn't want her to change. He had fallen in love with her . . . moxie.

I'm in love with her.

Jack cleared his throat. "I'm standing in as acting director until Walsh returns. I spoke with Director Bob Perkins, who is working on questioning the three men with Venezuelan passports detained at the Miami airport about their connection to the weapons seized by CIA field officers."

"Did they find who provided the weapons?" Nic asked.

"All Director Perkins would give me was that the expediter was moving the rifles according to the bill of lading from the vendor, and they're looking into who placed the order."

"That's it?" Lyla said. "How is that helpful to our investigation?"

"It's not, but"—Jack looked at Ms. Bridges—"MI5 is asking for our assistance."

Ms. Bridges leaned forward, putting her elbows on the table. "Before we ever made it into that warehouse, Sean insisted an outside source was providing the weapons to the Real IRA and that was why the trade was arranged. But we never got a name. We continued to investigate, but our leads kept dying, sometimes literally."

Nic's grip tightened on Lyla's hand, and she responded with a squeeze.

"We hoped when Eamon Flannery was arrested, he'd give us a name. He didn't, and we believe that's because he was continuing to use that source to keep soliciting weapons deals throughout Eastern Europe. It wasn't until Ammar El-Din was arrested and gave the interview about an American involved in the smuggling that we reopened our case. Tom said you were looking into someone calling himself Michael O'Sullivan, who claimed his identity was outed after working as an informant for the Real IRA."

They nodded.

"Well, his body was discovered yesterday morning. An overdose."

Kekoa was putting news articles on the screens overhead that supported everything Ms. Bridges was saying. Nic looked to Jack, wondering where this was going and what MI5 needed from them.

"Unfortunately, we won't be able to prove why O'Sullivan was killed, but our suspicions are that whoever was behind it is working furiously and lethally to keep their identity a secret."

"Every person who's claimed to know that person's identity has been killed." Lyla released Nic's hand. "Do you think Walsh knew?"

"We won't know until we talk to him," Jack said. "But that's why we're meeting tonight. We believe there was more on that flash drive than an article pointing to Ammar El-Din. Likely a name, or names, maybe even photos."

"But the drive was corrupt." Nic looked at Kekoa. "We have nothing."

"Whoever is coming after us doesn't know that."

Nic looked at Lyla, and his heart writhed at the fire lighting in her eyes. The horrible memory of finding her on the floor next to Genevieve's lifeless body came back. The pieces were adding up to a reality he didn't want to accept—one he believed Lyla had already committed to before it was even asked of her.

"You're going to lure them out with the flash

drive." He could feel everyone's gaze turn on him, but his focus was one hundred percent on the woman he could see steeling herself for what was coming next. "What are you asking her to do?"

"I've spoken with Director Perkins," Ms. Bridges said, "and he's going to work with Mr. Hudson's wife to start spinning chatter that your agency has a flash drive containing the names of those involved in the arms trafficking in Venezuela. MI5 is going to corroborate the story. The ATF is coordinating with your Department of Defense to release a memo to Diplomatic Security Forces about the weapons recovered in Venezuela."

"What we need Lyla to do"—Jack hesitated, his serious expression meeting Nic's—"is deliver the flash drive."

Nic's heart pounded. "To who? Where?"

Lyla's hand slipped beneath the table and found his again. Her touch was both reassuring and also crushing to his soul. Could he sit here and watch her take this risk? Would his heart be able to handle it if she was the one in the hospital? He shoved the awful thought away and focused on Jack's answer.

"President Lawson is offering his full support," Jack said. "He suggested setting up a principals meeting with his national security advisor, the secretary of defense, secretary of state, the director of Homeland Security, and Lyla to play up the ploy."

"And you think it'll work?"

Ms. Bridges nodded. "I'd be convinced."

"It will work," Jack said. "We need to go on the offense on this one, but I want us all to be in agreement."

Kekoa's eyes darted between Lyla and Nic before he gave a nod.

"I'm in," Lyla said.

Nic drew on faith he knew could only come from God, because if it was up to him, he'd list a thousand and one reasons why this was a bad idea. Beginning with the fact that he'd finally acknowledged he loved Lyla—all of her—and now it was time to confront the risk that love posed to his heart. He took a fortifying breath, looked her in the eyes, and said, "Let's roll, Stinkerbell."

30

Honey, why didn't you tell Tori you were going to pick up Anthony from his therapy class?"

Brooks froze midstride and nearly caused the Army captain behind him to run into him. "Pardon me." He pressed the cell phone to his ear, not sure he'd heard his wife correctly, and weaved his way through harried military and government personnel foot traffic to get to the Pentagon's outer corridor windows for his best chance at solid phone reception. "Lydia, what did you say?"

"I asked Tori to go by the school and pick up Anthony from his therapy class, but his teacher told her she saw you pick him up."

Panic pushed Brooks to move, but if he did he might not be able to get the details he needed. "Lydia, is Tori there?"

"Yes, why?"

"Honey, put her on the phone, please." Static filled his ear, and he ground his teeth. "Lydia, did you hear me?"

"Yes, hold on." A second later Tori came on the phone. "Hey, Daddy."

"Tori, baby, did Anthony's teacher tell you she saw *me* pick him up?"

"Uh, I don't know. I think so."

Gripping his cell phone, Brooks forced himself not to be short with her. "Try to remember. Did she say she saw him go with me or get into my car?"

As he waited for her to remember, a message pinged on his work phone. He almost ignored it until he saw the first part of the message.

We're at the school.

"I think she said she saw Anthony go to your car."

Brooks's throat grew raw with anger. "Okay, baby. Tell Mom I'll be home with Anthony soon."

"Okay," Tori said, her chirpy tone rivaling the dread coiled around his gut. Then she ended the call.

It was nearing four o'clock, and in Pentagon time that meant rush hour. With over twenty-three thousand employees working various hours, most began their commute home around three thirty, congesting the Metro, buses, and parking lots.

He had to get out of there. Had to get to Anthony. Pushing his way down the escalator, he tried to apologize and then stopped. He didn't have time. Cutting across the throng of people waiting for the slug line, he stepped up to the first car he saw and got in, ignoring the unkind comments from those behind him for breaking the carpool system's rules.

The driver was in an Air Force uniform and was looking at him like he was crazy or about to call the Pentagon police over.

Brooks pulled out his wallet and counted his money. "I'll give you three hundred and eighteen dollars if you take me to my child's school."

The airman hesitated.

"Please, the nurse called, and he fell at the playground, and they think he may have broken his arm."

A few more seconds passed, and Brooks was about to get out of the car and commandeer the next one when the driver shrugged. "Okay, but I don't talk."

Fine by him. There were rules for commuters using the slug line. Don't speak unless spoken to. Don't mess with the air, window, radio. Don't talk on the phone. Brooks flipped his phone over in his hand and sent a quick message to his executive assistant letting him know an unexpected emergency had come up.

Call the police.

That would be the smart thing to do. The appropriate thing to do. But Brooks was in too deep, and he had no idea what she would do to Anthony. He couldn't take the risk. Glancing over to the speedometer, he was at least thankful the driver had a bit of a lead foot.

Gripping the phone in his hand, he sent a message back to her.

On my way. Please don't hurt him.

It made him sick that he'd even have to ask that of her. But he'd known her long enough, seen what she was capable of, and knew the compassionate, maternal instinct he loved about Lydia was glaringly missing from the woman he'd just asked to protect his son.

By the time the airman pulled up in front of Eisenhower Elementary, Brooks's emotions were fluctuating between fear and fury. He hopped out of the car and saw that the cement bench in front of the oak tree where Anthony would've been waiting for Tori was empty. A handful of cars were still in the parking lot and one, a black sedan, flashed its lights at him.

Brooks jogged over, looking for a brick or stick he could use to smash the window and grab his son. He slowed when he saw the man in the driver's seat. He didn't need to know his name or be introduced. Something in the man's sinister glare told him he was the one behind the phone call the other night, behind the death of Genevieve Miller and who knew how many others.

He needed to tread lightly.

The back window rolled down. "Dad!" Anthony

371

stuck his head out, a ring of ice cream circling his lips. "Look what I got."

Next to Anthony, Brooks's boss, Christine León, smiled like she hadn't just lured his son with dessert like some kind of psycho kidnapper.

"Buddy, you know Mom doesn't like you eating snacks before dinner."

He tilted his head to the side. "She said I don't have to tell."

Anger pumped through his veins. "What's the rule about secrets, Anthony?"

Dipping his chin, he sighed. "We don't keep secrets from Mom and Dad."

"You have a smart boy, Brooks."

He itched to open the door and scoop his son into his arms. "I'm going to have to remind him about getting into cars with strangers."

"She's not a stranger, Dad. She ate dinner with us, remember?"

On more than one occasion, which made this all the worse. Brooks had invited the devil into his home.

"Son, why don't you get out of the car, now."

"Okay." He started to open it, but Christine put a hand on the door.

"Why don't we have a conversation first."

Brooks looked around. There was maybe a handful of teachers still inside the school, perhaps some janitorial staff, based on the number of cars in the lot. A Little League team was arriving at the field adjacent to the playground. Would Christine try something here? It frightened him that he didn't know.

"Anthony, do you want to play on the playground for a few minutes?"

"Yessss!" He play growled, and it was like Brooks had said the magic words. Anthony wriggled around in the back seat, anxious to get out of the car and stepping all over Christine. "I want to go on the swings. No, the monkey bars. No, the swings. Dad, will you push me high, high, high in the sky?"

"Sure, buddy."

Christine sent him a scathing look but allowed Anthony to climb out. Brooks lifted him up into his arms and hugged him fiercely.

"Dad, let me go."

"Yes, Dad, let him go so he can play and we can talk." Christine exited her car and brushed the dirt from her slacks. "My driver will keep an eye on him."

"No." Brooks knelt down. "Stay close so we can get home and eat some of Mom's famous meatloaf."

"Okay," Anthony agreed, then ran through the fence and lunged onto a swing, stomach on the seat part, arms spread wide like he was flying. "Wheee!"

"Why did you do this?" Brooks growled.

"The shipment of rifles didn't make it."

373

Brooks glanced down at her. His six feet could easily take her five-four frame, but part of him was worried a gun was pointed on him from the driver's seat. The last thing he'd want was for Anthony to be left with the memory of seeing him murdered.

"Did you hear me?"

"Yes, ma'am." He watched Anthony soar back and forth on the swing, pretending to be an airplane. Maybe his son would be a pilot. Christine stepped into his line of sight, and he narrowed his eyes on her. "What happened?"

"Homeland Security stopped the couriers at the airport, and next thing I hear, the CIA's confiscated our shipment." Her eyes narrowed on him. "You know they're going to start investigating."

Relief scaled his shoulders. "Maybe we should consider this a warning for us to pull back. Too many people have their noses to the ground after the girl was murdered and your buddy over there"—Brooks eyed the driver—"decided to poke a hornet's nest by targeting that woman from the SNAP Agency. You know Tom Walsh. He has deep connections. If he catches wind—"

"Oh, you didn't hear?" Mock concern tugged Christine's brows together. "Tom Walsh was the victim of a random shooting last night. He's in critical condition. Might not make it."

Brooks's breathing grew shallow. "You had him shot?"

"I have no idea what you're talking about."

"Christine, we need to let this go. We need to just take a pause and—"

"No, we need to get another shipment out to Colombia." Christine didn't raise her voice. There was no question, just a statement that it would be done.

"Ma'am." He hated calling her that, but he knew which boundaries to push—and that wasn't one of them. "If the CIA is looking into this, they're going to be watching. There's no inventory to skim from, and I can't divert another order without raising flags."

Christine walked to the fence and waved at Anthony as he climbed the steps to go down a yellow plastic slide. "Do you remember what you asked me a few minutes ago?"

Brooks sighed, replaying their conversation, but his concern for Anthony had his mind going blank.

She looked up at him. "You asked me why I did this." Anthony squealed as he slid down the slide. "Remember?"

"Yes."

"I did this to make sure you understand . . . I can get to you. I can get to your son. I can get to your family." She waved at Anthony. "Bye, buddy. See you next time."

Brooks curled his hands into fists to control the rage that made him want to wrap his fingers around her neck and squeeze the life out of her. A murder charge would be more merciful than what she was putting him through. Life in prison, or even on death row, would at least rid the world of this evil.

Christine looked over her shoulder before she got into the car. "Remember that, Brooks."

31

Lyla replayed the plan in her head once more, avoiding the way Nicolás kept looking at her. She'd thought he would try to talk her out of it, but his attention was more affirming than questioning. It bolstered her courage, giving her the strength she needed to quell the nervousness about possibly coming face-to-face with the person who put Walsh in the hospital, where he was fighting for his life.

Last night Lyla stayed at Jack and Brynn's house but sent both of her parents a text message saying she was okay and would check in with them later. It was hard. She hadn't felt that kind of separation from them since she was a child, and it broke her heart.

"President Lawson has scheduled the principals meeting," Jack said. "You're going to run three errands before coming back to the office, where a White House driver will pick you up and take you to the West Wing."

"If she's not intercepted before then."

"Right." Jack nodded at Nicolás. "If it doesn't happen before then, we can assume the plan is a bust."

Lyla checked her watch. "So, I'm heading to the hospital, where Agent Bridges will be stationed. Then stopping by Lulu's, where Kekoa will be, to pick up food. And then I'm supposed to stop by Crystal City Mall to pick up a gift." She looked at Jack. "Where you and Brynn will be."

"And Garcia will be with you the entire time," Jack confirmed.

"You have Cupcake?" Nicolás pointed to her purse. "Loaded?"

"Yes." Her stomach erupted in butterflies—and not the kind the little looks from Nicolás caused to flutter in her stomach. "I'm armed and ready."

"Shootz, you gonna take that braddah *down*." Kekoa came behind her and lifted up her arms. "Cupcake has nothing on these guns. Flex 'em, sis. Flex 'em."

Lyla rolled her eyes but needed this. She gave in and flexed her biceps, which were puny next to Kekoa's.

"Sis, you flexing or what?"

"Stop!" She twisted and playfully slapped Kekoa on the chest. He gripped her in his arms, crushing her in a bear hug. "K-koa ywoo . . . breav." Around her she could hear the other boys laughing and realized it had been a while since she'd heard a simple expression of happiness. It sounded like they all needed this.

When Kekoa finally released her, she reached around him and gave him a real hug. "Thanks, Kekoa." Emotion passed through his eyes, and she had to turn away. Nope, she was leaving on a high note. "Okay, let's get to the hospital."

In Nicolás's truck, they rode in silence for a few minutes. "Thank you for having my back, Nicolás. It means a lot."

"I'm not trying to talk you out of this, but if you want to change your mind, I'll drive this truck back to the office and barricade you in there. I have no doubt Jack, Kekoa, and I can keep you safe until we figure out another way to catch this person."

"Wow." She smiled. "You've really thought about this."

"Jack's mom will provide Italian food, Brynn will be our eyes on the outside, and Elinor has promised to redirect satellites to potentially make it look like our building is radioactive or something like that." He frowned. "There were a lot of technical science terms I didn't understand, but yes, Lyla, I've thought about a thousand ways to keep you safe, including whisking you away with me to Syria."

This time she laughed. "You think I'm safer in Syria than here?"

"Possibly." He tilted his head. "Or I could turn the job down and take you to a remote island somewhere."

"Nah, the mountains—North Carolina or Tennessee."

He looked confused. "You love the beach."

"But you love the mountains." She shrugged. "If we're going to be stuck together for a long time, I'd want you to be someplace you love."

His silence might've bothered her before, but the desire in his eyes meant more than anything he could've said.

Nicolás found a spot in the detached parking structure, and they walked the breezeway to the hospital. Lyla took a fortifying breath while keeping an eye on her surroundings. If a sniper wanted to take her out, there were a hundred places for them to hide. Okay, so maybe that was an exaggeration, but it was still unnerving to think someone might be out there, ready to take a shot if given the chance.

She'd realized, after a fitful night of sleep, that it was a much different ball game when she was making split-second decisions regarding risks than when she was willingly choosing to say, "Hey, bad guy, take your best shot." That realization shifted her perspective when she thought about what Nicolás had told her last night over chocolate fondue. She'd never really considered how her decisions might affect her family, her team . . . Nicolás.

That thought made her think of Jerry's family. Mrs. Miller had lost both of her children, and now her daughter-in-law and grandchildren were in hiding somewhere. R.D., where was she? Was she safe? Was her family?

And what about Lyla's family? Her grandparents? Walsh? What had caused him to lie to her all these years? What risks had Sean Murphy been facing? So much loss, and it made her realize not all risks held the same value.

"Lyla." Nicolás put his hand at the small of her back.

She hadn't realized they were already on the ICU floor and her mom was standing in the hallway, staring at her like she wanted to run to her but also fearfully rooted to the spot.

"Hi, Mom."

They met in the middle, followed by awkward seconds where neither one of them knew what to say or do.

"How's Tom?"

"It's still touch and go. They've had to put in a trach, and the doctors think it's better to keep him in the coma. They'll let you go back and see him."

Lyla felt timid, like she both knew the woman in front of her but also didn't. She was grateful Nicolás was with her. "Okay."

"Your dad is back there with Sam and someone from work, I think." Her mom looked at Nicolás. "They allow only four guests."

"I'll wait out here."

Lyla walked down the ICU hallway, where rooms on both sides were occupied by patients hooked up to beeping monitors and breathing machines. It made her a little woozy. Or maybe it was the antiseptic smell. Whatever it was, she didn't want to hang around here long.

Her heart sank when she came to Walsh's room. On his bed, in a hospital gown with wires attached all over him, he didn't look like the vigorous man she loved so much. He looked older and . . . human. Her eyes filled with tears. Walsh wasn't invincible.

"Lyla." Her father's voice called to her, and she found him standing next to Sam, who was sitting on the couch with a woman Lyla didn't know. "Are you . . . how are you?"

"I'm good." Lyla swallowed against the knot building in her throat. She looked at Sam. "How are you?"

Sam rose from the couch and wrapped her in a hug. "Better than I was last night. Tom's strong and showing some minor improvement that's making the doctors happy."

"That's really good to hear."

Stepping back, Sam gestured to the other woman. "Do you know Christine León?"

"I don't." Lyla shook the woman's hand.

"I work for the secretary of defense. He wanted me to deliver those"—she indicated a beautiful bouquet of flowers on a hospital table next to a few others and gave Sam a sympathetic smile—"and his prayers for a full recovery."

Her father walked over. "Lyla, do you have time to talk?"

Lyla breathed out slowly and gave a quick nod. She wasn't sure she was ready for this conversation, but standing next to Walsh's frail body was cracking her composure, and she needed to be strong for whatever the next couple of hours would bring.

They walked back to the same room where Lyla had discovered the truth about her life. Her mother stood up from a chair next to a window.

Glancing back down the hallway and then back to her mom, she asked, "Where's Agent Bridges?"

Her mom frowned. "Oh, you mean Sophie? She went to get some food for Sam from the cafeteria. We've been trying to make sure she eats. She won't be any help to Tom if she doesn't take care of herself."

"That's true," Lyla said, rubbing her arm. "So, um . . ."

"Lyla, we are so sorry for . . ." Her father pressed his lips together. "Everything. Well, not everything. We are not sorry that you came to be our daughter. We are sorry for the circumstances behind it, but from the moment you were placed in our arms—you were ours."

"I've always felt like I didn't fit in." Lyla's throat ached with emotion. "I didn't . . . match."

"You may not have our DNA, but you were—

are—the missing piece to our family. We were incomplete without you." Her mom wiped at tears streaming down her cheek. "You are our daughter."

Her father swiped under his eyes, clearing his throat. "We knew this day would come but weren't sure how it was going to happen. If you have questions, we'll answer them as best we can, but a lot of what you might want to know can only be answered by Tom."

"Agent Bridges explained a little about my . . ." She didn't feel right calling them her parents. "About Sean and Annie Murphy. It's a lot to take in."

"It is, honey." Lyla's mom reached a tentative hand to Lyla's shoulder. "And we completely understand if you need time to process it all. We want you to know that we love you so very much, and no matter what kind of relationship you feel comfortable with, we will be here for you."

Nicolás's words came back to her. She was fiercely loved. The two people in front of her knew she wasn't theirs, a fact she'd grappled with all night and kept coming to the same conclusion—they loved her unconditionally. No matter what she'd put them through, the risks she'd taken, her adolescent defiance, they never once gave up loving her.

Her watch pinged with an alert that said it was time to run her next errand. She sniffled and wiped away the moisture in the corners of her eyes. "I, um, have to go to work."

"We understand." Her dad wrapped an arm around her mom's shoulders. "Please be careful."

"I will." With a peace she couldn't understand, Lyla moved in and surprised both of her parents when she hugged them. They hugged her back. Hard. "I love you, Mom and Dad."

She hugged them a little longer before promising to be back later this evening for another visit. On her way out, she found Christine León also leaving.

"Lyla, right?"

"Yes."

The woman shifted and gave Lyla a strange smile. "Would you mind walking me out?"

"Actually, I need to meet my friend."

"He can wait, dear." Christine shifted her coat, which was folded over her arm, revealing the steel muzzle of a gun. "Let's take the stairs."

32

Nic checked his watch. Lyla was running late, but he didn't want to rush a conversation he knew she needed to have with her parents. He prayed again for their reconciliation. His phone buzzed with another message from Kekoa checking on their status.

He was nervous. Kekoa wasn't a fan of carrying the weight of personal protection even though he would demolish mountains for the people he cared about. But his nervousness was making Nic nervous.

Checking his watch again, he moved to the nurses' station to see if he could maybe call Walsh's room and check on her.

A man walked over with a bouquet of flowers, bumping into Nic. "Follow me."

Nic glanced around him, confused as to who the man was speaking to.

The man set the flowers on the counter. "You work for SNAP. The girl, Ms. Fox, is in danger. You need to come with me now."

Alarm set his adrenaline pumping. He tried to step around the man, but he caught Nic's arm. Nic was about to throw a punch when a flash of recognition hit him.

"Do I know you?"

"Probably, yes, but that's not important right now. They've already left, and I'm afraid if we wait another second, your friend won't be alive."

It was the lack of exaggeration in the man's tone that drove Nic to follow him. On his way, he pulled out his phone and sent a group text that the plan had gone bad. He kept an eye on the man in front of him and then lifted his phone to take a photo. The camera sound pulled the man's attention back to him.

"What are you doing?"

"Identifying you."

A rigid expression was the only reaction he got. That made Nic feel only slightly more sure that he wasn't being tricked. The next message he sent was to Kekoa about the cameras in the hospital, but midtext a message came in with a video that showed Lyla leaving with a woman. Nic was in full panic mode.

"Who's Lyla with?"

"Christine León. Under secretary of defense for acquisitions and sustainment. She's behind the arms deals to Venezuela and Ireland. I have a list. And she coordinated the shooting of your boss and Genevieve Miller."

"Where is she taking Lyla?"

"I don't know." He held up his phone. "But I have a tracker on her car. We need to take your truck, because I'm pretty sure she's got someone following me."

Nic's gaze moved around him. "Who?"

"One of her henchmen. Prior military guys who she pays well." He tilted his head. "Or at least it would be well if the money were real."

"What kind of device do you have on her car?"

"What?"

Nic unlocked his truck and they both jumped in. "On the car. Is it a generic brand? Military grade? Spy tech?"

"Generic."

Nic dialed Kekoa's number and handed his phone to the man. "Give me your phone and give him the details."

Starting his engine, Nic accelerated out of the hospital parking lot, following the tracker's blinking dot on the man's cell phone. He prayed Lyla was still alive. He wouldn't allow himself to consider any other alternative.

"He says they're tracking them now." The man next to him set down the phone. "I'm so sorry. I never meant for this to get so out of hand."

"Who are you?"

"Richard Vale. We met at the drag hunt."

Nic had a vague recollection. "You work for the secretary of defense."

"Yes."

"And your office . . ."

"Acquisitions and sustainment."

"Deals with weapons?"

"Yes," Vale answered Nic. "We coordinate

defense acquisitions and foreign military sales."

That at least explained the origin of the weapons. It didn't explain the how or why. Nic focused on the cell phone. They were headed out of the city on Route 223 and entering a densely forested area.

"I know where she's taking her," Vale said. "There's a hunting property that she purchased several years ago. She doesn't use it herself, but it's . . . uh . . ."

Nic looked at Vale, whose face had paled. "What?"

"I don't know this for sure, but it's the kind of place people are taken to and never heard from again."

The pressure of his foot on the accelerator pushed him deeper into his seat. Nic picked up his phone and dialed Jack's number. Jack answered right away.

"Jack, get a chopper out here, and SWAT. I have a feeling this is going to turn into a hostage situation. Subject is Christine León, under sec—"

"Got it, Garcia. FBI has been notified. Wheels up with an ETA of thirteen minutes."

Thirteen minutes. Nic looked at Vale. "How much farther?"

Vale pointed to the screen. "It's just there."

Nic slammed on the brakes, nearly missing the dirt road where he needed to turn. He jerked the wheel hard, the back of his truck fishtailing on he road. They bounced over the unpaved path, and Nic slowed only when he caught sight of the log cabin structure with a car parked in front of it.

He blocked the car in with his truck, threw it into park, and jumped out. Richard Vale yelled after him, but Nic ignored him, his boots hitting the porch steps just as he heard Lyla scream.

33

"Nicolás, stop!" Lyla screamed again when the front door swung open. She kept still, not moving, barely gathering breath to fill her lungs. "Please don't come in."

His attention moved to where she was standing, and when she saw the realization on his face, it made her understand just how bad this was. Nicolás took a step inside of the cabin, holding his hands up when Christine lifted her aim. He didn't flinch, just kept his steady gaze focused on Lyla. "I know it's rare for you to listen to my instructions, but please do it this time."

Lyla's lips quivered with a nervous laugh. "Just this one time, okay?"

"Well, we can all be grateful you didn't make us go *kaboom*." Christine León stepped back. "But I'm sorry to say this is goodbye."

"No." Lyla moved her foot, but she caught Nic shaking his head. Glancing down, she saw the cuff of her jeans was caught on the edge of a wire connected to a blue plastic box about the size of one of Etta's Kentucky Derby hatboxes.

"Lyla." Nicolás's voice was low and steady. His gaze moved to the bomb, where it stayed, assessing. "Please."

"We can't just let her get away, Nicolás."

He lifted his eyes to meet hers. "It's not worth the risk."

Lyla narrowed her eyes on Christine. How much danger was she in? Were they all in? She needed to give him time to figure it out. "What kind of a person are you?"

"The kind who learned that if she wanted to make things happen, she had to do it herself."

"Something tells me you're not the type to get your hands dirty."

Christine's smile was wicked. "And you would know. Must be hard to live a life of luxury—rich parents. You never had to want for anything."

"You don't know anything about my life," Lyla hissed, and then she thought about her parents and was grateful she'd told them she loved them. *Were those my last words to them?* Her knees started to shake.

"So you know what it's like to live under a regime of evil and corruption like my family in Venezuela?" Christine huffed. "You have no idea."

"And you thought distributing weapons to the very regimes that oppress and violate women was the answer?" Lyla couldn't control her sarcasm. "You really are the change the world needs."

"No!" Christine's irritation almost drove her to take a step forward, but her eyes dropped to the bomb next to Lyla. "What I saw was an opportunity to level the playing fields. If you

think your country is immune to someone
Alberto Guzman rising to power, you're bl
I was providing my people a way to fight be
just like your country does when it suits the
agenda."

"And what was Genevieve Miller? The innocent victims in Omagh? And countless others
who died because of the weapons you stole?"
Lyla thought about Sean and Annie and how
she'd never get a chance to know them. "If you
say collateral damage, you're just as evil as
Guzman."

The back door swung open, and a man stepped
in and fired a shot. Lyla flinched and had no idea
how she managed to keep still. She watched
Christine crumple forward and drop to her knees
before collapsing to the ground. Lyla sucked in a
breath, trying not to panic.

The man in the doorway lowered the gun and
looked at her. "She's just evil."

"Nicolás."

"Don't move, Lyla. Stay still." Nicolás locked
eyes with her. "I'll be right back."

"Don't leave me." Her body began to tremble.
"Please don't leave me."

"Vale, come back around to the front of the
house," Nicolás said to the man staring absently
at Christine's body. "Lyla, do you trust me?"

Lyla gave a little nod.

"I will be right back."

e watched Nicolás drag Christine's body out ne house and heard the woman moaning. She sn't dead, and Lyla didn't know if she should el relieved or worried that she might try to run or attack them.

A tremor she couldn't control was beginning to take over her ability to stay still. "Nicolás."

Sirens echoed, and then she heard a thumping noise that sounded like a helicopter. Or was that her pulse pumping loudly in her ears? She glanced down at the device and prayed it wasn't timed or remote detonated . . .

Lyla's knees wobbled. She was going to fall, and the whole place was going to explode. Closing her eyes, she thought back to the verse Nicolás had given her—the one on the coin Walsh had handed to them when they were officially a team.

The Lord is my shepherd . . . I will fear no evil.

Non timebo mala.

"I will fear no evil." Her whisper came out shaky, but the words filled her soul with a steadying strength she knew was not her own. "The Lord is my Shepherd."

"Lyla." Nicolás was back. He walked toward her slowly. "The bomb squad is a few minutes out. I just need you to hold out a little longer. Can you do that?"

The Lord is my shepherd. Lyla nodded. *I will fear no evil.* She was certain there were more

words to the verses, but for now that's all ⸱
could cling to.

"I'm going to step back out and get ready."

"Get ready?" Her knees nearly buckled.
"You're . . . you're going to—"

"Be right here with you."

Lyla wanted to tell him no, wanted to tell him
to leave, but she was afraid if she tried to speak,
she'd lose the last of her strength and then they'd
both die. *We both might die anyway.* "The Lord is
my shepherd."

Nicolás nodded at her whisper. "Yes, he is."

Lyla watched him leave and kept repeating the
verse. She didn't know how many minutes she
stood there praying for her legs to keep her up,
but soon the room was filled with bomb squad
members wearing green body armor and helmets
that made them look like they were going to
space.

Nicolás was wearing the bomb gear too, and
he looked at her through the protective shield. "I
make this look good, don't I?"

"Really?" Lyla said through gritted teeth.
"Jokes *now?*" Nicolás wiggled his brows, and
she knew it was an attempt to keep her calm—
and she loved him for it. *Loved him.* Nothing felt
truer than that and . . . *And of course I finally
acknowledge my feelings for him when he's
standing next to a bomb.* Who did she think she
was? Sandra Bullock?

While you consider my good looks, this is remy." Nicolás pointed to the man next to him. He's going to start working on the device, and I'm going to stay right here with you. Okay?"

"I d-don't want you to die."

"No one wants anyone to die." Nicolás took a cautious step toward her and reached for her hand with his, the only part of him not protected from a blast. The warmth from his touch calmed her. "Just think of this as an exercise in patience."

Adrenaline or shock was causing her teeth to rattle, and her jaw ached trying to stop it. "You know I-I don't have patience."

"Yes, I do."

The sound of radio chatter echoed, and Lyla's eyes moved to where Jeremy had slid open the lid of the device, revealing a bunch of wires. The trembling began again, and she knew she wasn't going to be able to keep standing much longer.

"Lyla." Nicolás squeezed her fingers, pulling her attention back to him. "Don't look down there, look at me. I know I'm not as handsome as Kekoa, but I have really good cholesterol numbers."

"What?" She gasped. "Why are you telling me about your cholesterol numbers?"

"Because I want you to know I'm going to be around for a long time." His gaze deepened. "Just in case you'd consider having me around."

Her heart beat against her ribs. "Nicolás—"

"Garcia."

Nicolás turned to Jeremy, and she saw the subtle shake of his head, the look that caused her heart to slow down.

"Lyla"—Nicolás turned back to her—"I need you to listen to me. I have to look at the device, and I need you to stay perfectly still for me."

34

Two seconds ago, the only thing Nic saw lighting Lyla's blue-green eyes was fear, but now he saw trust. She released his hand and stood still. Nic moved to where Jeremy was and knelt next to him. The bomb technician had used tape and a magnet to bypass the sensor on the locking hinge to open the case, revealing wires, fuses, and an internal sensor panel.

Nic studied the wires, lights, and switches. It took a few minutes, but he realized he was staring at a trap. If he didn't determine which of the components were sensors or which were pressure sensitive, it would lead to an explosion.

"Nicolás?"

He took a steadying breath and looked down at his hands. *Lord, guide my hands to undo the work of evil. Protect us.* Nic reached for the tools he needed and focused on the spring-loaded trigger.

"How did the conversation with your parents go?" Nic heard Lyla let out a breath. "I never got a chance to ask you."

"You mean because I was being kidnapped by a disgruntled government employee?"

He smiled. "Not even a bomb can squash your snark." He looked at Jeremy. "I told you she was plucky."

Jeremy grinned and handed Nic a shim that he carefully slid into place to keep the trigger in the armed position. After determining the orange fuses were touch sensors, he cautiously worked around them.

"We didn't get to talk much, but I'm hoping I'll get that chance."

Nic opened the next panel and blew out a breath. Three switches connected to a mess of wires that would make an eager or unexperienced bomb tech assume only one of them would lead to detonation. But that assumption would mean certain death, because this was another trap. He'd seen it before in Afghanistan. All three switches would detonate the bomb.

"How you doing, Nicolás?" Lyla's voice shook. "I bet Kekoa would've had me out of here by now."

"Really?" He smiled. "Jokes *now?*"

"I'm sorry."

"That's okay." Nic carefully unlatched a canister. Inside was a bottle braced sideways in a fixture with liquid inside. His breathing slowed. *This is it.* "Jokes are calming."

Using a USB endoscope and a cell phone, Nic recorded the bottle and discovered wires and a sensor attached to a liquid-lever trigger that would explode if moved too much.

"I meant I'm sorry about driving you to leave the agency. That my impulsive actions cause you to doubt yourself or what you mean to the team."

Nic's eyes flickered to Jeremy, who tried to look like he wasn't at all interested in this confessional. Nic reached for the pickup tool and said another prayer before sliding it into the narrow bottle. Sweat dripped down his back, and his fingers were vibrating with adrenaline. He forced himself to take another breath before continuing. The pickup tool slipped, and the water line moved. Nic froze.

The liquid stilled, and he started breathing again. *Come on.* Moving the device once more, the prongs were nearly at the sensor . . .

"I love you, Nicolás."

A yellow light flickered on the device, and the air in Nic's lungs whooshed out. Jeremy, with beads of sweat rolling down his brow, pushed back and visibly released his own breath before giving Nic a nod.

Nic stabilized the pickup tool with a piece of foam and ignored the painful ache in his knees when he stood and faced Lyla. "Really? You waited until my hands were literally on the wires of a bomb to tell me you love me?"

"I have impeccable timing." She breathed out. "Is it over?"

"It's over." Nic was glad he was there, because Lyla collapsed into his arms, and through the protective gear, he felt her sobs. He scooped her up and carried her out of the cabin. "I got Lyla."

Nic didn't know how many hours had passe but it was enough time for the police, ATF, an FBI to arrive on scene, take statements, snap photographs, and argue over who was going to run the follow-up investigation into Christine León's double life.

An ambulance had taken her to the hospital with a nonfatal gunshot wound, and the FBI had taken Richard Brooks Vale into custody. Nic was left with a hundred questions, but right now he cared about the answer to only one.

He walked over to where the FBI had set up a mobile unit, and Lyla was sitting in a camping chair with a clipboard and pen in her hand.

"Are you sure you're okay?"

She glanced up. "Are you?"

"Lyla, life is not a competition of wills."

"I know that." She signed the bottom of the page and set the clipboard aside. "But if it was, I'd win."

Nic rolled his eyes. "If you're done, they said we can leave. Jack called and said the secretary of defense, secretary of state, and national security advisor want a debrief but that we can go in tomorrow."

"Good, because I'm too exhausted to repeat myself one more time."

helped her out of the chair. "I was kind of
_ng you might repeat some things."
_yla's coy gaze met his under dark lashes.
_ike what?"

"Was it duress?"

"What?"

Nic rubbed a hand on the back of his neck. "I
know people say things under duress, and—"

"Nicolás." Lyla grabbed a hold of his belt
loops and pulled him to her. "I don't know why it
took me so long to figure it out, but I love you."
She smiled up at him, the skin around her eyes
creasing. "Willfully, stubbornly, recklessly, and
completely."

Inexplicable peace consumed him, and he
threaded an arm around her waist and cupped her
chin in his hand. "I obstinately love you too."

Lyla nestled into his embrace, her lips parting
as her eyes moved to his lips. He leaned in,
wanting to answer the yearning he saw in her
face.

"Ms. Fox?"

They both jerked back, Nic left dizzy by the
unfulfilled desire. A man in an FBI jacket was
holding up a cell phone.

"Someone named CocaKoa or Koakoa . . ." He
shook his head. "You have a call."

Nic rolled his eyes. "Even miles away, his
timing is unbelievable."

Lyla giggled and took the cell phone from the

FBI agent. Nic tugged off his cap and ran fingers through his hair. *She loves me.* And loved her.

What did that mean for his future?

"Nicolás, we need to go to the hospital." Lyla smiled. "Walsh is awake."

35

Two Weeks Later

Lyla could barely contain herself. She looked around the Galaxy Bowl-O-Rama and smiled. Balloons and crepe-paper streamers matching the retro colors of the bowling alley enhanced the festive atmosphere, and she couldn't wait to see Nicolás's face.

Who was she kidding? She wanted more than to see him—she wanted to hug him, feel his hand in hers, kiss him.

Va-va-voom.

Nicolás definitely gave her the va-va-vooms. Her insides wriggled with the kind of anticipation she'd get before Christmas as a child when she knew the gift waiting under the tree for her was the very thing she'd been hoping for most. *Nicolás.*

Lyla planned to make the most of the time they had together before he left for Syria, something she knew he needed to do, but her heart was already aching for the absence she knew was coming.

"The cake and the rest of the food is set up." Lyla's mom walked over and set down some napkins. "Now we just need the birthday boy to show up."

"Jack said they're on their way." Lyla check her watch. "Five minutes or so."

"You haven't stopped smiling all day." He. mother's soft tone drew Lyla's gaze up. "Are you happy, Lyla Anne?"

Anne, Lyla had learned, was a variation of her biological mother's name, Annie. When Keith and Catherine Fox adopted Lyla, they wanted to make sure she had a connection to the parents who had sacrificed their lives for their country and their daughter.

There were still days when the reality of the truth behind her birth and life left her feeling unsteady, and both her parents and her grand-parents allowed her space, but she realized that while she was heartbroken to have been kept in the dark for so long, it was a risk they took to protect her. And it was a risk to accept that one day Lyla would learn the truth and they could lose her for good.

Hearing her mom and dad speak those words, revealing their hearts, made Lyla see that she was more like them than she believed, and they would be all right.

"I'm happy, Mom."

Her mother's eyes glistened with emotion. Lyla's own throat ached, but she wouldn't cry today. Sniffling, Lyla hugged her mom and then walked to where her dad was talking with Tom and Sam at a table.

Lyla drew her arm around her father's waist, and he cradled her against his side, kissing her forehead. "Dad, would you help the DJ pick some music?"

"Sure, honey." He kissed her head again before letting her go. He paused. "What kind do you kids listen to these days?"

"I was thinking some of that dorky music from the seventies you forced me to listen to as a kid. Nicolás will probably like that."

"Donny Osmond and The Carpenters coming up." Her dad pointed double-gun fingers at her before doing a dance that was right up Kekoa's alley.

"I'm going to go see if your mom needs any help," Sam said, squeezing Tom's hand before walking away. "Don't let him get up no matter what he tells you."

Lyla nodded, then looked to Tom. "Shouldn't you be at home, recovering?"

"I could sit there or I could sit here." Tom glanced around him. "This is healing." He tipped his head to where her parents were standing. "I never meant to hurt you or them."

She swallowed. "I know."

"Sean was a good friend." Tom choked on the words, and Lyla's throat ached at the loss of a relationship she'd never know. "He wanted to protect you above all else, and we weren't sure if whoever killed him would come after you. I thought this was the best way to do it." He shifted on the seat and reached into his pocket. When he opened his hand, a gold chain with a trinity knot lay in his palm. "This was his, and I've been saving it to give to you."

Lyla took the necklace in her hand, and a tear slipped down her cheek. "Thank you, Tom."

"Jack just pulled up," Brynn said as she walked over. "You ready?"

When Lyla put on the necklace and touched it, an indescribable contentment seemed to fill the void she'd felt in her life. This was where she belonged—with her parents, Tom, and her team.

Her eyes moved to the door of the bowling alley, and she smiled. In one minute, she'd be in Nicolás's arms, where she most definitely belonged.

"Surprise!"

Nic walked into the bowling alley to an eruption of hoots and hollers. Around him, his friends, some familiar colleagues from the CIA and FBI, and Lyla's family clapped for him, but his gaze zeroed in on the woman in a bubble-gum-colored bowling shirt, her eyes sparkling brighter than the turquoise-blue décor.

It had been thirteen days since Lyla declared she loved him. And because of the gravity of Christine León's crimes, they'd been separated by extensive daily debriefings that kept them from exploring their feelings.

Torture. That's what it had felt like to be limited to quick phone conversations before fatigue forced them to sleep, leaving them aching for more. If he hadn't already committed to General DeAntona, he would've backed out of the Syria mission, because Nic wasn't sure he'd be able to handle one day without Lyla in his life.

I was crazy to think I could ever leave her.

And now, on the first day free from the inquisition of lawyers, members of Congress, and the Department of Defense, the laws of attraction buzzing through Nic pushed him toward the woman he loved.

"Hau'oli lā hānau e, Garcia!" Kekoa stepped in front of Nic and wrapped him in a bone-crushing hug. "Happy birthday, brah."

"Thanks," Nic said once Kekoa released him and he was able to breathe again. His eyes found Lyla's again. "I'm just going to go—"

"Happy birthday, Garcia." Brynn and Jack intercepted his attempt to get to Lyla. "Jack didn't give it away? He's a terrible secret keeper."

"Hey!" Jack said. "I told him we were coming here to pick up the surveillance video from the other night."

"And you believed him?" Kekoa teased.

"I did." Nic gave a polite smile. It had seemed odd, but he was too exhausted to question Jack.

He took a few more steps in Lyla's direction. "
like to—"

"Happy birthday, soldier." His neighbor, M
Brandt, ambled over with Lyla's great-aunt Effie
by his side.

"Thank you, Mr. Brandt."

Nic was going to lose his ever-loving mind if
he didn't get to Lyla.

"Aunt Effie, Mr. Brandt, why don't I get you
something to drink?" Lyla's mom, Catherine,
gave Nic a knowing smile before escorting the
elderly couple away.

Nic could have hugged the woman right there
if he had a second to spare, but with Lyla in his
sights—the wait was over. He closed the distance
between them, and even though he wanted to
scoop her into his arms and feel her lips on his,
he restrained himself out of respect for her family
and settled—very reluctantly—for a hug.

Torture.

This close to her, Nic wondered how rude it
would be to whisk her away. He eyed a semi-
private spot behind some lockers and wondered
if they could sneak off like a couple of teenagers
and he could give in to the desire pulsing through
him to kiss her madly. From the hungry look in
Lyla's eyes, he sensed the feeling was mutual.

His gaze dipped to her lips. He fought the
heady temptation to kiss her and instead forced
himself to release her.

yla, her cheeks pink, looked a bit flustered as ⸺e brushed her hair from her forehead. She bit ⸺r lip. "I'll go get the shoes."

With Lyla grabbing their bowling shoes, Nic finished greeting Lyla's parents, grandparents, and Director Walsh and his wife, Sam, before he walked back to where Kekoa, Elinor, and Jack were putting on their shoes. Brynn was typing their names into the bowling lineup.

"Jack was just telling us that President Guzman declared Christine León a war criminal for her role in providing weapons to rebel forces attacking his soldiers." Elinor shook her head. "You guys handle some really crazy assignments."

"Which is why we're always glad when they're finished," Jack said.

Lyla sat next to Nicolás and handed him his shoes, their eyes meeting in agreement that they, too, were glad the assignment was over.

Christine León and Richard Brooks Vale were connected to multiple arms trafficking deals that stretched over two decades. Christine León was facing numerous charges. She'd also had her naturalization revoked for crimes against the United States. It was one of many conspiracy-related headlines that had R.D. Leto busy.

"Okay, no more work chat." Brynn raised her brows at Kekoa. "Let's bowl."

Nic rolled up his jeans and pulled off his

boots, only to realize his mistake when he hea
Kekoa's hoot.

"What are those?"

Nic wiggled his toes in the armadillo socks
Lyla had given him. "Armadillos." His cheeks
warmed. "Lyla gave them to me."

"You have it bad, brah."

"Don't listen to him." Elinor smacked Kekoa's
arm. "Love looks good on you."

"You wore them."

Nic glanced up and found Lyla standing with
her hands clasped under her chin. She walked
toward him, reached for his hand, and brought
him up to his feet. His heart pounded heavy
against his ribs. He brushed his knuckles along
her cheek.

"Go on, brah, kiss her."

Laughter echoed around them, causing Nic's
cheeks to burn and Lyla to smile. He gently
cradled the back of her neck as Lyla wound her
arms around his waist. Built-up anticipation had
led to this moment, and he wanted to savor every
second of it.

"Lyla, with your family, our boss and friends as
witnesses, even the crazy Hawaiian, with me in
my armadillo socks, I'd like to ask permission to
kiss y—"

She kissed him, silencing the rest of his
request, and he closed his eyes. The noise around
him disappeared as her lips softly explored his

several seconds. When she pulled back, the intensity in her gaze stole his breath.

"Finally," Elinor said.

"Maestro," Kekoa called out to the DJ, and the music in the bowling alley changed to the twangy song "Rhinestone Cowboy."

Nic shook his head as Lyla giggled, but before the moment was gone—or Kekoa interrupted— he twisted her around in his arms, dipped her backward, and kissed her with all the passion of someone who'd risk his heart over and over again for the chance to be loved by such a woman as Lyla Anne Fox.

ACKNOWLEDGMENTS

Dear readers, I can't believe we've come to the end of another series, and I'll be honest—this one hurts a little. I have come to love the SNAP Agency team and had the greatest time writing their stories. But the best part has truly been watching you love them as much as I do! If you read the prequel novella, Initium, then you know a bit about the background to Director Walsh's story and Lyla's beginning. Although the bombing in Omagh, Ireland, was an actual event, I took some creative liberties crafting their stories around details like the Real Irish Republican Army's involvement, the miscommunicated intel, even the devastating destruction of the bombing that did take the life of a pregnant woman. Several other areas in this story were inspired by fact, including counterfeit supernotes, the smuggling of money in double-sided suitcases, and the gun smuggling and cover-ups within government agencies. Let me tell you, it was a whole lot of fun to dream up scenarios to include in this book. I'm so thankful to all my readers who willingly and enthusiastically trust me to take them with me on these crazy adventures. You guys are the best!

None of this could have happened without

incredible team at Revell. My editors, Vicki rumpton and Amy Ballor, are the best and made ure that even among the edits, their enthusiasm and love for the characters and story pushed me to keep going. Brianne Dekker and Karen Steele are the fun behind the process, and I'm grateful for their constant encouragement and support. My agent, Tamela Hancock-Murray, is the sunshine to the cloudy hard days, and I wouldn't want anyone else by my side.

If any of you have been following my journey with this story, then you know Lyla and Garcia gave me a very hard time. I was ready to toss in the towel on these two if not for the best tribe of friends and readers who prayed, talked me through plot issues, convinced me not to torture Lyla and Garcia out of spite, and sent me chocolate. Emilie, Christen, Steff, Joy, Crissy, Amy, and Ashley—readers can thank you for this book!

None of what I do would matter without the unconditional love and support of GI JOE and my kids. Being an author is awesome, but being a wife and mother is even better, and I'm lucky I get to do it all.

And finally, but most importantly, I'm so thankful the Lord put the love of story in my heart and opened doors to give me the opportunity and blessing to do something I love.

ABOUT THE AUTHOR

Natalie Walters is the author of *Lights Out* and *Fatal Code*, as well as the Harbored Secrets series. A military wife, she currently resides in Texas with her soldier husband and is the proud mom of three. She loves traveling, spending time with her family, and connecting with readers on Instagram and Facebook. Learn more at www.nataliewalterswriter.com.

Center Point Large Print
600 Brooks Road / PO Box 1
Thorndike, ME 04986-0001 USA

(207) 568-3717

US & Canada:
1 800 929-9108
www.centerpointlargeprint.com